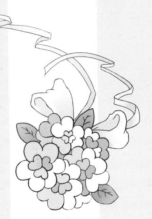

CHII PRESENTS

The Bride was
a Boy

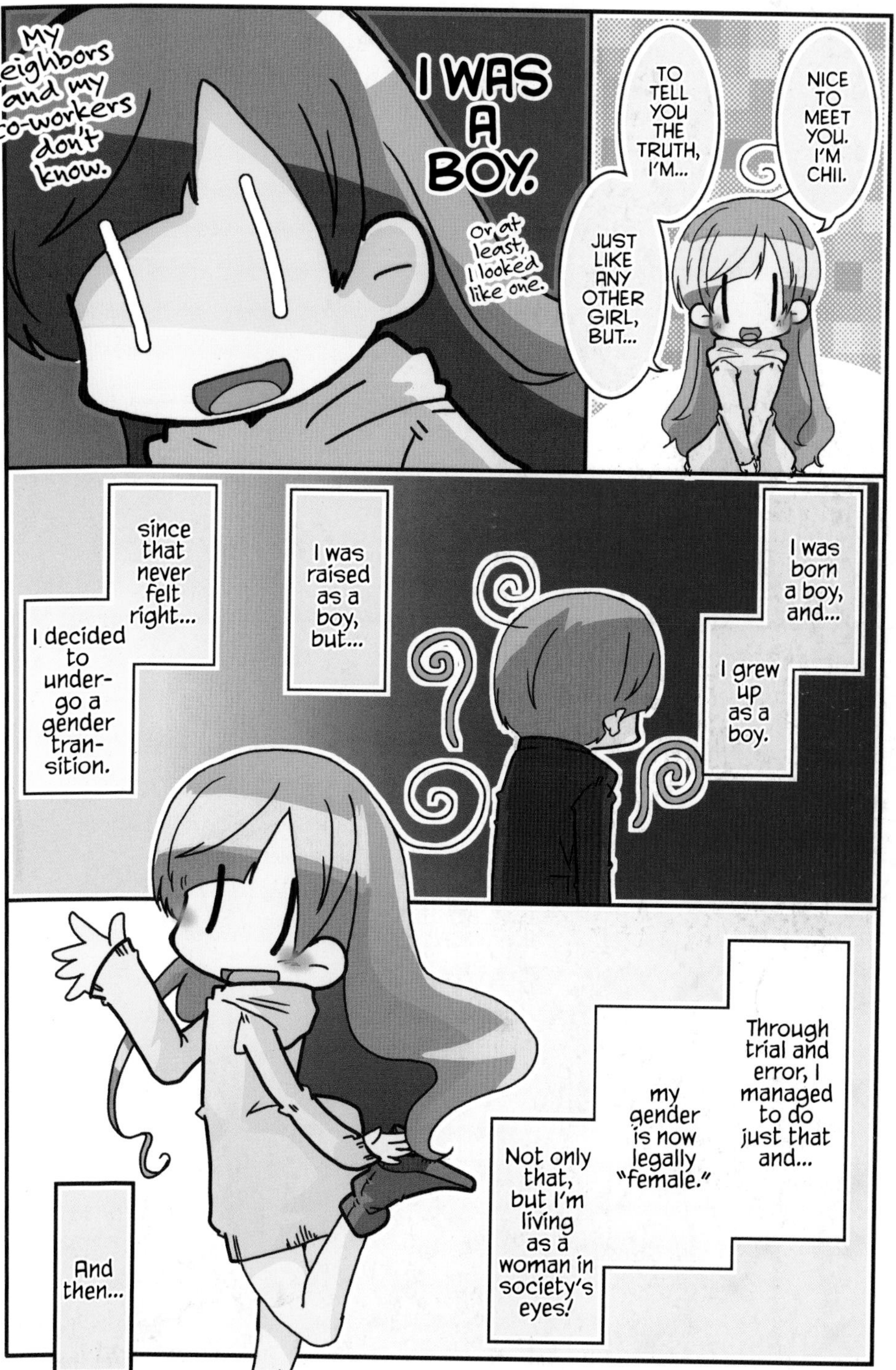
NICE TO MEET YOU. I'M CHII.
TO TELL YOU THE TRUTH, I'M...
JUST LIKE ANY OTHER GIRL, BUT...
I WAS A BOY.
Or at least, I looked like one.
My neighbors and my co-workers don't know.
I was born a boy, and...
I grew up as a boy.
I was raised as a boy, but...
since that never felt right...
I decided to undergo a gender transition.
Through trial and error, I managed to do just that and...
my gender is now legally "female."
Not only that, but I'm living as a woman in society's eyes!
And then...

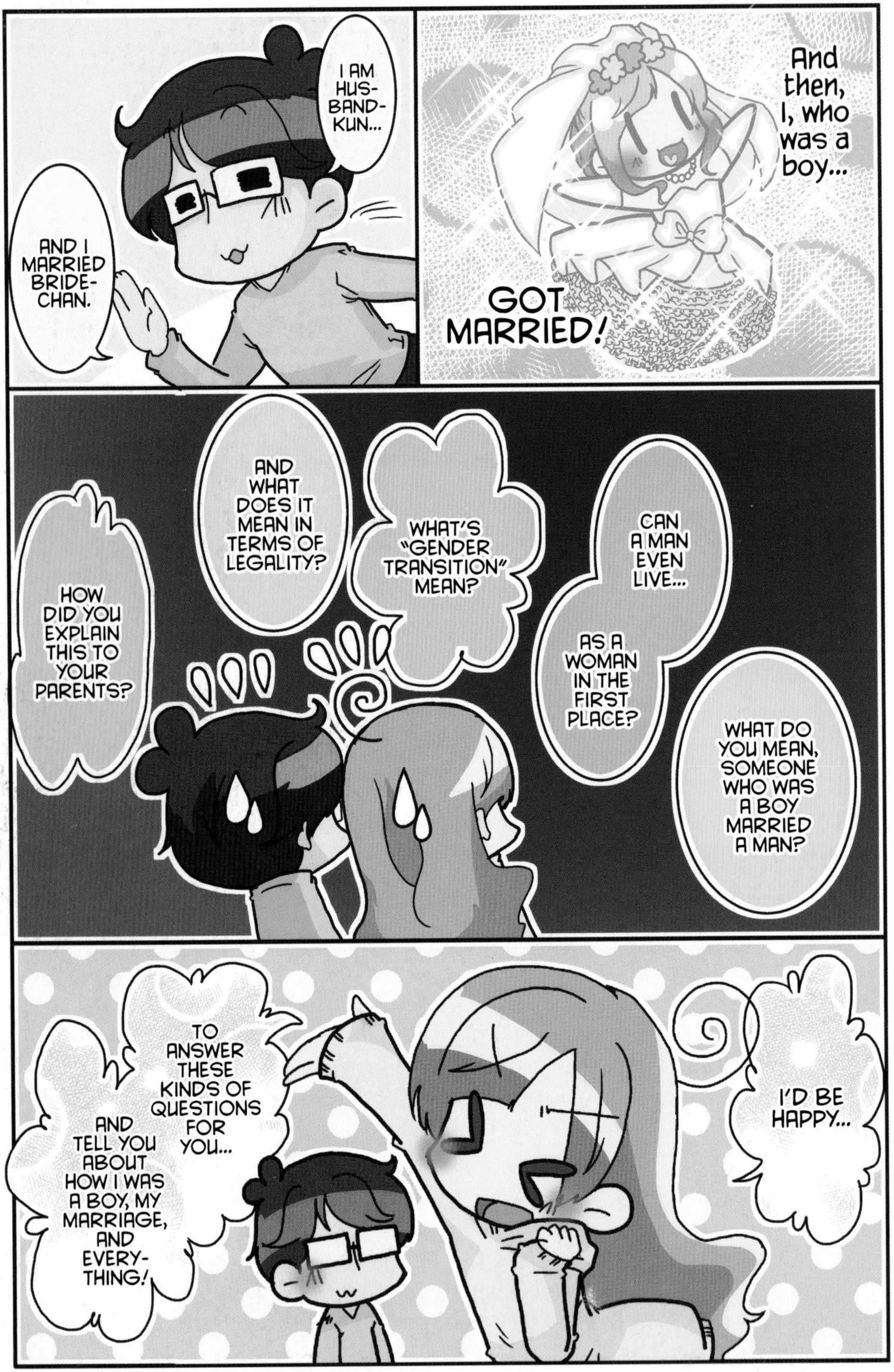
And then, I, who was a boy...
GOT MARRIED!
I AM HUS-BAND-KUN...
AND I MARRIED BRIDE-CHAN.
CAN A MAN EVEN LIVE...
AS A WOMAN IN THE FIRST PLACE?
WHAT DO YOU MEAN, SOMEONE WHO WAS A BOY MARRIED A MAN?
WHAT'S "GENDER TRANSITION" MEAN?
AND WHAT DOES IT MEAN IN TERMS OF LEGALITY?
HOW DID YOU EXPLAIN THIS TO YOUR PARENTS?
I'D BE HAPPY...
TO ANSWER THESE KINDS OF QUESTIONS FOR YOU...
AND TELL YOU ABOUT HOW I WAS A BOY, MY MARRIAGE, AND EVERY-THING!

The Bride was a Boy
CONTENTS

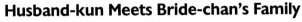

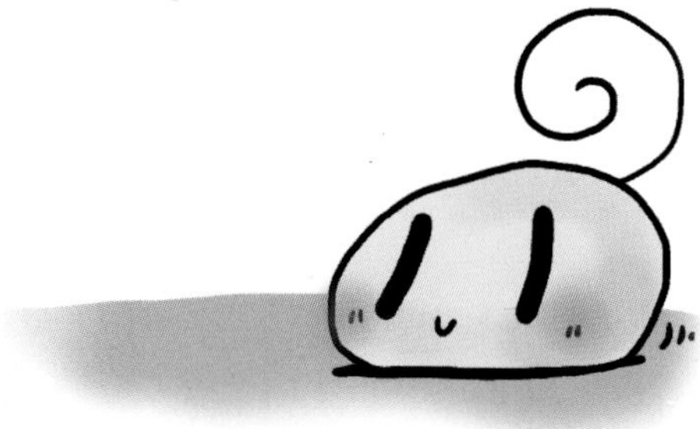

CHAPTER 1

How We Met

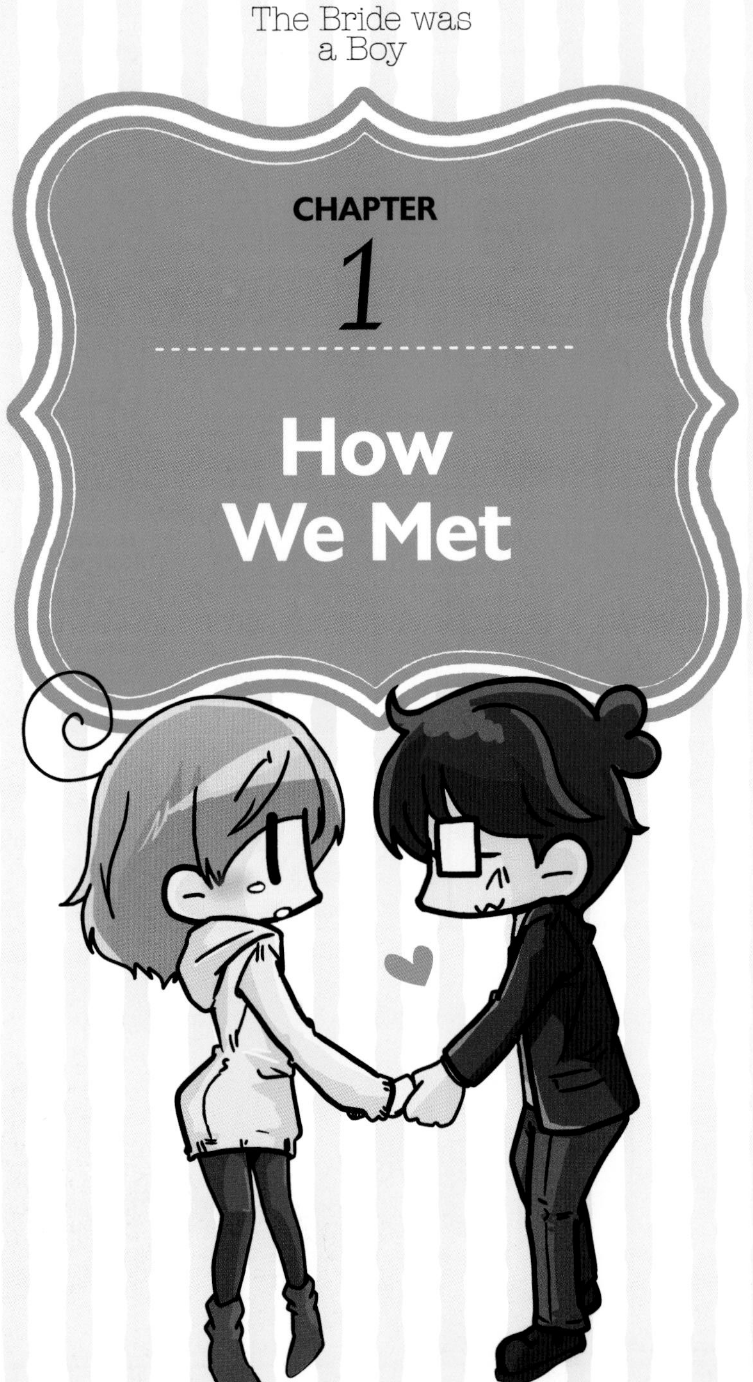

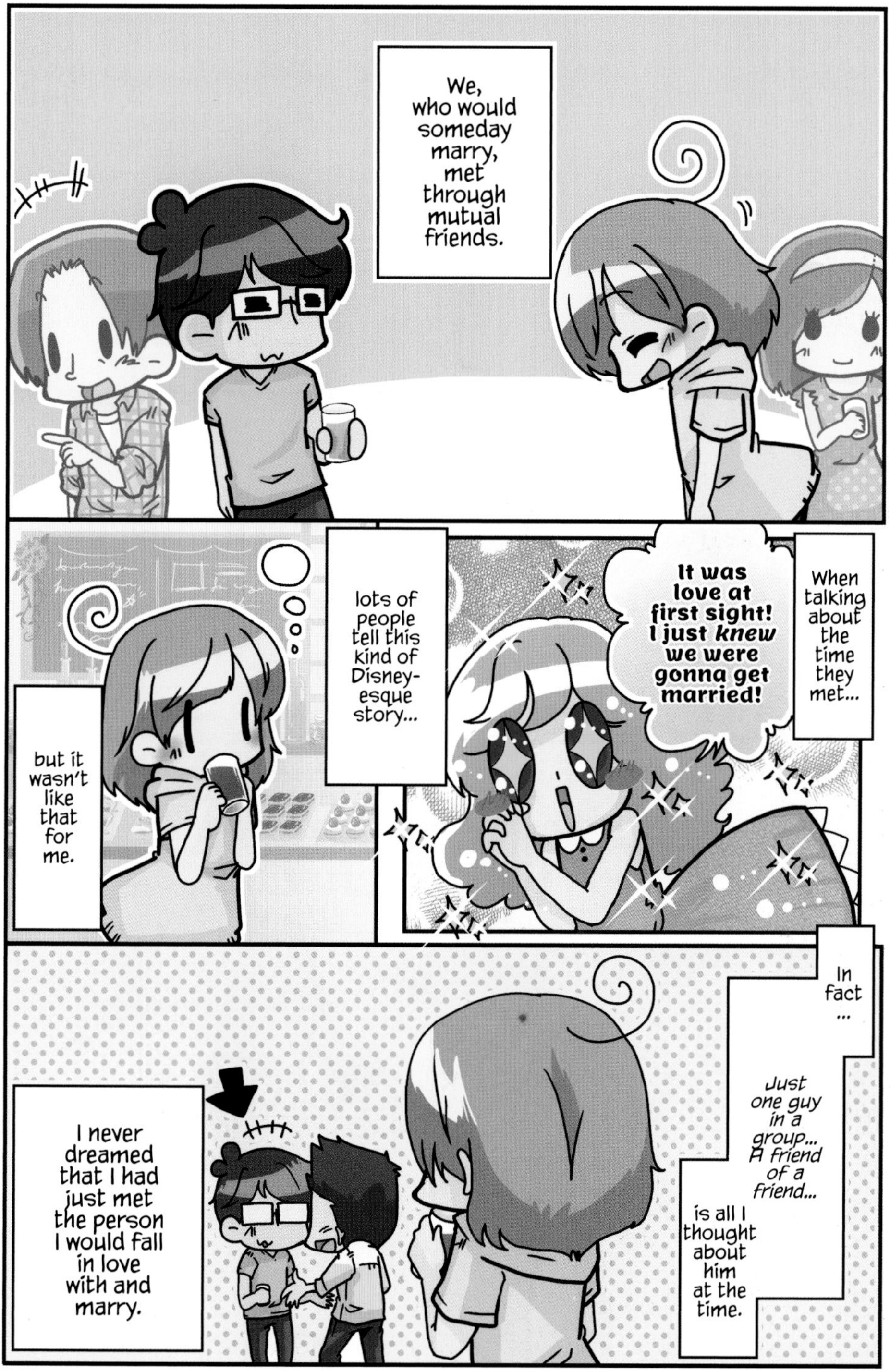
We, who would someday marry, met through mutual friends.
When talking about the time they met...
It was love at first sight! I just *knew* we were gonna get married!
lots of people tell this kind of Disney-esque story...
but it wasn't like that for me.
In fact...
Just one guy in a group... A friend of a friend...
is all I thought about him at the time.
I never dreamed that I had just met the person I would fall in love with and marry.

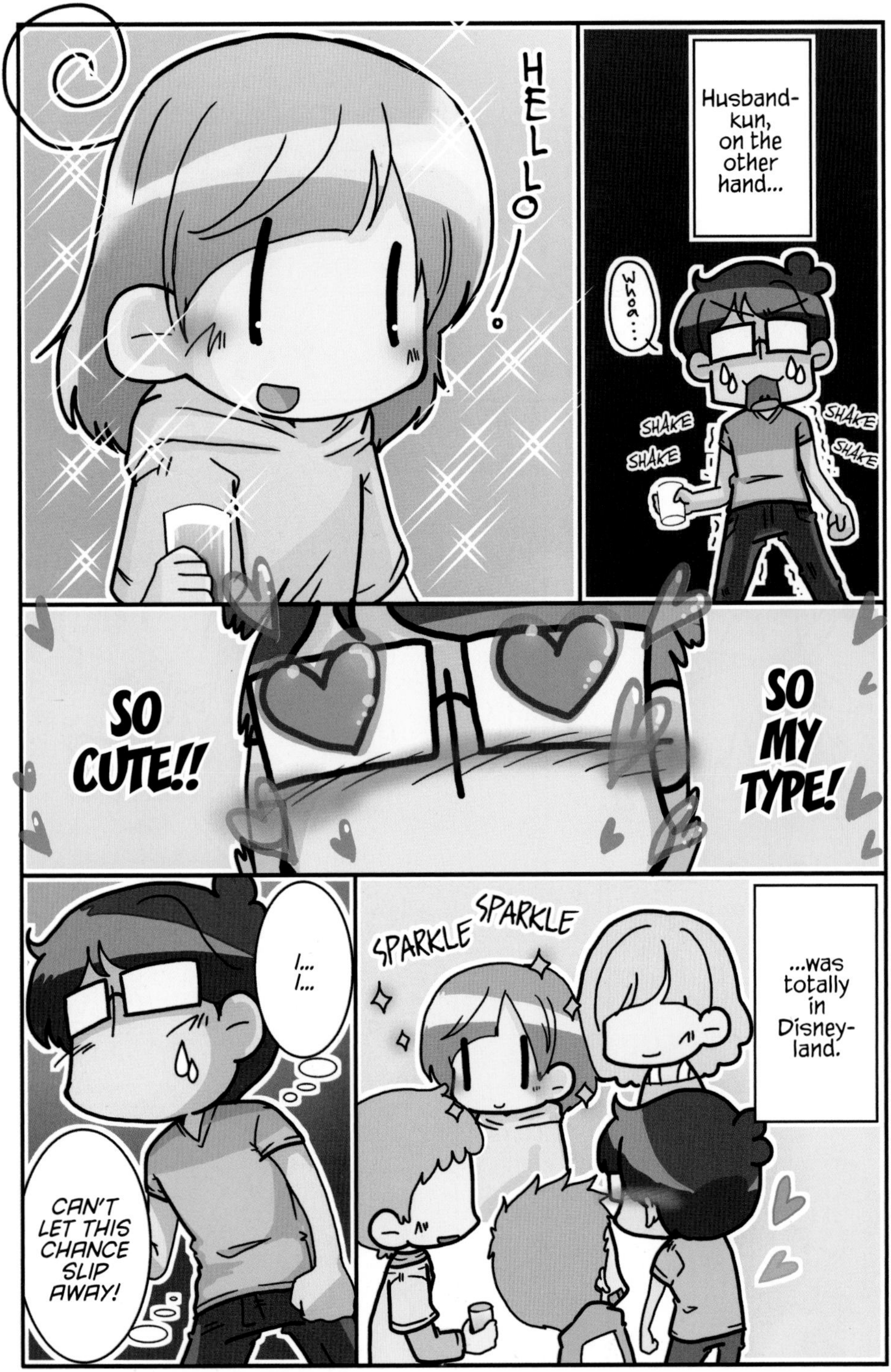
Husband-kun, on the other hand...
Whoa...
SHAKE
SHAKE
SHAKE
SHAKE
HELLO!
SO MY TYPE!
SO CUTE!!
...was totally in Disneyland.
SPARKLE SPARKLE
I... I...
CAN'T LET THIS CHANCE SLIP AWAY!

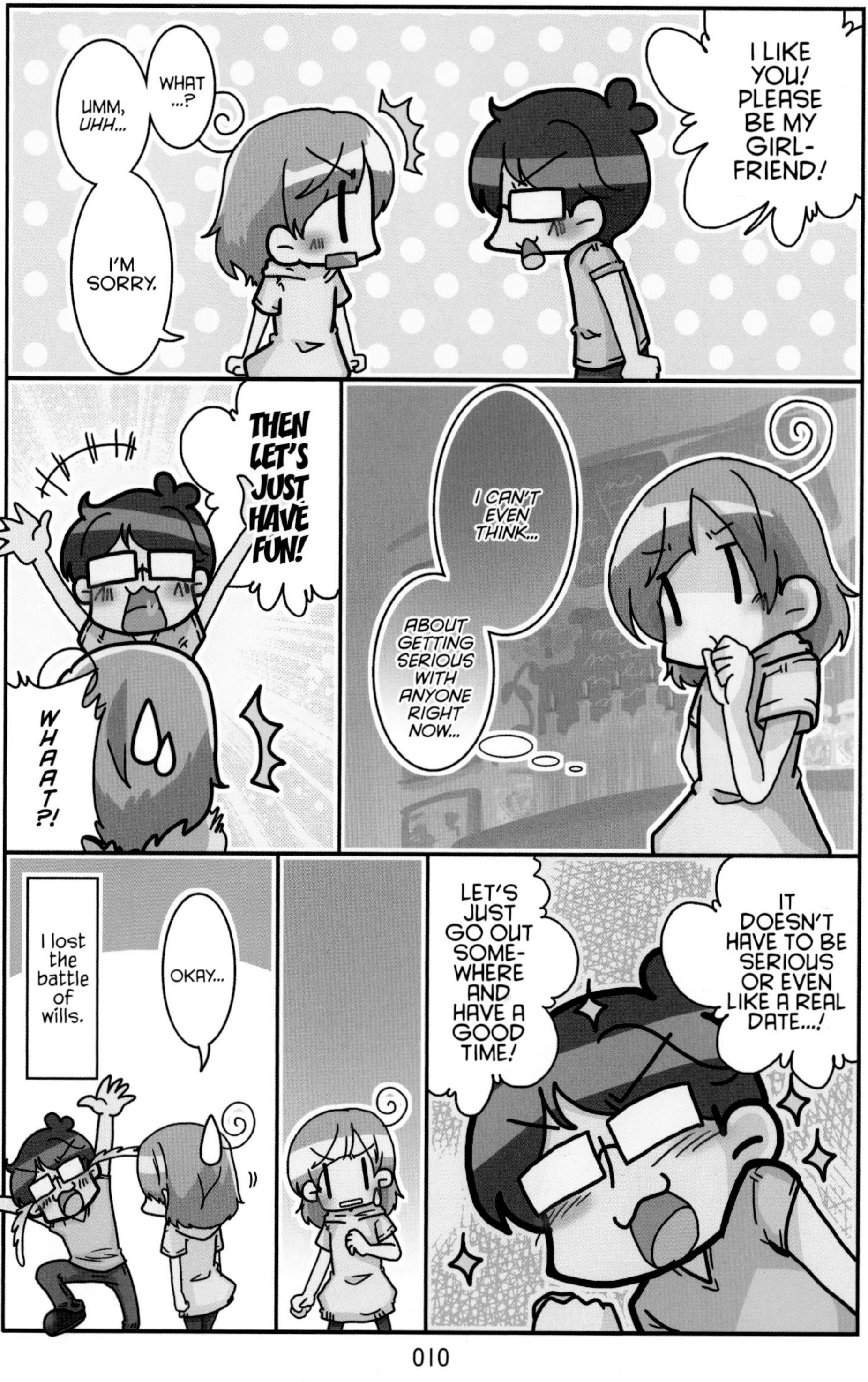
I LIKE YOU! PLEASE BE MY GIRL-FRIEND!
WHAT ...?
UMM, UHH... I'M SORRY.
I CAN'T EVEN THINK... ABOUT GETTING SERIOUS WITH ANYONE RIGHT NOW...
THEN LET'S JUST HAVE FUN!
WHAAAT?!
IT DOESN'T HAVE TO BE SERIOUS OR EVEN LIKE A REAL DATE...!
LET'S JUST GO OUT SOMEWHERE AND HAVE A GOOD TIME!
OKAY...
I lost the battle of wills.

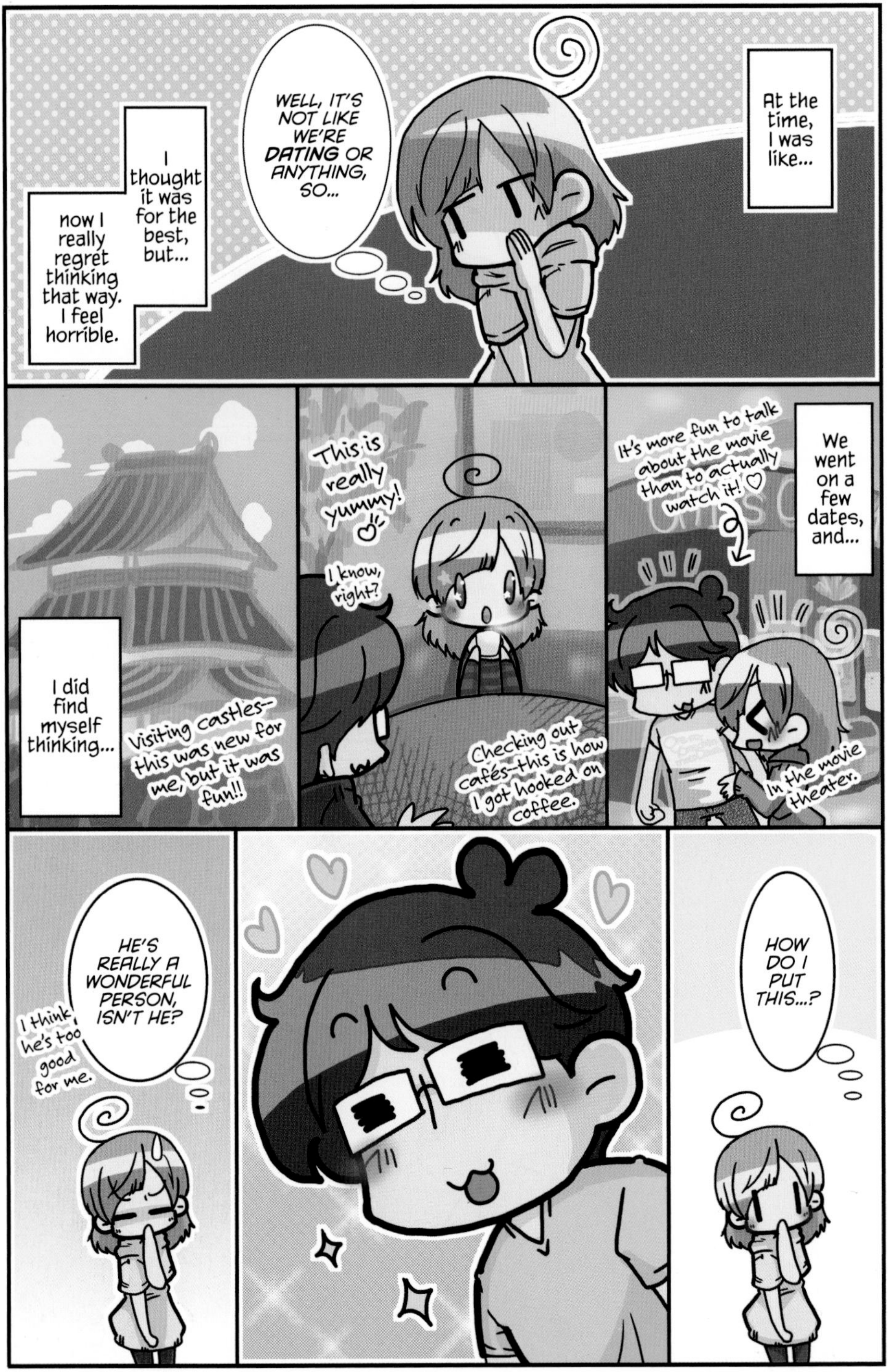
At the time, I was like...
WELL, IT'S NOT LIKE WE'RE DATING OR ANYTHING, SO...
I thought it was for the best, but...
now I really regret thinking that way. I feel horrible.
We went on a few dates, and...
It's more fun to talk about the movie than to actually watch it! ♡
In the movie theater.
This is really yummy!
I know, right?
Checking out cafés--this is how I got hooked on coffee.
I did find myself thinking...
Visiting castles--this was new for me, but it was fun!!
HOW DO I PUT THIS...?
HE'S REALLY A WONDERFUL PERSON, ISN'T HE?
I think he's too good for me.

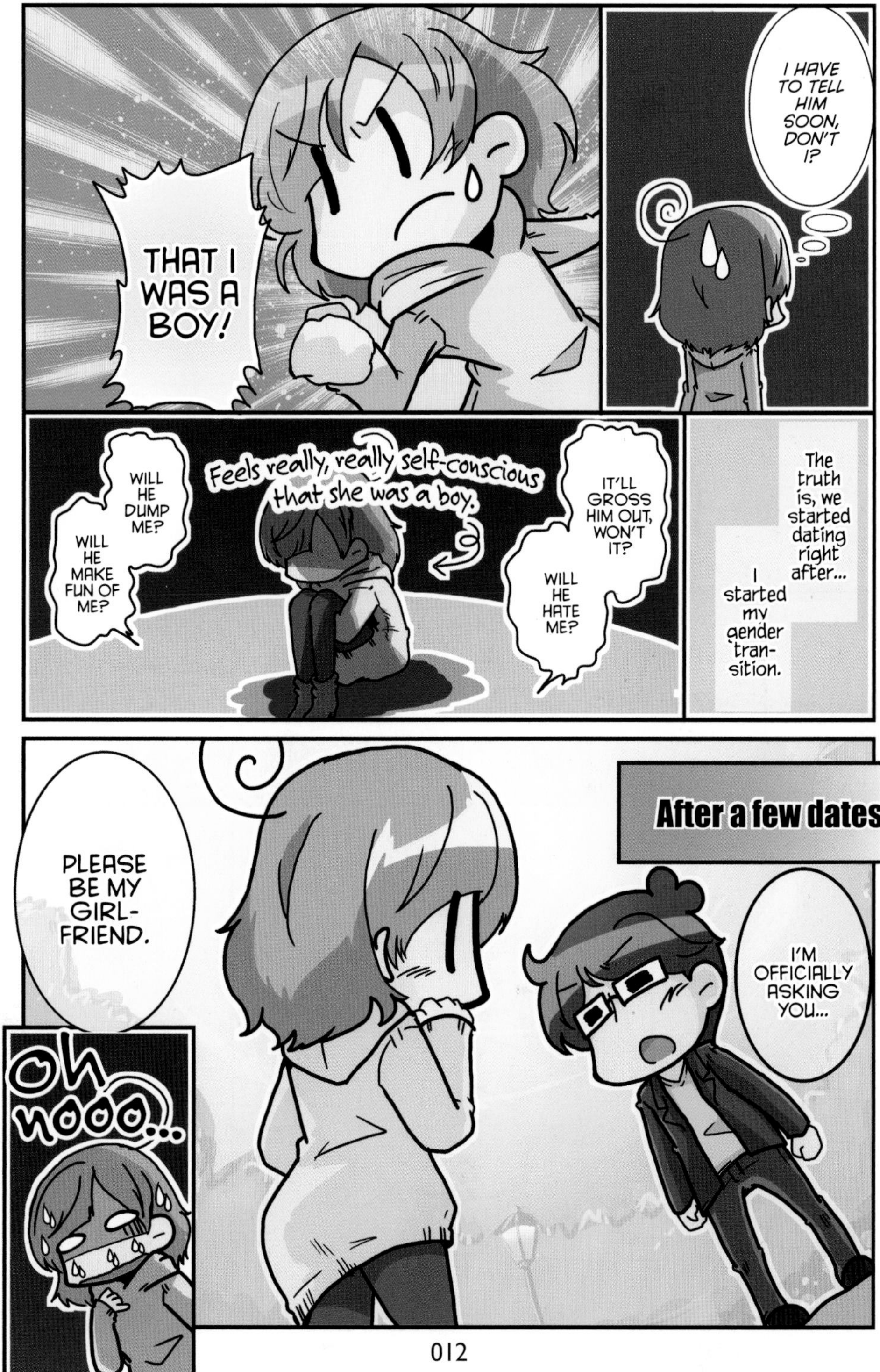
I HAVE TO TELL HIM SOON, DON'T I?
THAT I WAS A BOY!
The truth is, we started dating right after...
I started my gender tran-sition.
IT'LL GROSS HIM OUT, WON'T IT?
WILL HE HATE ME?
Feels really, really self-conscious that she was a boy.
WILL HE DUMP ME?
WILL HE MAKE FUN OF ME?
After a few dates...
I'M OFFICIALLY ASKING YOU...
PLEASE BE MY GIRL-FRIEND.
Oh nooo...

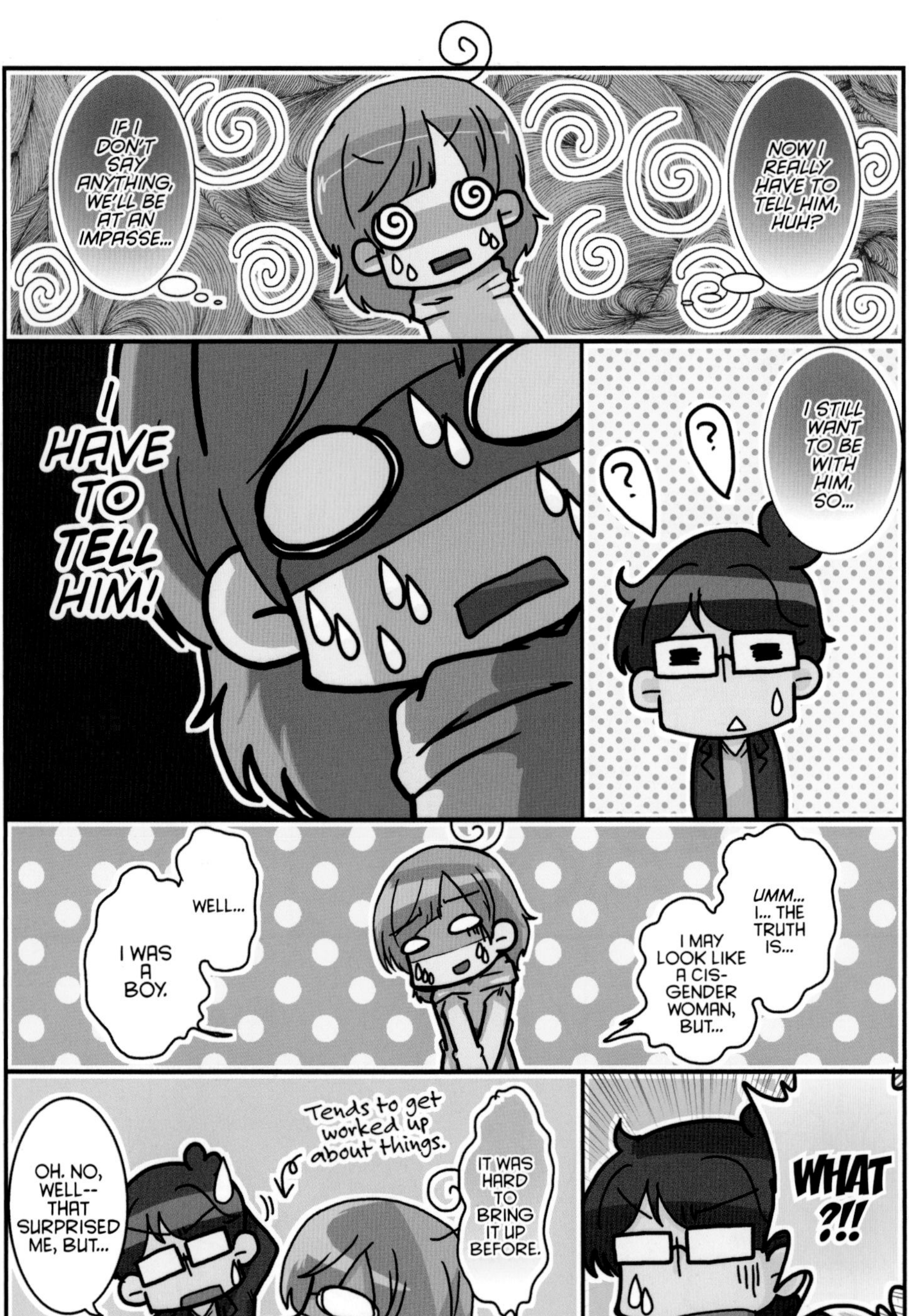
NOW I REALLY HAVE TO TELL HIM, HUH?
IF I DON'T SAY ANYTHING, WE'LL BE AT AN IMPASSE...
I STILL WANT TO BE WITH HIM, SO...
I HAVE TO TELL HIM!
UMM... I... THE TRUTH IS...
I MAY LOOK LIKE A CIS-GENDER WOMAN, BUT...
WELL...
I WAS A BOY.
WHAT ?!!
IT WAS HARD TO BRING IT UP BEFORE.
Tends to get worked up about things.
OH. NO, WELL-- THAT SURPRISED ME, BUT...

※Cisgender: Refers to an individual whose gender identity matches what they were assigned at birth.

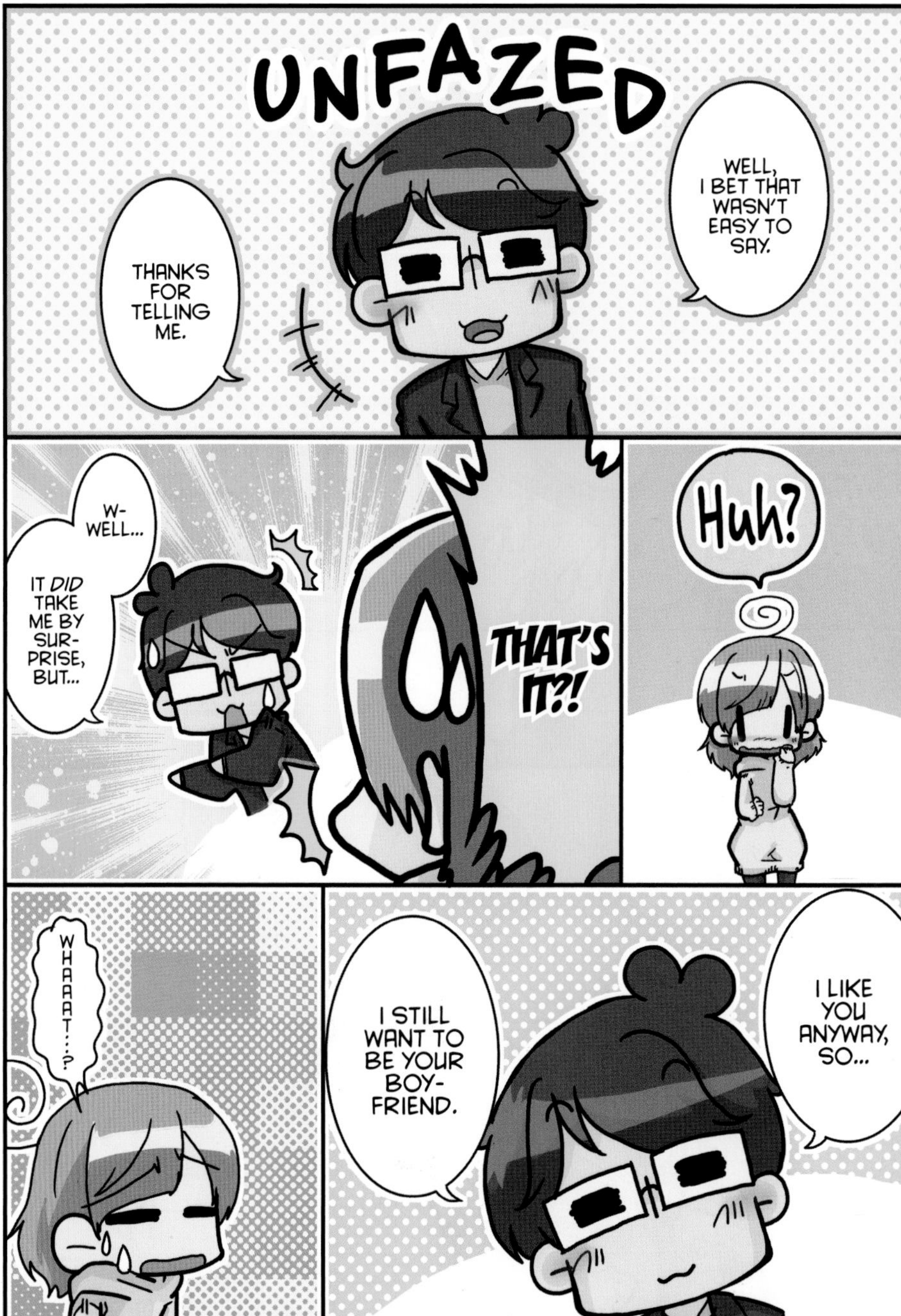
UNFAZED
WELL, I BET THAT WASN'T EASY TO SAY.
THANKS FOR TELLING ME.
Huh?
THAT'S IT?!
W- WELL... IT *DID* TAKE ME BY SURPRISE, BUT...
I LIKE YOU ANYWAY, SO...
I STILL WANT TO BE YOUR BOY-FRIEND.
WHAAAT...?

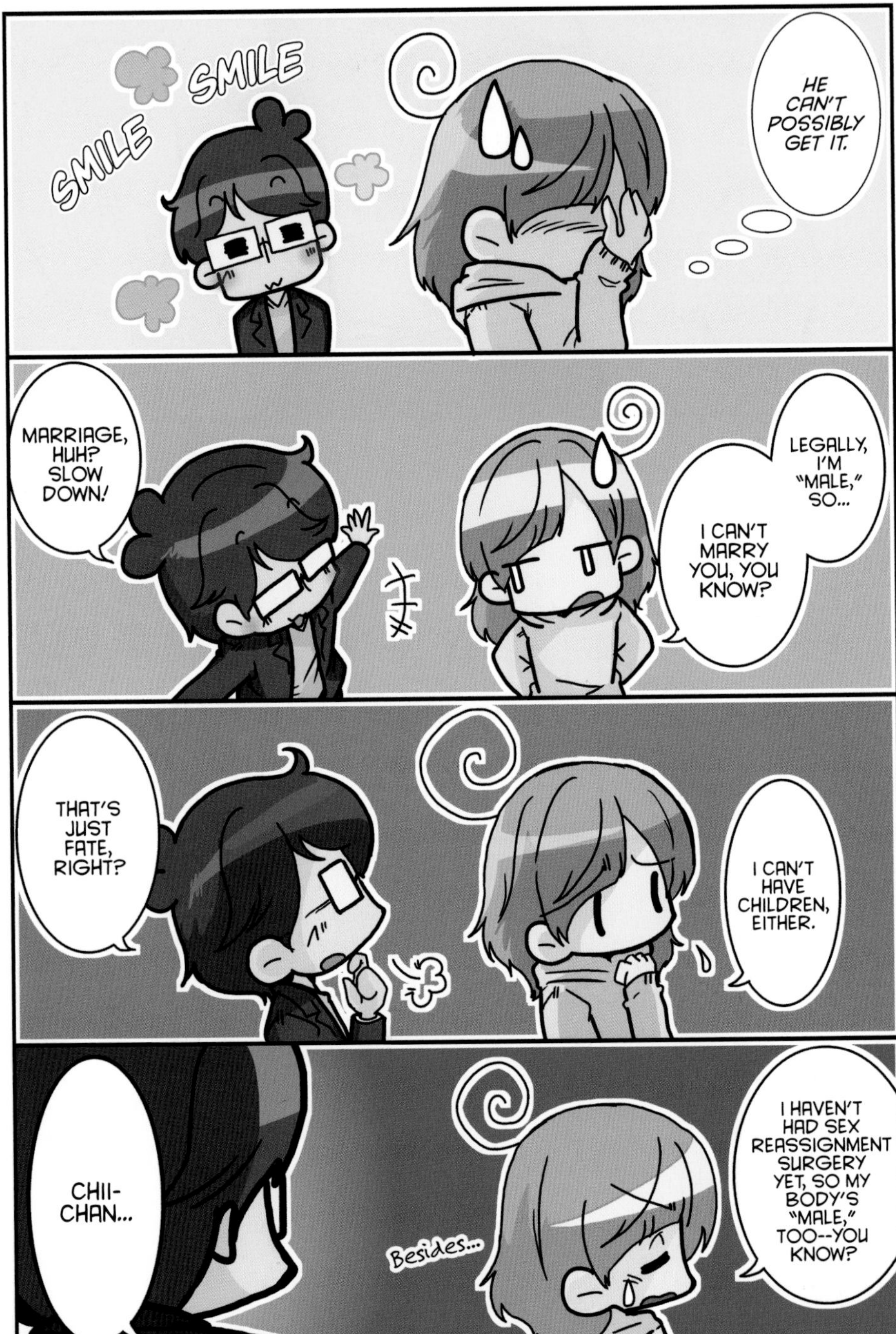
HE CAN'T POSSIBLY GET IT.
SMILE SMILE
LEGALLY, I'M "MALE," SO...
I CAN'T MARRY YOU, YOU KNOW?
MARRIAGE, HUH? SLOW DOWN!
I CAN'T HAVE CHILDREN, EITHER.
THAT'S JUST FATE, RIGHT?
I HAVEN'T HAD SEX REASSIGNMENT SURGERY YET, SO MY BODY'S "MALE," TOO--YOU KNOW?
Besides...
CHII-CHAN...

※*As of the time of this publication in English, same-sex partnerships aren't legal in most of Japan.*

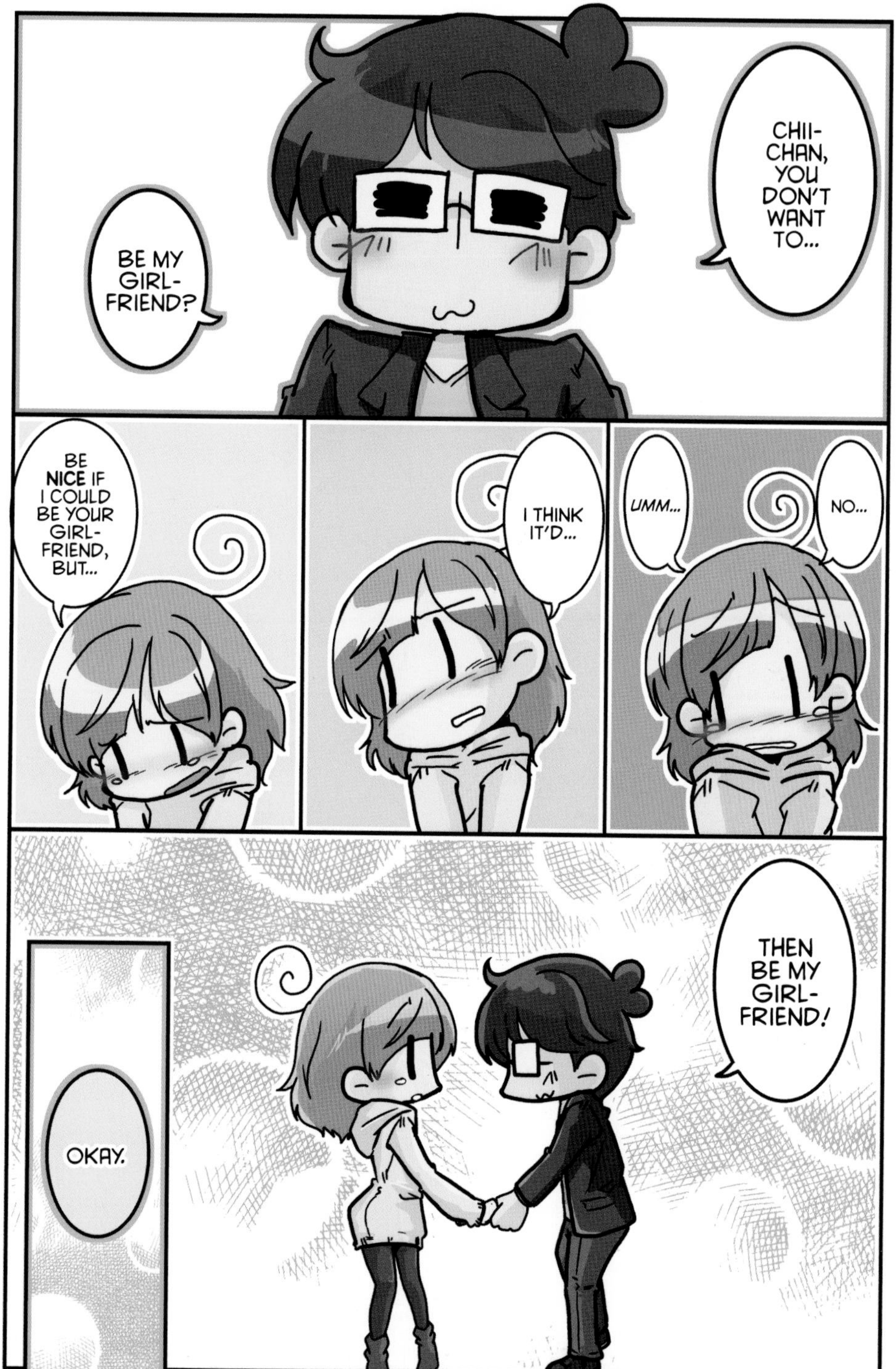
CHII-CHAN, YOU DON'T WANT TO...
BE MY GIRL-FRIEND?
NO...
UMM...
I THINK IT'D...
BE NICE IF I COULD BE YOUR GIRL-FRIEND, BUT...
THEN BE MY GIRL-FRIEND!
OKAY.

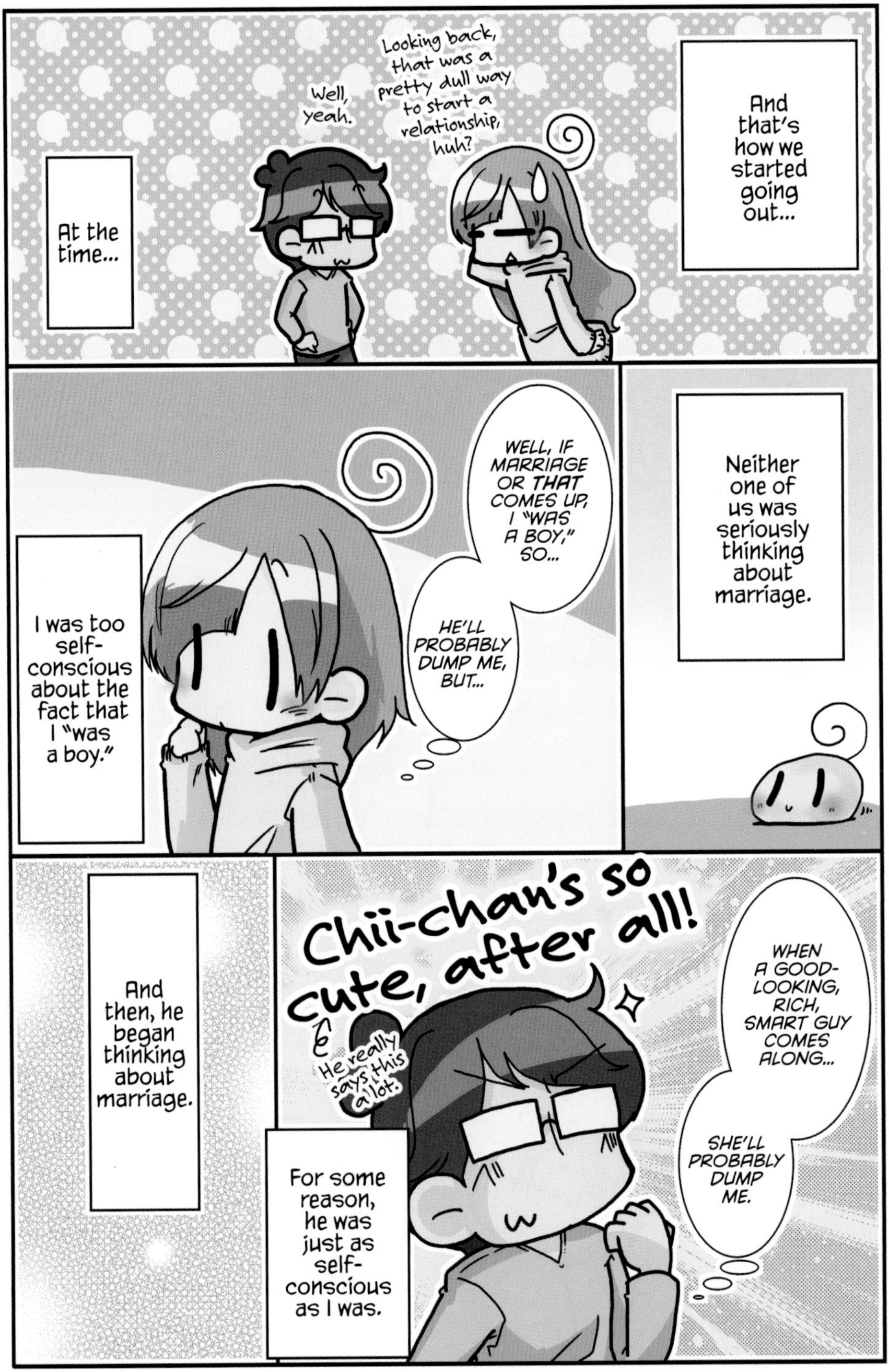
And that's how we started going out...
Looking back, that was a pretty dull way to start a relationship, huh?
Well, yeah.
At the time...
Neither one of us was seriously thinking about marriage.
WELL, IF MARRIAGE OR THAT COMES UP, I "WAS A BOY," SO...
HE'LL PROBABLY DUMP ME, BUT...
I was too self-conscious about the fact that I "was a boy."
WHEN A GOOD-LOOKING, RICH, SMART GUY COMES ALONG...
SHE'LL PROBABLY DUMP ME.
Chii-chan's so cute, after all!
He really says this a lot.
For some reason, he was just as self-conscious as I was.
And then, he began thinking about marriage.

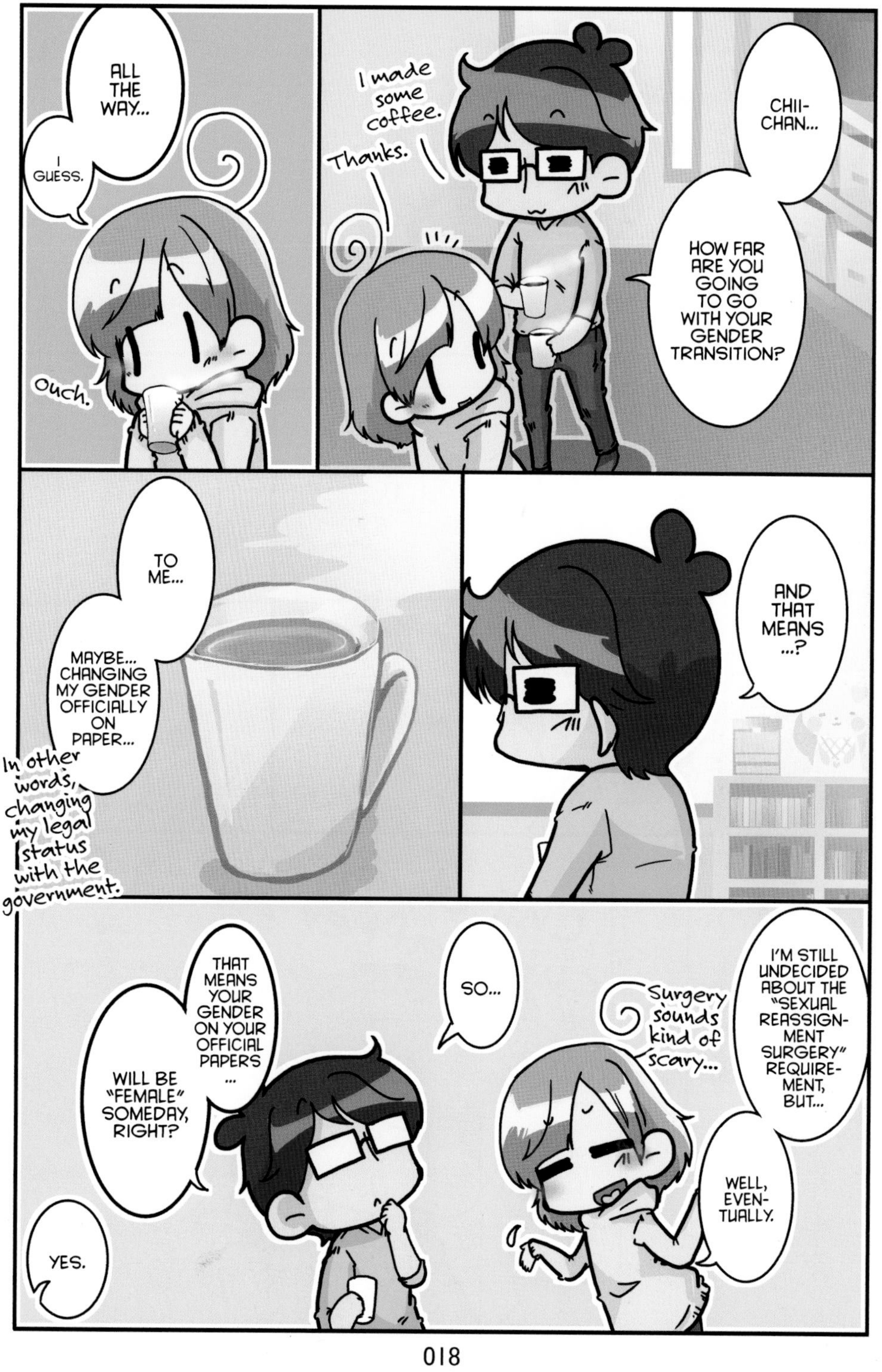
CHII-CHAN...
HOW FAR ARE YOU GOING TO GO WITH YOUR GENDER TRANSITION?
I made some coffee.
Thanks.
ALL THE WAY...
I GUESS.
Ouch.
AND THAT MEANS ...?
TO ME...
MAYBE... CHANGING MY GENDER OFFICIALLY ON PAPER...
In other words, changing my legal status with the government.
I'M STILL UNDECIDED ABOUT THE "SEXUAL REASSIGNMENT SURGERY" REQUIREMENT, BUT...
Surgery sounds kind of scary...
SO...
WELL, EVENTUALLY.
THAT MEANS YOUR GENDER ON YOUR OFFICIAL PAPERS ...
WILL BE "FEMALE" SOMEDAY, RIGHT?
YES.

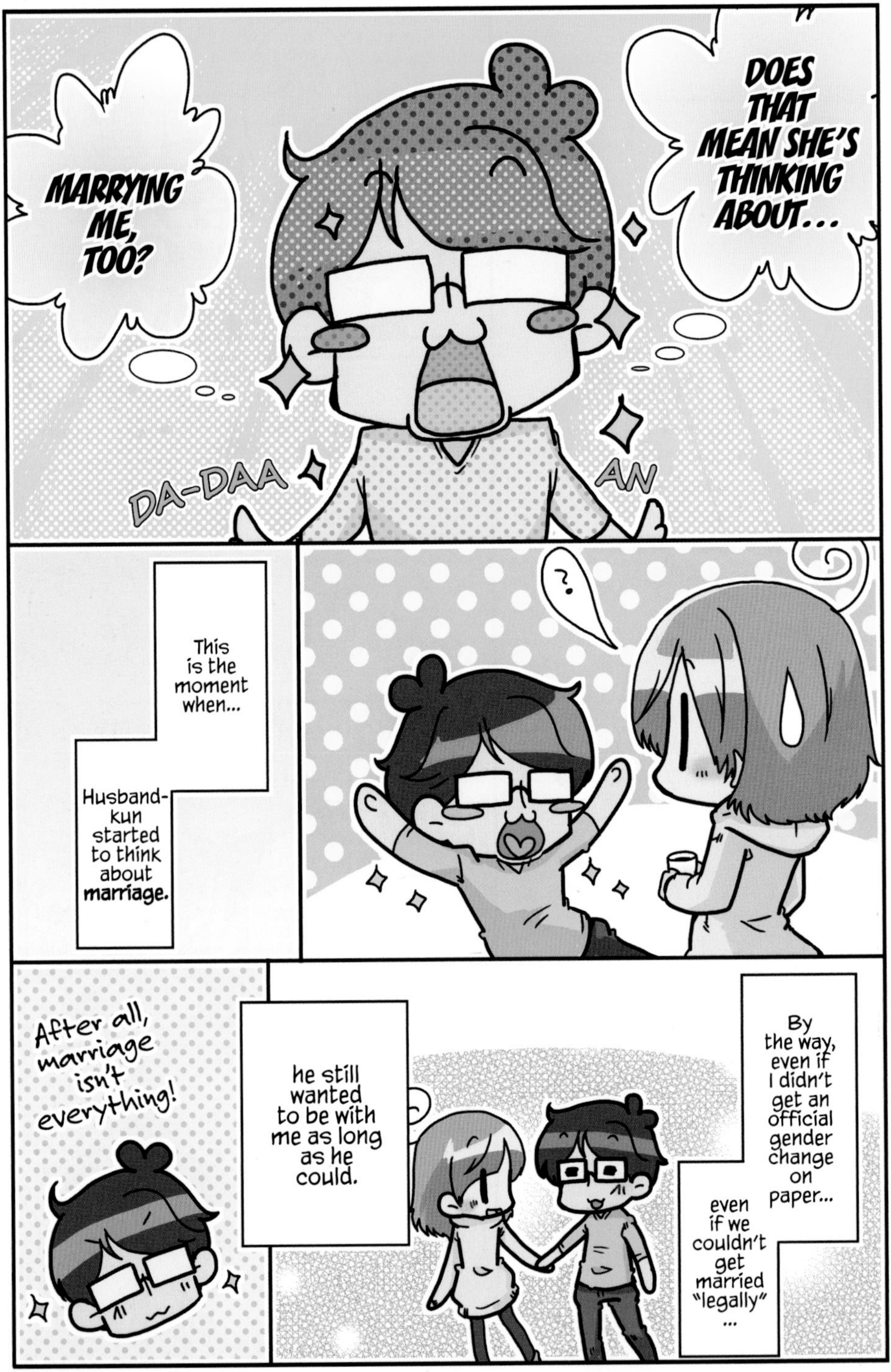
DOES THAT MEAN SHE'S THINKING ABOUT...
MARRYING ME, TOO?
DA-DAA
AN
?
This is the moment when...
Husband-kun started to think about marriage.
By the way, even if I didn't get an official gender change on paper...
even if we couldn't get married "legally"...
he still wanted to be with me as long as he could.
After all, marriage isn't everything!

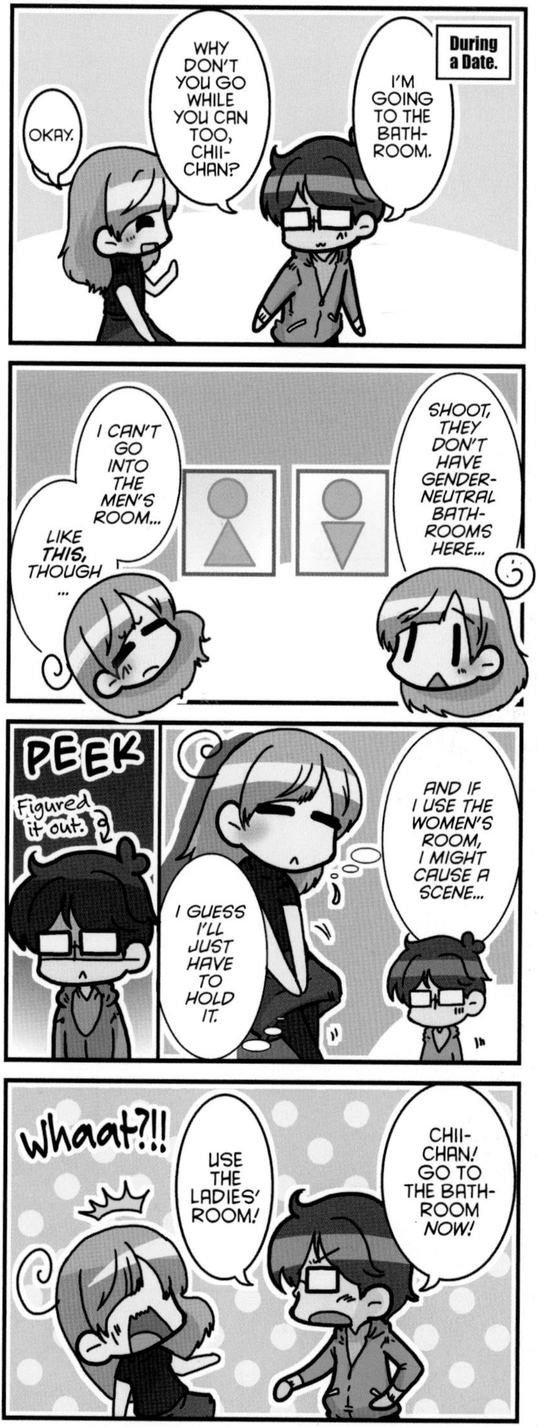
During a Date.
I'M GOING TO THE BATH-ROOM.
WHY DON'T YOU GO WHILE YOU CAN TOO, CHII-CHAN?
OKAY.
SHOOT, THEY DON'T HAVE GENDER-NEUTRAL BATH-ROOMS HERE...
I CAN'T GO INTO THE MEN'S ROOM... LIKE THIS, THOUGH...
AND IF I USE THE WOMEN'S ROOM, I MIGHT CAUSE A SCENE...
I GUESS I'LL JUST HAVE TO HOLD IT.
PEEK
Figured it out.
CHII-CHAN! GO TO THE BATH-ROOM NOW!
USE THE LADIES' ROOM!
Whaat?!!

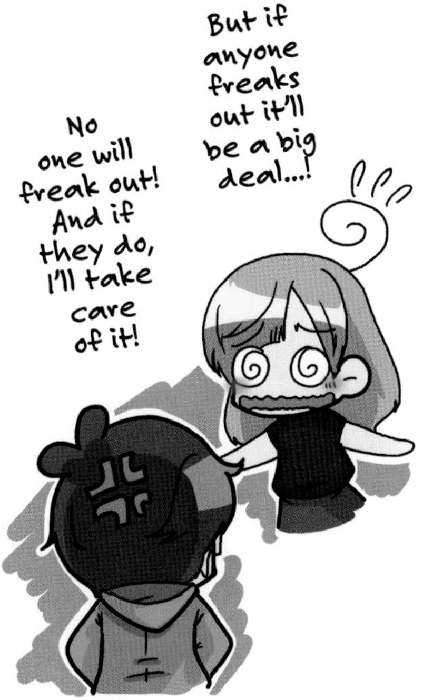
But if anyone freaks out it'll be a big deal...!
No one will freak out! And if they do, I'll take care of it!

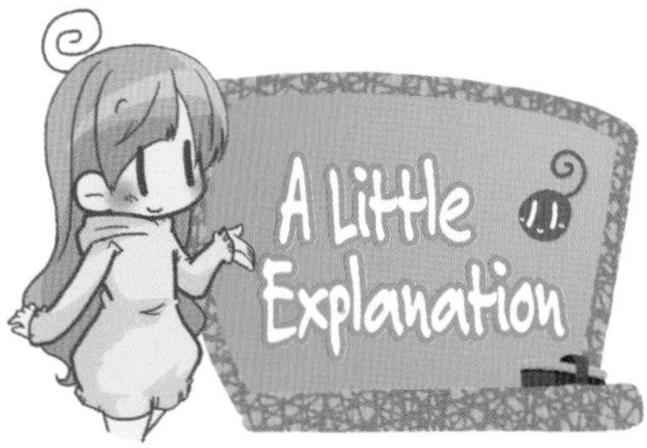

A Little Explanation

Rainbow Flag

The six-color rainbow--made up of red, orange, yellow, green, blue, and purple--is probably the main and most well-known symbol of diverse sexualities and genders.

Displaying a rainbow flag symbolizes the pride and social activism of these different sexualities and genders. The Rainbow Flag is also commonly known as the Gay Pride Flag or LGBT Pride Flag.

During the 2013 LGBT Pride Weekend, the Empire State Building in New York was lit up in rainbow colors. The White House was also lit up in rainbow colors on June 26, 2015, when the Supreme Court ruled that same-sex couples could marry in the United States. These are just two of the many amazing displays of iconography that have been in support of the LGBT movement over the years, and there are countless more!

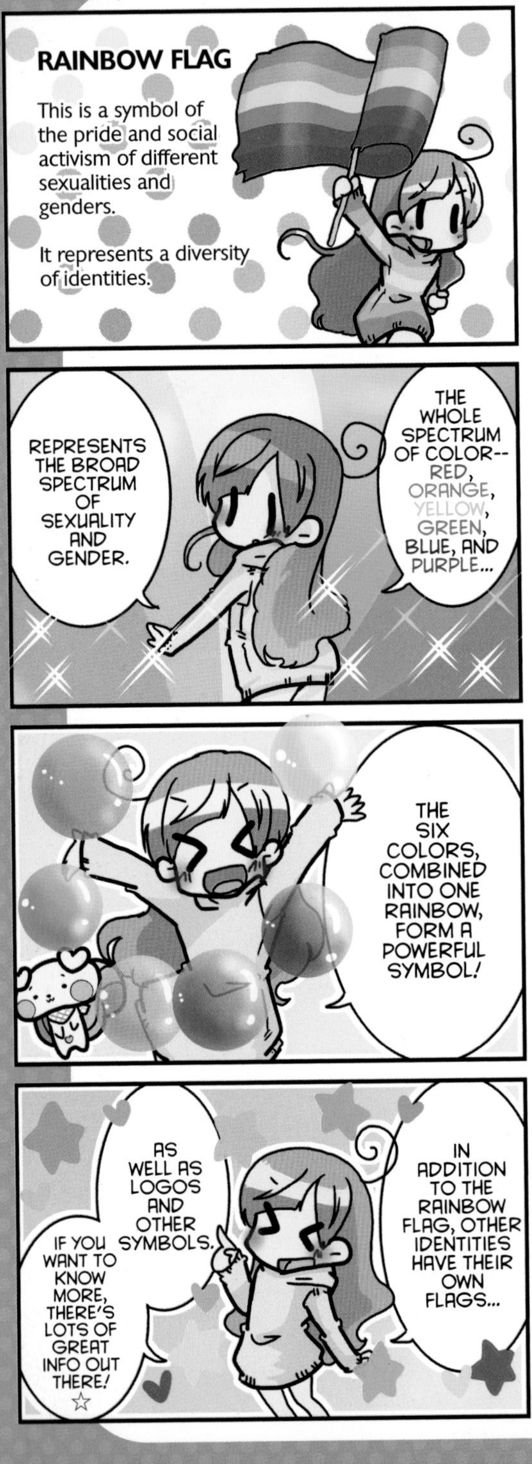

RAINBOW FLAG
This is a symbol of the pride and social activism of different sexualities and genders.
It represents a diversity of identities.
THE WHOLE SPECTRUM OF COLOR-- RED, ORANGE, YELLOW, GREEN, BLUE, AND PURPLE...
REPRESENTS THE BROAD SPECTRUM OF SEXUALITY AND GENDER.
THE SIX COLORS, COMBINED INTO ONE RAINBOW, FORM A POWERFUL SYMBOL!
IN ADDITION TO THE RAINBOW FLAG, OTHER IDENTITIES HAVE THEIR OWN FLAGS...
AS WELL AS LOGOS AND OTHER SYMBOLS.
IF YOU WANT TO KNOW MORE, THERE'S LOTS OF GREAT INFO OUT THERE! ☆

“I’m so jealous! You understand how a man *and* a woman feels!”

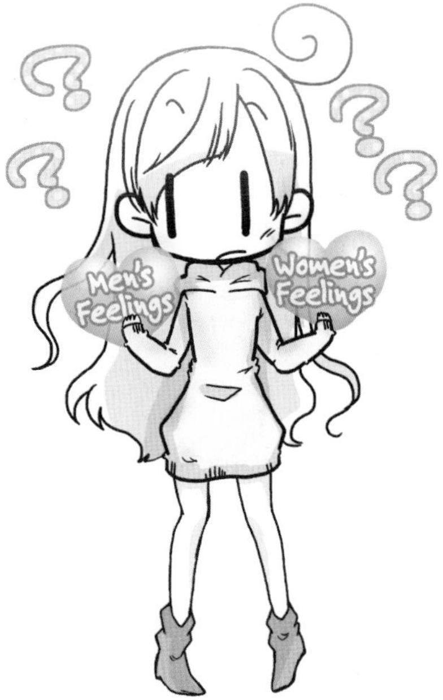
Men's Feelings
Women's Feelings

I’m sure there are some people for whom this is true, but it’s not so easy for me. I understand my own heart well enough, but when other people say, “You understand how a man *and* a woman feels,” I want to tell them, “I don’t know anything about either of them!” I think that it’s really hard to understand how *anyone* feels.

CHAPTER 2

Bride-chan's Time as a Boy

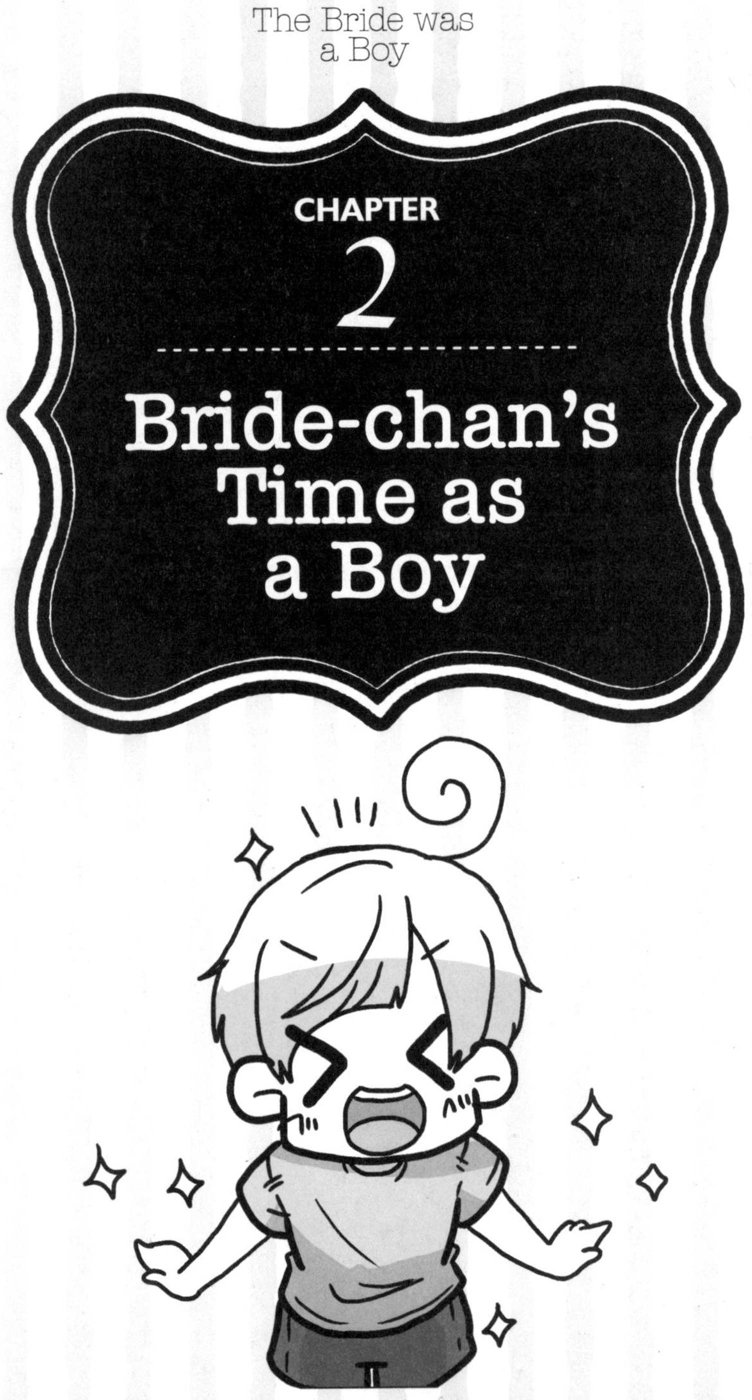

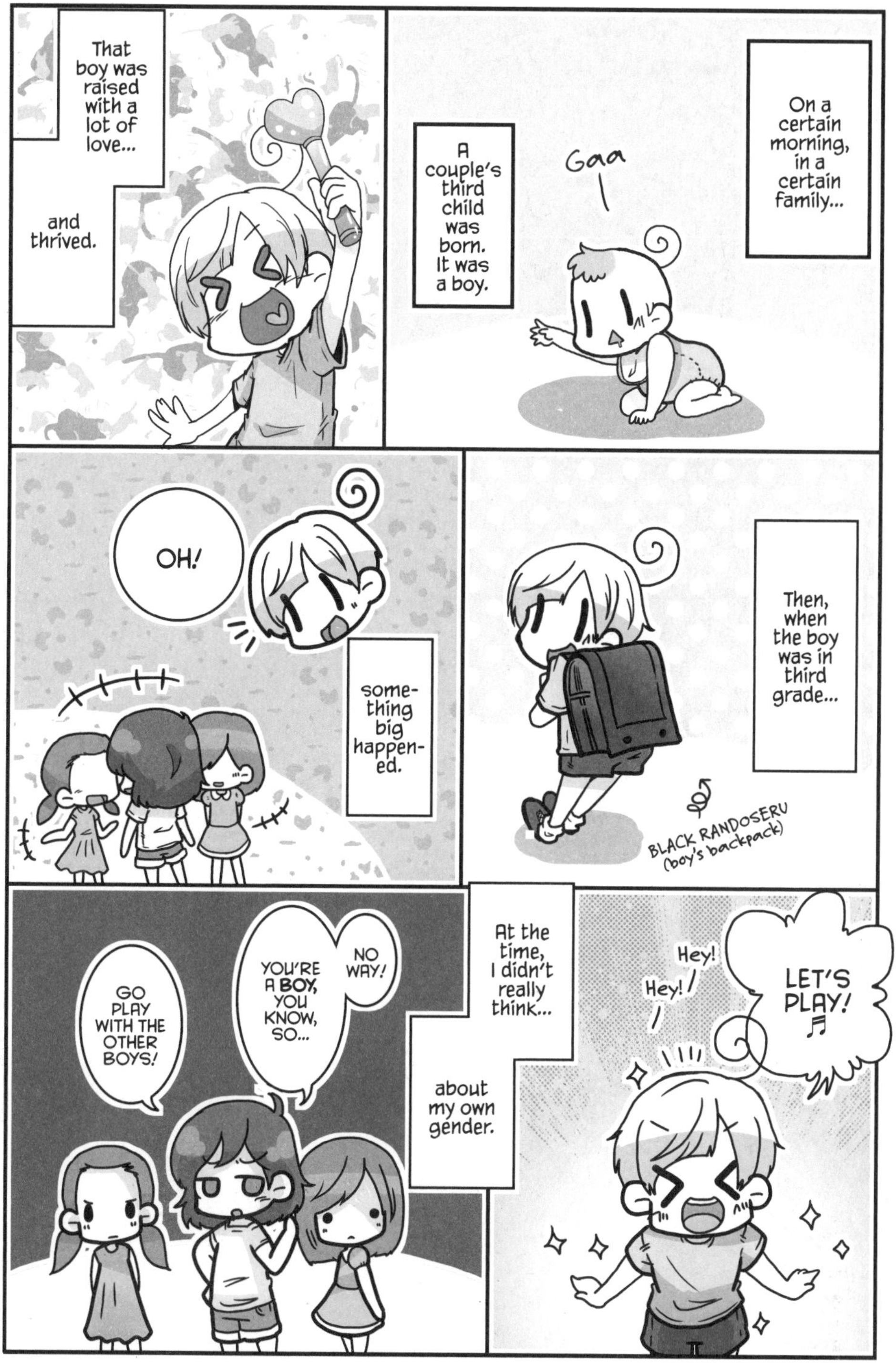
On a certain morning, in a certain family...
A couple's third child was born. It was a boy.
Gaa
That boy was raised with a lot of love...
and thrived.
Then, when the boy was in third grade...
BLACK RANDOSERU (boy's backpack)
OH!
some-thing big happen-ed.
Hey!
Hey!
LET'S PLAY! ♫
At the time, I didn't really think...
about my own gender.
NO WAY!
YOU'RE A **BOY**, YOU KNOW, SO...
GO PLAY WITH THE OTHER BOYS!

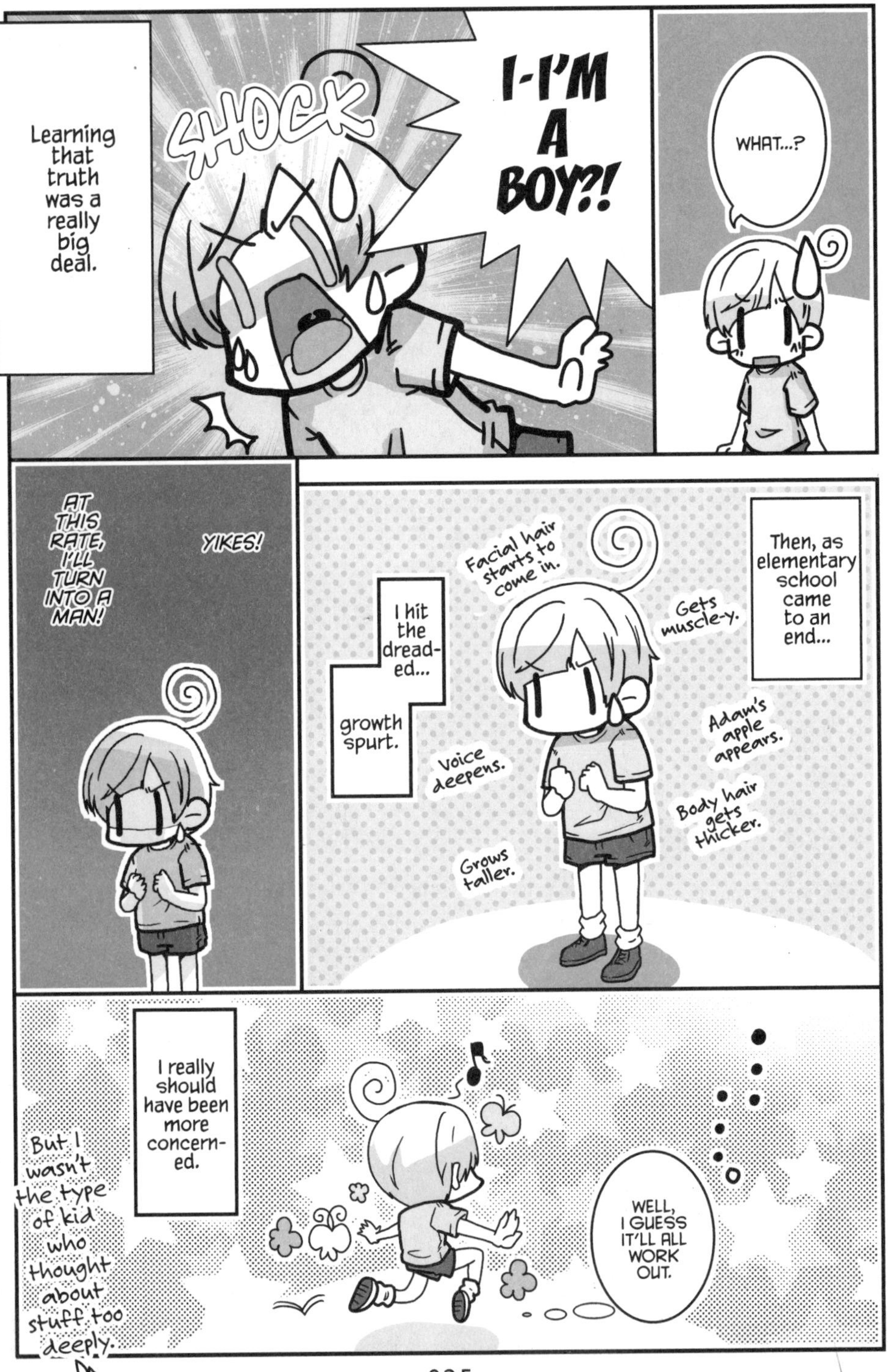
WHAT...?
I-I'M A BOY?!
SHOCK
Learning that truth was a really big deal.
Then, as elementary school came to an end...
Facial hair starts to come in.
Gets muscle-y.
I hit the dreaded... growth spurt.
Adam's apple appears.
Voice deepens.
Body hair gets thicker.
Grows taller.
YIKES!
AT THIS RATE, I'LL TURN INTO A MAN!
WELL, I GUESS IT'LL ALL WORK OUT.
I really should have been more concerned.
But I wasn't the type of kid who thought about stuff too deeply.

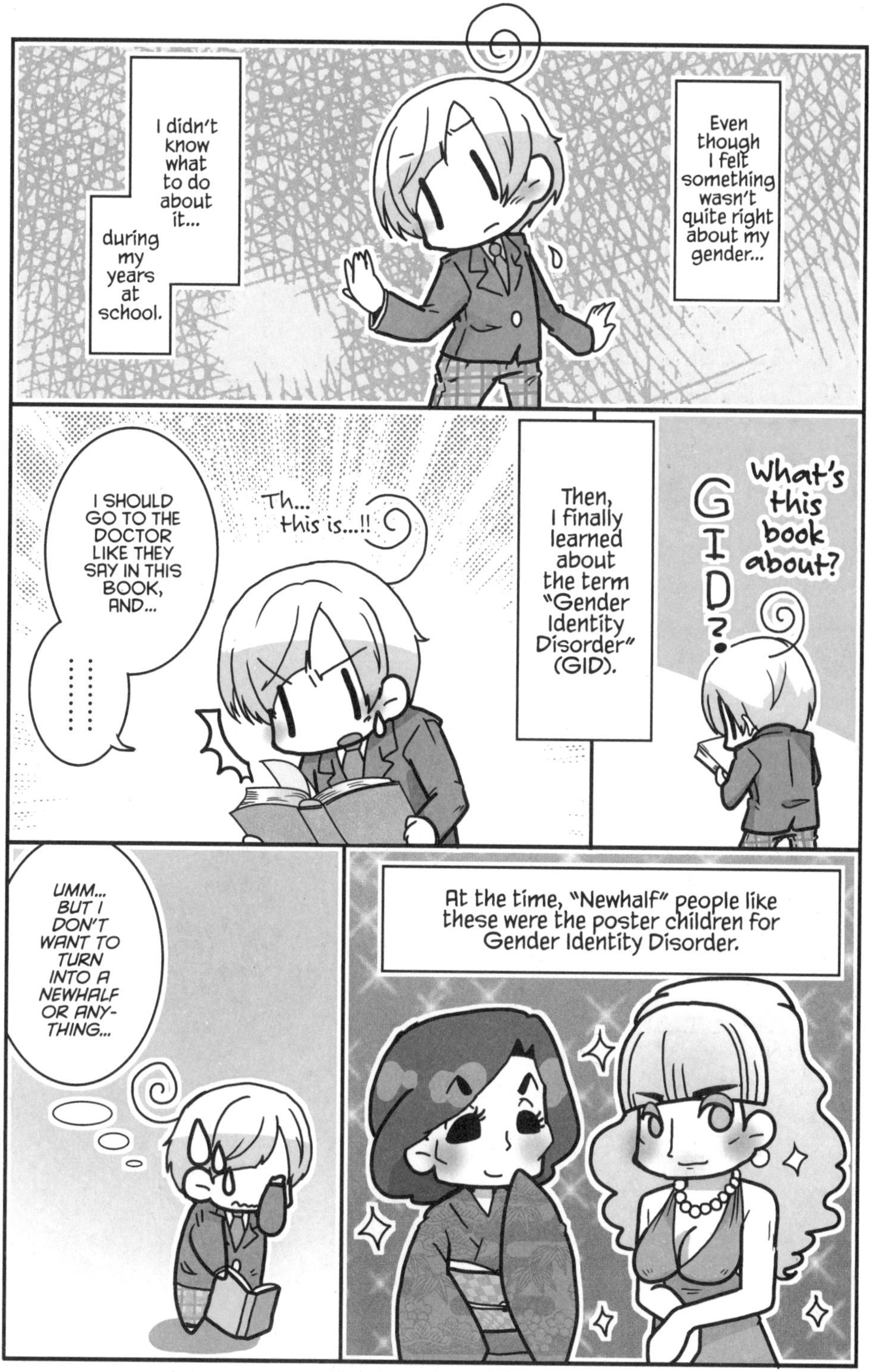

Even though I felt something wasn't quite right about my gender...
I didn't know what to do about it...
during my years at school.
What's this book about?
GID?
Then, I finally learned about the term "Gender Identity Disorder" (GID).
Th... this is...!!
I SHOULD GO TO THE DOCTOR LIKE THEY SAY IN THIS BOOK, AND... ......
At the time, "Newhalf" people like these were the poster children for Gender Identity Disorder.
UMM... BUT I DON'T WANT TO TURN INTO A NEWHALF OR ANY-THING...

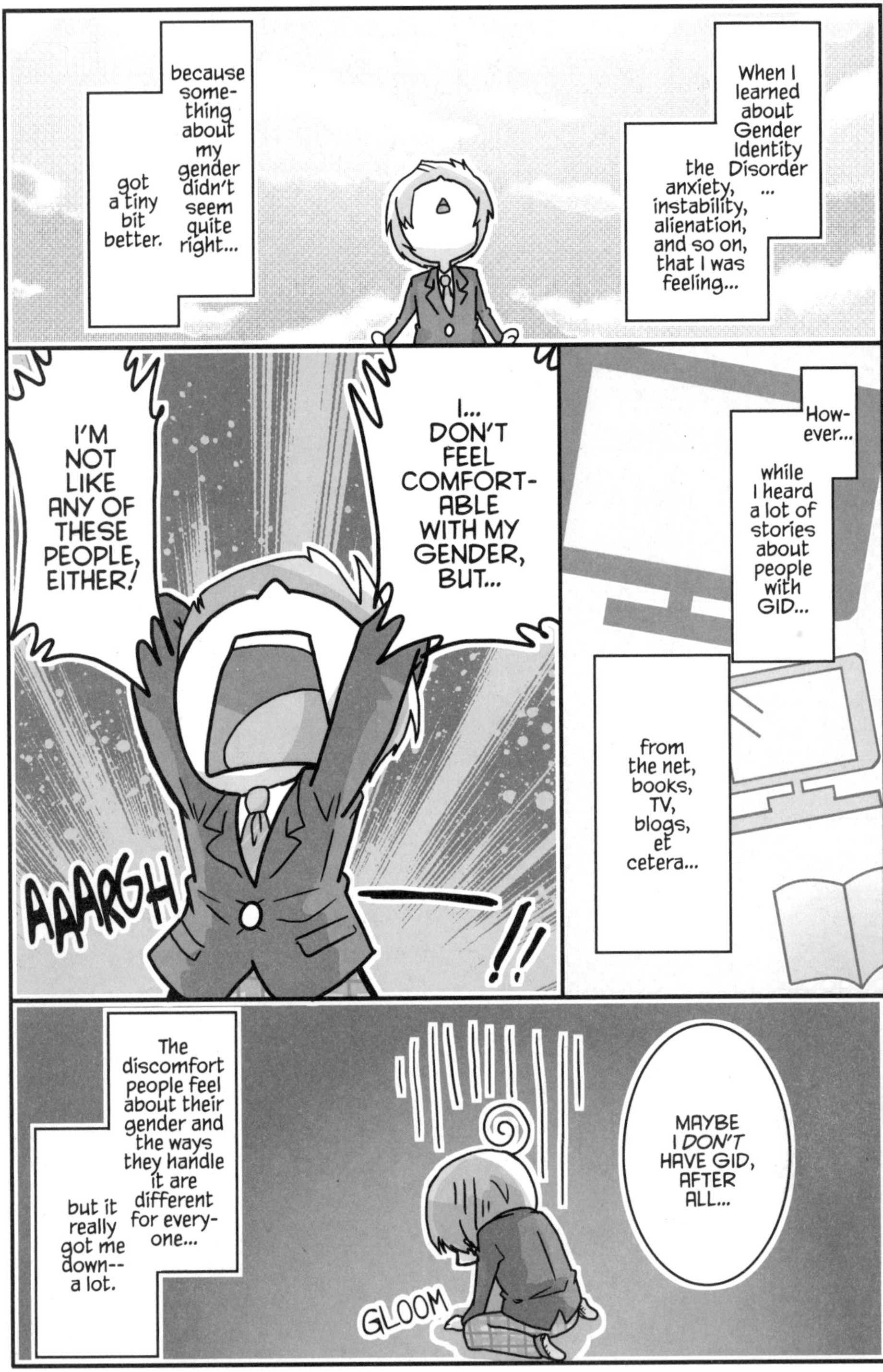
When I learned about Gender Identity Disorder...
the anxiety, instability, alienation, and so on, that I was feeling...
because some-thing about my gender didn't seem quite right...
got a tiny bit better.
How-ever...
while I heard a lot of stories about people with GID...
from the net, books, TV, blogs, et cetera...
I... DON'T FEEL COMFORT-ABLE WITH MY GENDER, BUT...
I'M NOT LIKE ANY OF THESE PEOPLE, EITHER!
AAARGH!!
MAYBE I *DON'T* HAVE GID, AFTER ALL...
GLOOM
The discomfort people feel about their gender and the ways they handle it are different for every-one...
but it really got me down--a lot.

※ *Gender Identity Disorder: Seidouissei Shougai is the Japanese name for people who identify with a gender that isn't the one that they were assigned at birth. This is also called "gender dysphoria."*

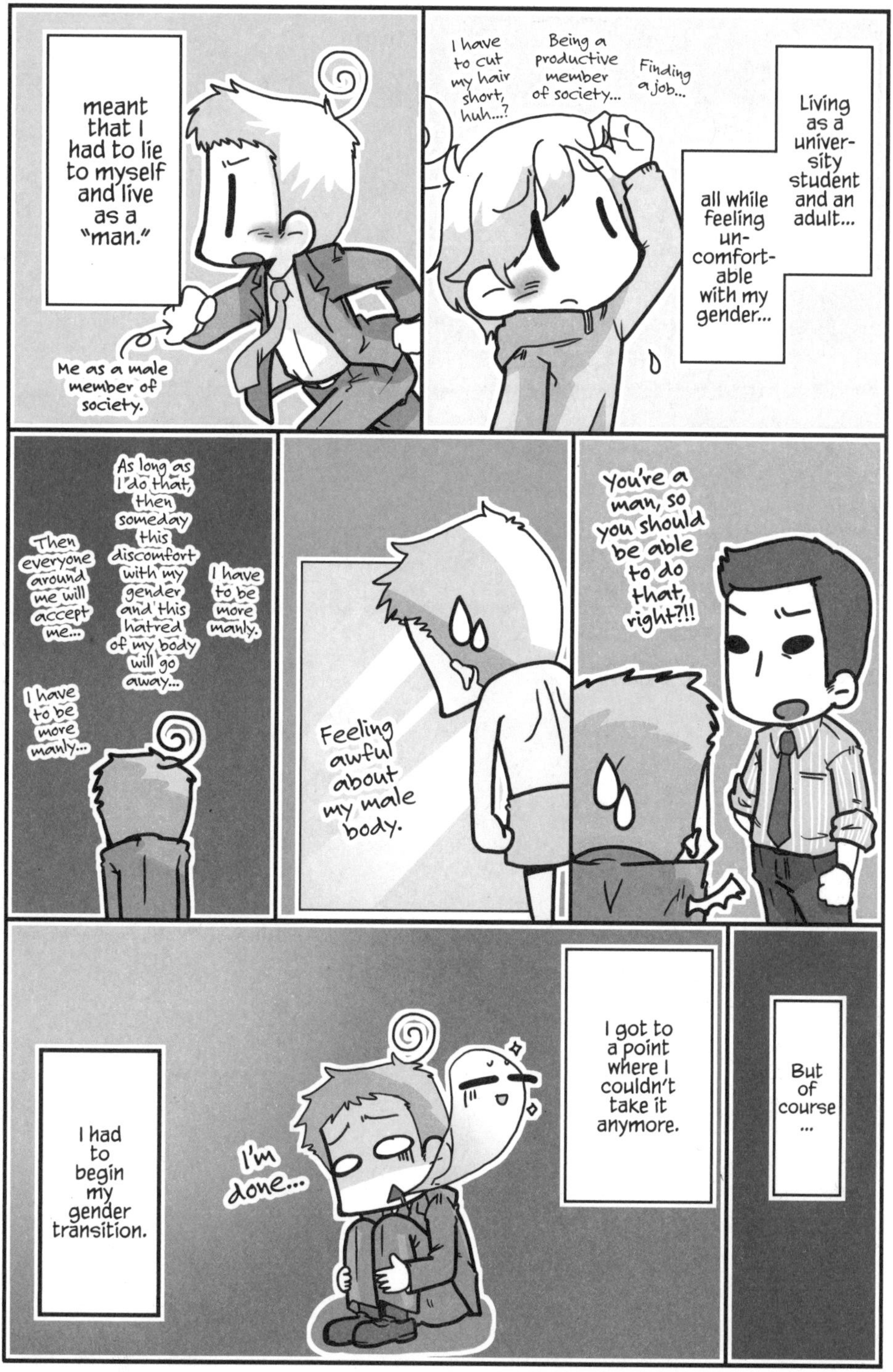
Living as a university student and an adult...
all while feeling uncomfortable with my gender...
Finding a job...
Being a productive member of society...
I have to cut my hair short, huh...?
meant that I had to lie to myself and live as a "man."
Me as a male member of society.
You're a man, so you should be able to do that, right?!!
Feeling awful about my male body.
As long as I do that, then someday this discomfort with my gender and this hatred of my body will go away...
I have to be more manly.
Then everyone around me will accept me...
I have to be more manly...
But of course...
I got to a point where I couldn't take it anymore.
I'm done...
I had to begin my gender transition.

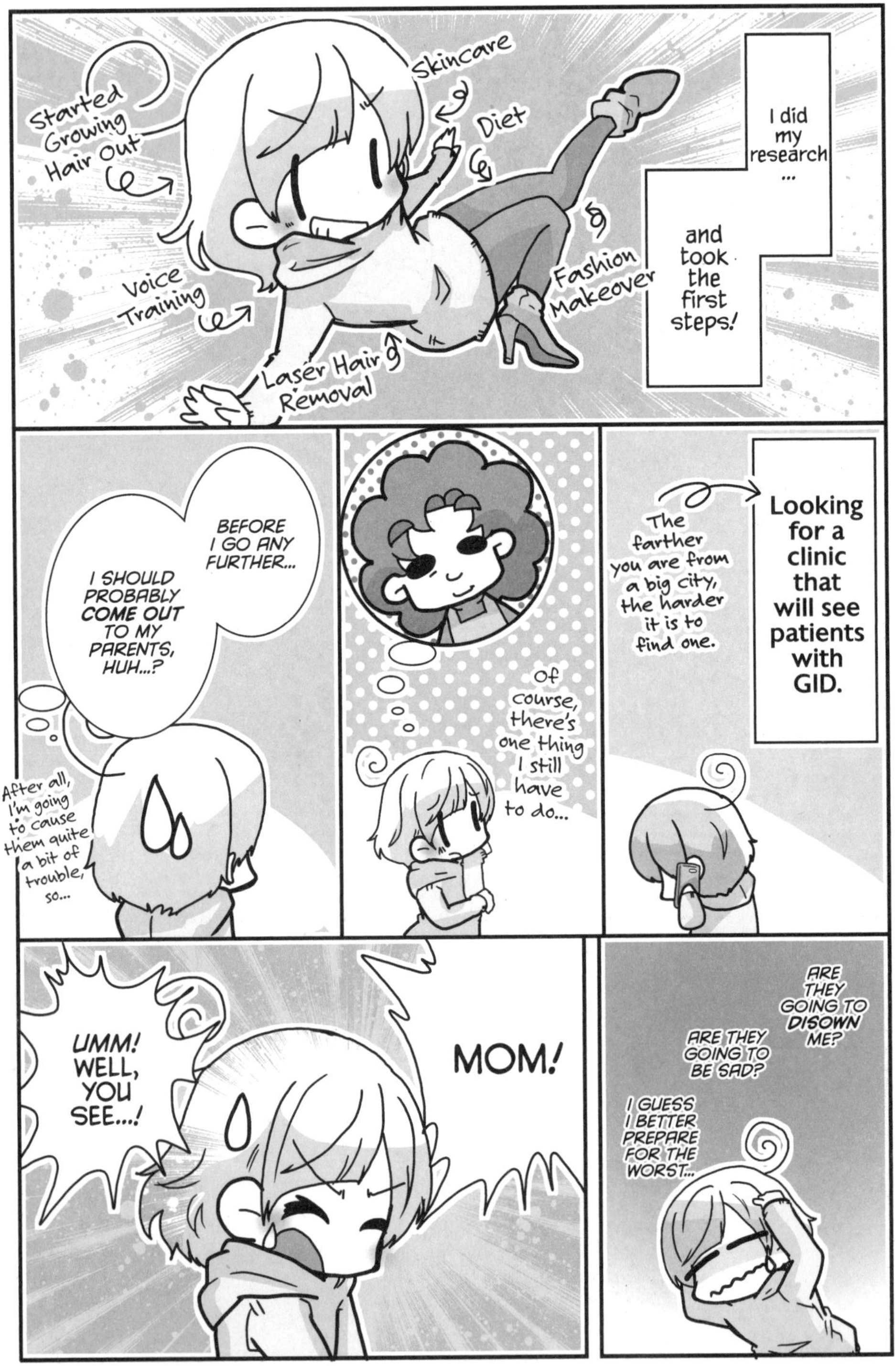
I did my research...
and took the first steps!
Skincare
Diet
Fashion Makeover
Started Growing Hair Out
Voice Training
Laser Hair Removal
Looking for a clinic that will see patients with GID.
The farther you are from a big city, the harder it is to find one.
Of course, there's one thing I still have to do...
BEFORE I GO ANY FURTHER...
I SHOULD PROBABLY **COME OUT** TO MY PARENTS, HUH...?
After all, I'm going to cause them quite a bit of trouble, so...
ARE THEY GOING TO **DISOWN** ME?
ARE THEY GOING TO BE SAD?
I GUESS I BETTER PREPARE FOR THE WORST...
MOM!
UMM! WELL, YOU SEE...!

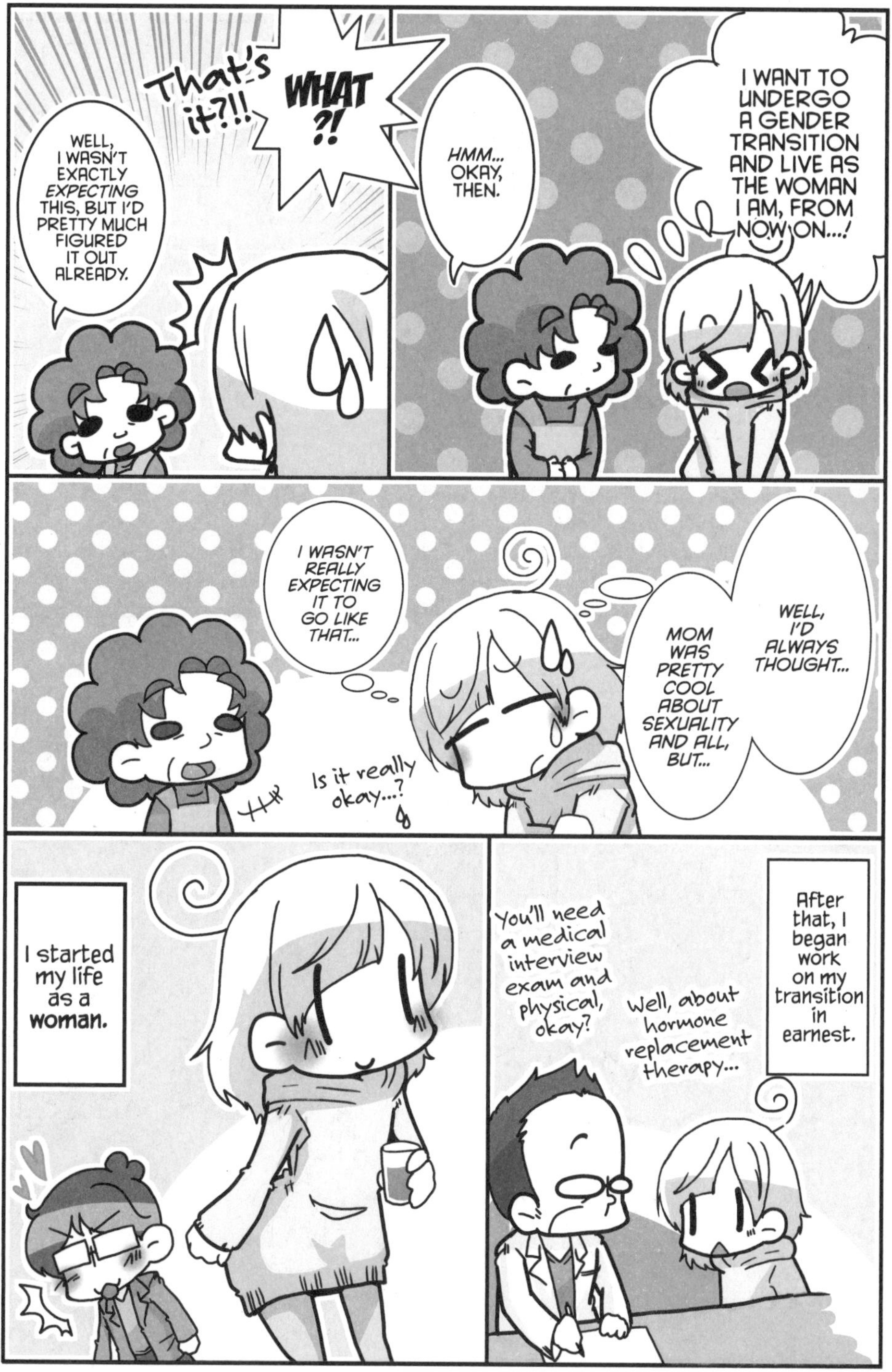
I WANT TO UNDERGO A GENDER TRANSITION AND LIVE AS THE WOMAN I AM, FROM NOW ON...!
HMM... OKAY, THEN.
WHAT ?!
That's it?!!
WELL, I WASN'T EXACTLY EXPECTING THIS, BUT I'D PRETTY MUCH FIGURED IT OUT ALREADY.
WELL, I'D ALWAYS THOUGHT...
MOM WAS PRETTY COOL ABOUT SEXUALITY AND ALL, BUT...
I WASN'T REALLY EXPECTING IT TO GO LIKE THAT...
Is it really okay...?
After that, I began work on my transition in earnest.
You'll need a medical interview exam and physical, okay?
Well, about hormone replacement therapy...
I started my life as a woman.

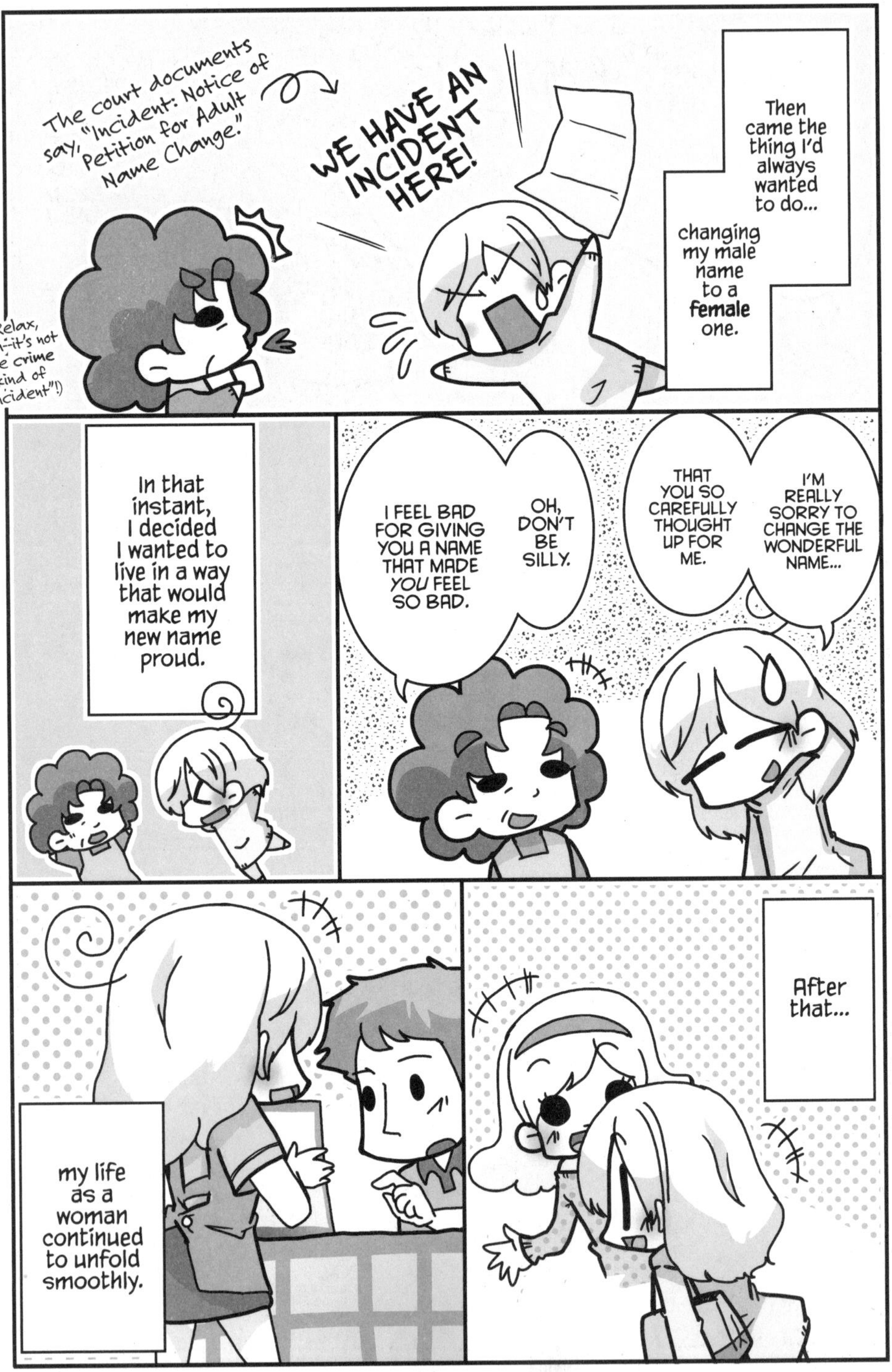
Then came the thing I'd always wanted to do...
changing my male name to a **female** one.
WE HAVE AN INCIDENT HERE!
The court documents say, "Incident: Notice of Petition for Adult Name Change."
(Relax, Mom–it's not the crime kind of "Incident"!)
I'M REALLY SORRY TO CHANGE THE WONDERFUL NAME...
THAT YOU SO CAREFULLY THOUGHT UP FOR ME.
OH, DON'T BE SILLY.
I FEEL BAD FOR GIVING YOU A NAME THAT MADE *YOU* FEEL SO BAD.
In that instant, I decided I wanted to live in a way that would make my new name proud.
After that...
my life as a woman continued to unfold smoothly.

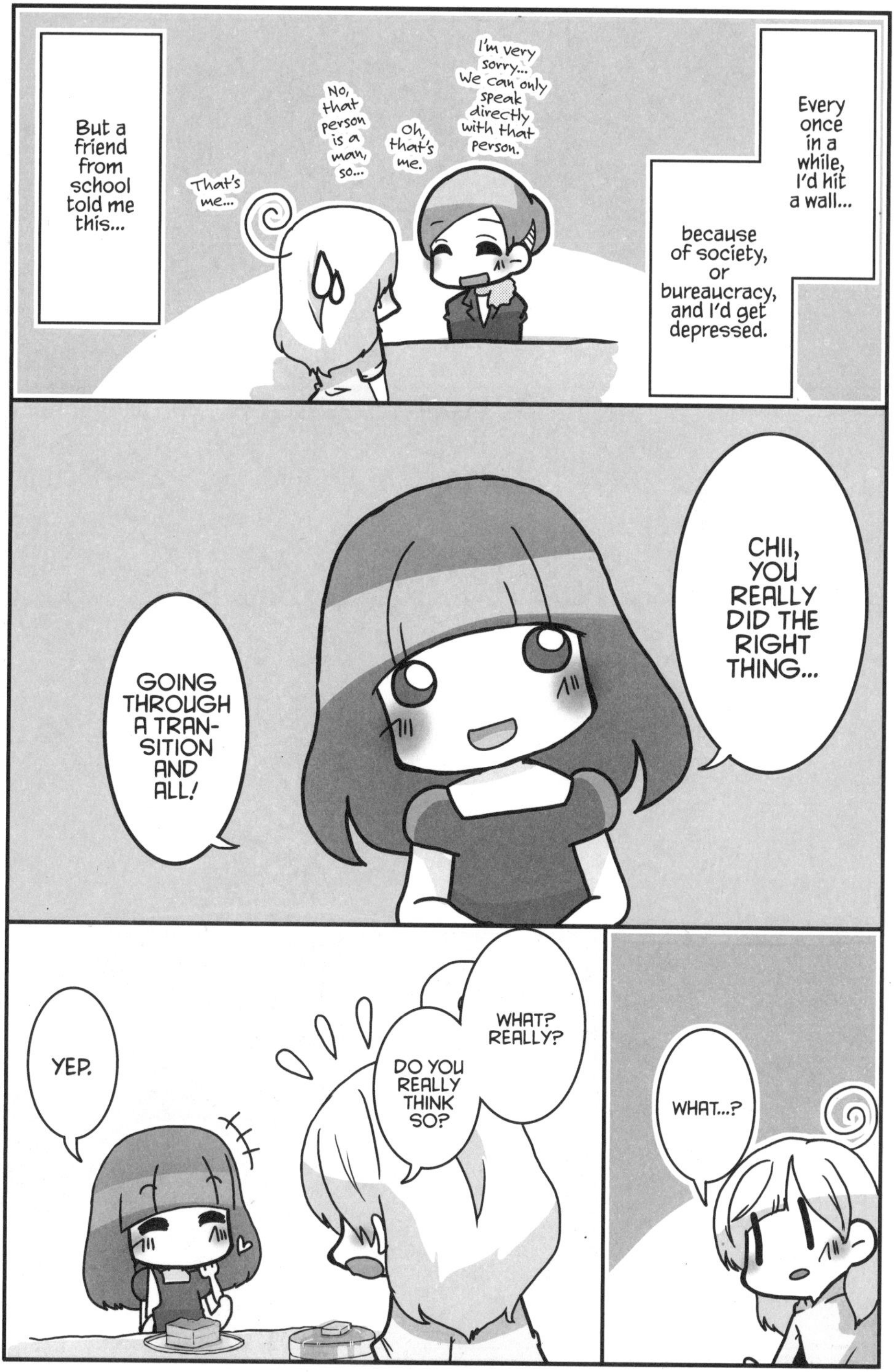
Every once in a while, I'd hit a wall...
because of society, or bureaucracy, and I'd get depressed.
I'm very sorry... We can only speak directly with that person.
Oh, that's me.
No, that person is a man, so...
That's me...
But a friend from school told me this...
CHII, YOU REALLY DID THE RIGHT THING...
GOING THROUGH A TRANSITION AND ALL!
WHAT...?
WHAT? REALLY?
DO YOU REALLY THINK SO?
YEP.

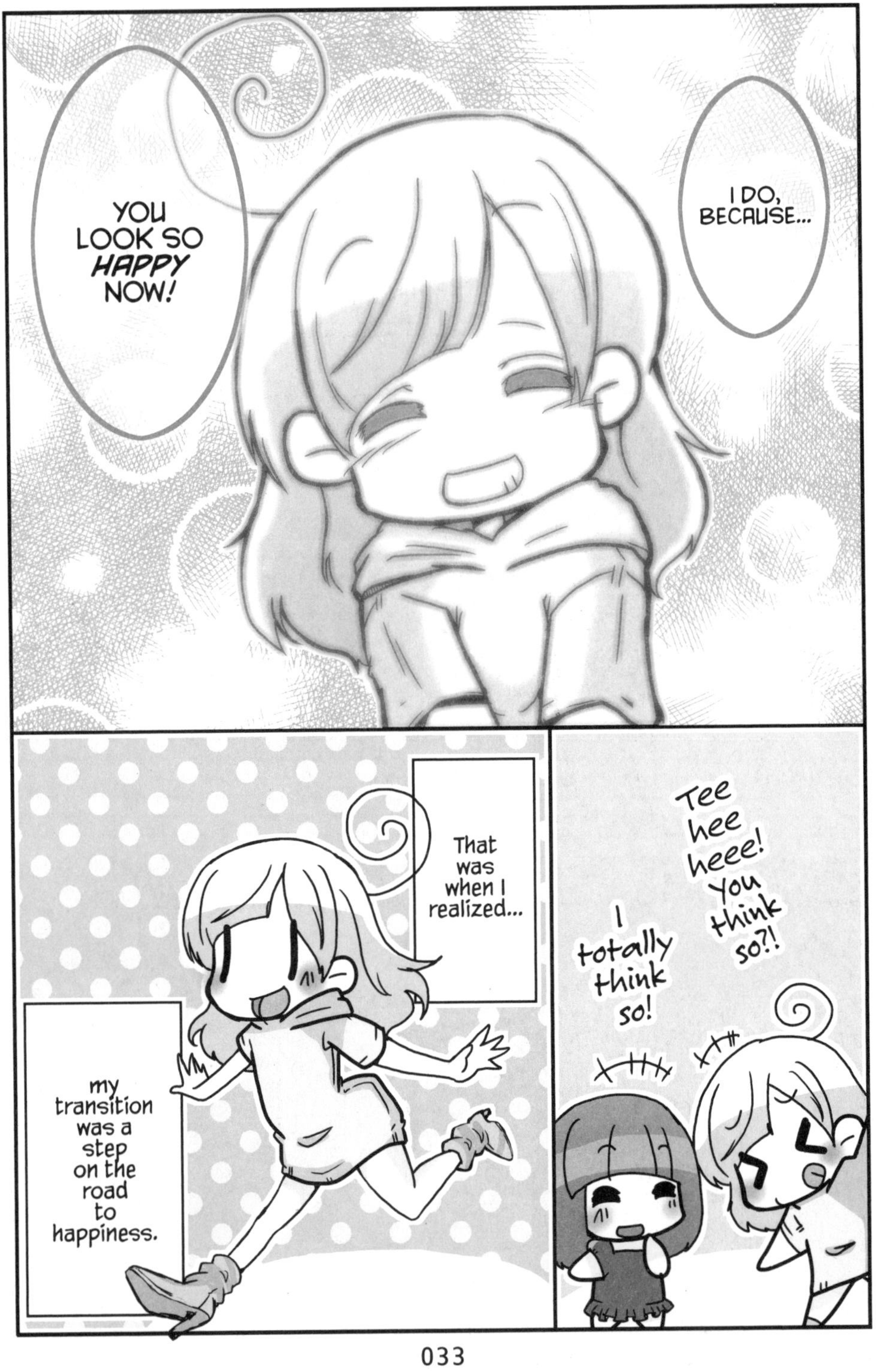
YOU LOOK SO *HAPPY* NOW!
I DO, BECAUSE...
Tee hee heee! You think so?!
I totally think so!
That was when I realized...
my transition was a step on the road to happiness.

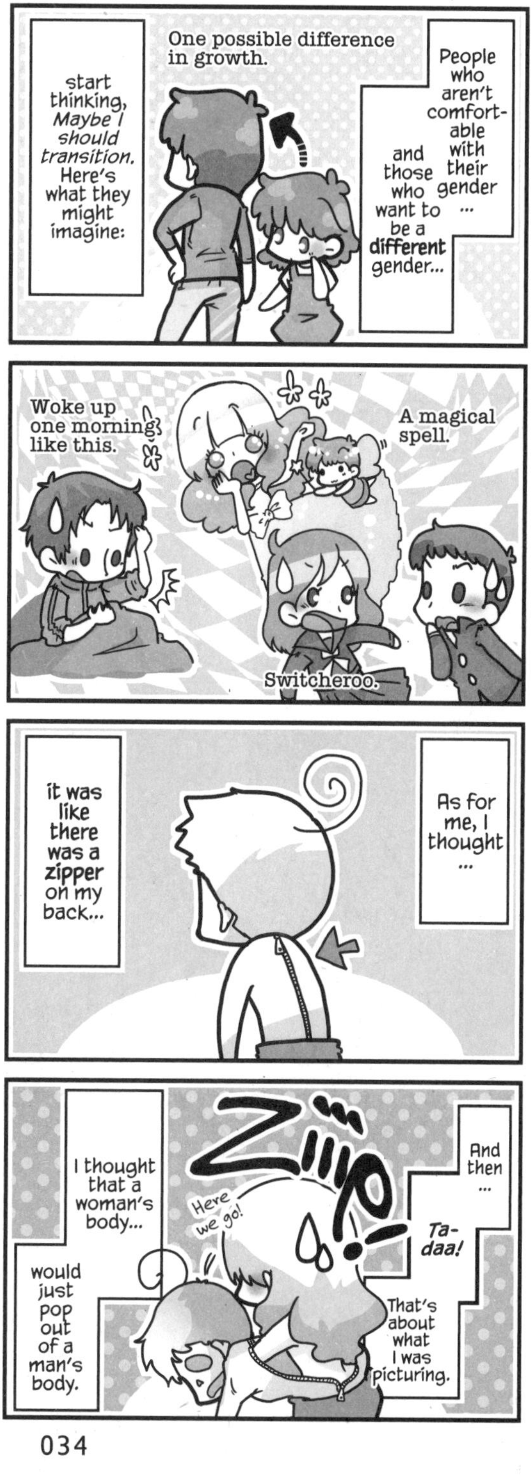
People who aren't comfortable with their gender...
and those who want to be a **different** gender...
One possible difference in growth.
start thinking, *Maybe I should transition.* Here's what they might imagine:
A magical spell.
Woke up one morning like this.
Switcheroo.
As for me, I thought...
it was like there was a **zipper** on my back...
And then...
Ziiip!
Ta-daa!
Here we go!
I thought that a woman's body...
would just pop out of a man's body.
That's about what I was picturing.

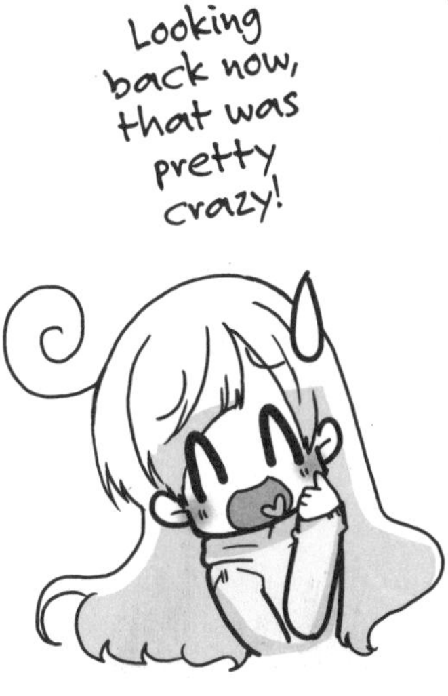
Looking back now, that was pretty crazy!

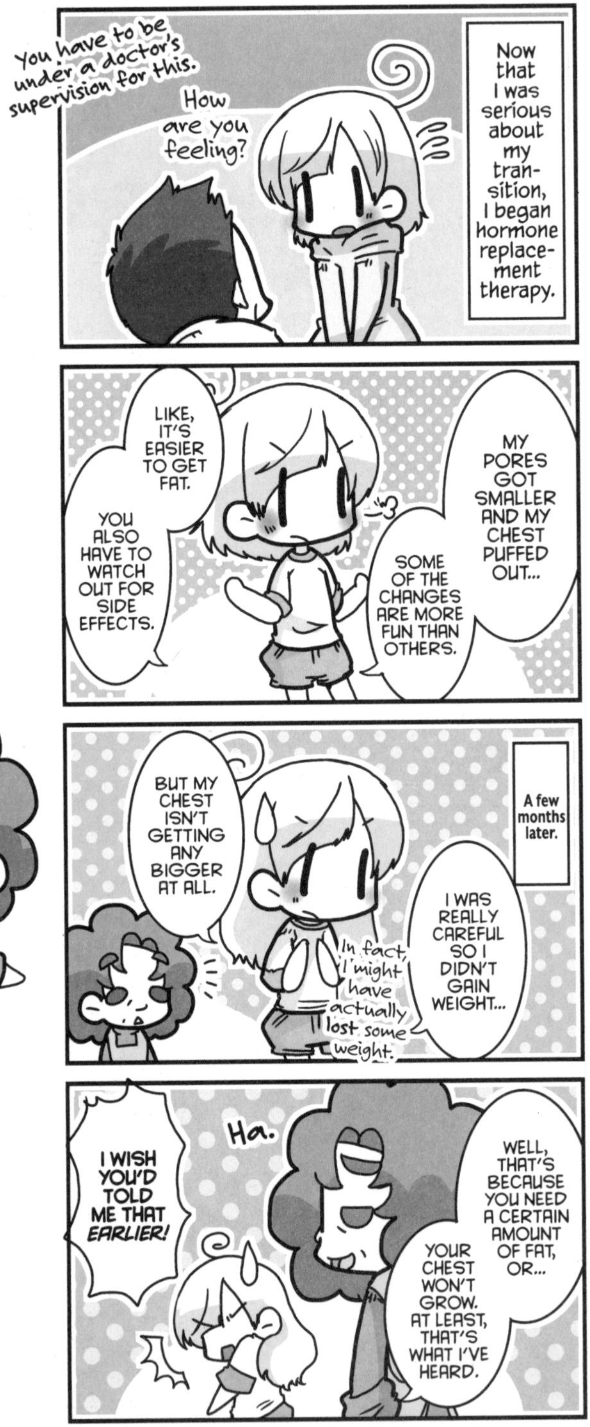

Now that I was serious about my transition, I began hormone replacement therapy.
How are you feeling?
You have to be under a doctor's supervision for this.
MY PORES GOT SMALLER AND MY CHEST PUFFED OUT...
SOME OF THE CHANGES ARE MORE FUN THAN OTHERS.
LIKE, IT'S EASIER TO GET FAT.
YOU ALSO HAVE TO WATCH OUT FOR SIDE EFFECTS.
A few months later.
I WAS REALLY CAREFUL SO I DIDN'T GAIN WEIGHT...
In fact, I might have actually lost some weight.
BUT MY CHEST ISN'T GETTING ANY BIGGER AT ALL.
WELL, THAT'S BECAUSE YOU NEED A CERTAIN AMOUNT OF FAT, OR...
YOUR CHEST WON'T GROW. AT LEAST, THAT'S WHAT I'VE HEARD.
Ha.
I WISH YOU'D TOLD ME THAT *EARLIER*!

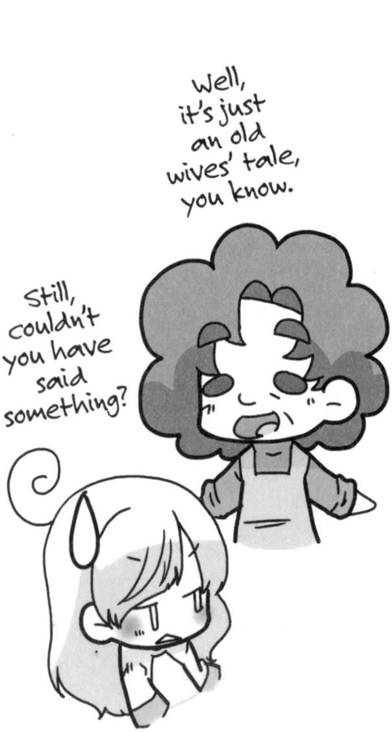

Well, it's just an old wives' tale, you know.
Still, couldn't you have said something?

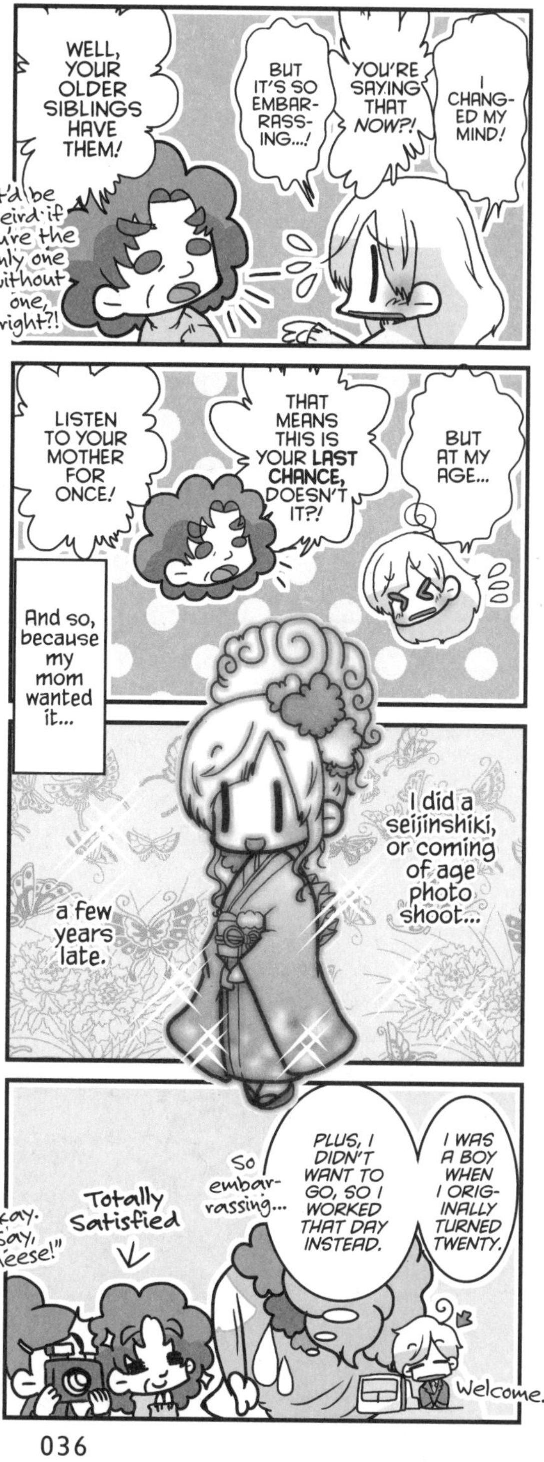
I CHANGED MY MIND!
YOU'RE SAYING THAT NOW?!
BUT IT'S SO EMBARRASSING...!
WELL, YOUR OLDER SIBLINGS HAVE THEM!
It'd be weird if you're the only one without one, right?!
BUT AT MY AGE...
THAT MEANS THIS IS YOUR **LAST CHANCE,** DOESN'T IT?!
LISTEN TO YOUR MOTHER FOR ONCE!
And so, because my mom wanted it...
I did a seijinshiki, or coming of age photo shoot...
a few years late.
I WAS A BOY WHEN I ORIGINALLY TURNED TWENTY.
PLUS, I DIDN'T WANT TO GO, SO I WORKED THAT DAY INSTEAD.
So embarrassing...
Totally Satisfied
Okay. Say, "Cheese!"
Welcome.

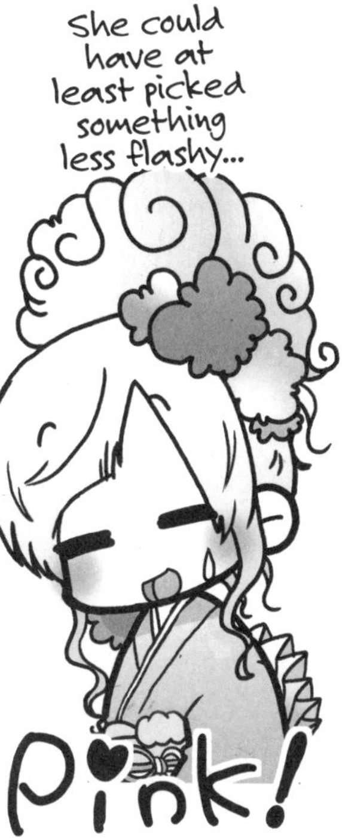
She could have at least picked something less flashy...
Pink!

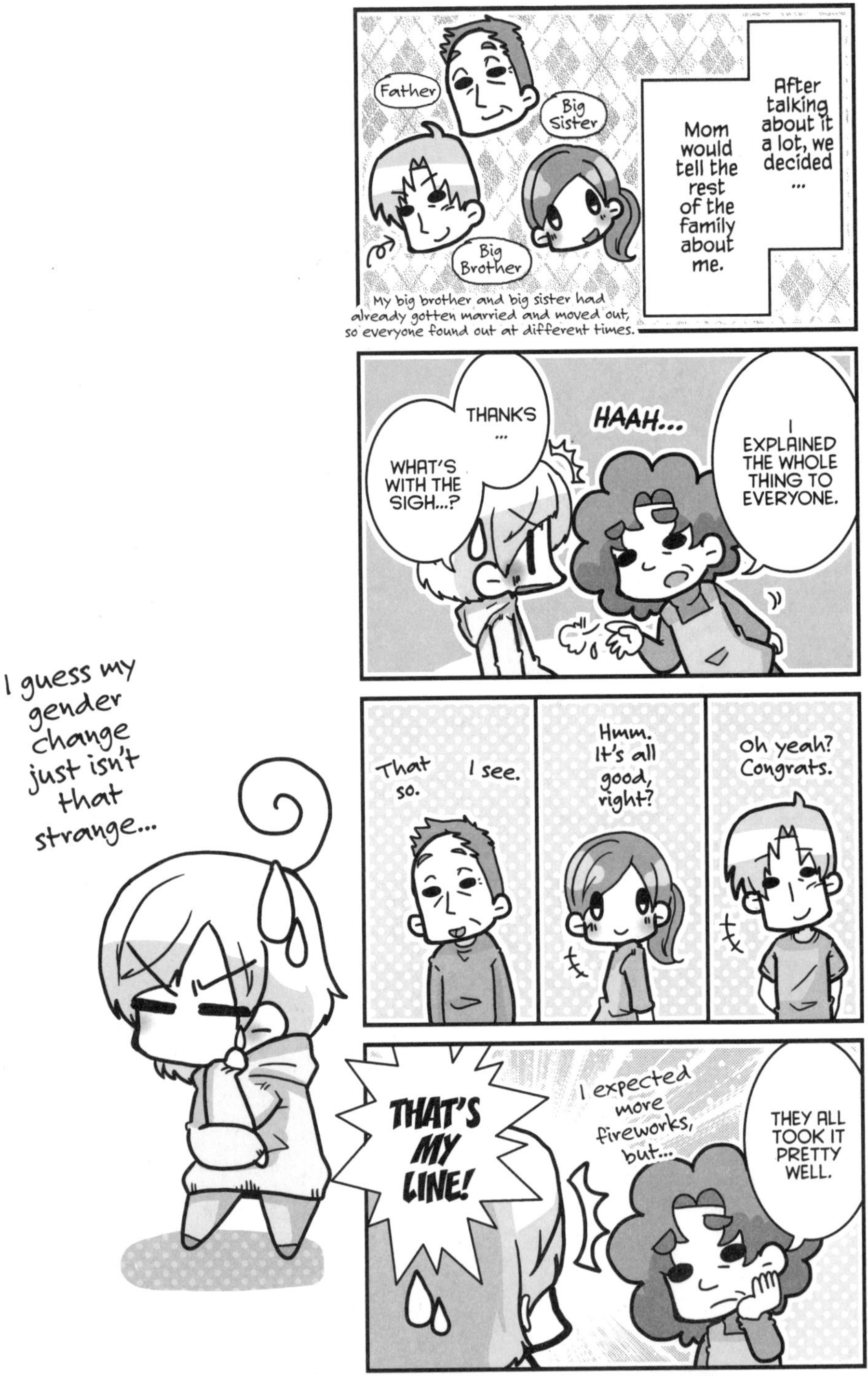
After talking about it a lot, we decided ...
Mom would tell the rest of the family about me.
Father
Big Sister
Big Brother
My big brother and big sister had already gotten married and moved out, so everyone found out at different times.
I EXPLAINED THE WHOLE THING TO EVERYONE.
HAAH...
THANKS ...
WHAT'S WITH THE SIGH...?
Oh yeah? Congrats.
Hmm. It's all good, right?
I see.
That so.
THEY ALL TOOK IT PRETTY WELL.
I expected more fireworks, but...
THAT'S MY LINE!
I guess my gender change just isn't that strange...

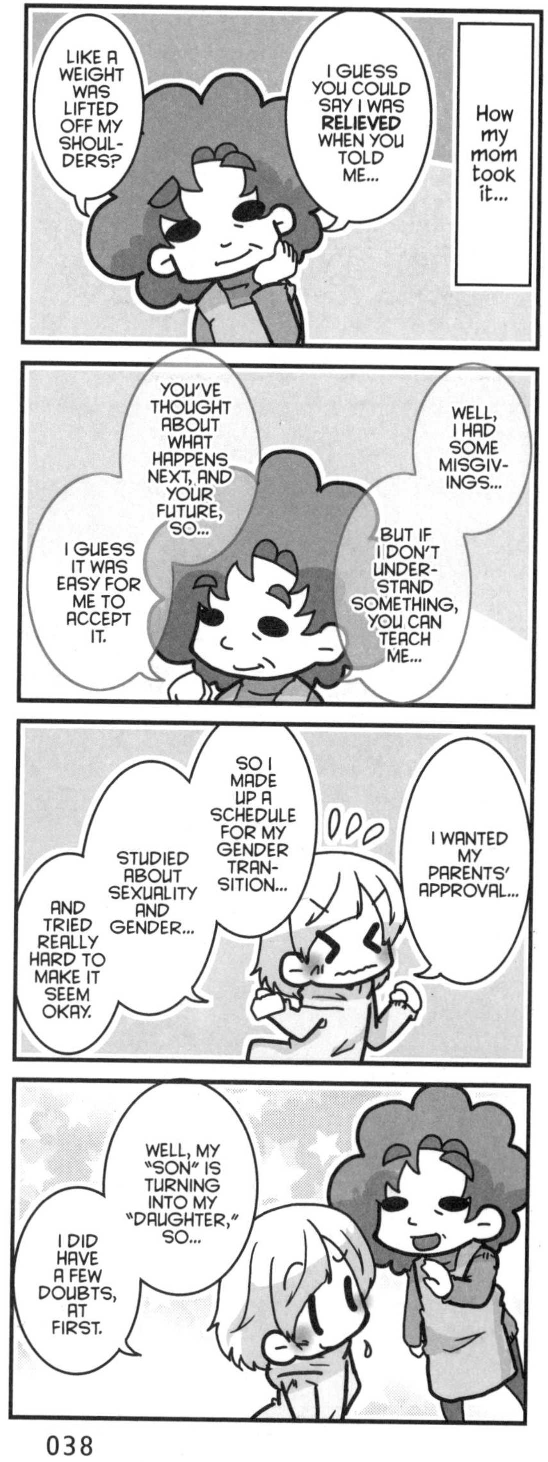
How my mom took it...
I GUESS YOU COULD SAY I WAS **RELIEVED** WHEN YOU TOLD ME...
LIKE A WEIGHT WAS LIFTED OFF MY SHOUL-DERS?
WELL, I HAD SOME MISGIV-INGS...
BUT IF I DON'T UNDER-STAND SOMETHING, YOU CAN TEACH ME...
YOU'VE THOUGHT ABOUT WHAT HAPPENS NEXT, AND YOUR FUTURE, SO...
I GUESS IT WAS EASY FOR ME TO ACCEPT IT.
I WANTED MY PARENTS' APPROVAL...
SO I MADE UP A SCHEDULE FOR MY GENDER TRAN-SITION...
STUDIED ABOUT SEXUALITY AND GENDER...
AND TRIED REALLY HARD TO MAKE IT SEEM OKAY.
WELL, MY "SON" IS TURNING INTO MY "DAUGHTER," SO...
I DID HAVE A FEW DOUBTS, AT FIRST.

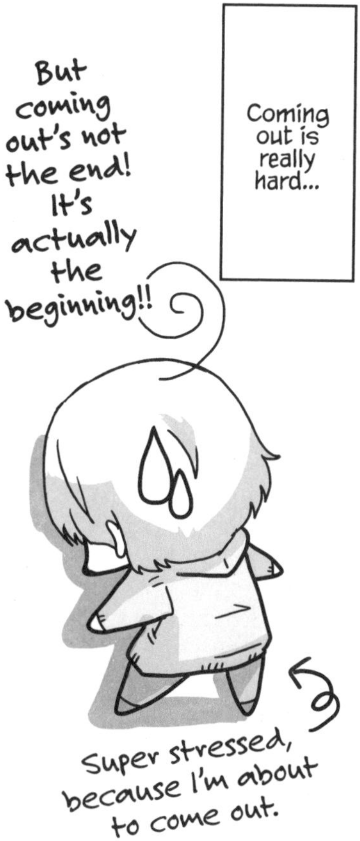
Coming out is really hard...
But coming out's not the end! It's actually the beginning!!
Super stressed, because I'm about to come out.

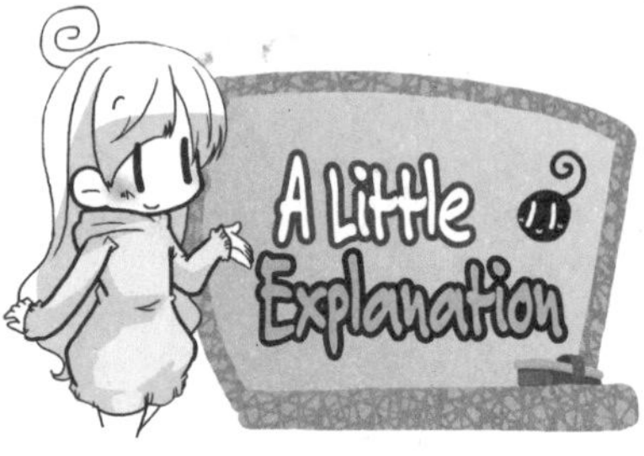
A Little Explanation

Gender Identity Disorder (GID)

Some people describe this as a "mismatch between your soul and your body," but that expression is easily misunderstood, so, although it's a hassle, I try to give people a more detailed explanation. A lot of people think "sex change" when they hear the phrase, "Gender Identity Disorder," but it's a personal decision to transition, or not transition.

Starting with the 2013 publication of the *DSM-5*, a book of guidelines put out by the American Psychiatric Association, Gender Identity Disorder has been changed to Gender Dysphoria. Because this is not a mental illness, it is no longer called a "disorder." However, because counseling and physical gender transition require appropriate medical care, the diagnostic name of "Gender Dysphoria" was adopted. The new name is gradually being used more and more.

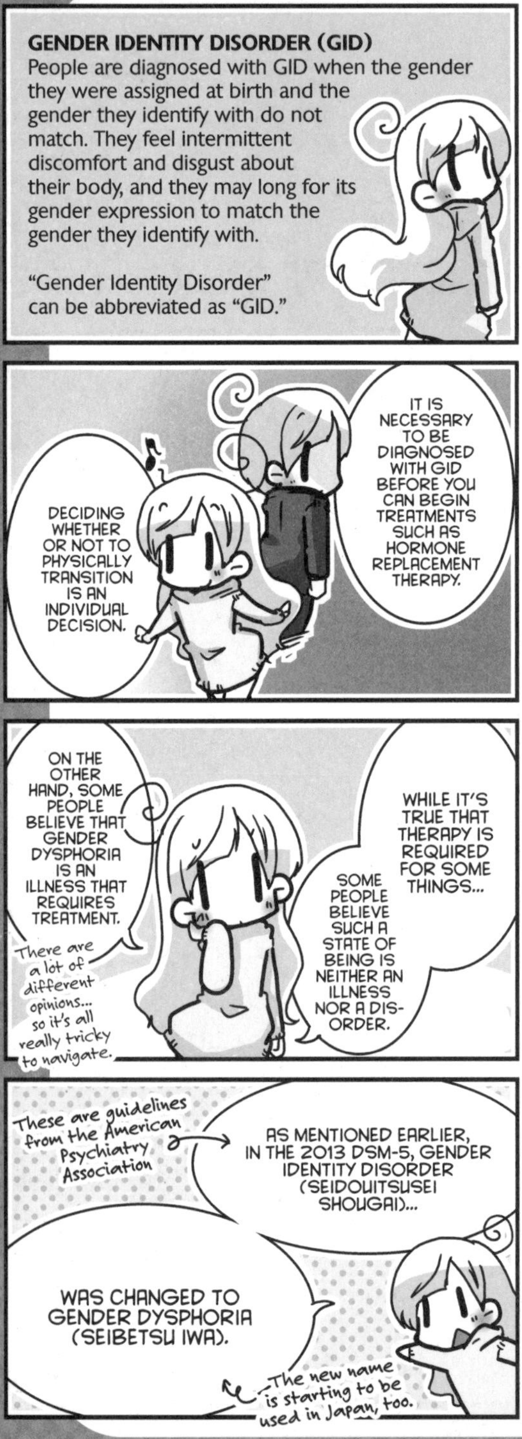
GENDER IDENTITY DISORDER (GID)
People are diagnosed with GID when the gender they were assigned at birth and the gender they identify with do not match. They feel intermittent discomfort and disgust about their body, and they may long for its gender expression to match the gender they identify with.
"Gender Identity Disorder" can be abbreviated as "GID."
IT IS NECESSARY TO BE DIAGNOSED WITH GID BEFORE YOU CAN BEGIN TREATMENTS SUCH AS HORMONE REPLACEMENT THERAPY.
DECIDING WHETHER OR NOT TO PHYSICALLY TRANSITION IS AN INDIVIDUAL DECISION.
WHILE IT'S TRUE THAT THERAPY IS REQUIRED FOR SOME THINGS...
SOME PEOPLE BELIEVE SUCH A STATE OF BEING IS NEITHER AN ILLNESS NOR A DISORDER.
ON THE OTHER HAND, SOME PEOPLE BELIEVE THAT GENDER DYSPHORIA IS AN ILLNESS THAT REQUIRES TREATMENT.
There are a lot of different opinions... so it's all really tricky to navigate.
These are guidelines from the American Psychiatry Association
AS MENTIONED EARLIER, IN THE 2013 DSM-5, GENDER IDENTITY DISORDER (SEIDOUITSUSEI SHOUGAI)...
WAS CHANGED TO GENDER DYSPHORIA (SEIBETSU IWA).
The new name is starting to be used in Japan, too.

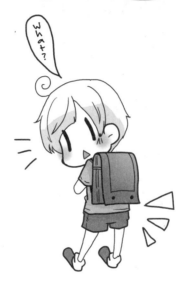

"Like, you just
wanted to wear a skirt
or something,
didn't you?"

What?

People express gender through their clothes in many
different and personal ways. Some women like masculine
fashion, while others prefer a more boyish style. Everyone is
different. So, just because some lived as "boys," that doesn't
mean that they all love feminine fashion.

As for me, I wear skirts now, but when I was little I wasn't
particularly attracted to skirts or red randoseru (girls'
backpacks).

CHAPTER 3

My Love Life as a Boy

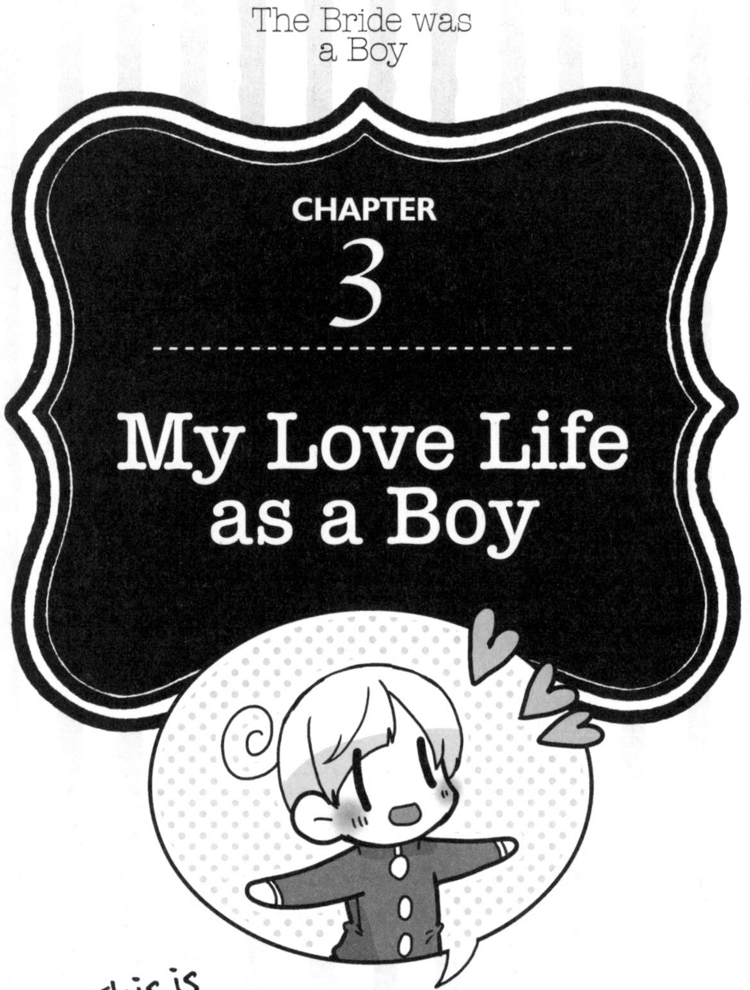

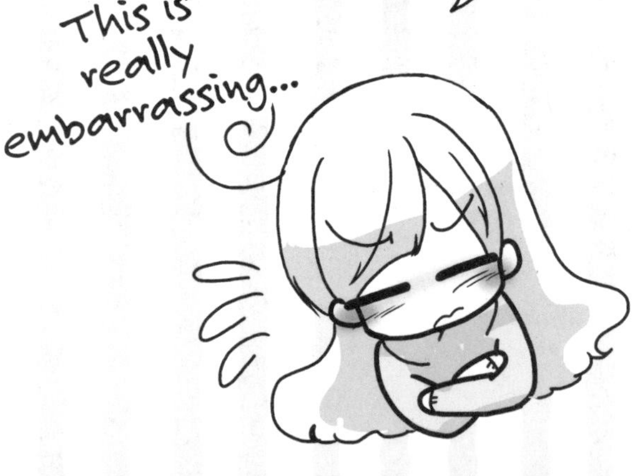
This is really embarrassing...

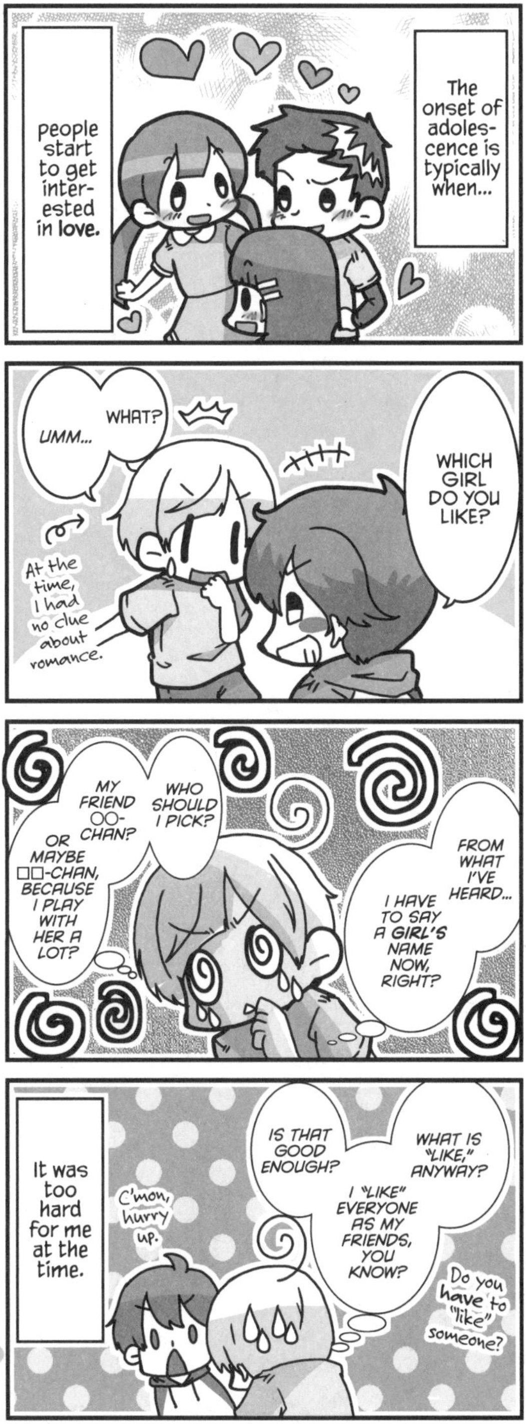
The onset of adolescence is typically when...
people start to get interested in love.
WHICH GIRL DO YOU LIKE?
WHAT?
UMM...
At the time, I had no clue about romance.
FROM WHAT I'VE HEARD...
I HAVE TO SAY A GIRL'S NAME NOW, RIGHT?
WHO SHOULD I PICK?
MY FRIEND ○○-CHAN?
OR MAYBE □□-CHAN, BECAUSE I PLAY WITH HER A LOT?
WHAT IS "LIKE," ANYWAY?
I "LIKE" EVERYONE AS MY FRIENDS, YOU KNOW?
Do you have to "like" someone?
IS THAT GOOD ENOUGH?
C'mon, hurry up.
It was too hard for me at the time.

Romantic Challenges I Faced as a BOY

I got nervous because I couldn't keep up with other people when they talked about sexual things.

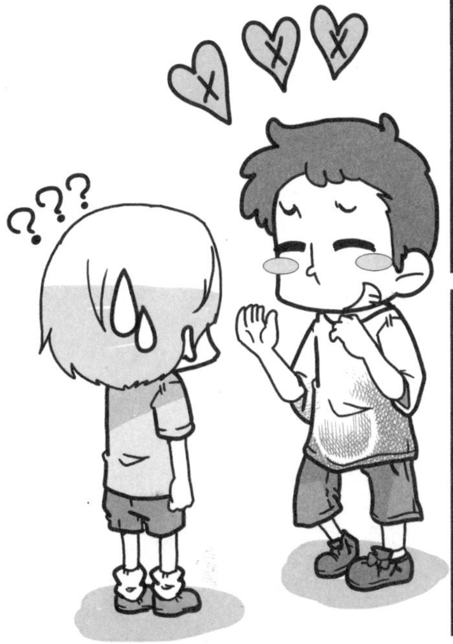
???

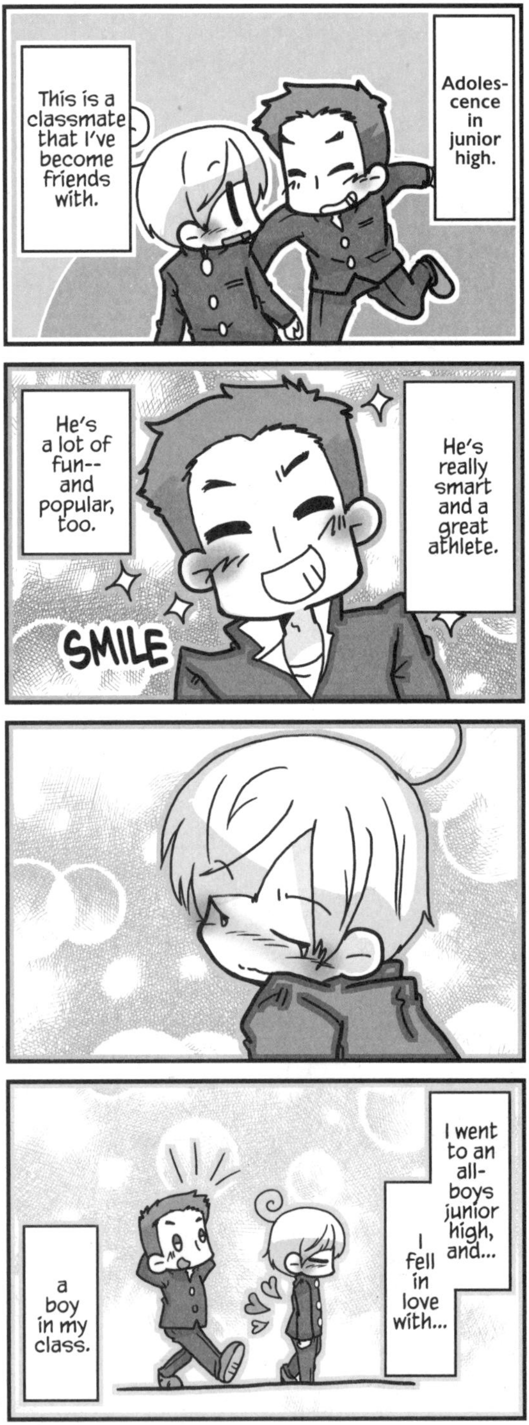
Adolescence in junior high.
This is a classmate that I've become friends with.
He's really smart and a great athlete.
He's a lot of fun--and popular, too.
SMILE
I went to an all-boys junior high, and...
I fell in love with...
a boy in my class.

Romantic Challenges I Faced as a BOY

Being called "homosexual," "homo," and "gay."

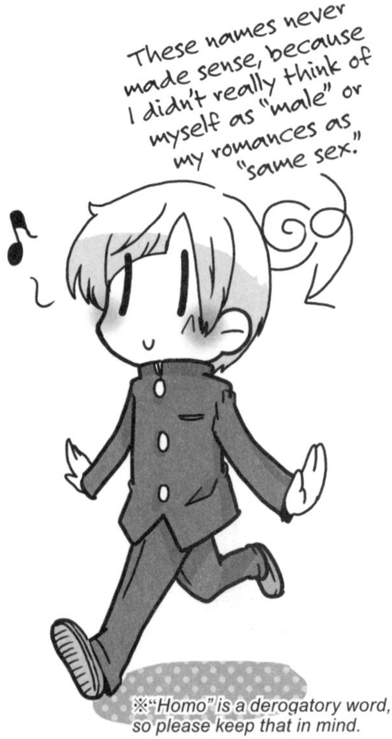
These names never made sense, because I didn't really think of myself as "male" or my romances as "same sex."

※"Homo" is a derogatory word, so please keep that in mind.

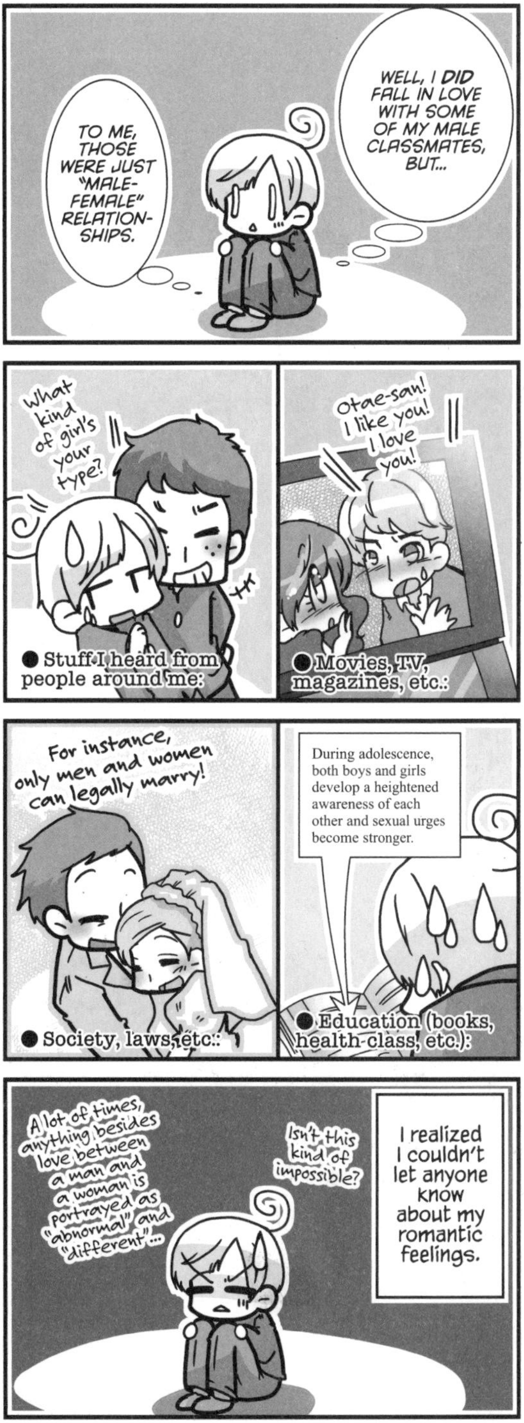
WELL, I **DID** FALL IN LOVE WITH SOME OF MY MALE CLASSMATES, BUT...
TO ME, THOSE WERE JUST "MALE-FEMALE" RELATIONSHIPS.
Otae-san! I like you! I love you!
● Movies, TV, magazines, etc.:
What kind of girl's your type?
● Stuff I heard from people around me:
During adolescence, both boys and girls develop a heightened awareness of each other and sexual urges become stronger.
● Education (books, health class, etc.):
For instance, only men and women can legally marry!
● Society, laws, etc.:
I realized I couldn't let anyone know about my romantic feelings.
Isn't this kind of impossible?
A lot of times, anything besides love between a man and a woman is portrayed as "abnormal" and "different"...

Romantic Challenges I Faced as a BOY

Hiding feelings of love because I was afraid of being judged.

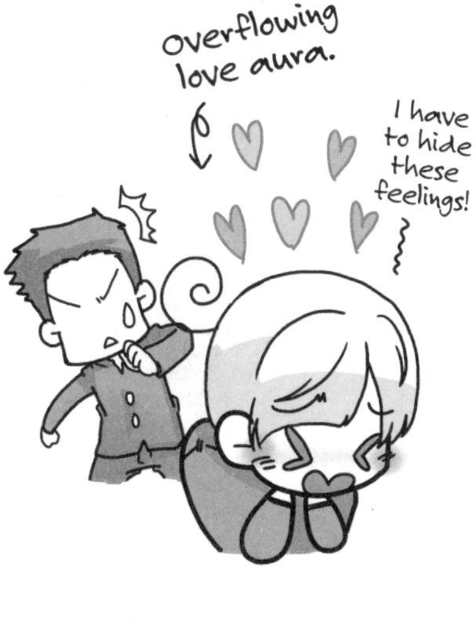
Overflowing love aura.
I have to hide these feelings!

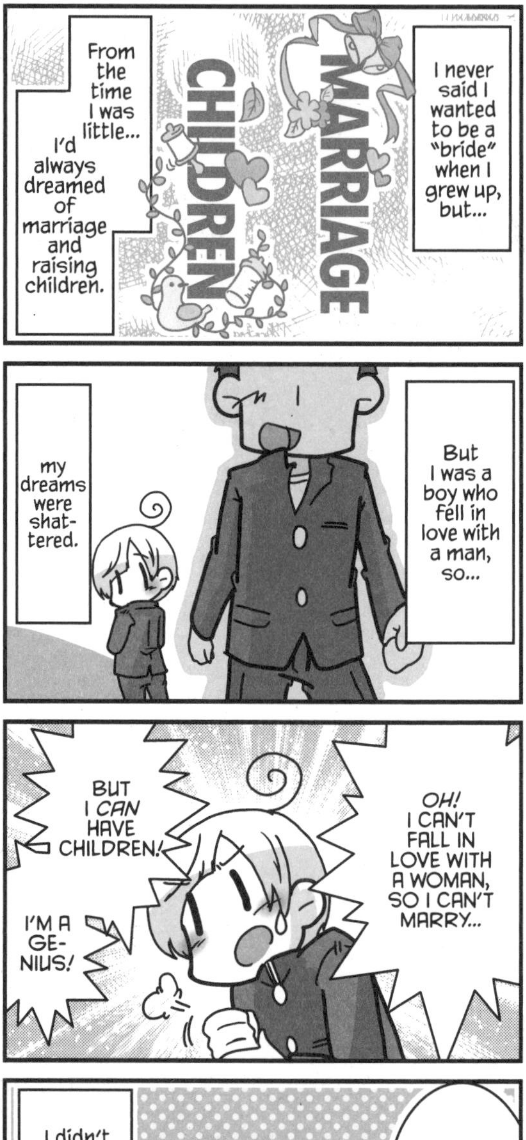
I never said I wanted to be a "bride" when I grew up, but...
MARRIAGE
CHILDREN
From the time I was little...
I'd always dreamed of marriage and raising children.
But I was a boy who fell in love with a man, so...
my dreams were shat-tered.
OH! I CAN'T FALL IN LOVE WITH A WOMAN, SO I CAN'T MARRY...
BUT I CAN HAVE CHILDREN!
I'M A GE-NIUS!
I CAN'T GET MARRIED, BUT I WANT CHILDREN.
What are you even saying?
I didn't really under-stand much in my junior high years.

Romantic Challenges I Faced as a BOY

I can't marry the person I love.

This was a pretty bitter truth for an adolescent in the throes of love.

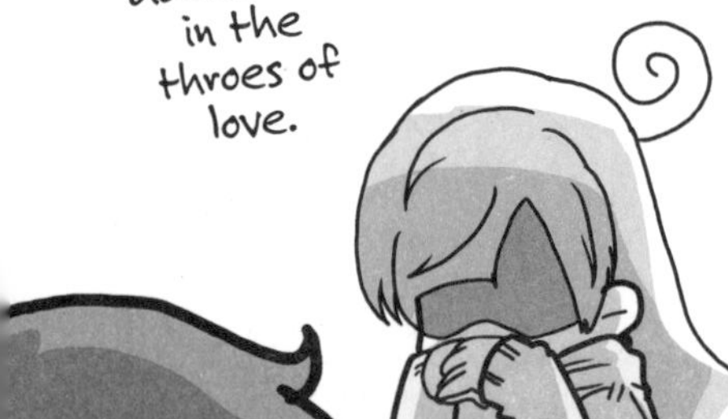

※At this time, same-sex marriages weren't allowed, much less changing one's gender.

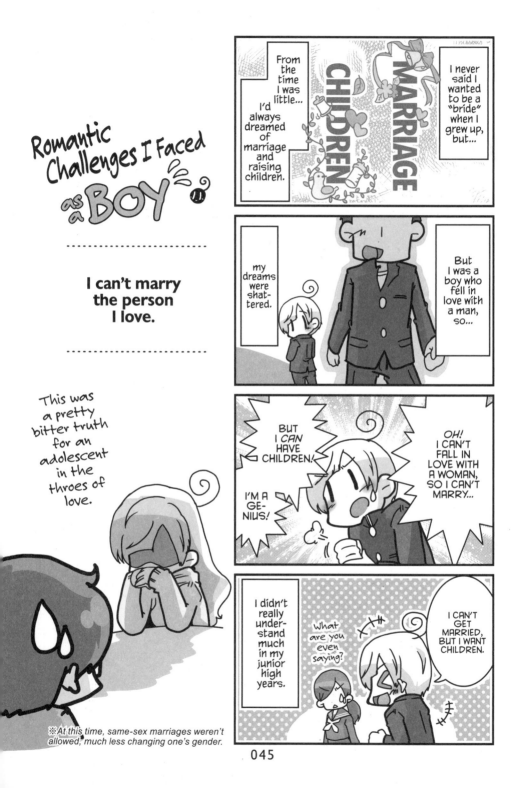

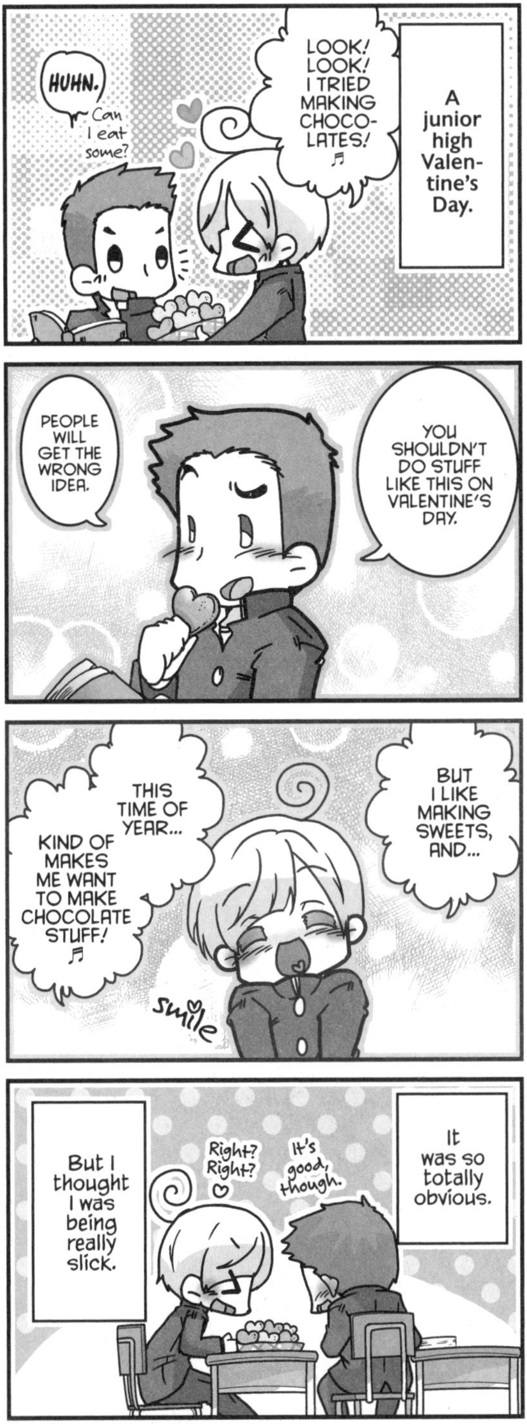
A junior high Valentine's Day.
LOOK! LOOK! I TRIED MAKING CHOCOLATES! ♬
HUHN.
Can I eat some?
YOU SHOULDN'T DO STUFF LIKE THIS ON VALENTINE'S DAY.
PEOPLE WILL GET THE WRONG IDEA.
BUT I LIKE MAKING SWEETS, AND...
THIS TIME OF YEAR...
KIND OF MAKES ME WANT TO MAKE CHOCOLATE STUFF! ♬
smile
It was so totally obvious.
It's good, though.
Right? Right? ♡
But I thought I was being really slick.

Romantic Challenges I Faced as a BOY 11

Unlike Valentine's Day, I wasn't too excited about White Day.

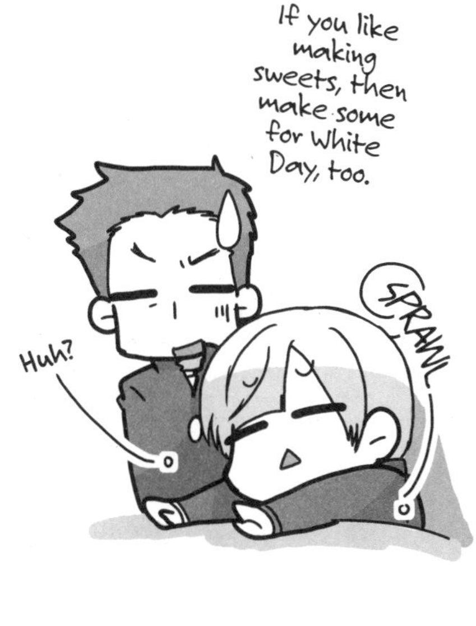
If you like making sweets, then make some for White Day, too.
SPRAWL
Huh?

※*On Valentine's Day (Feb 14) in Japan, women give honmei-choco (love chocolate) or giri-choco (courtesy chocolate) to men they like or know. On White Day (March 14), men return the favor by giving gifts in return.*

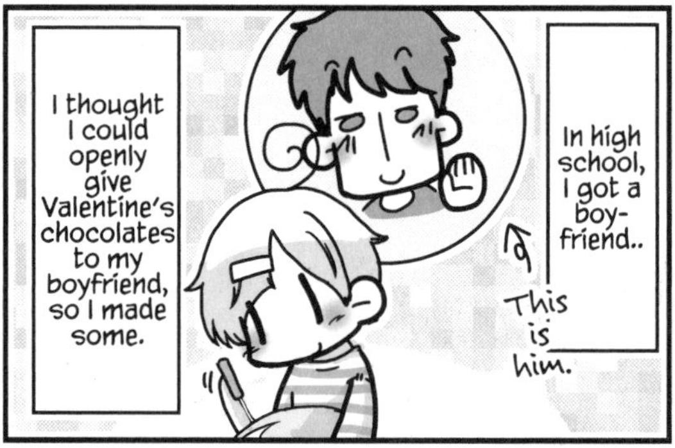
In high school, I got a boyfriend..
This is him.
I thought I could openly give Valentine's chocolates to my boyfriend, so I made some.

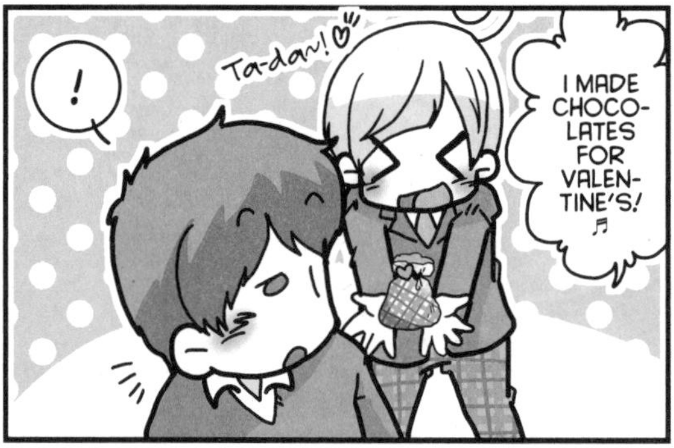
I MADE CHOCOLATES FOR VALENTINE'S! ♬
Ta-dah!♡
!

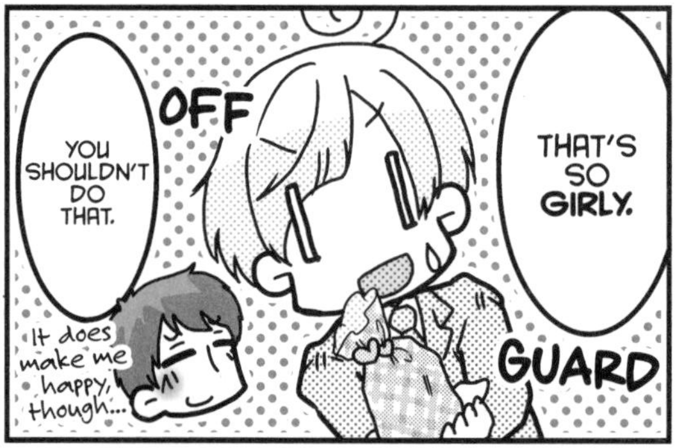
THAT'S SO GIRLY.
GUARD
OFF
YOU SHOULDN'T DO THAT.
It does make me happy, though...

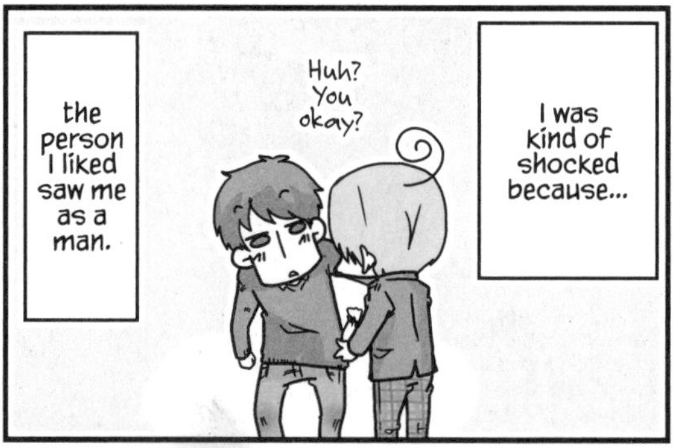
I was kind of shocked because...
Huh? You okay?
the person I liked saw me as a man.

Romantic Challenges I Faced as a BOY

My secret love.

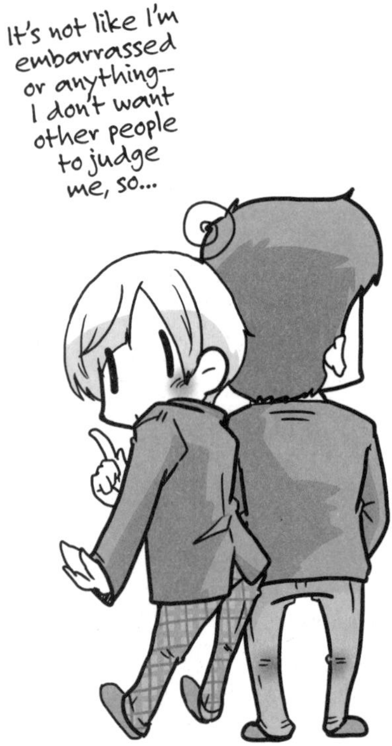
It's not like I'm embarrassed or anything-- I don't want other people to judge me, so...

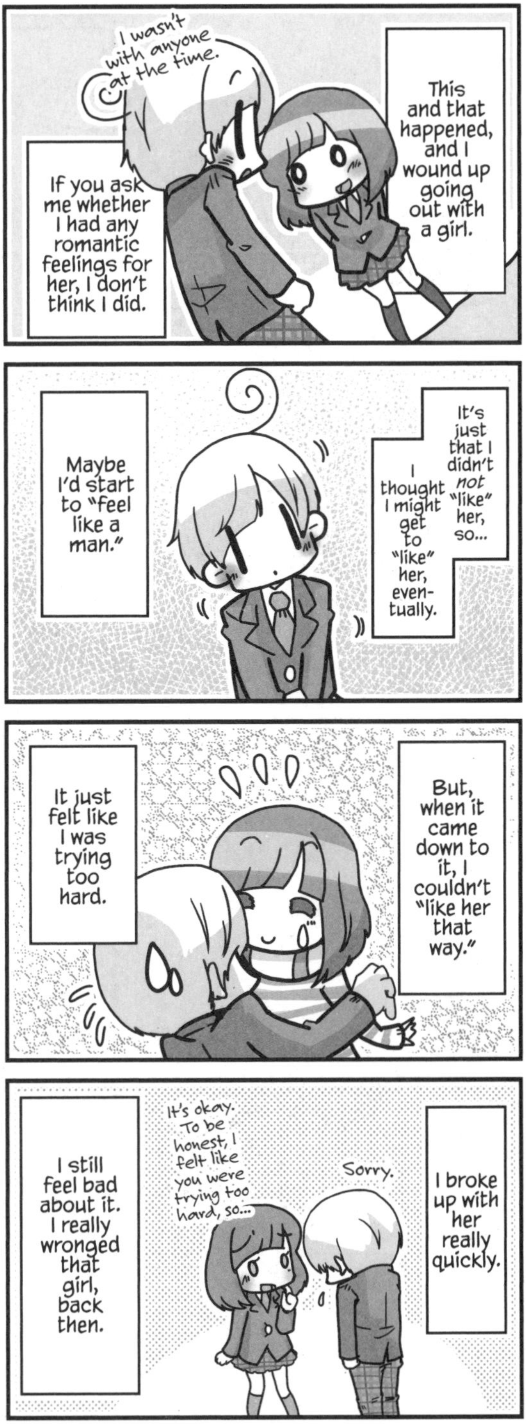
This and that happened, and I wound up going out with a girl.
I wasn't with anyone at the time.
If you ask me whether I had any romantic feelings for her, I don't think I did.
It's just that I didn't *not* "like" her, so...
I thought I might get to "like" her, eventually.
Maybe I'd start to "feel like a man."
But, when it came down to it, I couldn't "like her that way."
It just felt like I was trying too hard.
I broke up with her really quickly.
Sorry.
It's okay. To be honest, I felt like you were trying too hard, so...
I still feel bad about it. I really wronged that girl, back then.

Romantic Challenges I Faced as a BOY

A woman says she likes me.

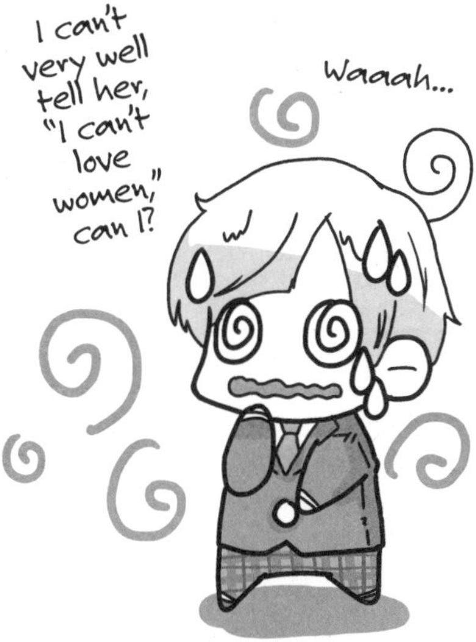
Waaah...
I can't very well tell her, "I can't love women," can I?

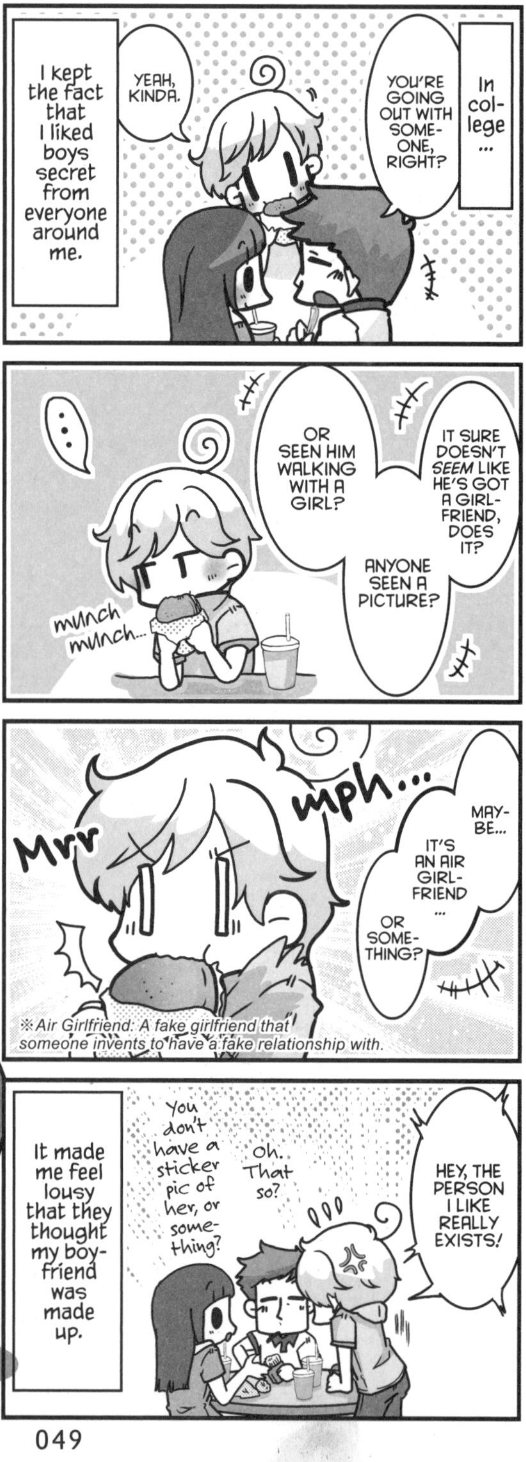
In college...
YOU'RE GOING OUT WITH SOMEONE, RIGHT?
YEAH, KINDA.
I kept the fact that I liked boys secret from everyone around me.
IT SURE DOESN'T *SEEM* LIKE HE'S GOT A GIRLFRIEND, DOES IT?
OR SEEN HIM WALKING WITH A GIRL?
ANYONE SEEN A PICTURE?
...
munch munch...
MAYBE... IT'S AN AIR GIRLFRIEND... OR SOMETHING?
Mrr mph...
※Air Girlfriend: A fake girlfriend that someone invents to have a fake relationship with.
HEY, THE PERSON I LIKE REALLY EXISTS!
Oh. That so?
You don't have a sticker pic of her, or something?
It made me feel lousy that they thought my boyfriend was made up.

Romantic Challenges I Faced as a BOY

When people talked about love, I wanted to join in, but couldn't.

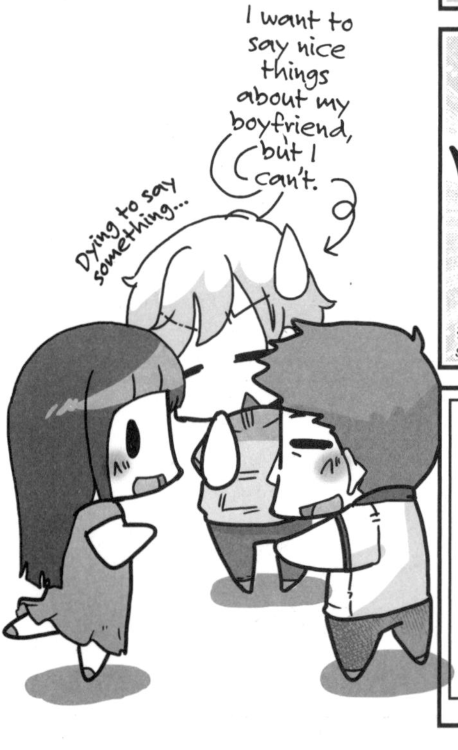
I want to say nice things about my boyfriend, but I can't.
Dying to say something...

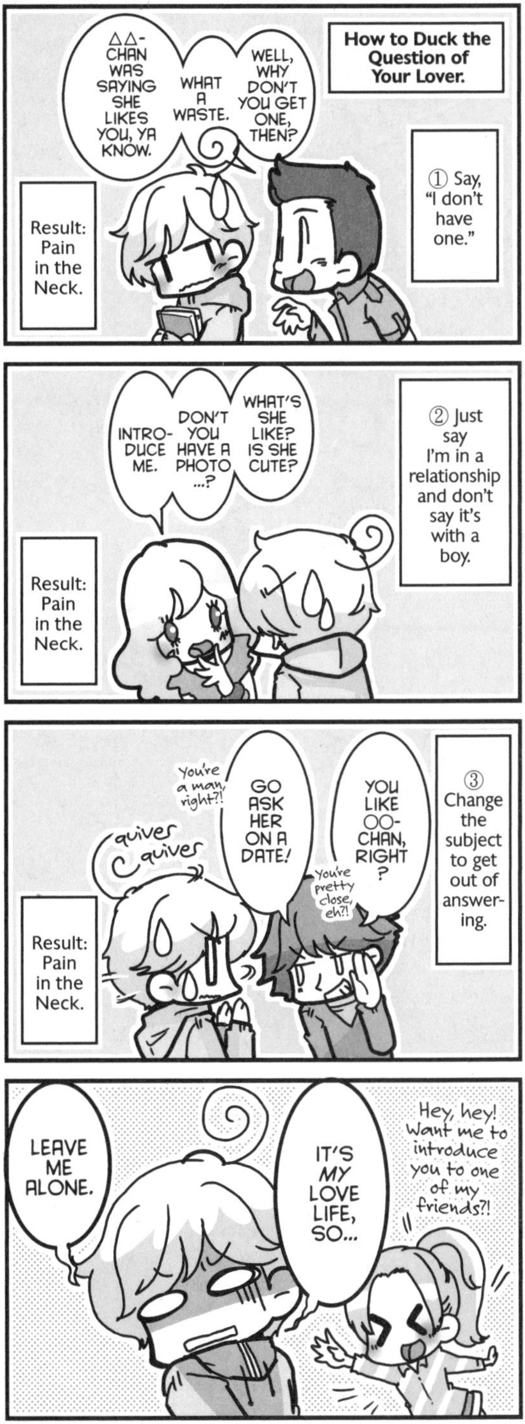
How to Duck the Question of Your Lover.
① Say, "I don't have one."
WELL, WHY DON'T YOU GET ONE, THEN?
WHAT A WASTE.
△△-CHAN WAS SAYING SHE LIKES YOU, YA KNOW.
Result: Pain in the Neck.
② Just say I'm in a relationship and don't say it's with a boy.
WHAT'S SHE LIKE? IS SHE CUTE?
DON'T YOU HAVE A PHOTO ...?
INTRO-DUCE ME.
Result: Pain in the Neck.
③ Change the subject to get out of answer-ing.
YOU LIKE ○○-CHAN, RIGHT?
You're pretty close, eh?!
GO ASK HER ON A DATE!
You're a man, right?!
quiver quiver
Result: Pain in the Neck.
Hey, hey! Want me to introduce you to one of my friends?!
IT'S MY LOVE LIFE, SO...
LEAVE ME ALONE.

Romantic Challenges I Faced as a BOY

The gōkon/group dating scene.

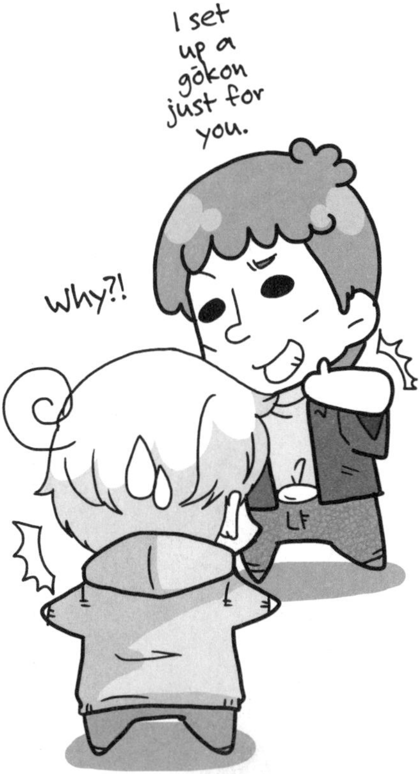
I set up a gōkon just for you.
Why?!
LF

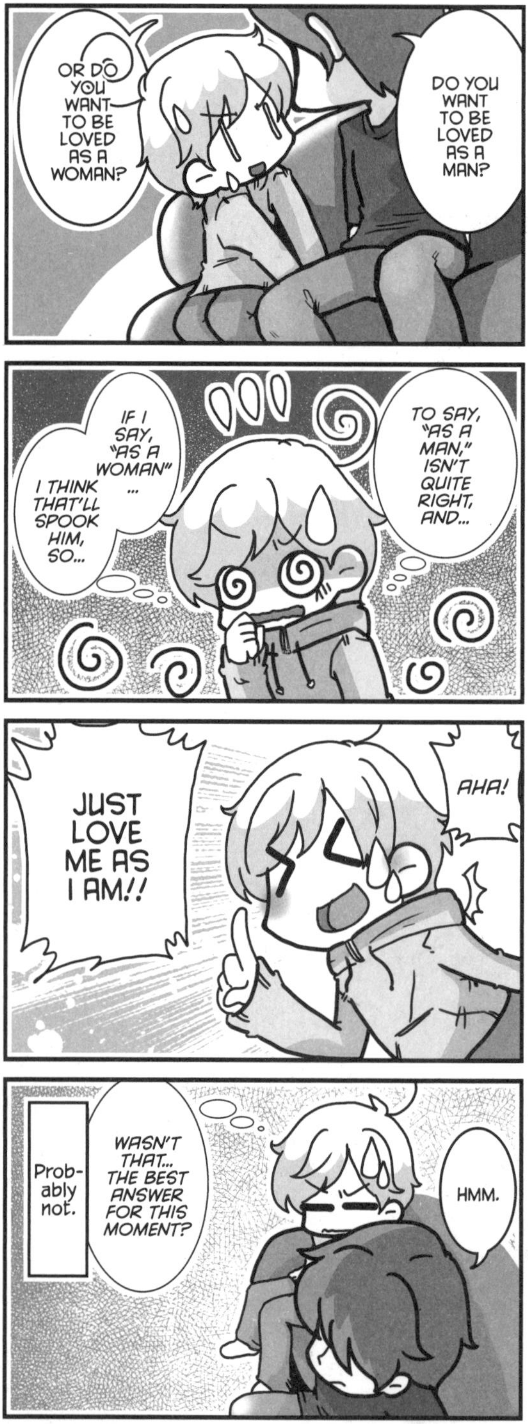
DO YOU WANT TO BE LOVED AS A MAN?
OR DO YOU WANT TO BE LOVED AS A WOMAN?
TO SAY, "AS A MAN," ISN'T QUITE RIGHT, AND...
IF I SAY, "AS A WOMAN"...
I THINK THAT'LL SPOOK HIM, SO...
AHA!
JUST LOVE ME AS I AM!!
HMM.
WASN'T THAT... THE BEST ANSWER FOR THIS MOMENT?
Probably not.

Romantic Challenges I Faced as a BOY 11

Talking about the future.

The future is kind of a forbidden topic.

It's hard, not being able to talk about the future with your lover.

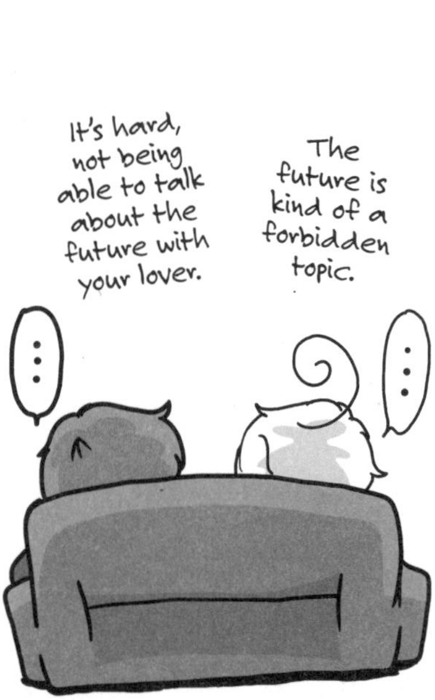
...
...

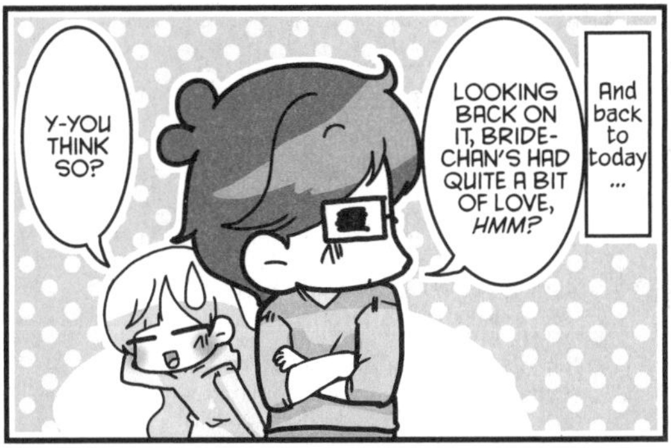
And back to today ...
LOOKING BACK ON IT, BRIDE-CHAN'S HAD QUITE A BIT OF LOVE, *HMM?*
Y-YOU THINK SO?

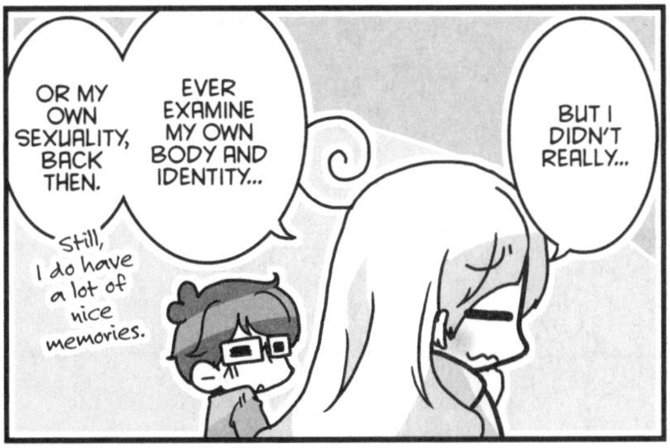
BUT I DIDN'T REALLY...
EVER EXAMINE MY OWN BODY AND IDENTITY...
OR MY OWN SEXUALITY, BACK THEN.
Still, I do have a lot of nice memories.

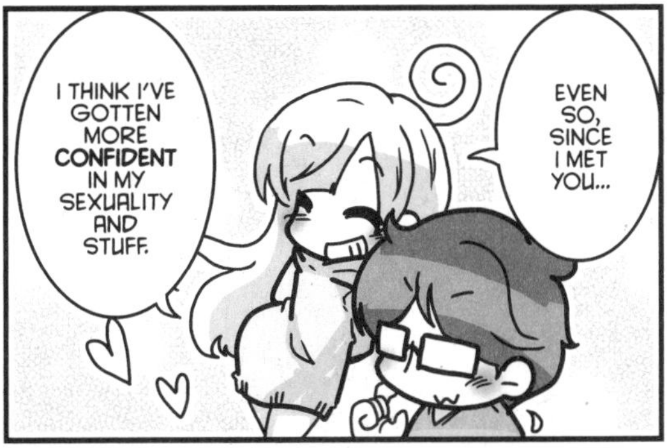
EVEN SO, SINCE I MET YOU...
I THINK I'VE GOTTEN MORE **CONFIDENT** IN MY SEXUALITY AND STUFF.

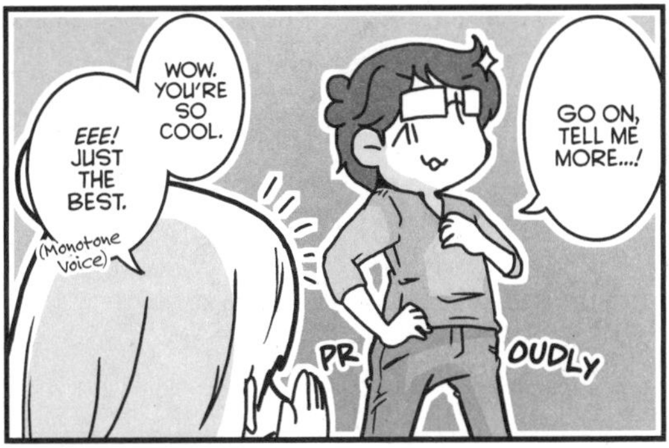
GO ON, TELL ME MORE...!
WOW. YOU'RE SO COOL.
EEE! JUST THE BEST.
(Monotone Voice)
PR OUDLY

Romantic Challenges I Faced as a BOY

Bride-chan deals with "How many people have you been with?"

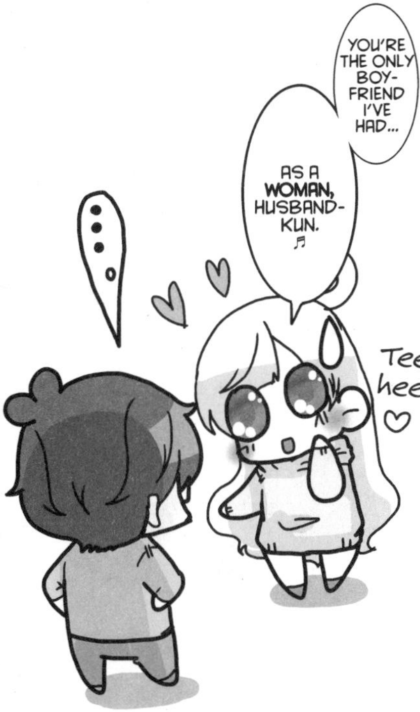
YOU'RE THE ONLY BOY-FRIEND I'VE HAD...
AS A **WOMAN,** HUSBAND-KUN. ♬
Tee hee!

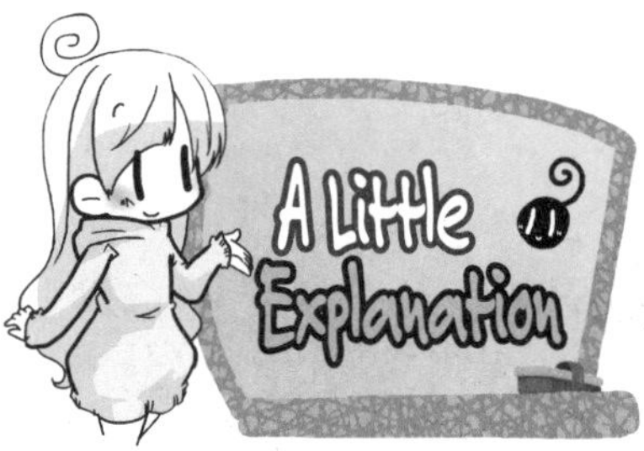
A Little Explanation

LGBT

"LGBT" is an acronym that is used as a shorthand for a number of different sexualities and genders. But the question of how LGBT feels if your identity is not included is one that gets a lot of debate.

After a while, an "s" was added to the acronym, to express the wide range of possible sexualities and genders, and that is how the term LGBTs came to be. I remember being grateful for this and thinking, "Now it can be used for all kinds of identities!" Of course, some people don't want to be categorized as LGBT, so you have to use the term with care.

To be honest, I didn't even know the term LGBT until I was an adult. Lately, I've started to think that if the media and schools had used it more back then, I wouldn't have had to take the long way to get to where I am now.

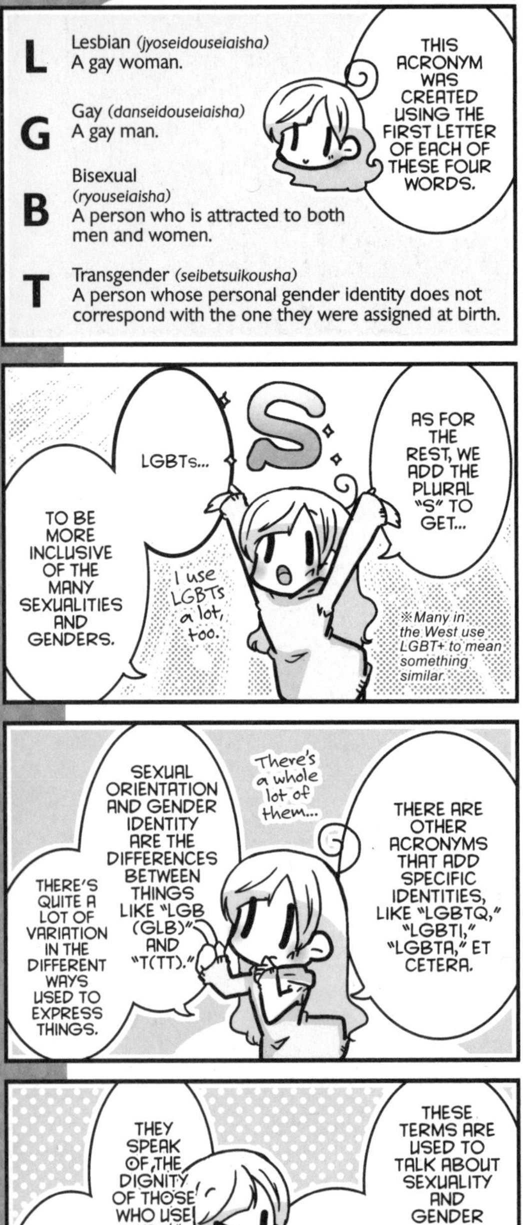
THIS ACRONYM WAS CREATED USING THE FIRST LETTER OF EACH OF THESE FOUR WORDS.
L Lesbian (jyoseidouseiaisha) A gay woman.
G Gay (danseidouseiaisha) A gay man.
B Bisexual (ryouseiaisha) A person who is attracted to both men and women.
T Transgender (seibetsuikousha) A person whose personal gender identity does not correspond with the one they were assigned at birth.
AS FOR THE REST, WE ADD THE PLURAL "S" TO GET...
S
LGBTs...
TO BE MORE INCLUSIVE OF THE MANY SEXUALITIES AND GENDERS.
I use LGBTs a lot, too.
※Many in the West use LGBT+ to mean something similar.
THERE ARE OTHER ACRONYMS THAT ADD SPECIFIC IDENTITIES, LIKE "LGBTQ," "LGBTI," "LGBTA," ET CETERA.
There's a whole lot of them...
SEXUAL ORIENTATION AND GENDER IDENTITY ARE THE DIFFERENCES BETWEEN THINGS LIKE "LGB (GLB)" AND "T(TT)."
THERE'S QUITE A LOT OF VARIATION IN THE DIFFERENT WAYS USED TO EXPRESS THINGS.
THESE TERMS ARE USED TO TALK ABOUT SEXUALITY AND GENDER IN A POSITIVE WAY...
THEY SPEAK OF THE DIGNITY OF THOSE WHO USE THEM!!
AND THEY SAY, "WE'RE HERE!"
AND ARE BEING WIDELY USED THESE DAYS!

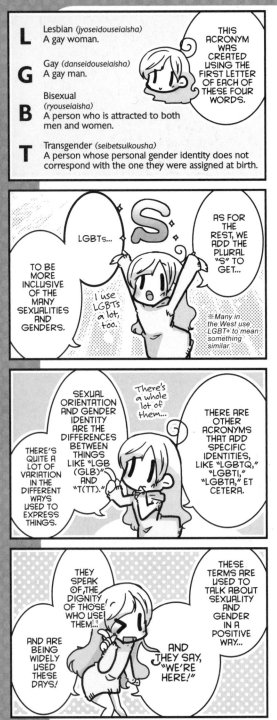

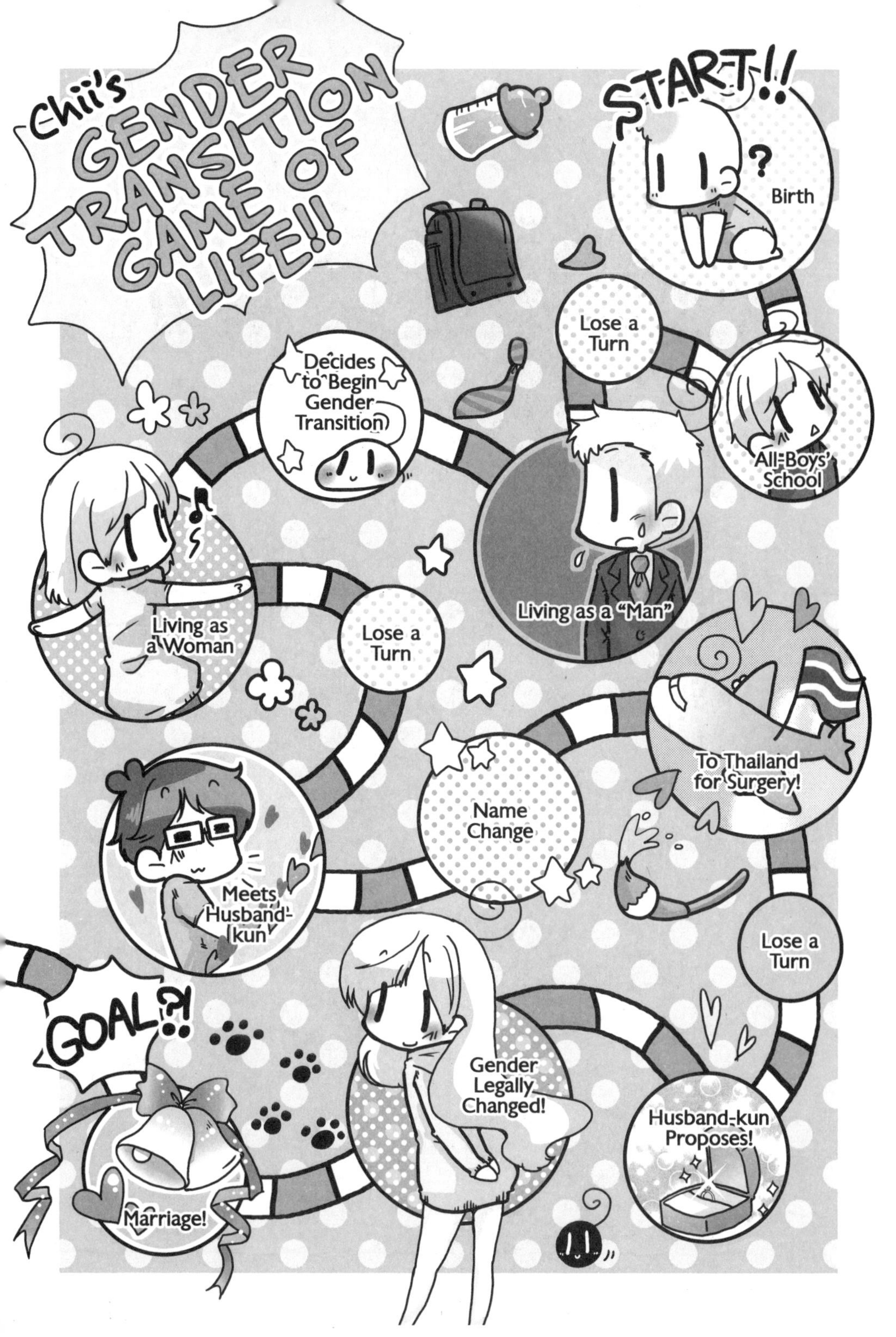
Chii's GENDER TRANSITION GAME OF LIFE!!
START!!
?
Birth
All-Boys' School
Lose a Turn
Living as a "Man"
Decides to Begin Gender Transition
Living as a Woman
Lose a Turn
Meets Husband-kun
Name Change
To Thailand for Surgery!
Lose a Turn
Husband-kun Proposes!
Gender Legally Changed!
GOAL?!
Marriage!

The Bride was
a Boy

CHAPTER 4

Bride-chan's Surgery

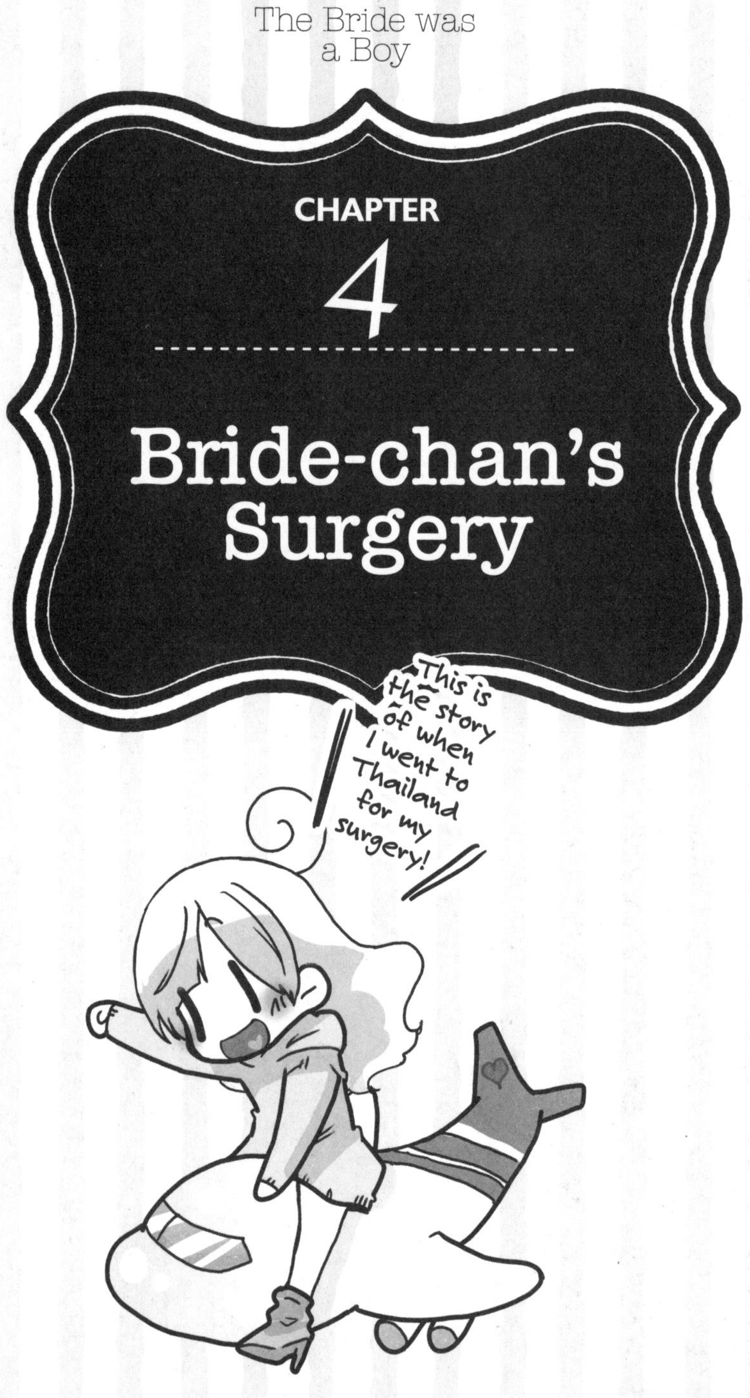
This is the story of when I went to Thailand for my surgery!

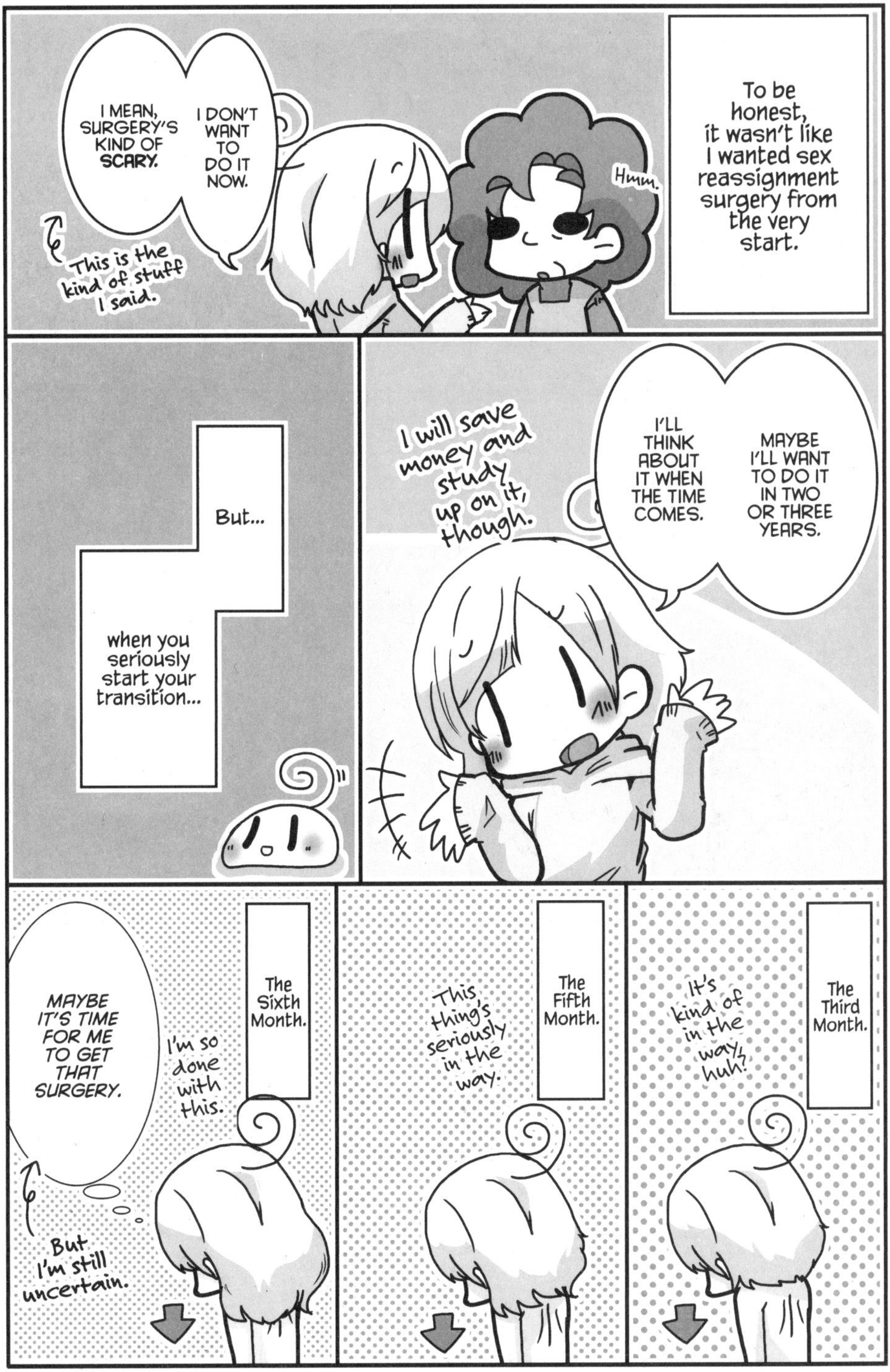
To be honest, it wasn't like I wanted sex reassignment surgery from the very start.
Hmm.
I DON'T WANT TO DO IT NOW.
I MEAN, SURGERY'S KIND OF SCARY.
This is the kind of stuff I said.
MAYBE I'LL WANT TO DO IT IN TWO OR THREE YEARS.
I'LL THINK ABOUT IT WHEN THE TIME COMES.
I will save money and study up on it, though.
But...
when you seriously start your transition...
The Third Month.
It's kind of in the way, huh?
The Fifth Month.
This thing's seriously in the way.
The Sixth Month.
I'm so done with this.
MAYBE IT'S TIME FOR ME TO GET THAT SURGERY.
But I'm still uncertain.

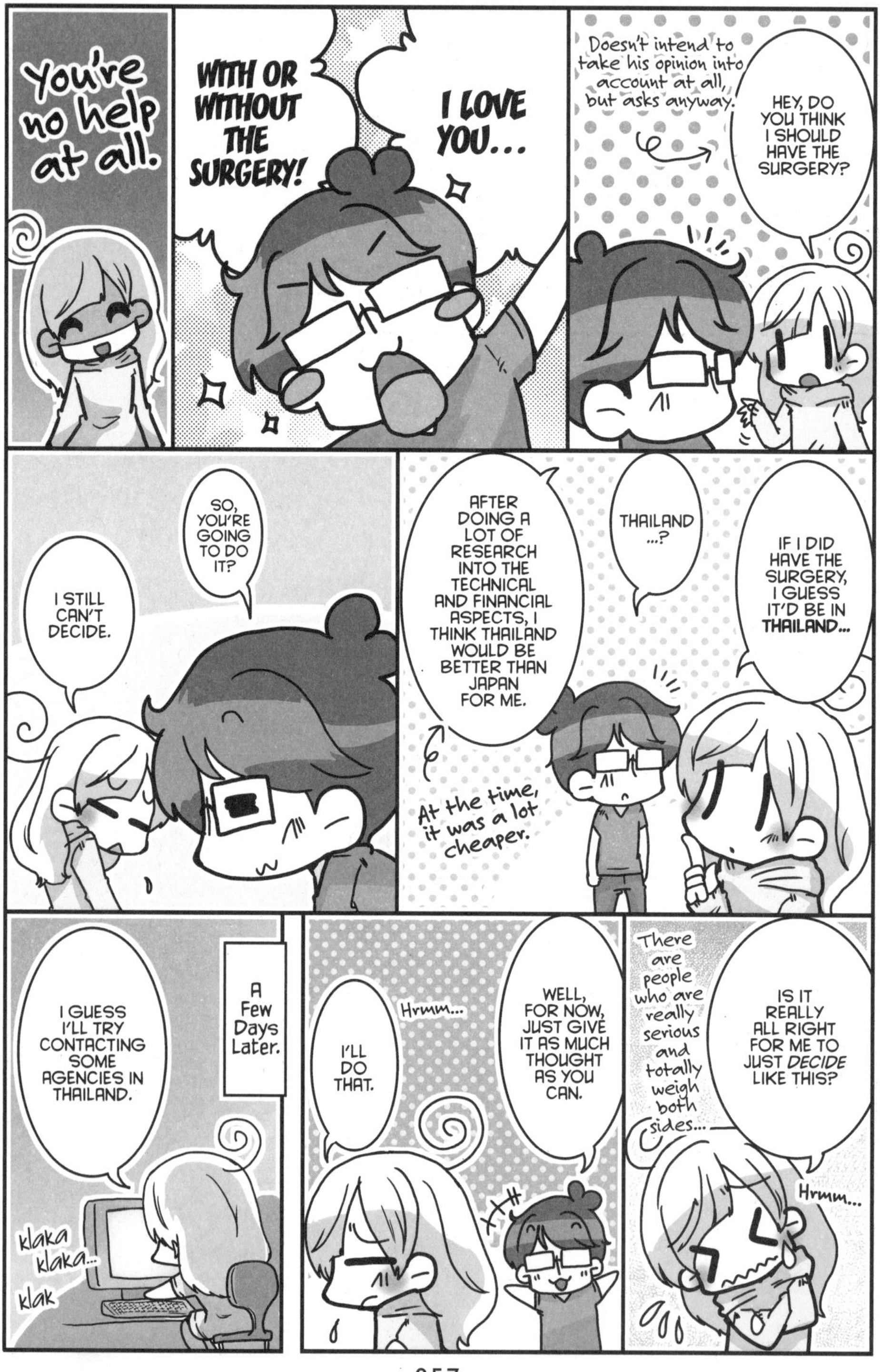
Doesn't intend to take his opinion into account at all, but asks anyway.
HEY, DO YOU THINK I SHOULD HAVE THE SURGERY?
I LOVE YOU...
WITH OR WITHOUT THE SURGERY!
You're no help at all.
IF I DID HAVE THE SURGERY, I GUESS IT'D BE IN THAILAND...
THAILAND ...?
AFTER DOING A LOT OF RESEARCH INTO THE TECHNICAL AND FINANCIAL ASPECTS, I THINK THAILAND WOULD BE BETTER THAN JAPAN FOR ME.
At the time, it was a lot cheaper.
SO, YOU'RE GOING TO DO IT?
I STILL CAN'T DECIDE.
IS IT REALLY ALL RIGHT FOR ME TO JUST DECIDE LIKE THIS?
There are people who are really serious and totally weigh both sides...
Hrmm...
WELL, FOR NOW, JUST GIVE IT AS MUCH THOUGHT AS YOU CAN.
Hrmm...
I'LL DO THAT.
A Few Days Later.
I GUESS I'LL TRY CONTACTING SOME AGENCIES IN THAILAND.
klaka klaka...
klak

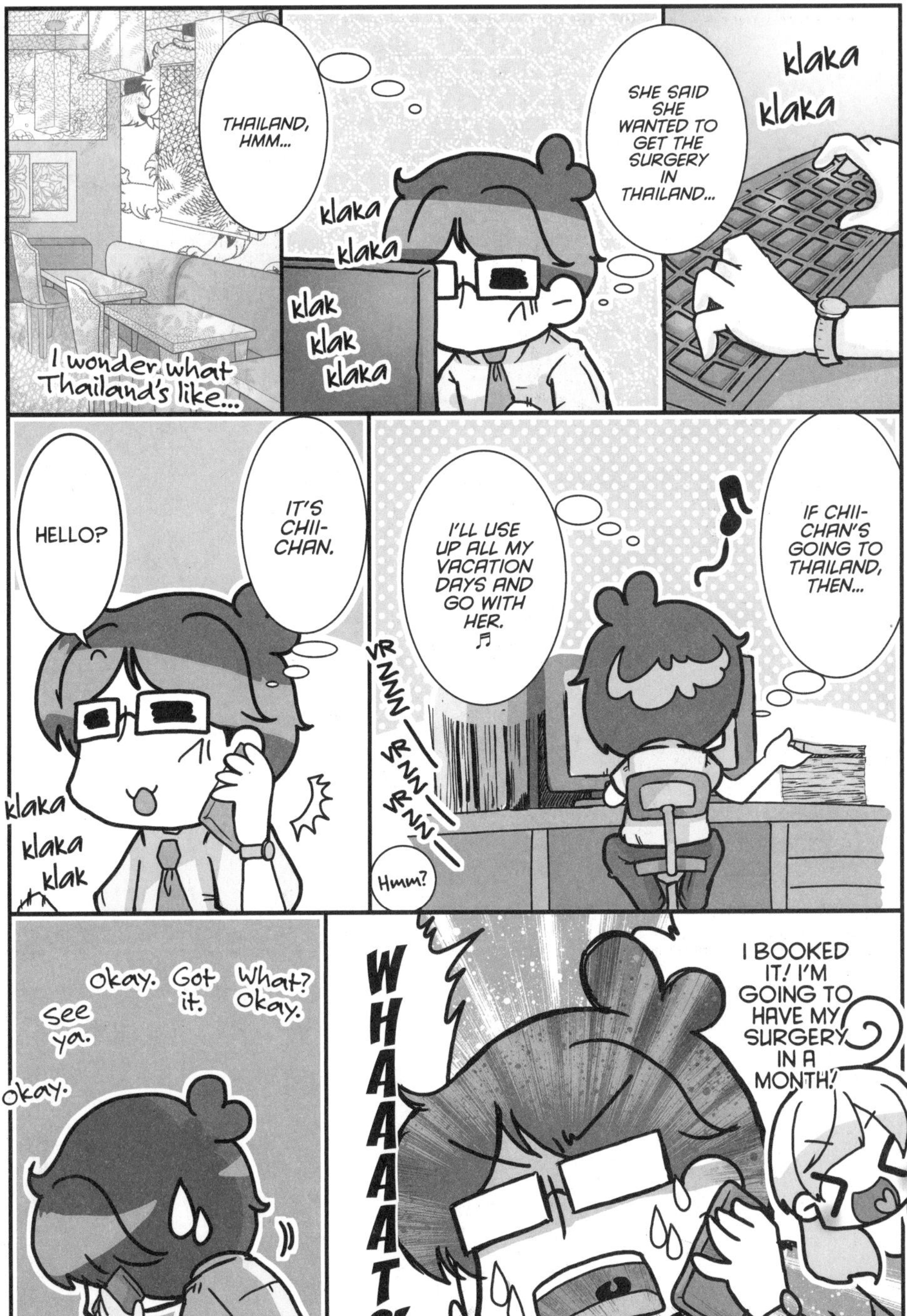
klaka
klaka
SHE SAID SHE WANTED TO GET THE SURGERY IN THAILAND...
THAILAND, HMM...
klaka
klaka
klak
klak
klaka
I wonder what Thailand's like...
IF CHII-CHAN'S GOING TO THAILAND, THEN...
I'LL USE UP ALL MY VACATION DAYS AND GO WITH HER. ♫
VRZZZ
VRNN
VRNN
Hmm?
IT'S CHII-CHAN.
HELLO?
klaka
klaka
klak
I BOOKED IT! I'M GOING TO HAVE MY SURGERY IN A MONTH!
WHAAAAAT?!
What? Okay.
Got it.
Okay.
See ya.
Okay.

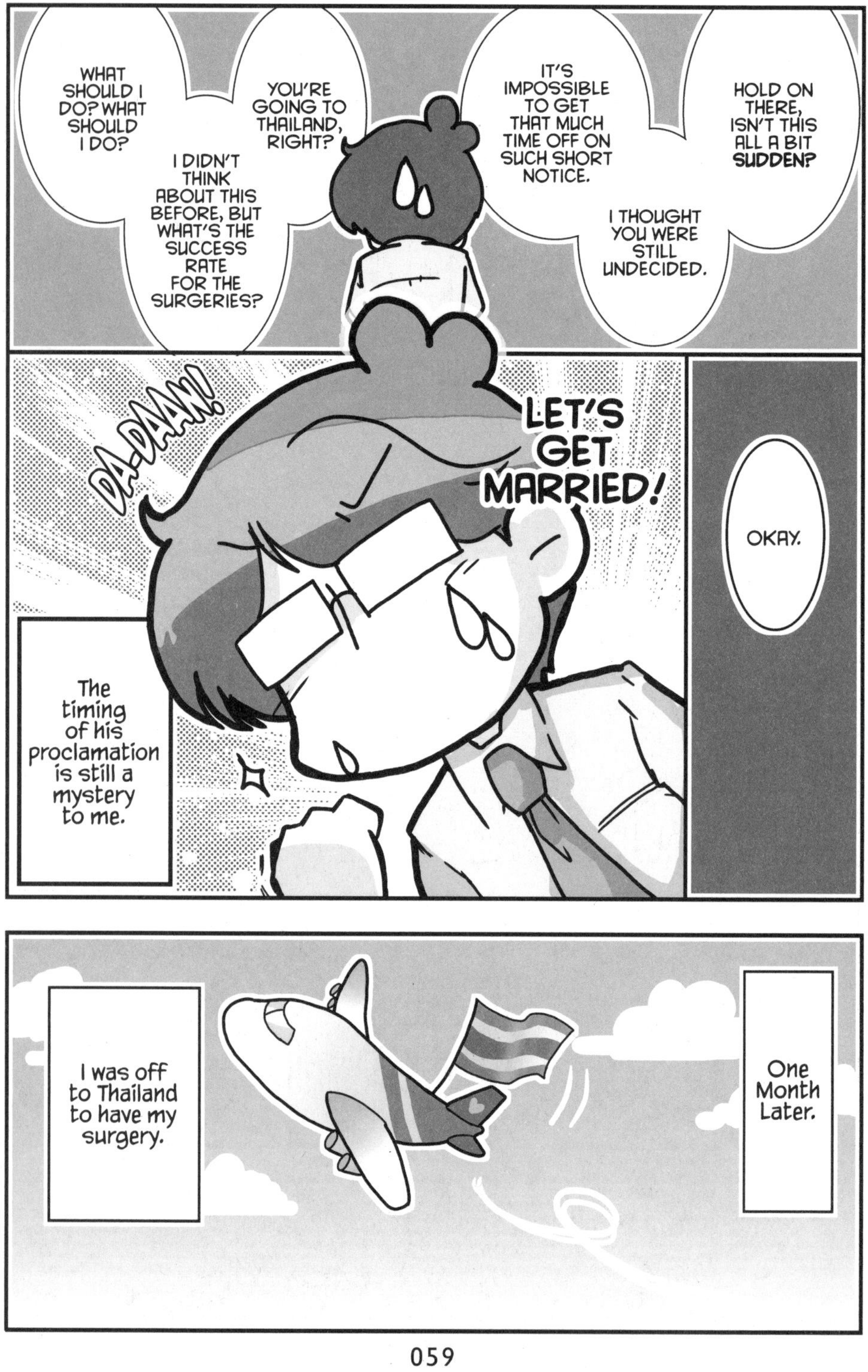
HOLD ON THERE, ISN'T THIS ALL A BIT SUDDEN?
I THOUGHT YOU WERE STILL UNDECIDED.
IT'S IMPOSSIBLE TO GET THAT MUCH TIME OFF ON SUCH SHORT NOTICE.
YOU'RE GOING TO THAILAND, RIGHT?
I DIDN'T THINK ABOUT THIS BEFORE, BUT WHAT'S THE SUCCESS RATE FOR THE SURGERIES?
WHAT SHOULD I DO? WHAT SHOULD I DO?
OKAY.
LET'S GET MARRIED!
DA-DAAN!
The timing of his proclamation is still a mystery to me.
One Month Later.
I was off to Thailand to have my surgery.

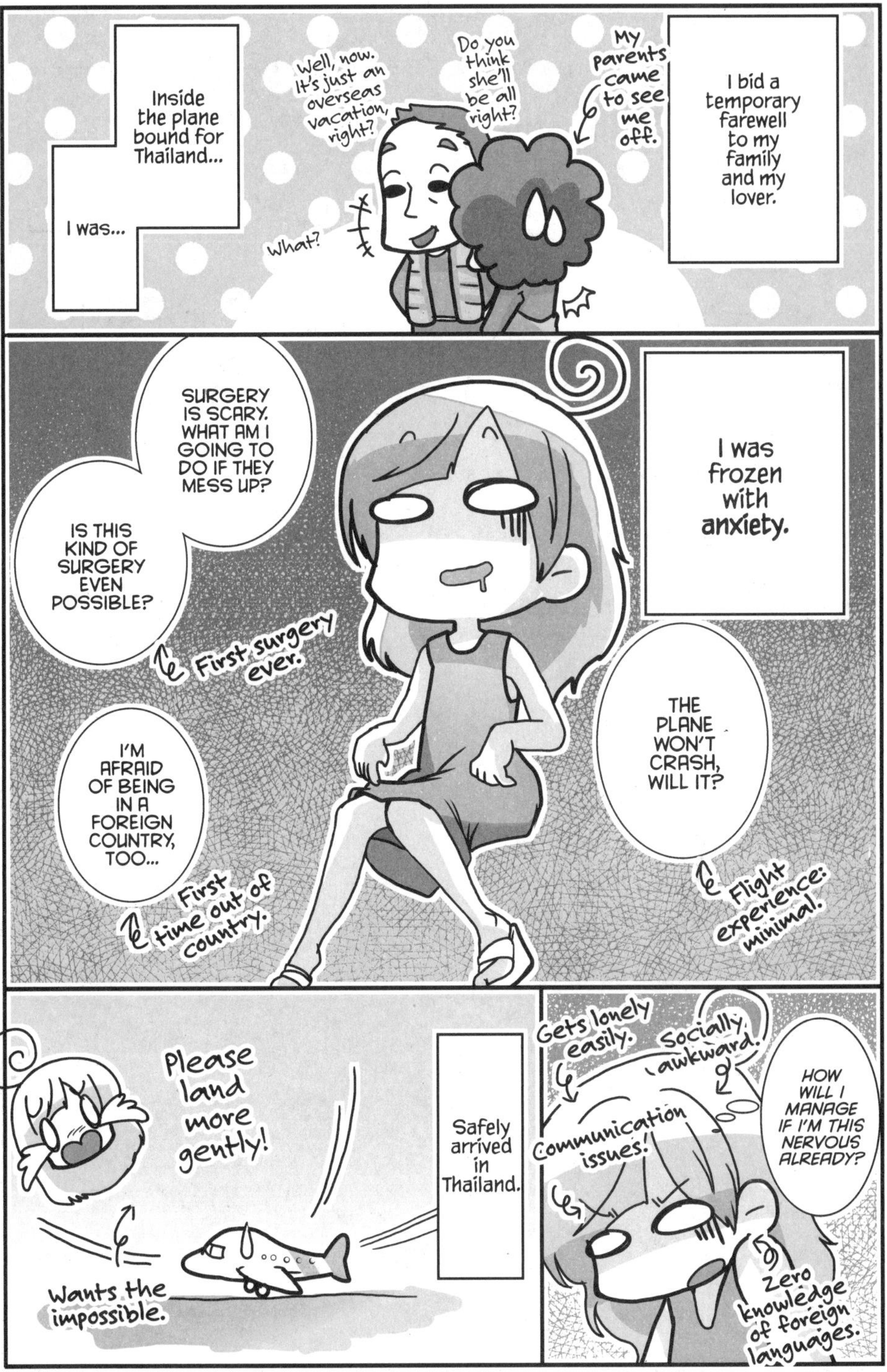
I bid a temporary farewell to my family and my lover.
My parents came to see me off.
Do you think she'll be all right?
Well, now. It's just an overseas vacation, right?
What?
Inside the plane bound for Thailand...
I was...
I was frozen with anxiety.
THE PLANE WON'T CRASH, WILL IT?
Flight experience: minimal.
SURGERY IS SCARY. WHAT AM I GOING TO DO IF THEY MESS UP?
IS THIS KIND OF SURGERY EVEN POSSIBLE?
First surgery ever.
I'M AFRAID OF BEING IN A FOREIGN COUNTRY, TOO...
First time out of country.
HOW WILL I MANAGE IF I'M THIS NERVOUS ALREADY?
Socially awkward.
Gets lonely easily.
Communication issues.
Zero knowledge of foreign languages.
Safely arrived in Thailand.
Please land more gently!
Wants the impossible.

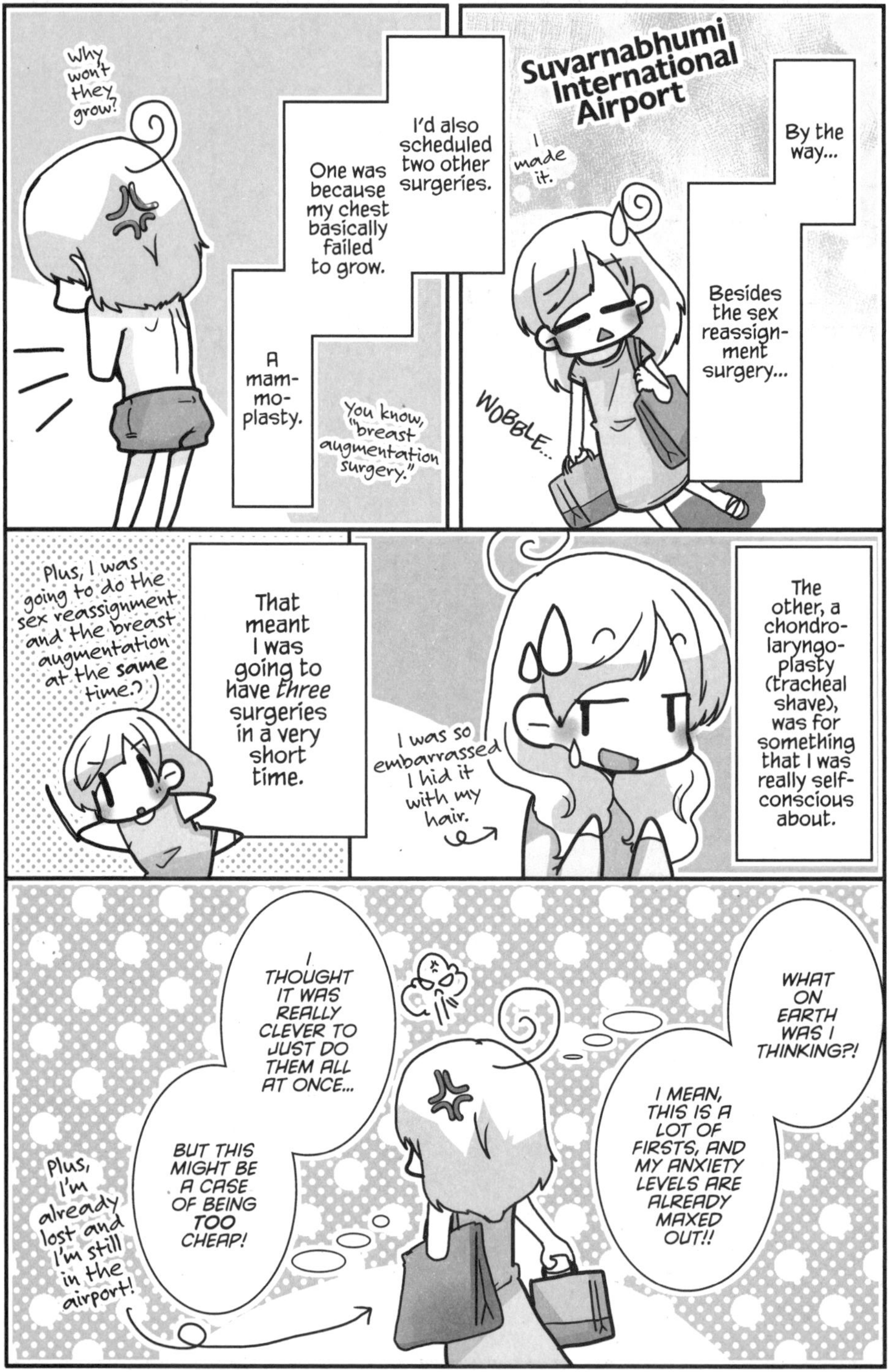
Suvarnabhumi International Airport
I made it.
By the way...
Besides the sex reassignment surgery...
WOBBLE...
I'd also scheduled two other surgeries.
One was because my chest basically failed to grow.
Why won't they grow?
A mammoplasty.
You know, "breast augmentation surgery."
The other, a chondrolaryngoplasty (tracheal shave), was for something that I was really self-conscious about.
I was so embarrassed I hid it with my hair.
That meant I was going to have *three* surgeries in a very short time.
Plus, I was going to do the sex reassignment and the breast augmentation at the **same** time.
WHAT ON EARTH WAS I THINKING?!
I MEAN, THIS IS A LOT OF FIRSTS, AND MY ANXIETY LEVELS ARE ALREADY MAXED OUT!!
I THOUGHT IT WAS REALLY CLEVER TO JUST DO THEM ALL AT ONCE...
BUT THIS MIGHT BE A CASE OF BEING **TOO** CHEAP!
Plus, I'm already lost and I'm still in the airport!

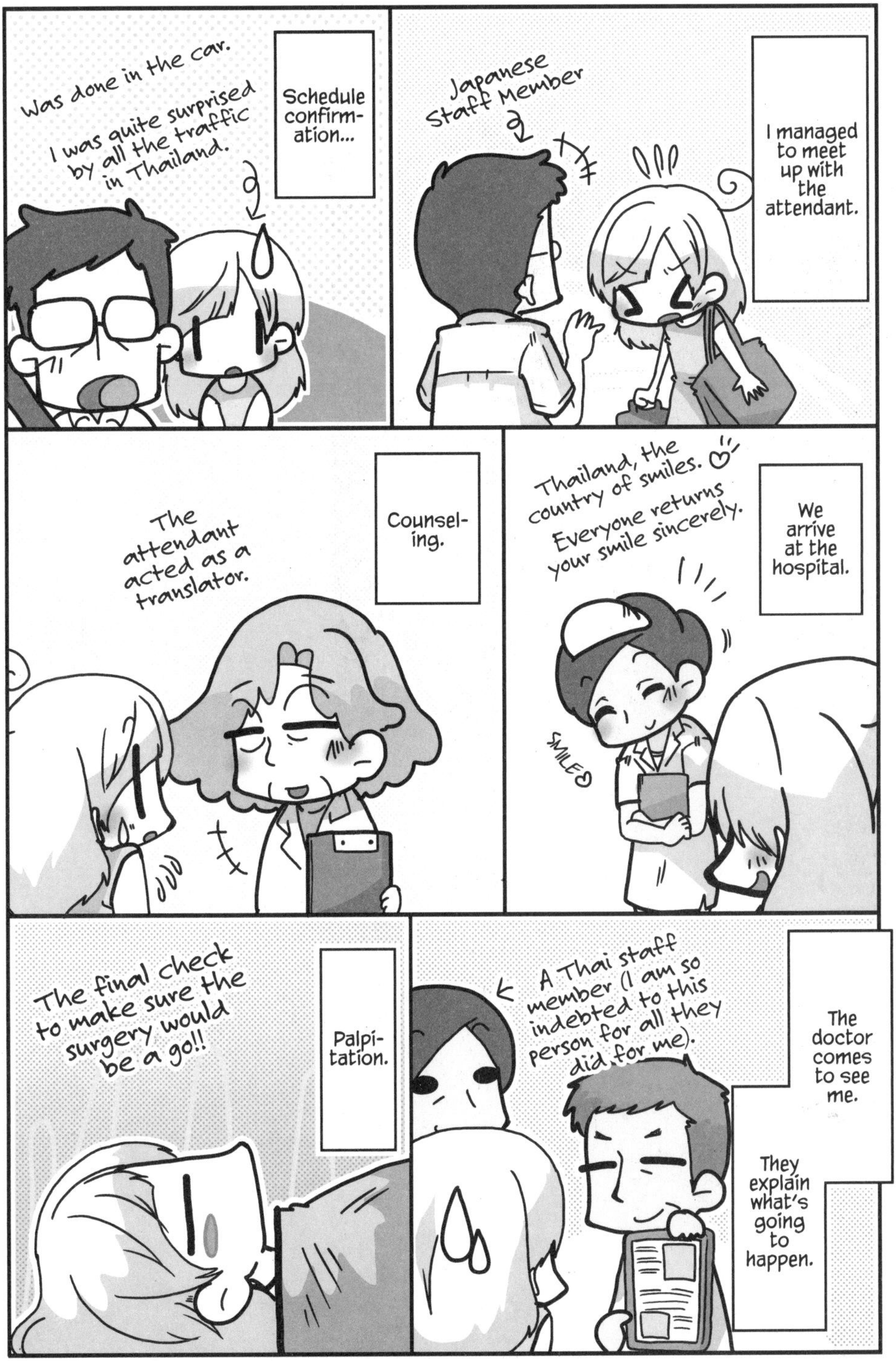
I managed to meet up with the attendant.
Japanese Staff Member
Schedule confirmation...
Was done in the car.
I was quite surprised by all the traffic in Thailand.
We arrive at the hospital.
Thailand, the country of smiles.
Everyone returns your smile sincerely.
SMILE
Counseling.
The attendant acted as a translator.
The doctor comes to see me.
They explain what's going to happen.
A Thai staff member (I am so indebted to this person for all they did for me).
Palpitation.
The final check to make sure the surgery would be a go!!

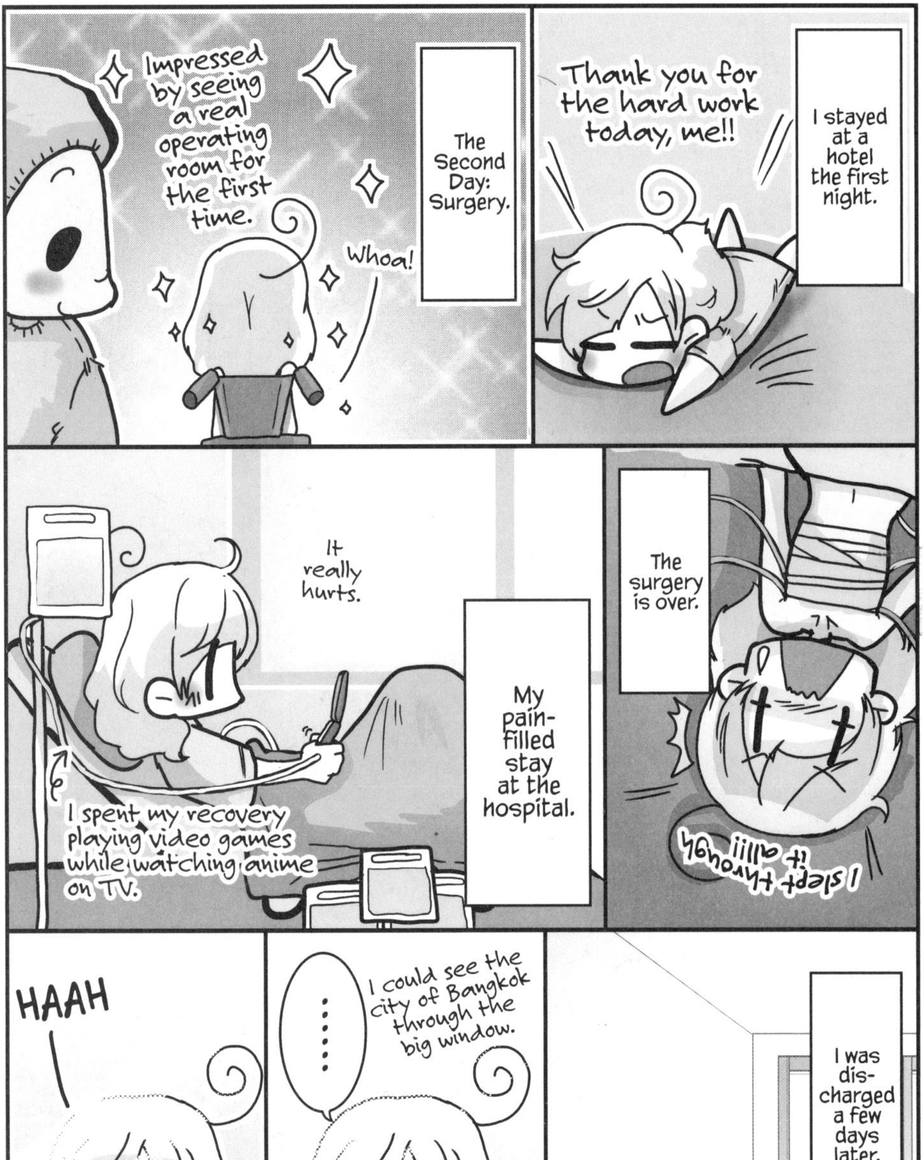
I stayed at a hotel the first night.
Thank you for the hard work today, me!!
The Second Day: Surgery.
Impressed by seeing a real operating room for the first time.
Whoa!
The surgery is over.
I slept through it all!!
My pain-filled stay at the hospital.
It really hurts.
I spent my recovery playing video games while watching anime on TV.
I was discharged a few days later.
I could see the city of Bangkok through the big window.
......
HAAH

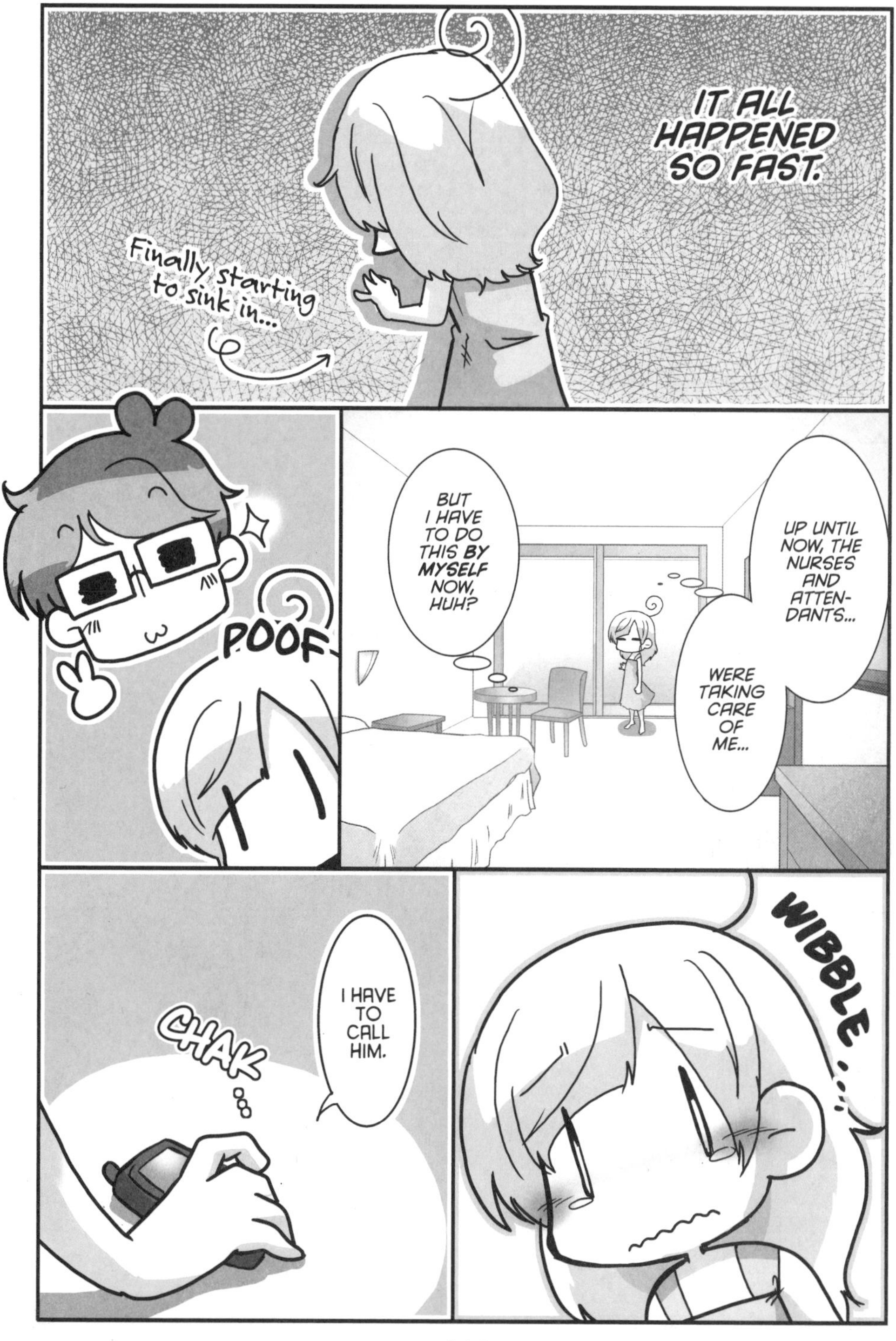
IT ALL HAPPENED SO FAST.
Finally starting to sink in...
UP UNTIL NOW, THE NURSES AND ATTEN-DANTS...
WERE TAKING CARE OF ME...
BUT I HAVE TO DO THIS **BY MYSELF** NOW, HUH?
POOF
WIBBLE...
I HAVE TO CALL HIM.
CHAK

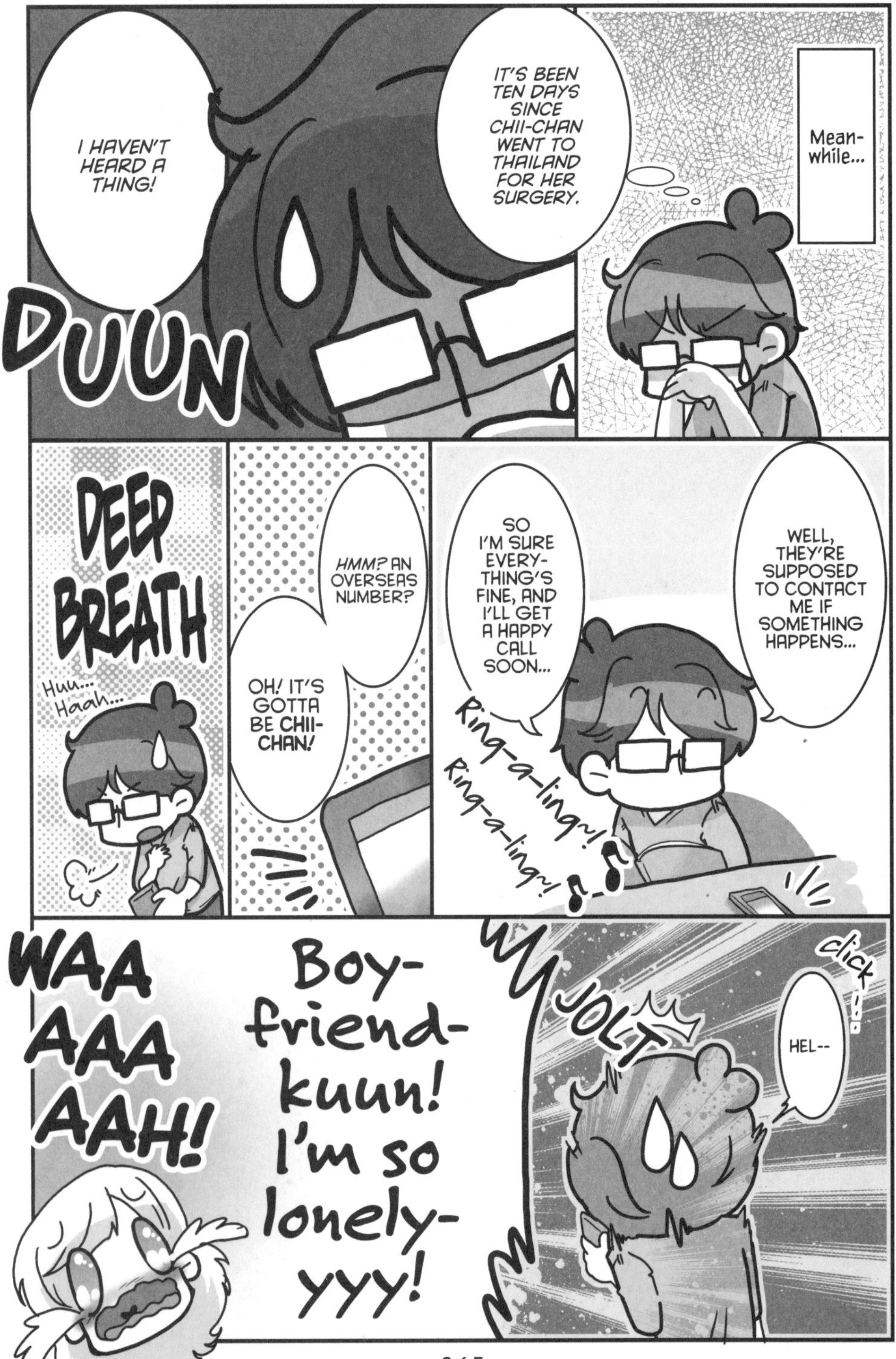
Mean-while...
IT'S BEEN TEN DAYS SINCE CHII-CHAN WENT TO THAILAND FOR HER SURGERY.
I HAVEN'T HEARD A THING!
DUUN
WELL, THEY'RE SUPPOSED TO CONTACT ME IF SOMETHING HAPPENS...
SO I'M SURE EVERY-THING'S FINE, AND I'LL GET A HAPPY CALL SOON...
Ring-a-ling~!
Ring-a-ling~!
HMM? AN OVERSEAS NUMBER?
OH! IT'S GOTTA BE CHII-CHAN!
DEEP BREATH
Huu... Haah...
click
HEL--
JOLT
WAA AAA AAH!
Boy-friend-kuun! I'm so lonely-yyy!

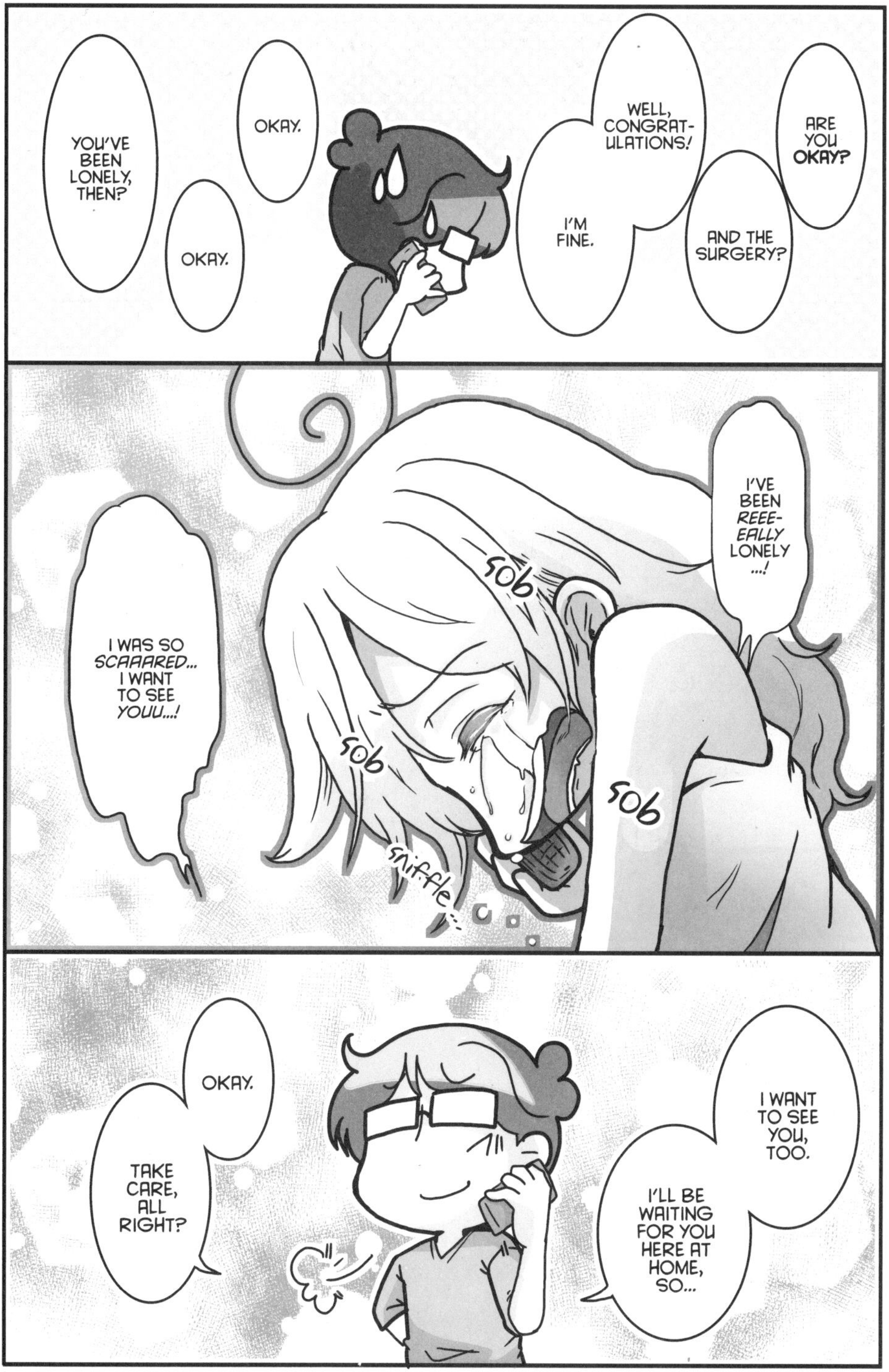
ARE YOU **OKAY?**
AND THE SURGERY?
WELL, CONGRAT- ULATIONS!
I'M FINE.
OKAY.
OKAY.
YOU'VE BEEN LONELY, THEN?
I'VE BEEN *REEE- EALLY* LONELY ...!
sob
sob
sob
sniffle...
I WAS SO *SCAAARED*... I WANT TO SEE *YOUU*...!
I WANT TO SEE YOU, TOO.
I'LL BE WAITING FOR YOU HERE AT HOME, SO...
OKAY.
TAKE CARE, ALL RIGHT?

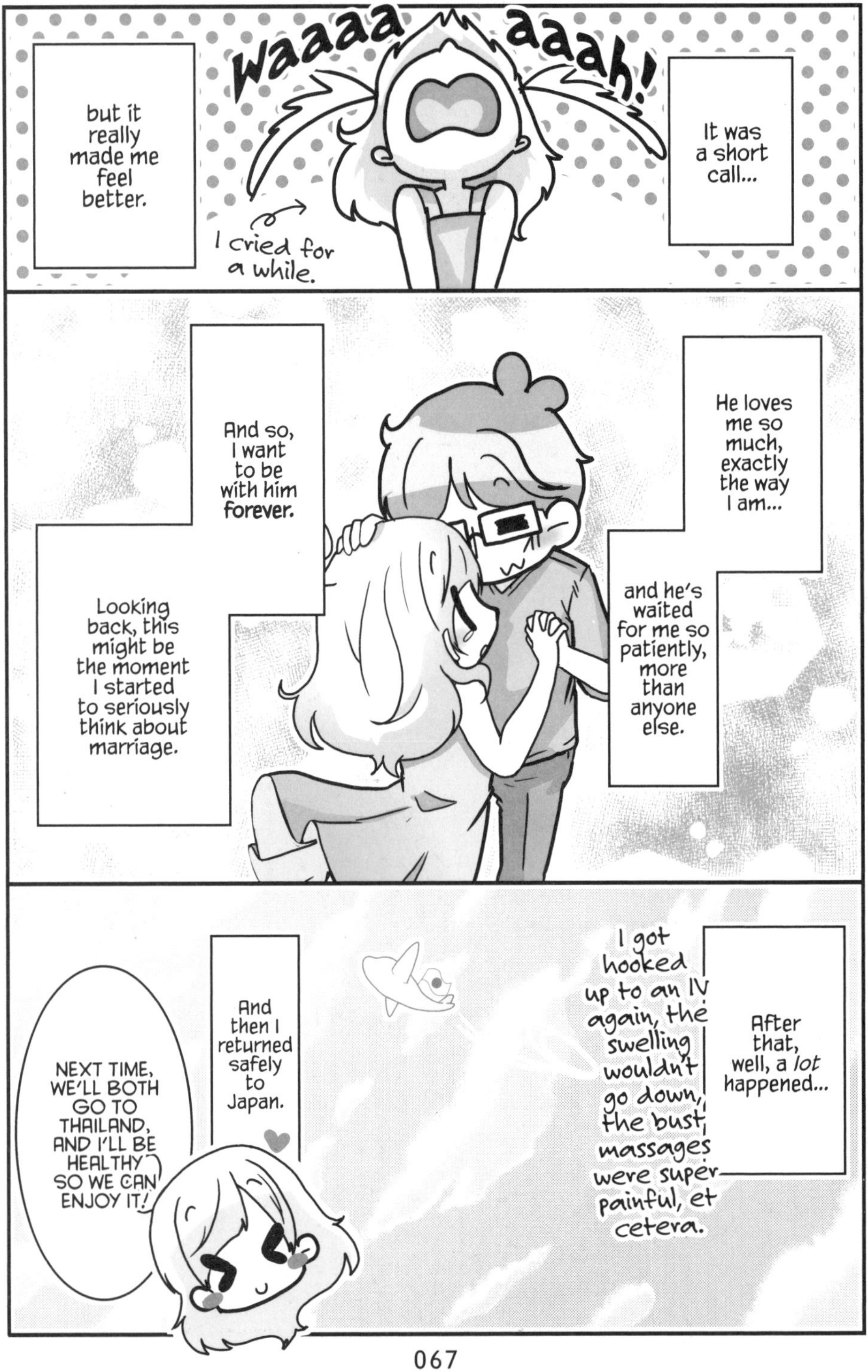
It was a short call...
waaaaa aaaah!
I cried for a while.
but it really made me feel better.
He loves me so much, exactly the way I am...
and he's waited for me so patiently, more than anyone else.
And so, I want to be with him forever.
Looking back, this might be the moment I started to seriously think about marriage.
After that, well, a lot happened...
I got hooked up to an IV again, the swelling wouldn't go down, the bust massages were super painful, et cetera.
And then I returned safely to Japan.
NEXT TIME, WE'LL BOTH GO TO THAILAND, AND I'LL BE HEALTHY SO WE CAN ENJOY IT!

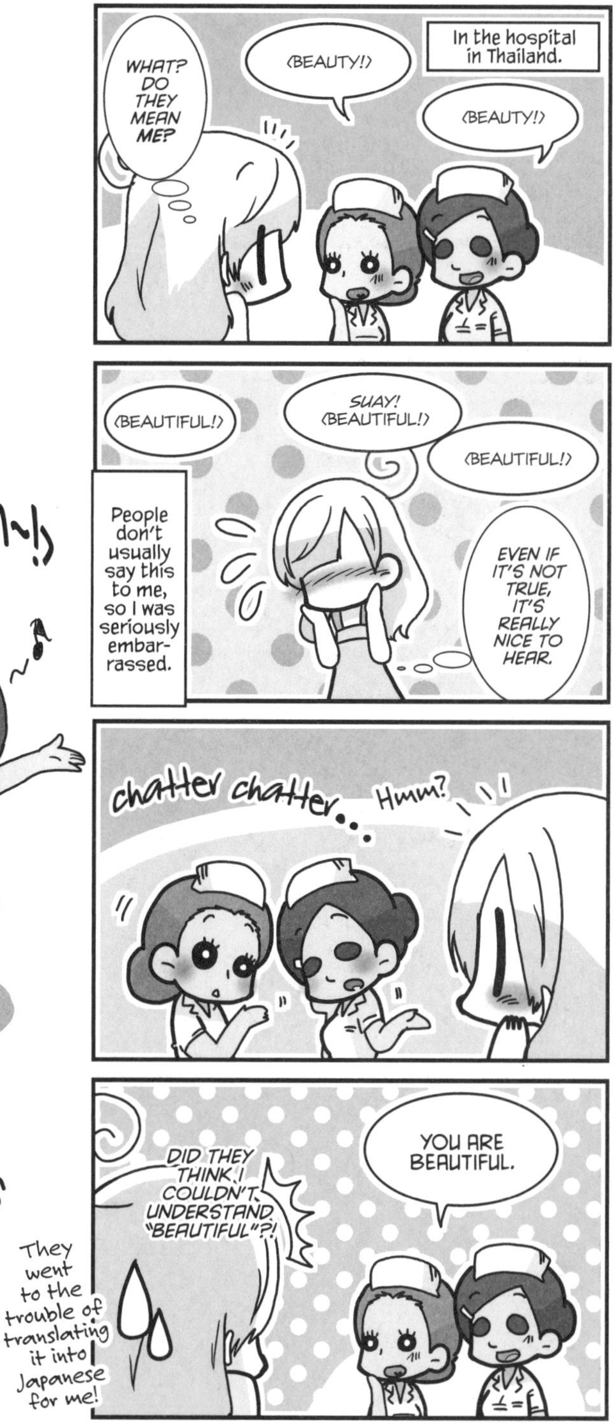
In the hospital in Thailand.
‹BEAUTY!›
‹BEAUTY!›
WHAT? DO THEY MEAN ME?
SUAY! ‹BEAUTIFUL!›
‹BEAUTIFUL!›
‹BEAUTIFUL!›
EVEN IF IT'S NOT TRUE, IT'S REALLY NICE TO HEAR.
People don't usually say this to me, so I was seriously embarrassed.
Hmm?
chatter chatter...
YOU ARE BEAUTIFUL.
DID THEY THINK I COULDN'T UNDERSTAND "BEAUTIFUL"?!
They went to the trouble of translating it into Japanese for me!

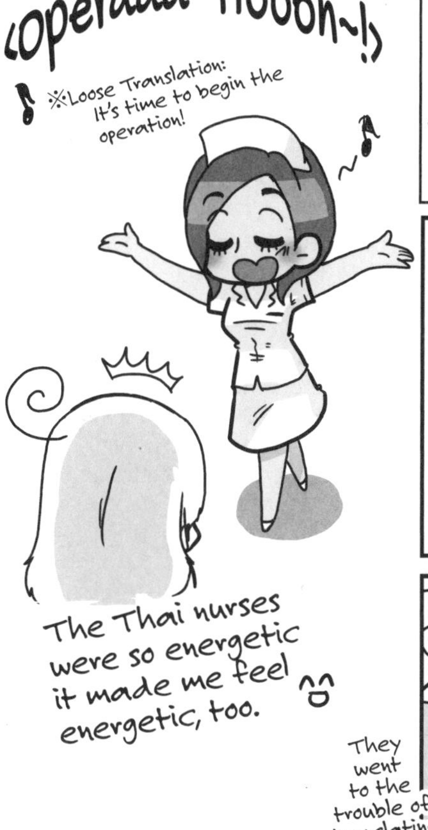
‹operaaa~tiooon~!›
※Loose Translation: It's time to begin the operation!
The Thai nurses were so energetic it made me feel energetic, too.

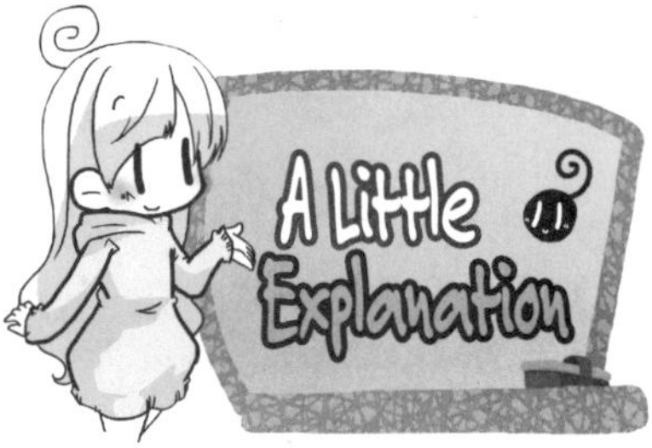

A Little Explanation

Sex Reassignment Surgery (SRS)

I'm often asked, "Is this different from sex change surgery?" It's true that name was used in the past, but considering the gender identity of the person in question, it's not that they're "changing their sex" but rather that they're "taking back their correct gender." Thus, people tend to avoid using phrases like "sex change surgery" or "sex change operation."

As for what goes on in the surgery, it varies quite a bit depending on the country or region, the state of one's health, the clinic, and so on. Things like cost, procedure name, and requirements differ quite a bit, too. Before my surgery, I had a lot of trouble choosing between clinics and deciding on all the details.

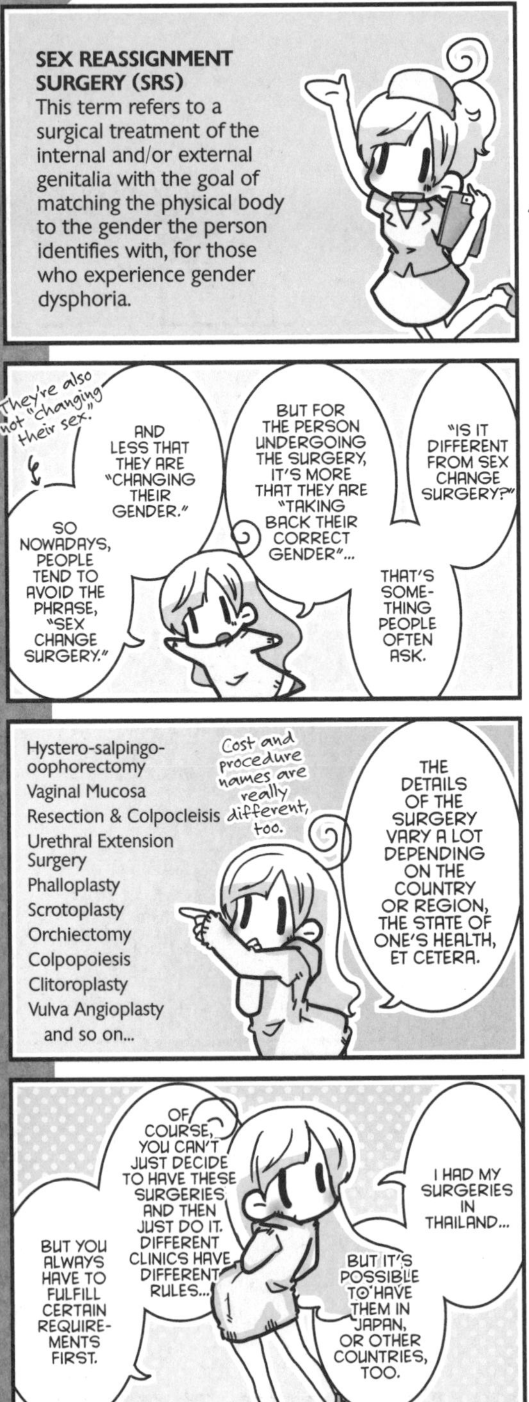

SEX REASSIGNMENT SURGERY (SRS)
This term refers to a surgical treatment of the internal and/or external genitalia with the goal of matching the physical body to the gender the person identifies with, for those who experience gender dysphoria.
"IS IT DIFFERENT FROM SEX CHANGE SURGERY?"
THAT'S SOMETHING PEOPLE OFTEN ASK.
BUT FOR THE PERSON UNDERGOING THE SURGERY, IT'S MORE THAT THEY ARE "TAKING BACK THEIR CORRECT GENDER"...
AND LESS THAT THEY ARE "CHANGING THEIR GENDER."
They're also not "changing their sex."
SO NOWADAYS, PEOPLE TEND TO AVOID THE PHRASE, "SEX CHANGE SURGERY."
THE DETAILS OF THE SURGERY VARY A LOT DEPENDING ON THE COUNTRY OR REGION, THE STATE OF ONE'S HEALTH, ET CETERA.
Cost and procedure names are really different, too.
Hystero-salpingo-oophorectomy
Vaginal Mucosa Resection & Colpocleisis
Urethral Extension Surgery
Phalloplasty
Scrotoplasty
Orchiectomy
Colpopoiesis
Clitoroplasty
Vulva Angioplasty
and so on...
I HAD MY SURGERIES IN THAILAND...
BUT IT'S POSSIBLE TO HAVE THEM IN JAPAN, OR OTHER COUNTRIES, TOO.
OF COURSE, YOU CAN'T JUST DECIDE TO HAVE THESE SURGERIES AND THEN JUST DO IT. DIFFERENT CLINICS HAVE DIFFERENT RULES...
BUT YOU ALWAYS HAVE TO FULFILL CERTAIN REQUIREMENTS FIRST.

"People who transition all have surgery and transition legally on paper, right?"

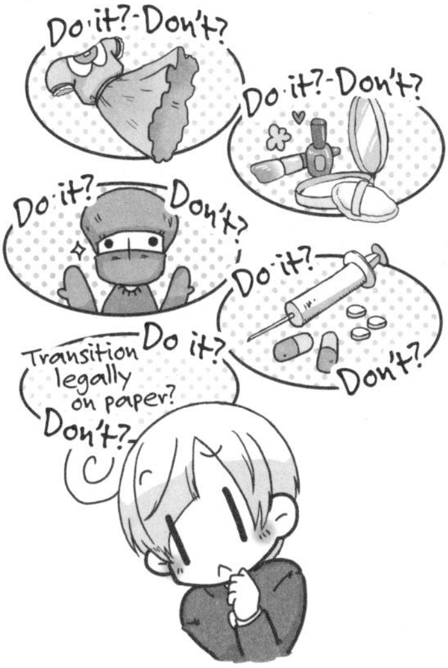
Do it?-Don't?
Do it?-Don't?
Do it? Don't?
Do it? Don't?
Transition legally on paper? Do it? Don't?

I hear this a lot and before I considered transitioning, I thought so myself, too. After speaking to a lot of people, though, I found out that it isn't actually the case; it varies from person to person. There are a lot of people who don't undergo sex reassignment surgery and/or don't want it. I was touched that such a choice existed.

However, there are those who want to have it but can't, and/or those who don't want to but have to have it. It's a very complex situation. Anyway, it'd make me happy for you to know that people who transition don't all have surgery or change their gender legally on paper.

The Bride was a Boy

CHAPTER 5

Husband-kun Proposes

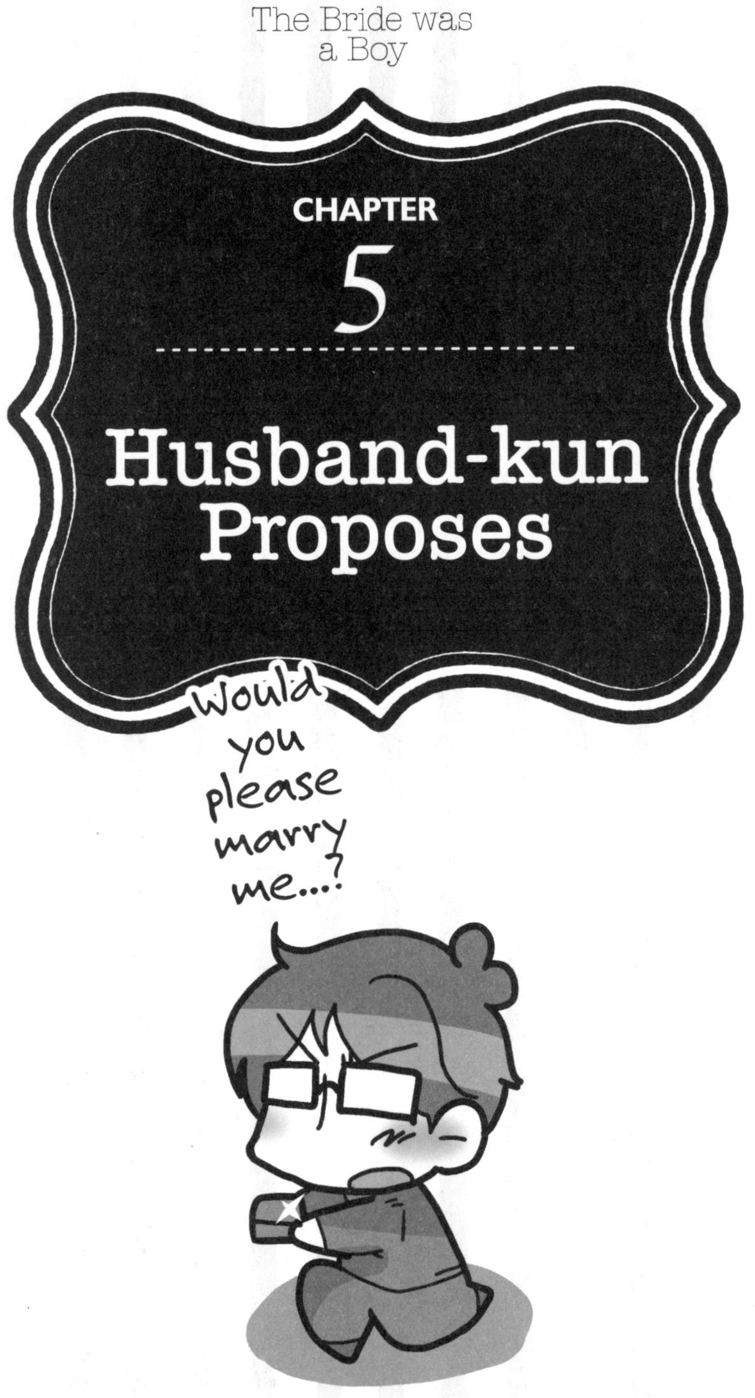
Would you please marry me...?

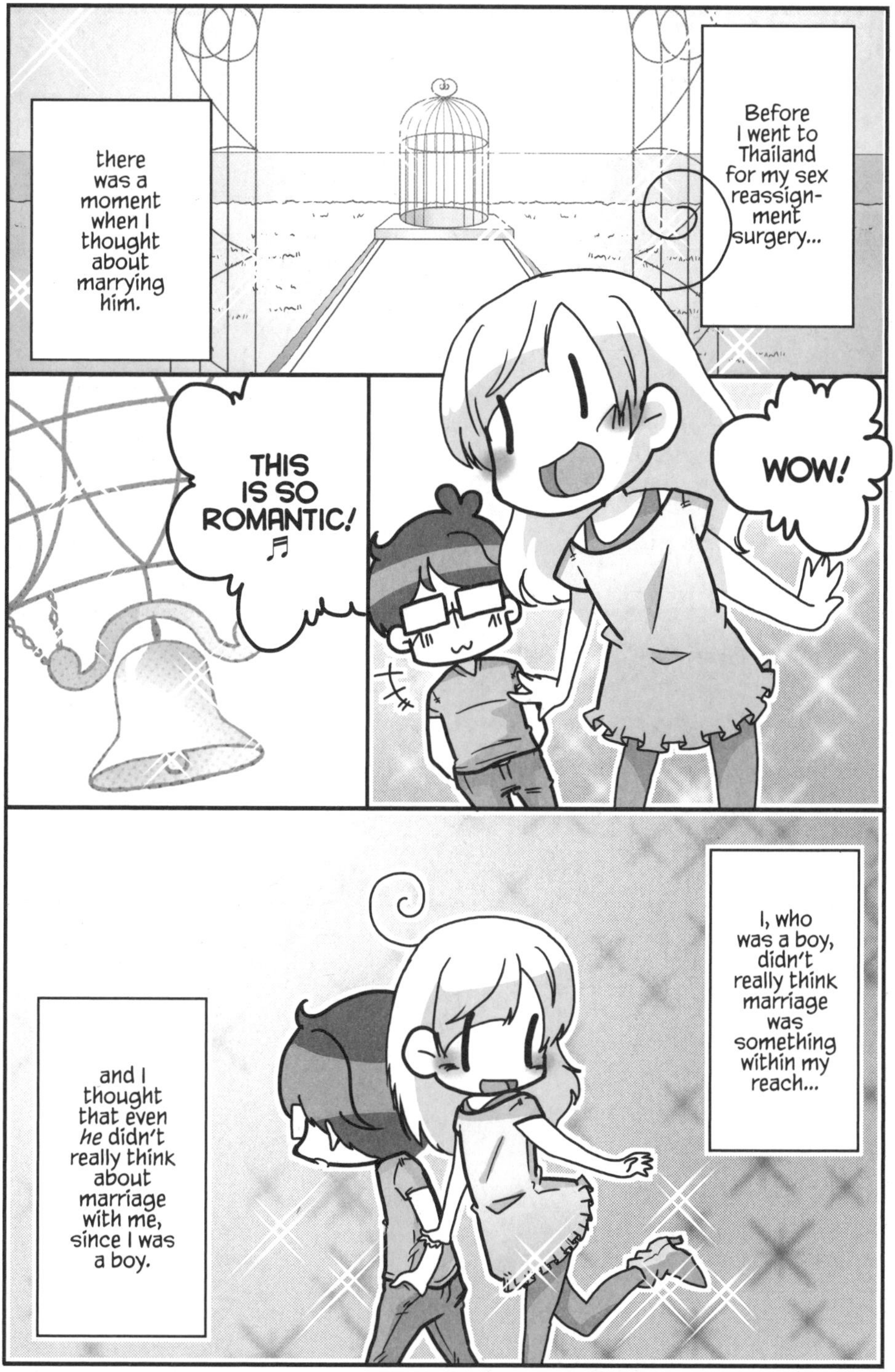
Before I went to Thailand for my sex reassignment surgery...
there was a moment when I thought about marrying him.
WOW!
THIS IS SO ROMANTIC! ♬
I, who was a boy, didn't really think marriage was something within my reach...
and I thought that even *he* didn't really think about marriage with me, since I was a boy.

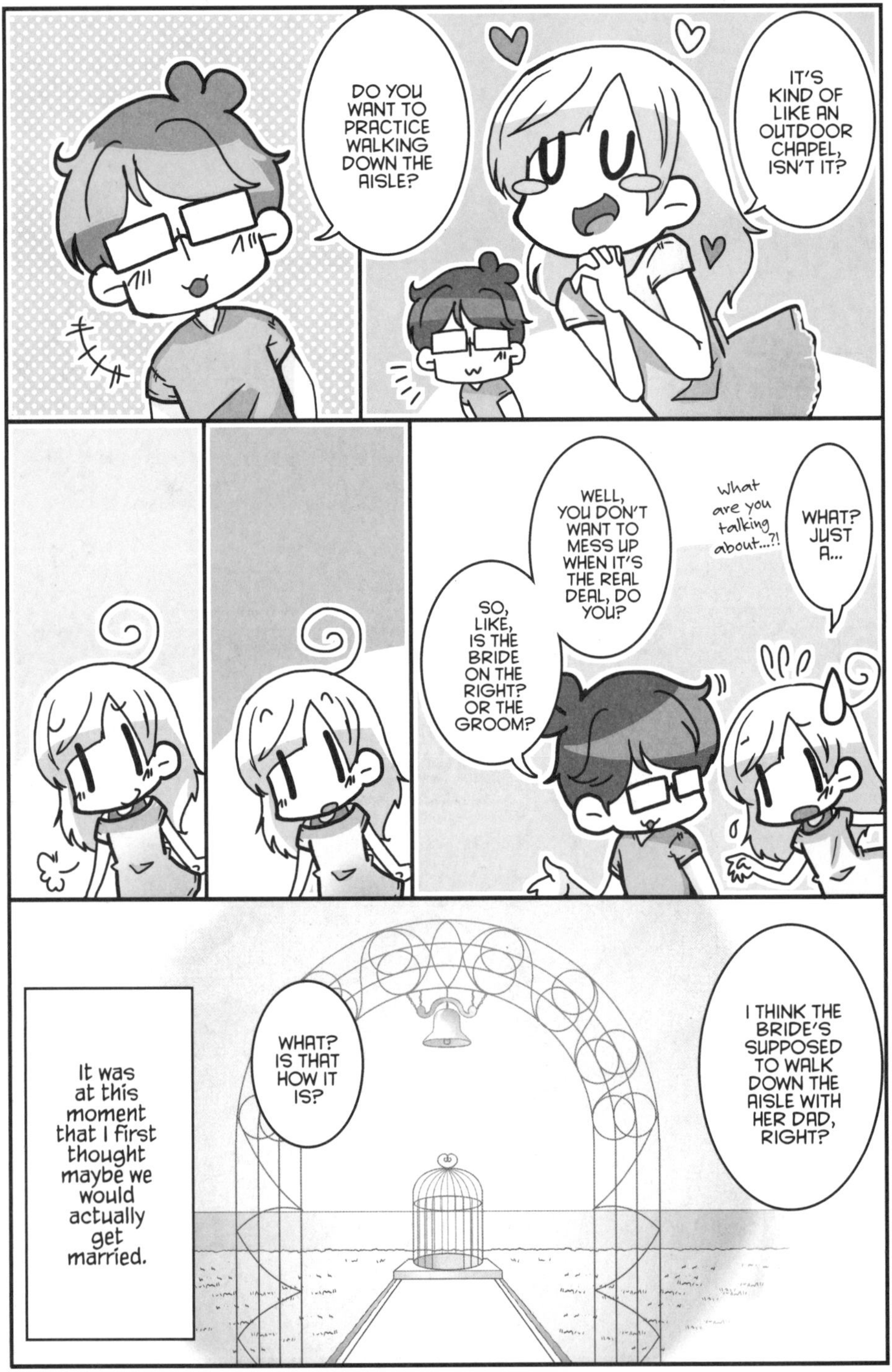
IT'S KIND OF LIKE AN OUTDOOR CHAPEL, ISN'T IT?
DO YOU WANT TO PRACTICE WALKING DOWN THE AISLE?
WHAT? JUST A...
What are you talking about...?!
WELL, YOU DON'T WANT TO MESS UP WHEN IT'S THE REAL DEAL, DO YOU?
SO, LIKE, IS THE BRIDE ON THE RIGHT? OR THE GROOM?
I THINK THE BRIDE'S SUPPOSED TO WALK DOWN THE AISLE WITH HER DAD, RIGHT?
WHAT? IS THAT HOW IT IS?
It was at this moment that I first thought maybe we would actually get married.

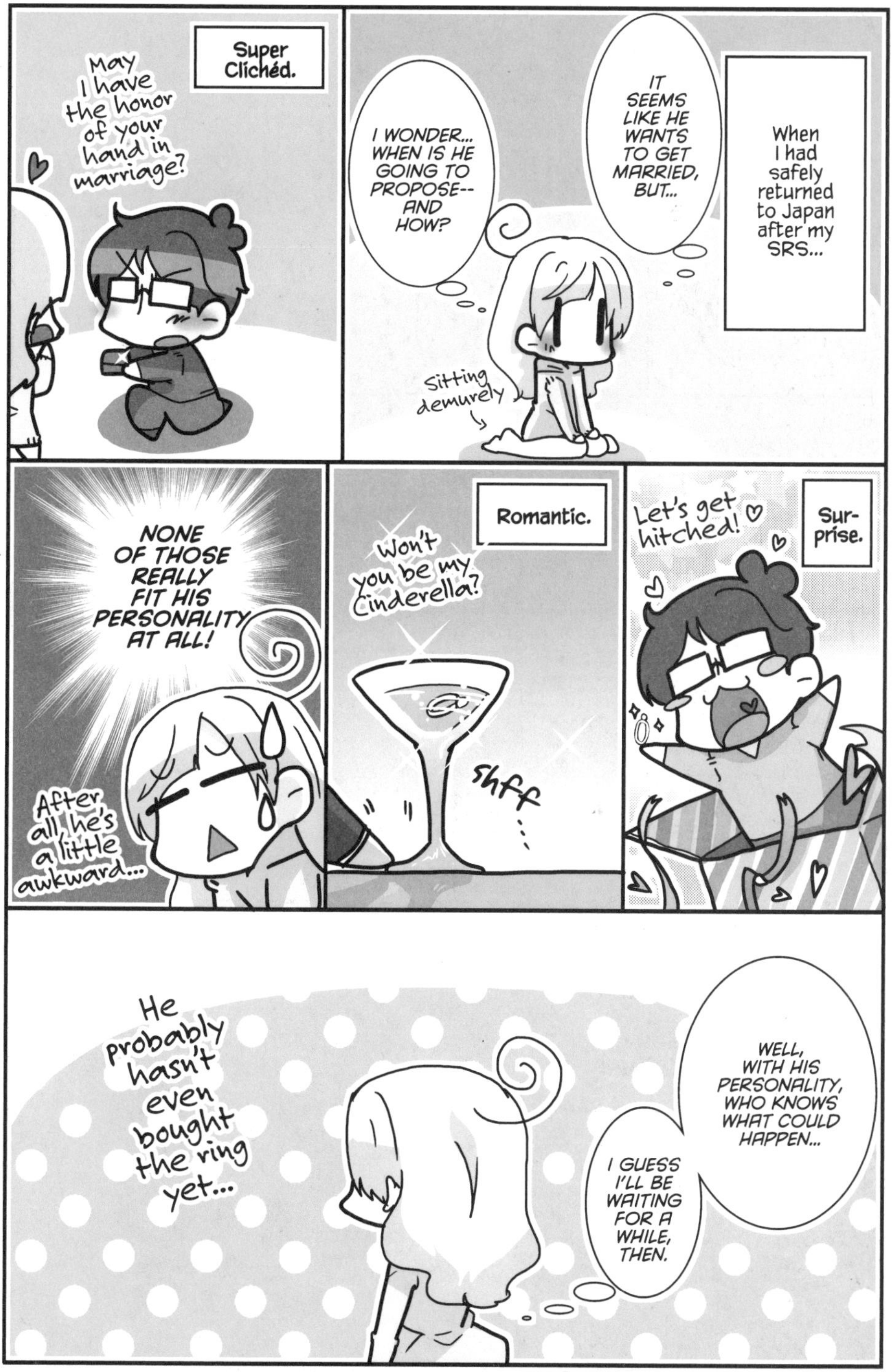
When I had safely returned to Japan after my SRS...
IT SEEMS LIKE HE WANTS TO GET MARRIED, BUT...
I WONDER... WHEN IS HE GOING TO PROPOSE--AND HOW?
Sitting demurely
Super Clichéd.
May I have the honor of your hand in marriage?
Sur-prise.
Let's get hitched!
Romantic.
Won't you be my Cinderella?
shff...
NONE OF THOSE REALLY FIT HIS PERSONALITY AT ALL!
After all, he's a little awkward...
WELL, WITH HIS PERSONALITY, WHO KNOWS WHAT COULD HAPPEN...
I GUESS I'LL BE WAITING FOR A WHILE, THEN.
He probably hasn't even bought the ring yet...

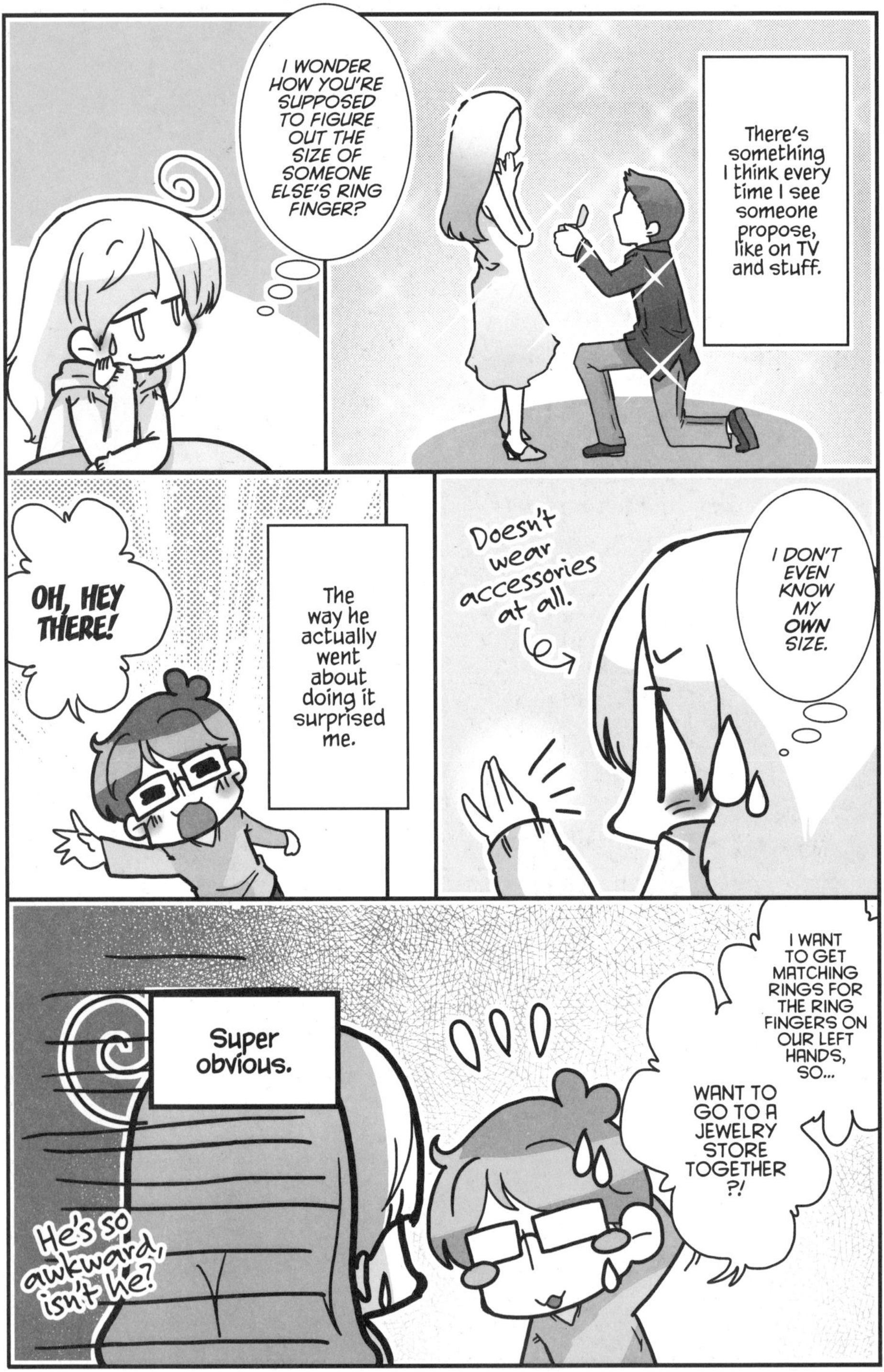
There's something I think every time I see someone propose, like on TV and stuff.
I WONDER HOW YOU'RE SUPPOSED TO FIGURE OUT THE SIZE OF SOMEONE ELSE'S RING FINGER?
I DON'T EVEN KNOW MY OWN SIZE.
Doesn't wear accessories at all.
The way he actually went about doing it surprised me.
OH, HEY THERE!
I WANT TO GET MATCHING RINGS FOR THE RING FINGERS ON OUR LEFT HANDS, SO...
WANT TO GO TO A JEWELRY STORE TOGETHER?!
Super obvious.
He's so awkward, isn't he?

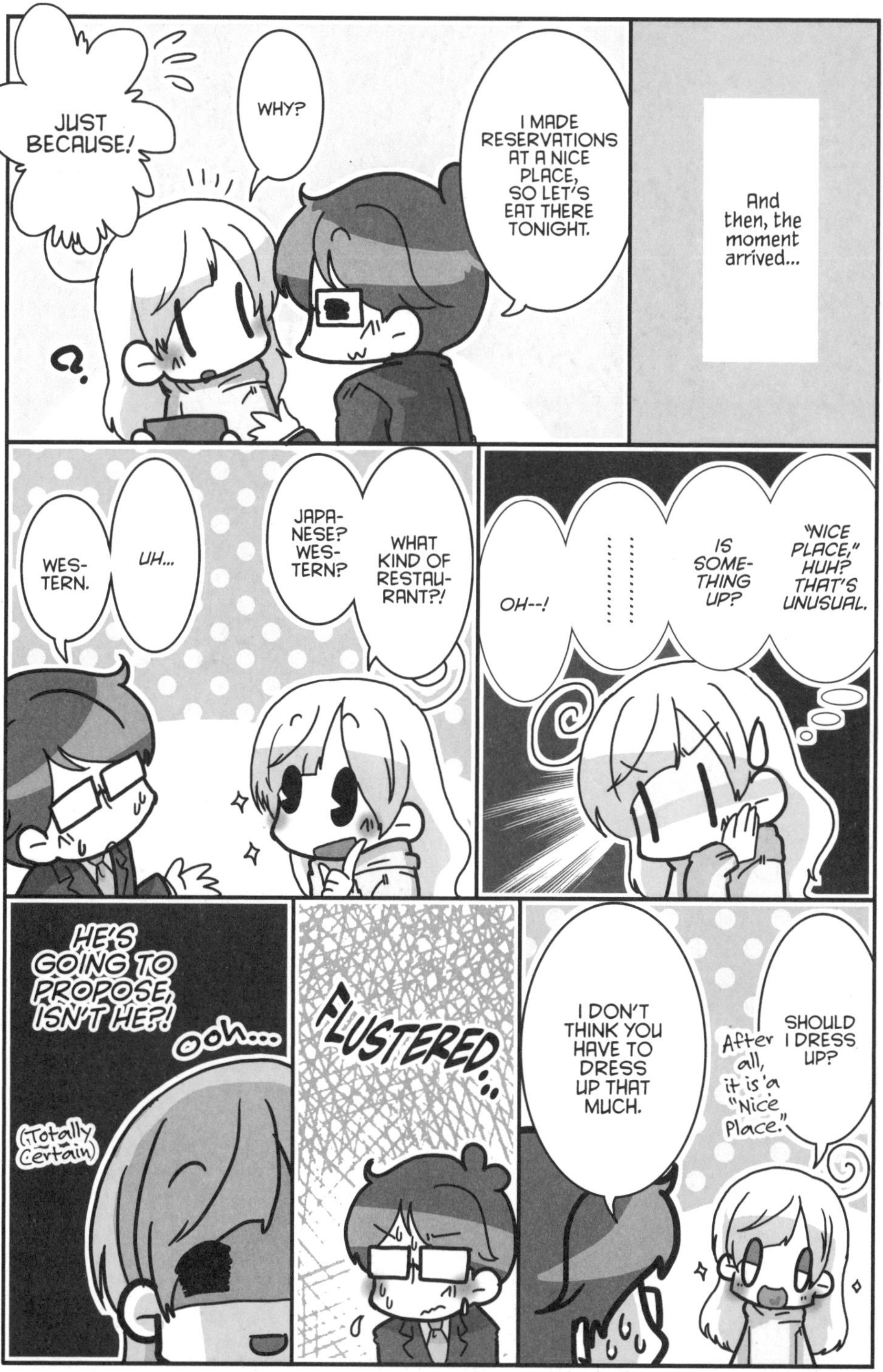
And then, the moment arrived...
I MADE RESERVATIONS AT A NICE PLACE, SO LET'S EAT THERE TONIGHT.
WHY?
JUST BECAUSE!
"NICE PLACE," HUH? THAT'S UNUSUAL.
IS SOMETHING UP?
......
OH--!
WHAT KIND OF RESTAURANT?!
JAPANESE? WESTERN?
UH...
WESTERN.
SHOULD I DRESS UP?
After all, it is a "Nice Place."
I DON'T THINK YOU HAVE TO DRESS UP THAT MUCH.
FLUSTERED...
HE'S GOING TO PROPOSE, ISN'T HE?!
ooh...
(Totally Certain)

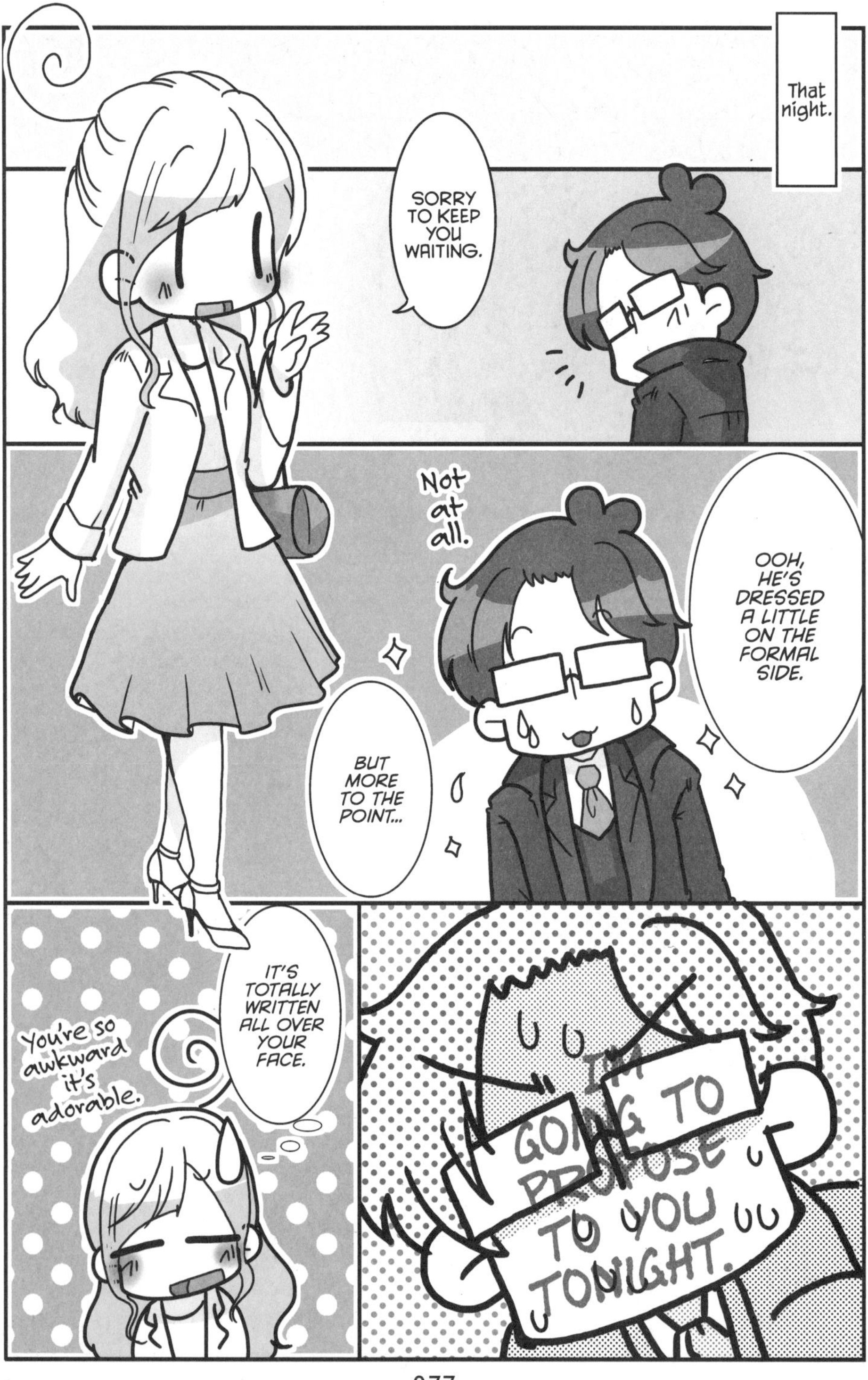
That night.
SORRY TO KEEP YOU WAITING.
Not at all.
OOH, HE'S DRESSED A LITTLE ON THE FORMAL SIDE.
BUT MORE TO THE POINT...
I'M GOING TO PROPOSE TO YOU TONIGHT.
IT'S TOTALLY WRITTEN ALL OVER YOUR FACE.
You're so awkward it's adorable.

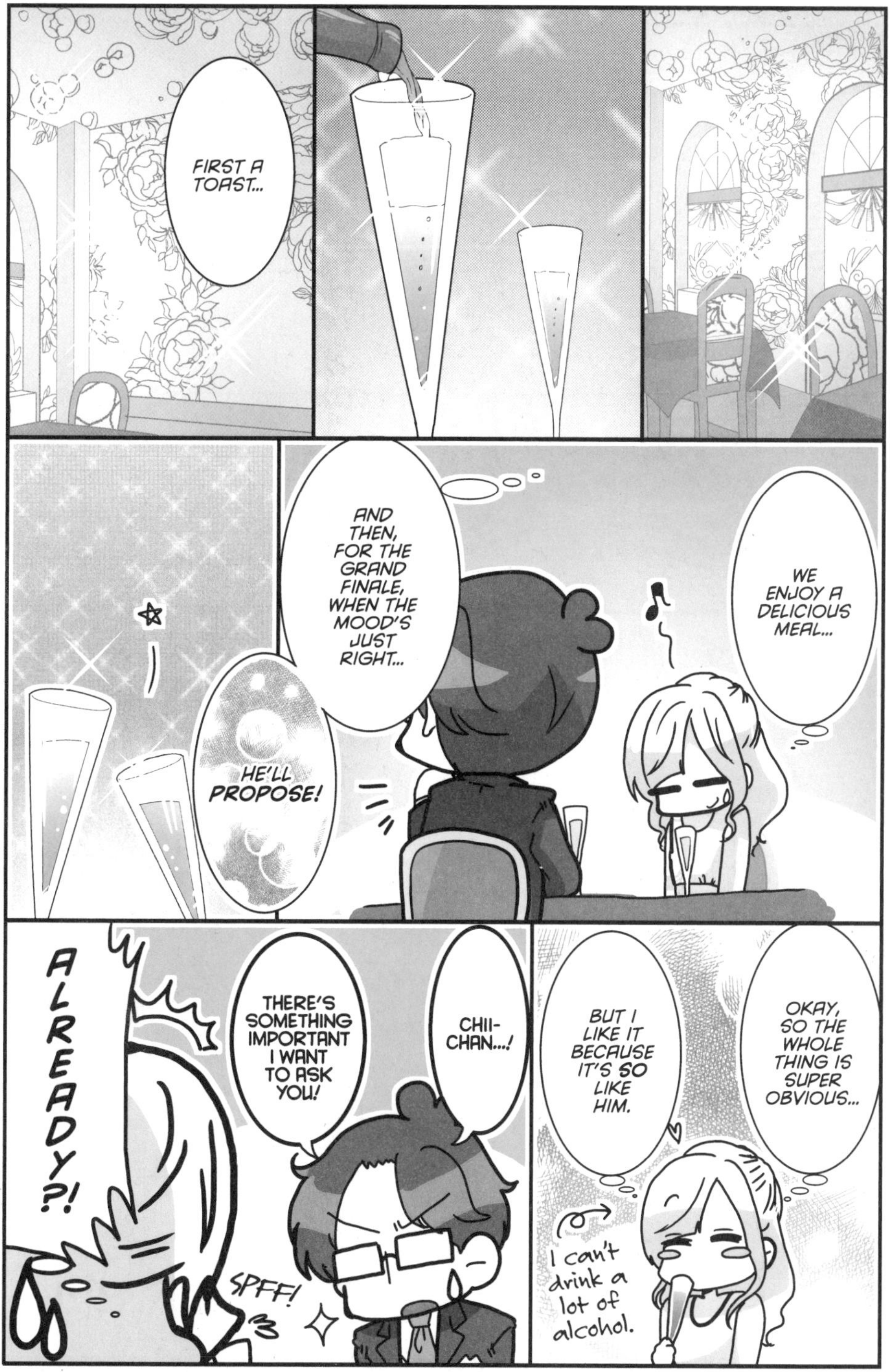
FIRST A TOAST...
WE ENJOY A DELICIOUS MEAL...
AND THEN, FOR THE GRAND FINALE, WHEN THE MOOD'S JUST RIGHT...
HE'LL PROPOSE!
OKAY, SO THE WHOLE THING IS SUPER OBVIOUS...
BUT I LIKE IT BECAUSE IT'S SO LIKE HIM.
I can't drink a lot of alcohol.
CHII-CHAN...!
THERE'S SOMETHING IMPORTANT I WANT TO ASK YOU!
SPFF!
ALREADY?!

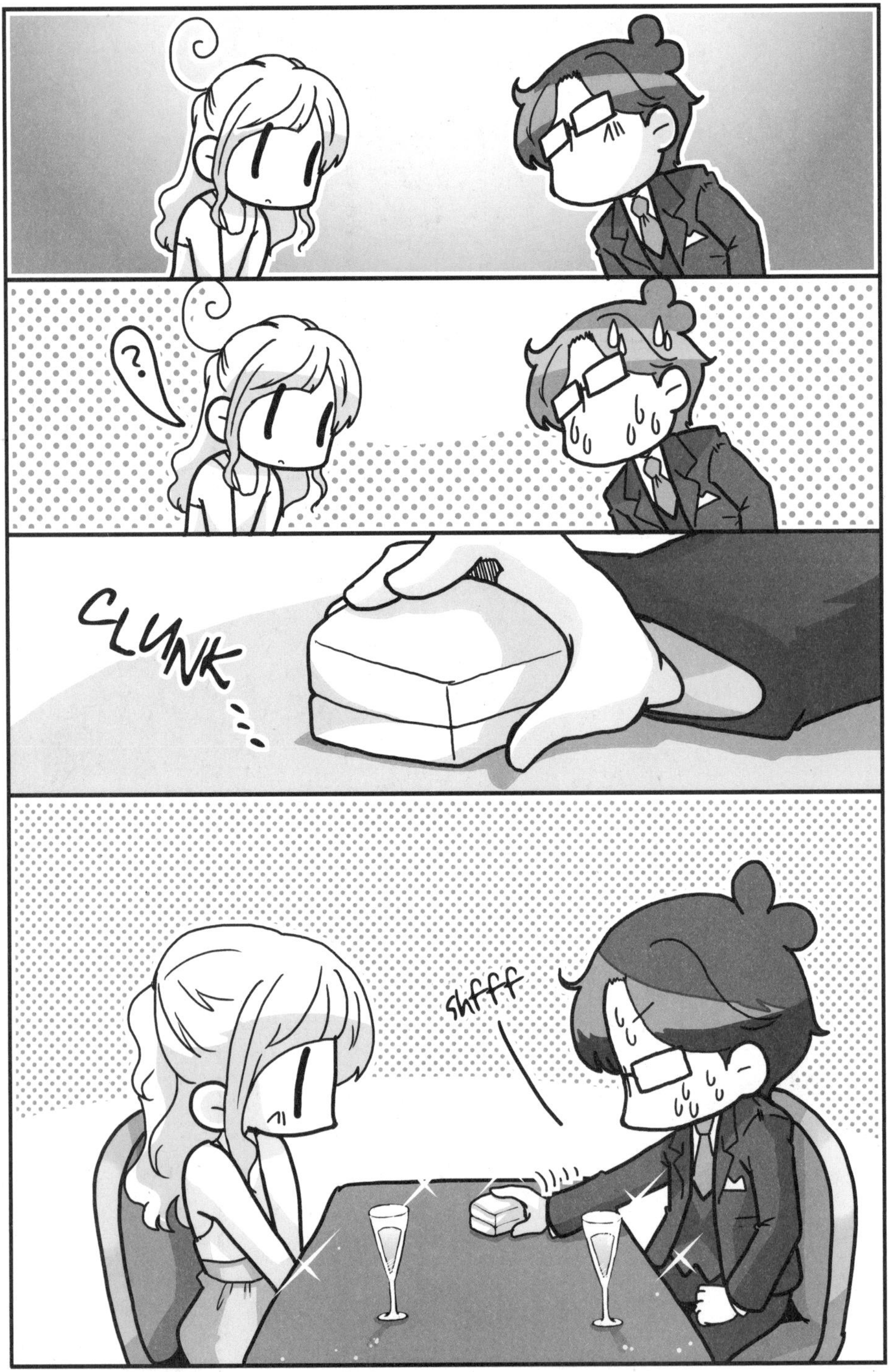
?
CLUNK...
shfff

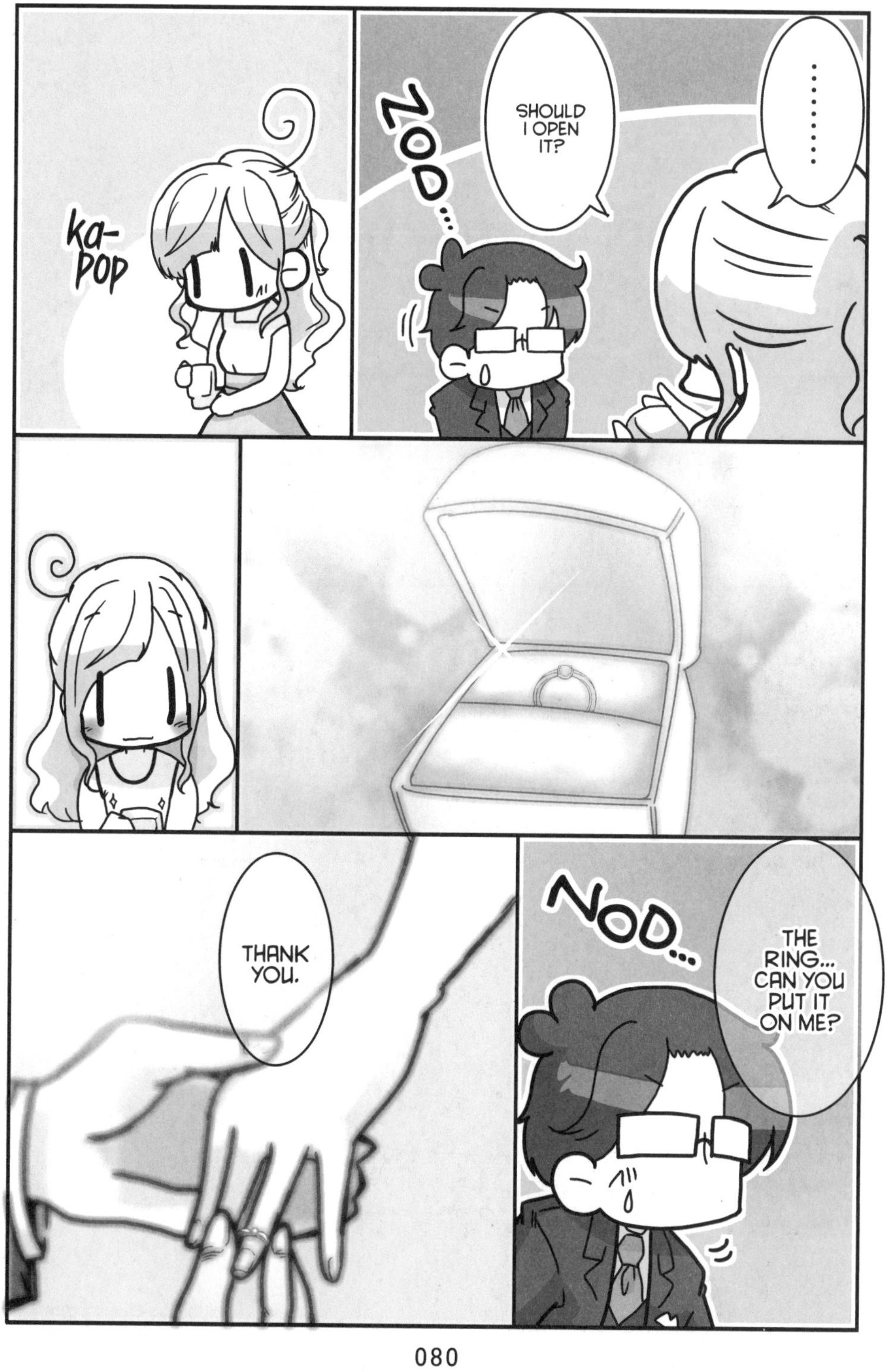

....
SHOULD I OPEN IT?
NOD...
ka-pop
THE RING... CAN YOU PUT IT ON ME?
NOD...
THANK YOU.

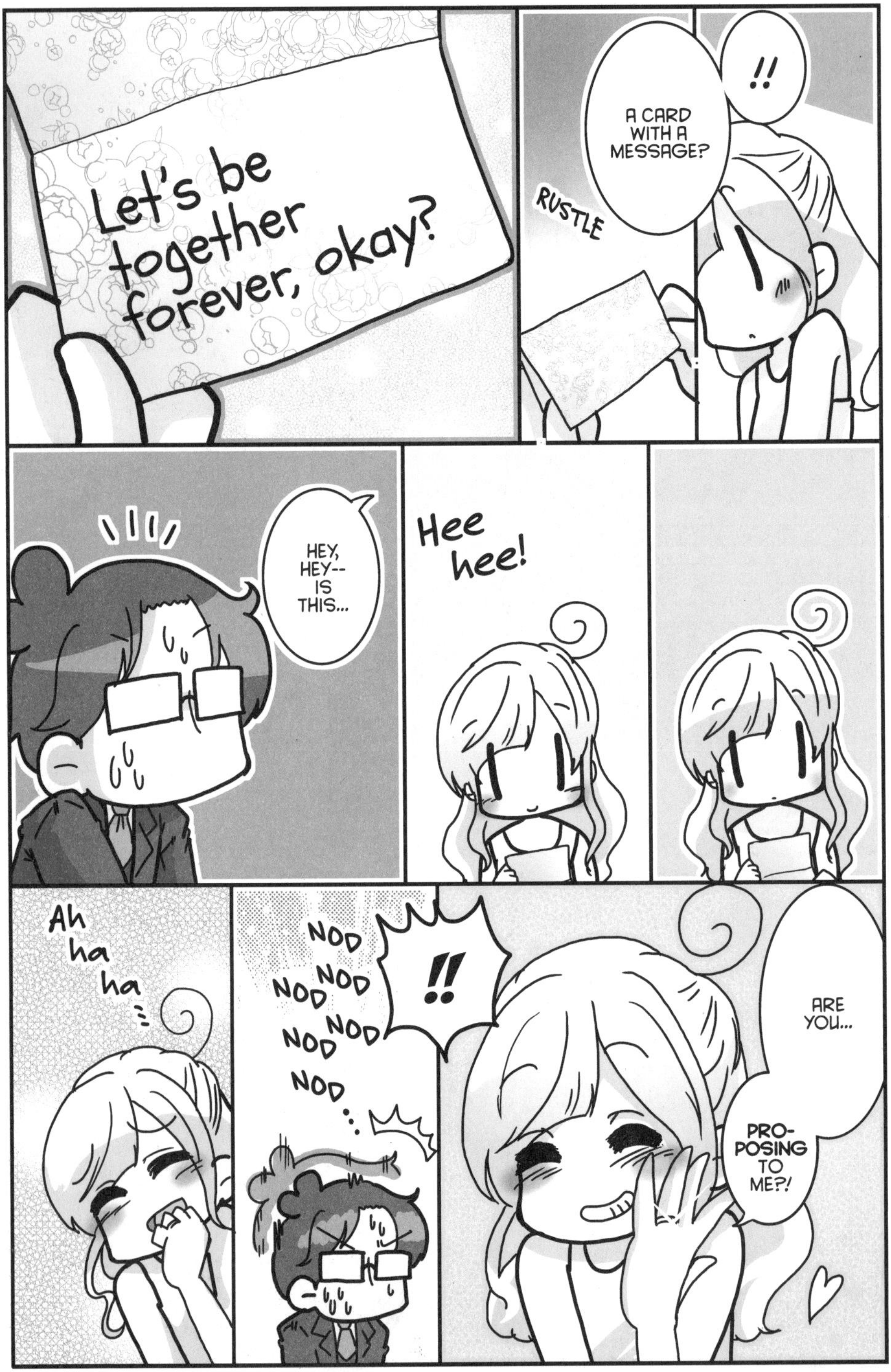

!!
A CARD WITH A MESSAGE?
RUSTLE
Let's be together forever, okay?
Hee hee!
HEY, HEY-- IS THIS...
ARE YOU...
PRO-POSING TO ME?!
!!
NOD NOD NOD NOD NOD NOD...
Ah ha ha

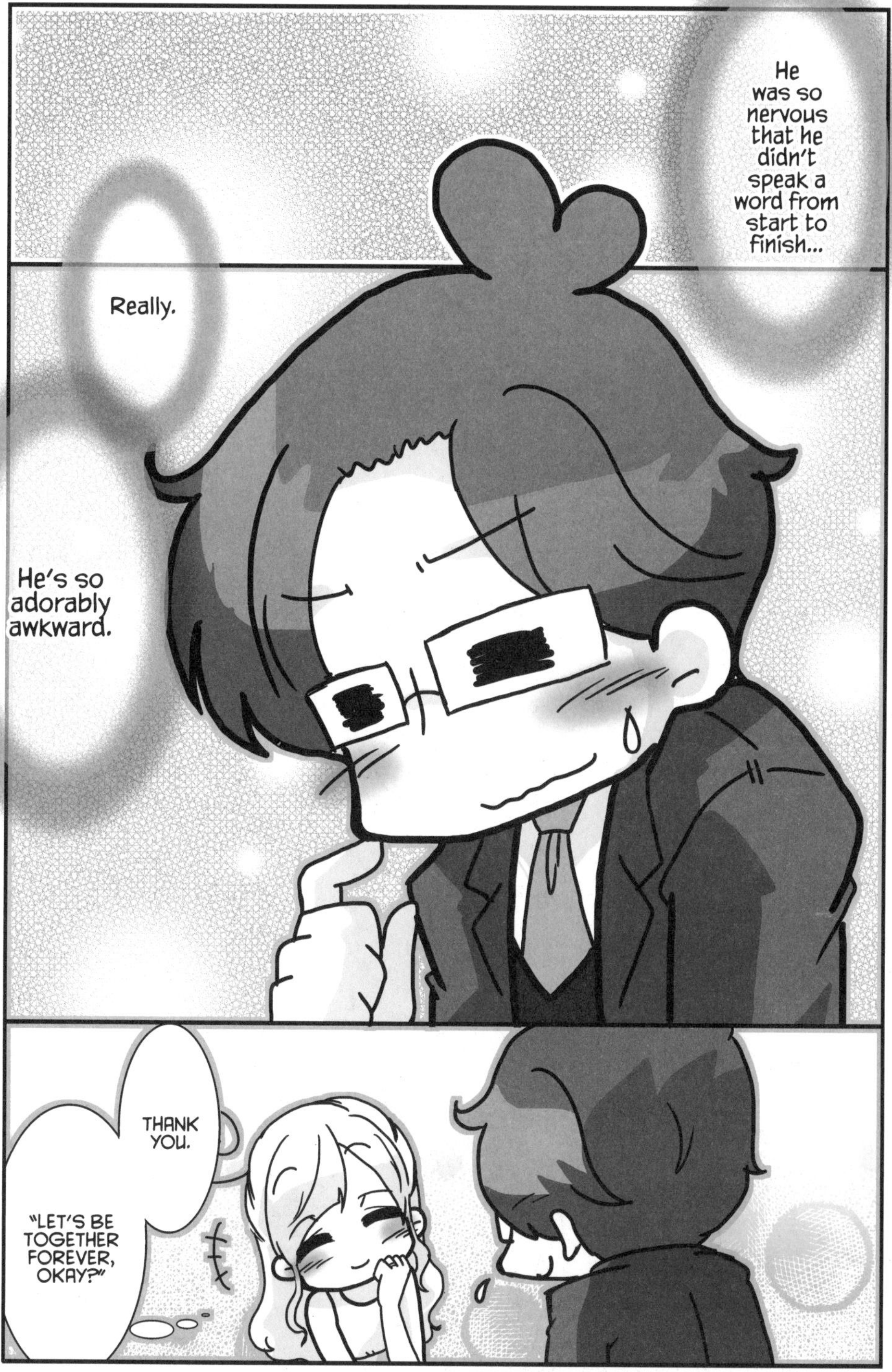
He was so nervous that he didn't speak a word from start to finish...
Really.
He's so adorably awkward.
THANK YOU.
"LET'S BE TOGETHER FOREVER, OKAY?"

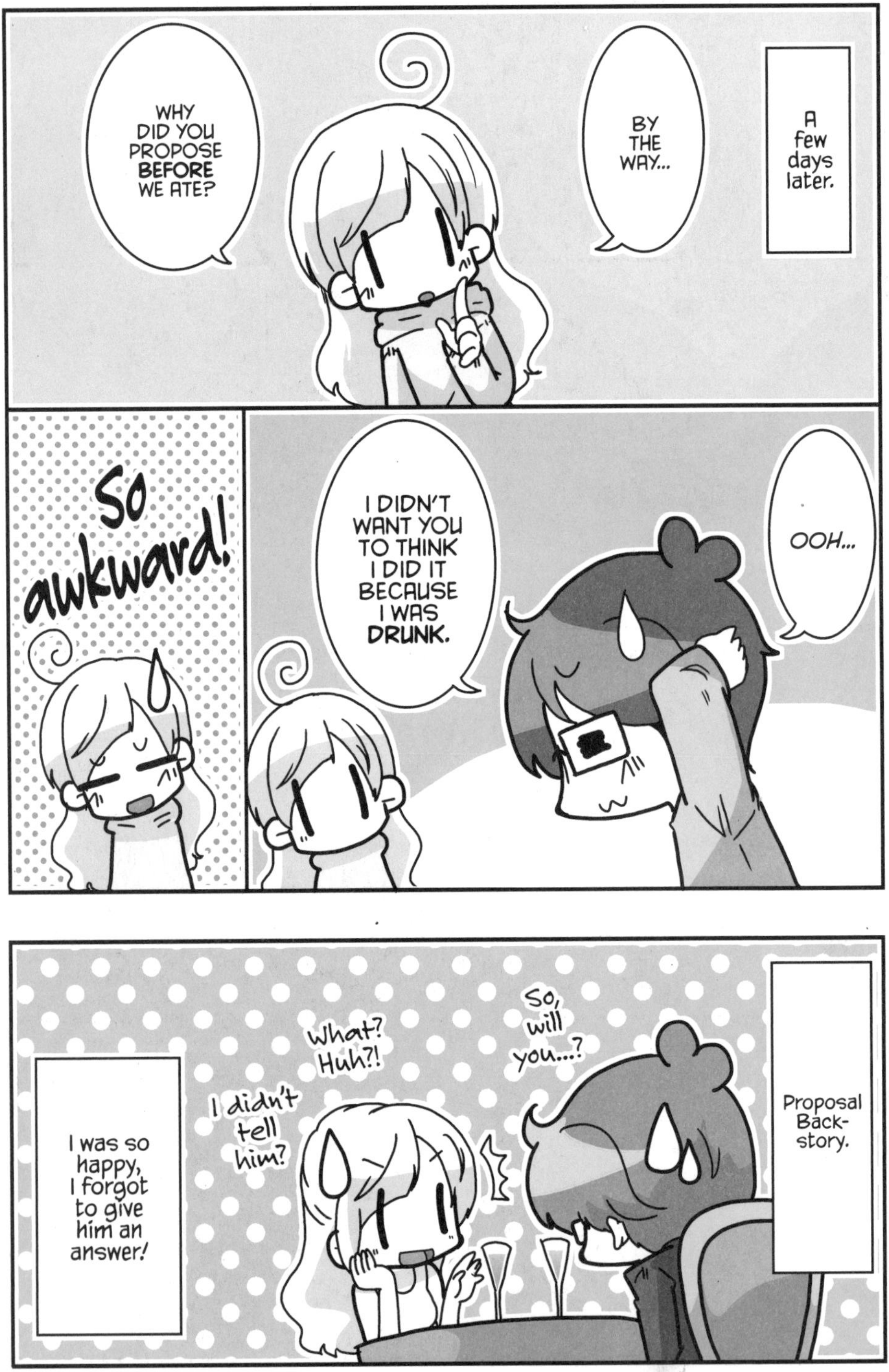
A few days later.
BY THE WAY...
WHY DID YOU PROPOSE BEFORE WE ATE?
OOH...
I DIDN'T WANT YOU TO THINK I DID IT BECAUSE I WAS DRUNK.
So awkward!
Proposal Back-story.
So, will you...?
What? Huh?!
I didn't tell him?
I was so happy, I forgot to give him an answer!

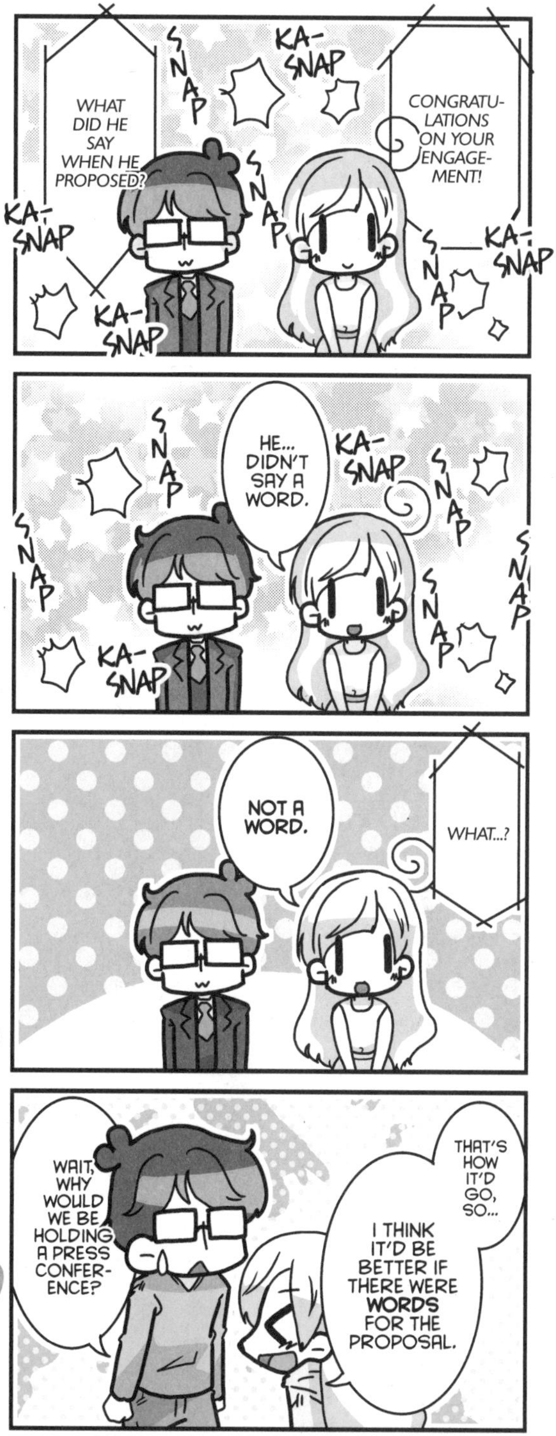
KA-SNAP
CONGRATULATIONS ON YOUR ENGAGEMENT!
SNAP
KA-SNAP
SNAP
WHAT DID HE SAY WHEN HE PROPOSED?
SNAP
KA-SNAP
KA-SNAP
SNAP
KA-SNAP
SNAP
SNAP
HE... DIDN'T SAY A WORD.
SNAP
SNAP
KA-SNAP
WHAT...?
NOT A WORD.
THAT'S HOW IT'D GO, SO...
I THINK IT'D BE BETTER IF THERE WERE **WORDS** FOR THE PROPOSAL.
WAIT, WHY WOULD WE BE HOLDING A PRESS CONFERENCE?

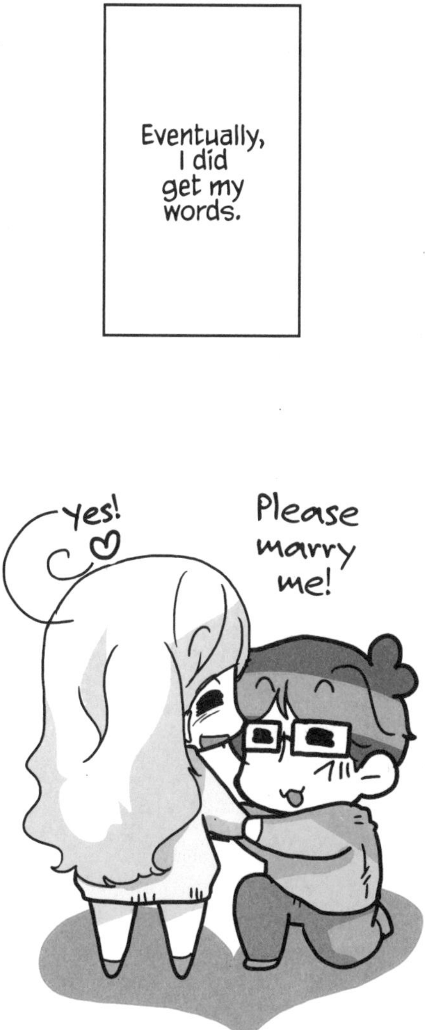
Eventually, I did get my words.
Please marry me!
Yes!

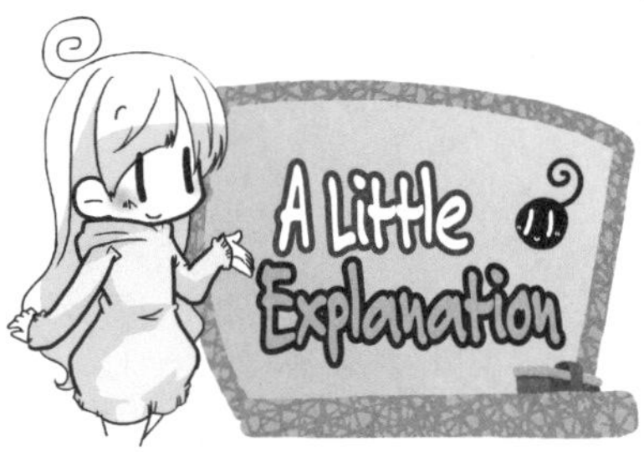
A Little Explanation

Gender Transition

Changing your gender in the eyes of society and in your own physical body is called "Gender Transition," and also "trans." A societal gender transition is when a person lives as the gender they identify with so that they can experience what it's like and learn how to adapt. The main goal is to improve their mental state and quality of life.

There is no set way to accomplish this, though. A person may take the steps needed to get along in society, like finding a new job. They might also live as the gender they identify with only on their days off. It varies a lot for each individual.

A "physical gender transition" makes it easier for someone to live in society as the gender they identify with, but the goal is more aimed at relieving the discomfort and disgust they may feel toward their current body.

Counseling and medical surgeries may also come into play, so appropriate medical care is often necessary. These choices also vary and depend on the individual.

The duration of a person's gender transition is also considered to be the duration that one is uncomfortable with their assigned gender, as well as the duration of their transition, and depends on whether they can reach some kind of peace within themselves. Of course, this varies according to the individual.

GENDER TRANSITION (TRANS)

This means transitioning to the gender one identifies with, physically and in terms of societal standards.

From a medical point of view, this is often referred to as "treatment" of Gender Identity Disorder. However, many individuals prefer to call it "gender transition" or "being trans."

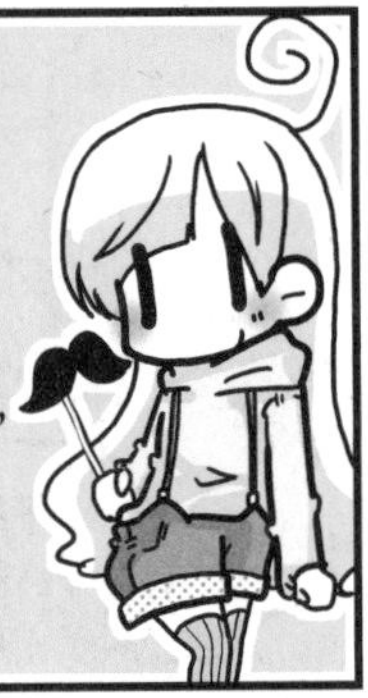

"SOCIETAL GENDER TRANSITION"

- By living as one's preferred gender, one can experience related issues and thus develop coping methods.
- This can result in an improvement in one's mental state by increasing self-esteem, quality of life, et cetera.

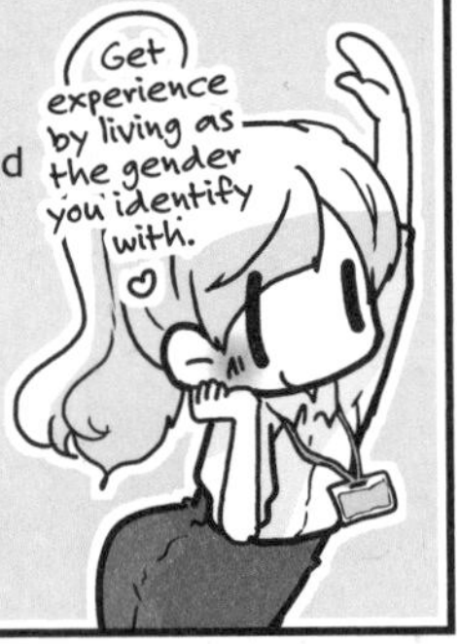
Get experience by living as the gender you identify with.

PHYSICAL GENDER TRANSITION

- **Hormone Therapy:** Secondary sex characteristics develop with the administration of hormones, thus bringing one's body closer to one's gender identity.
- **Breast Transition:** Mammoplasty/mastectomy. Breast Augmentation Surgery (implants), etc.

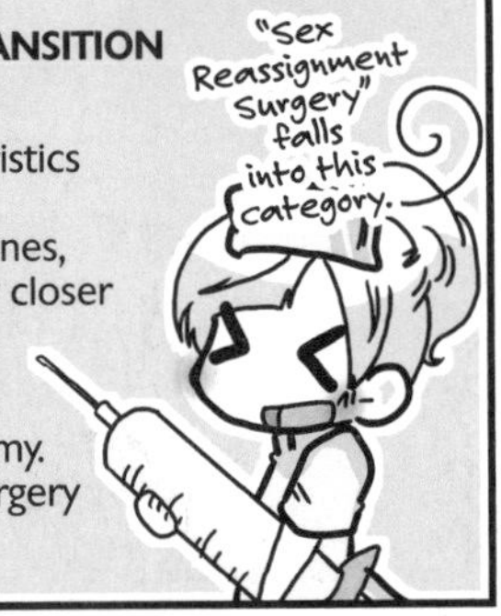
"Sex Reassignment Surgery" falls into this category.

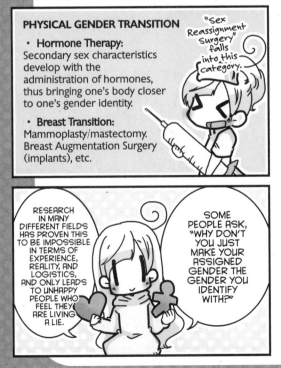

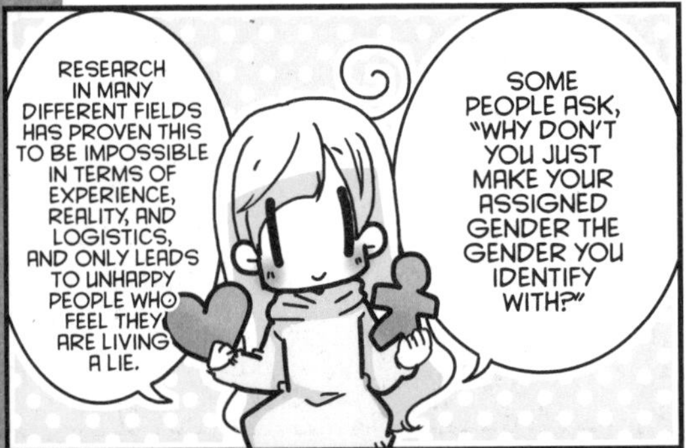
SOME PEOPLE ASK, "WHY DON'T YOU JUST MAKE YOUR ASSIGNED GENDER THE GENDER YOU IDENTIFY WITH?"
RESEARCH IN MANY DIFFERENT FIELDS HAS PROVEN THIS TO BE IMPOSSIBLE IN TERMS OF EXPERIENCE, REALITY, AND LOGISTICS, AND ONLY LEADS TO UNHAPPY PEOPLE WHO FEEL THEY ARE LIVING A LIE.

"Where do people who were boys work?"

WORK
NOW!

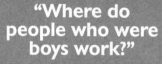

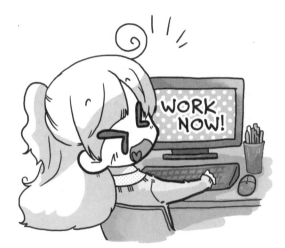

I think many people believe that everyone who's had a gender transition works at "Okama Bars" (transvestite bars) and as "Newhalfs" (transwomen who work in the entertainment industry). However, a person doesn't have to work at those places just because they're a woman who transitioned. It's really an individual preference.

There are those who do white collar work, those who work in the service industry, and even those who work in politics. However, there are housewives and househusbands, too.

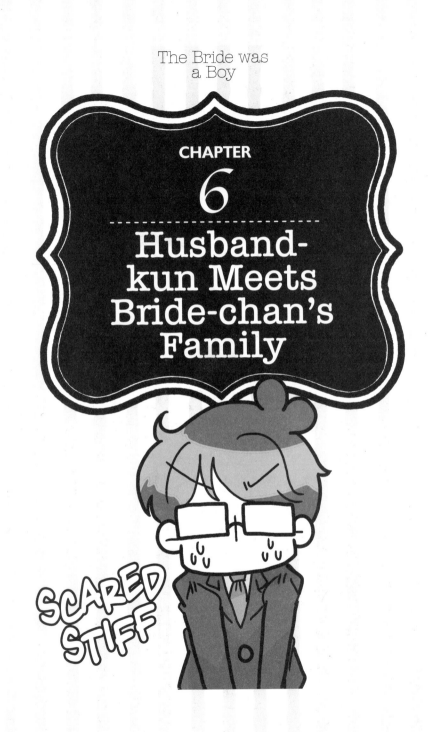

The Bride was a Boy

CHAPTER

6

Husband-kun Meets Bride-chan's Family

SCARED STIFF

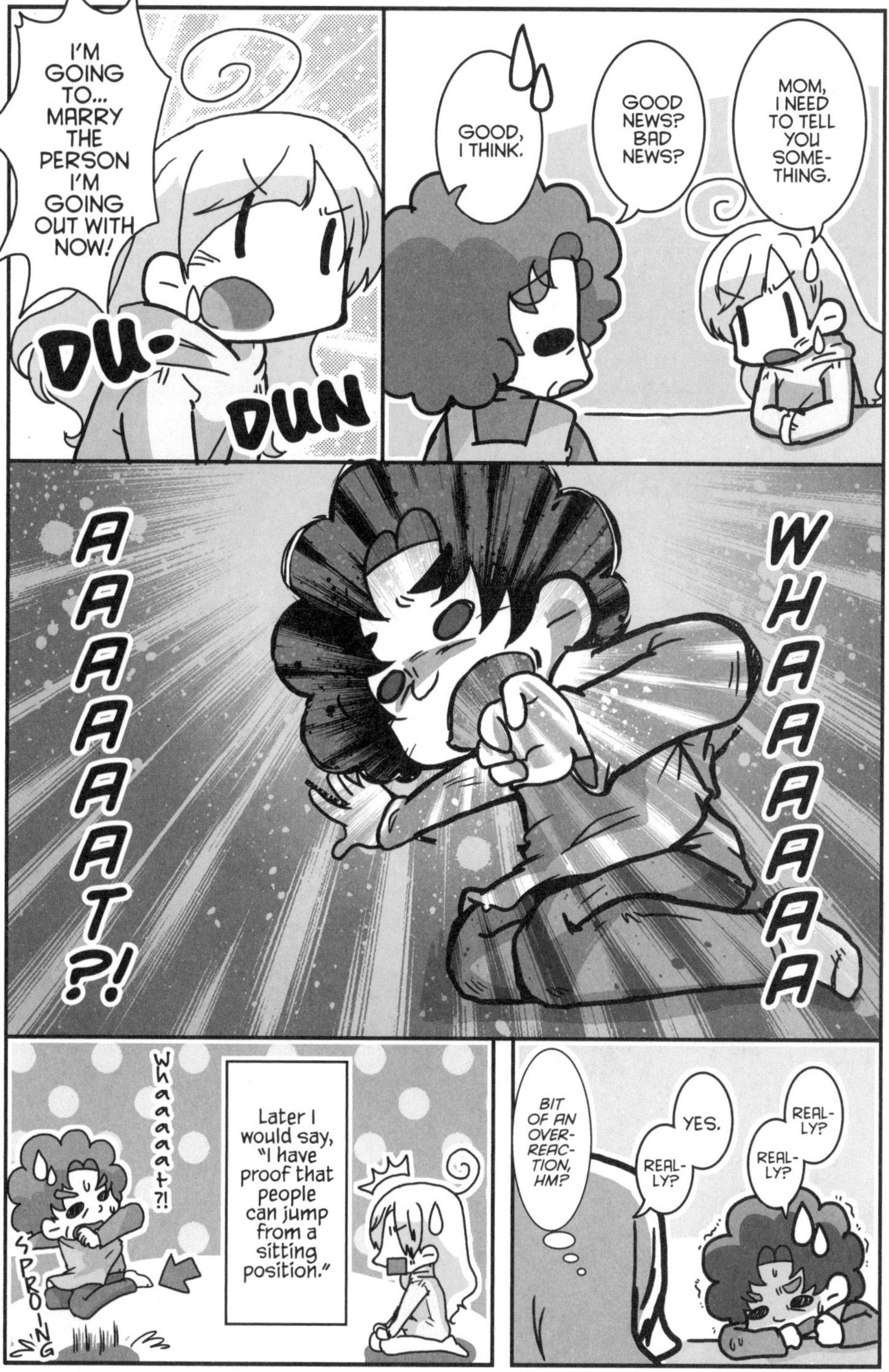
MOM, I NEED TO TELL YOU SOME-THING.
GOOD NEWS? BAD NEWS?
GOOD, I THINK.
I'M GOING TO... MARRY THE PERSON I'M GOING OUT WITH NOW!
DU-
DUN
WHAAAAAA
AAAAAAT?!
REAL-LY?
REAL-LY?
YES.
REAL-LY?
BIT OF AN OVER-REACTION, HM?
Later I would say, "I have proof that people can jump from a sitting position."
Whaaaaat?!
SPROING

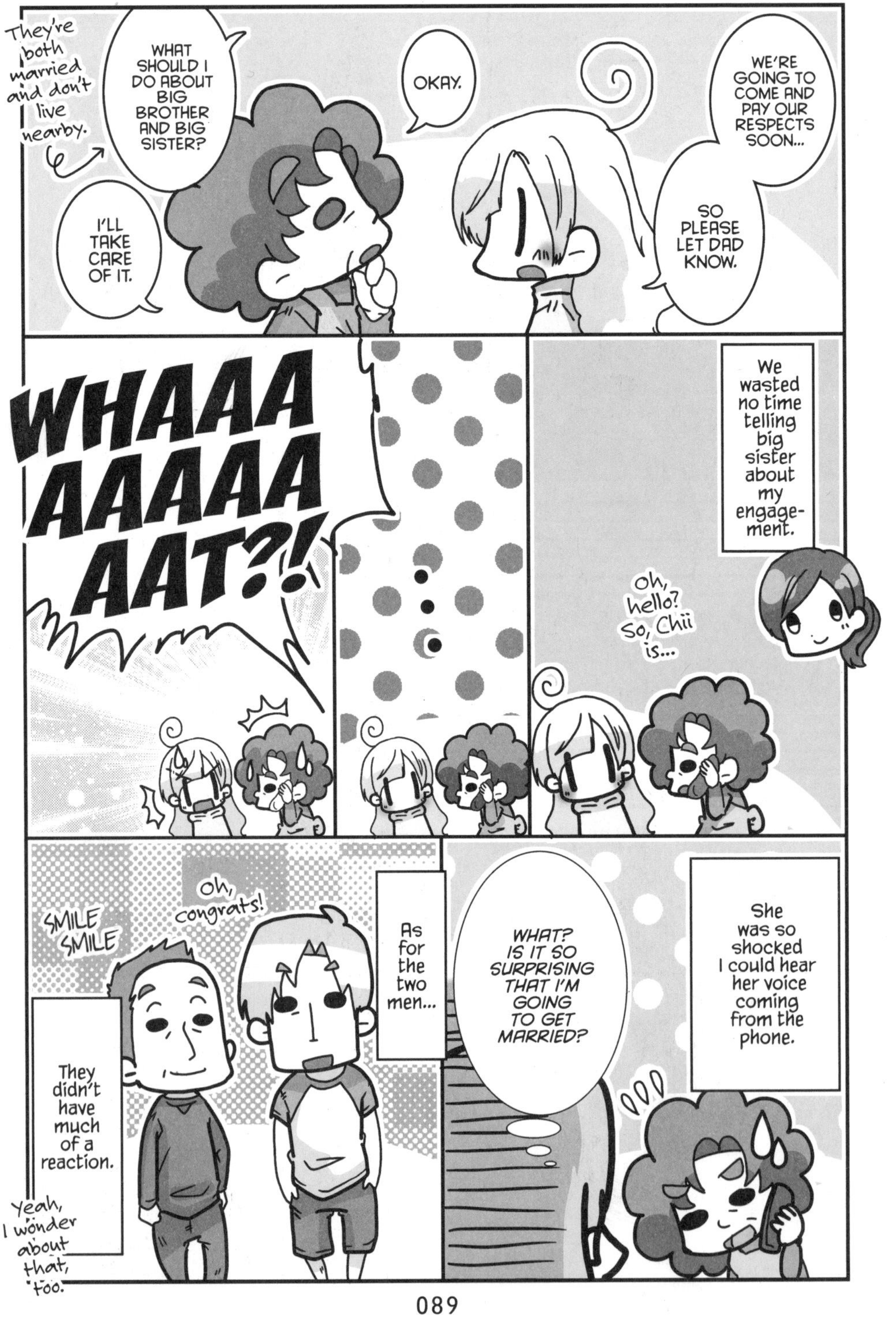
WE'RE GOING TO COME AND PAY OUR RESPECTS SOON...
SO PLEASE LET DAD KNOW.
OKAY.
WHAT SHOULD I DO ABOUT BIG BROTHER AND BIG SISTER?
I'LL TAKE CARE OF IT.
They're both married and don't live nearby.
We wasted no time telling big sister about my engagement.
Oh, hello? So, Chii is...
WHAAAAAAAAAAT?!
She was so shocked I could hear her voice coming from the phone.
WHAT? IS IT SO SURPRISING THAT I'M GOING TO GET MARRIED?
As for the two men...
Oh, congrats!
SMILE SMILE
They didn't have much of a reaction.
Yeah, I wonder about that, too.

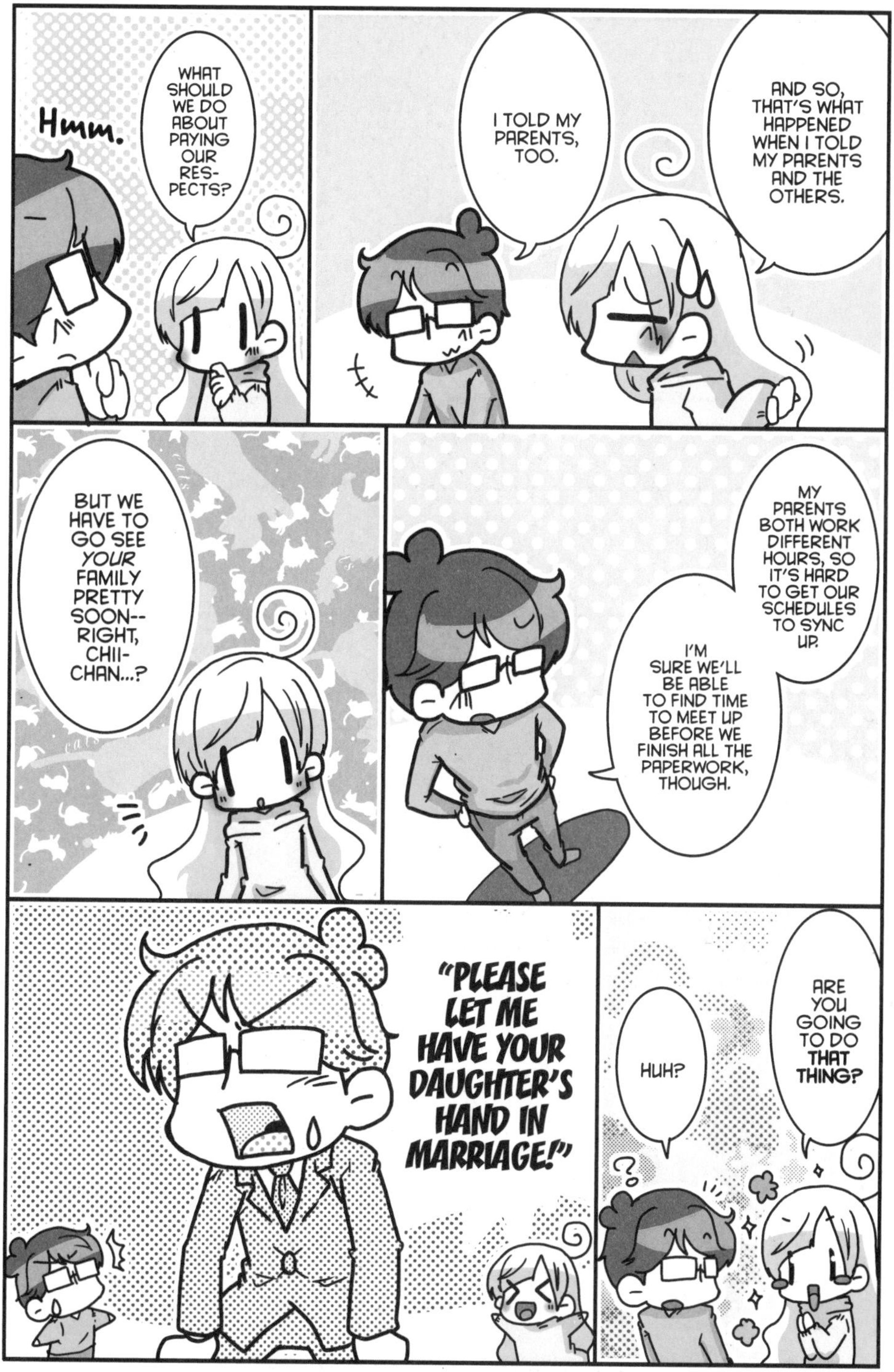
AND SO, THAT'S WHAT HAPPENED WHEN I TOLD MY PARENTS AND THE OTHERS.
I TOLD MY PARENTS, TOO.
WHAT SHOULD WE DO ABOUT PAYING OUR RES-PECTS?
Hmm.
MY PARENTS BOTH WORK DIFFERENT HOURS, SO IT'S HARD TO GET OUR SCHEDULES TO SYNC UP.
I'M SURE WE'LL BE ABLE TO FIND TIME TO MEET UP BEFORE WE FINISH ALL THE PAPERWORK, THOUGH.
BUT WE HAVE TO GO SEE *YOUR* FAMILY PRETTY SOON-- RIGHT, CHII-CHAN...?
ARE YOU GOING TO DO **THAT THING?**
HUH?
"PLEASE LET ME HAVE YOUR DAUGHTER'S HAND IN MARRIAGE!"

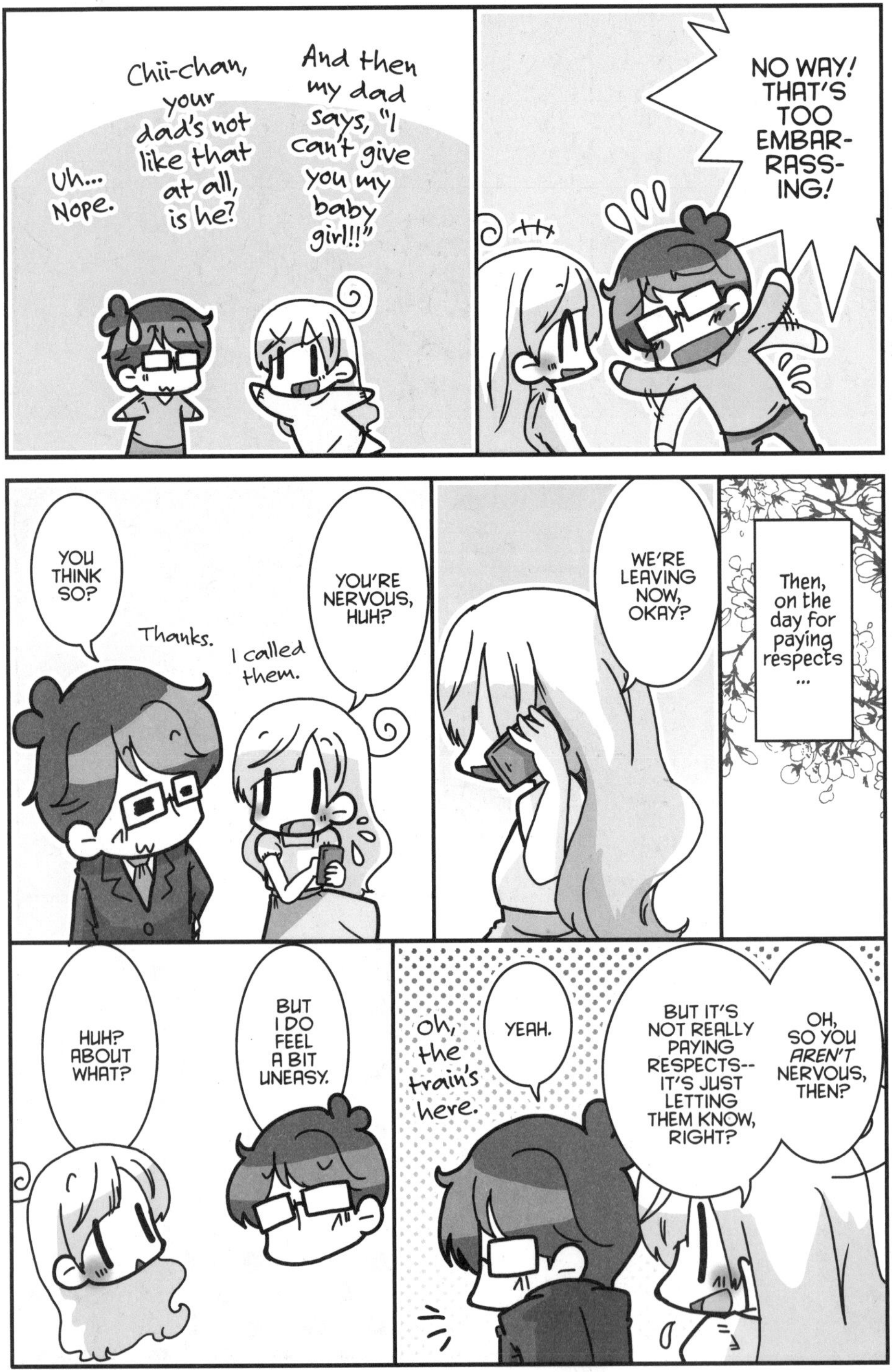

NO WAY! THAT'S TOO EMBARRASSING!
And then my dad says, "I can't give you my baby girl!!"
Chii-chan, your dad's not like that at all, is he?
Uh... Nope.
Then, on the day for paying respects...
WE'RE LEAVING NOW, OKAY?
YOU'RE NERVOUS, HUH?
I called them.
Thanks.
YOU THINK SO?
OH, SO YOU *AREN'T* NERVOUS, THEN?
BUT IT'S NOT REALLY PAYING RESPECTS-- IT'S JUST LETTING THEM KNOW, RIGHT?
YEAH.
Oh, the train's here.
BUT I DO FEEL A BIT UNEASY.
HUH? ABOUT WHAT?

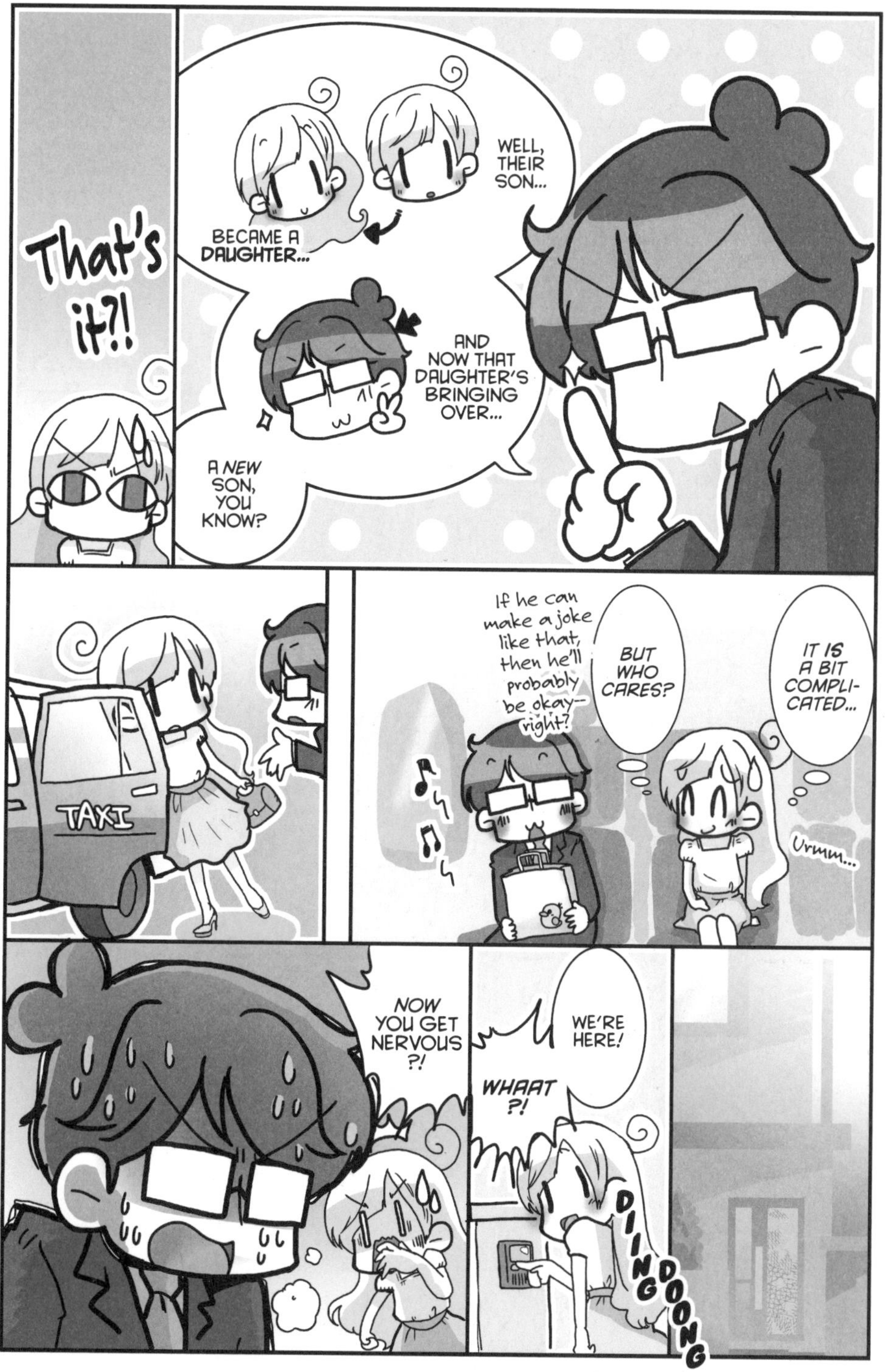
WELL, THEIR SON...
BECAME A DAUGHTER...
AND NOW THAT DAUGHTER'S BRINGING OVER...
A NEW SON, YOU KNOW?
That's it?!
IT IS A BIT COMPLICATED...
BUT WHO CARES?
If he can make a joke like that, then he'll probably be okay—right?
Urmm...
TAXI
WE'RE HERE!
WHAAT ?!
DIIING DOOONG
NOW YOU GET NERVOUS ?!

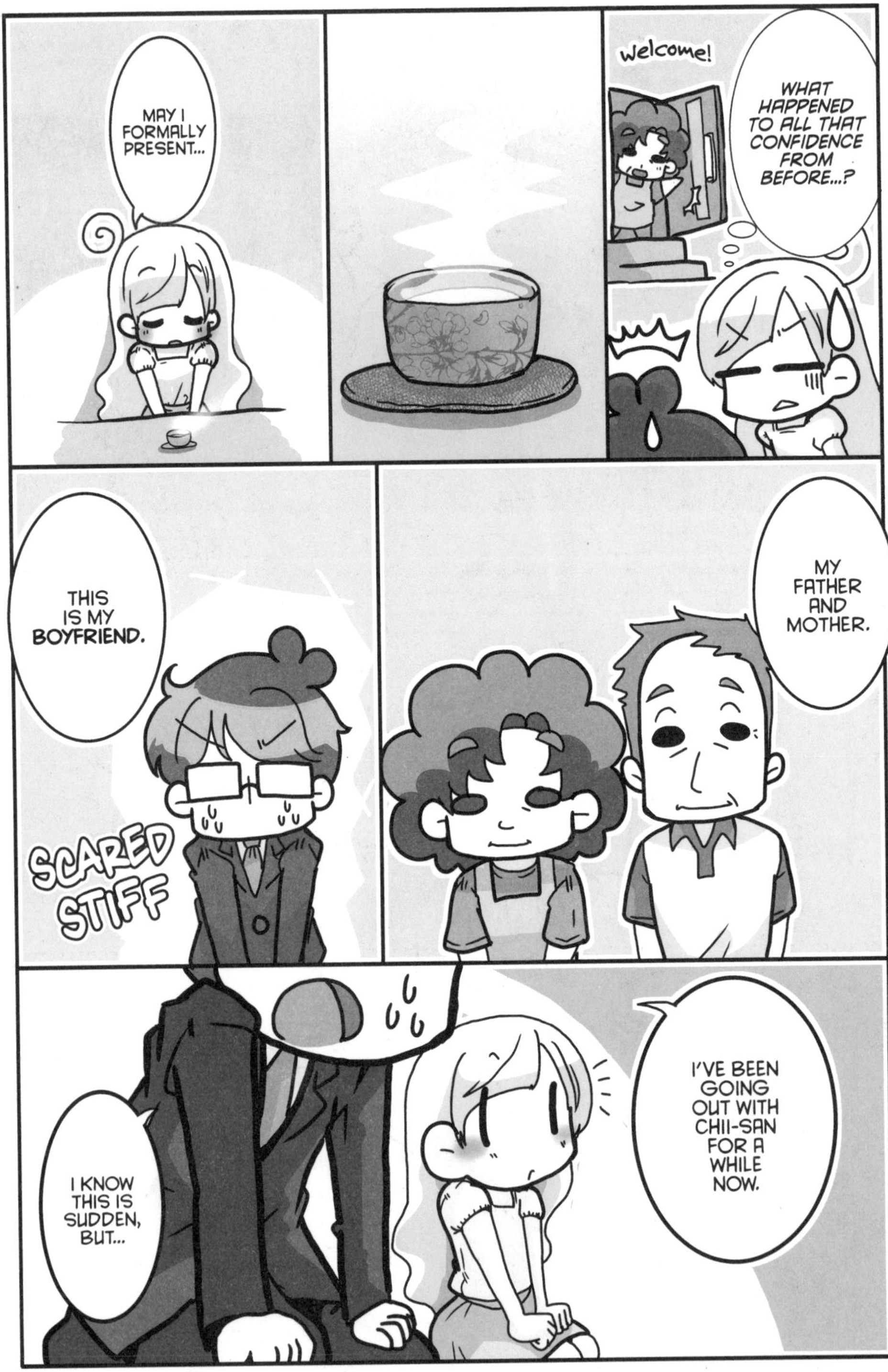
WHAT HAPPENED TO ALL THAT CONFIDENCE FROM BEFORE...?
Welcome!
MAY I FORMALLY PRESENT...
MY FATHER AND MOTHER.
THIS IS MY BOYFRIEND.
SCARED STIFF
I'VE BEEN GOING OUT WITH CHII-SAN FOR A WHILE NOW.
I KNOW THIS IS SUDDEN, BUT...

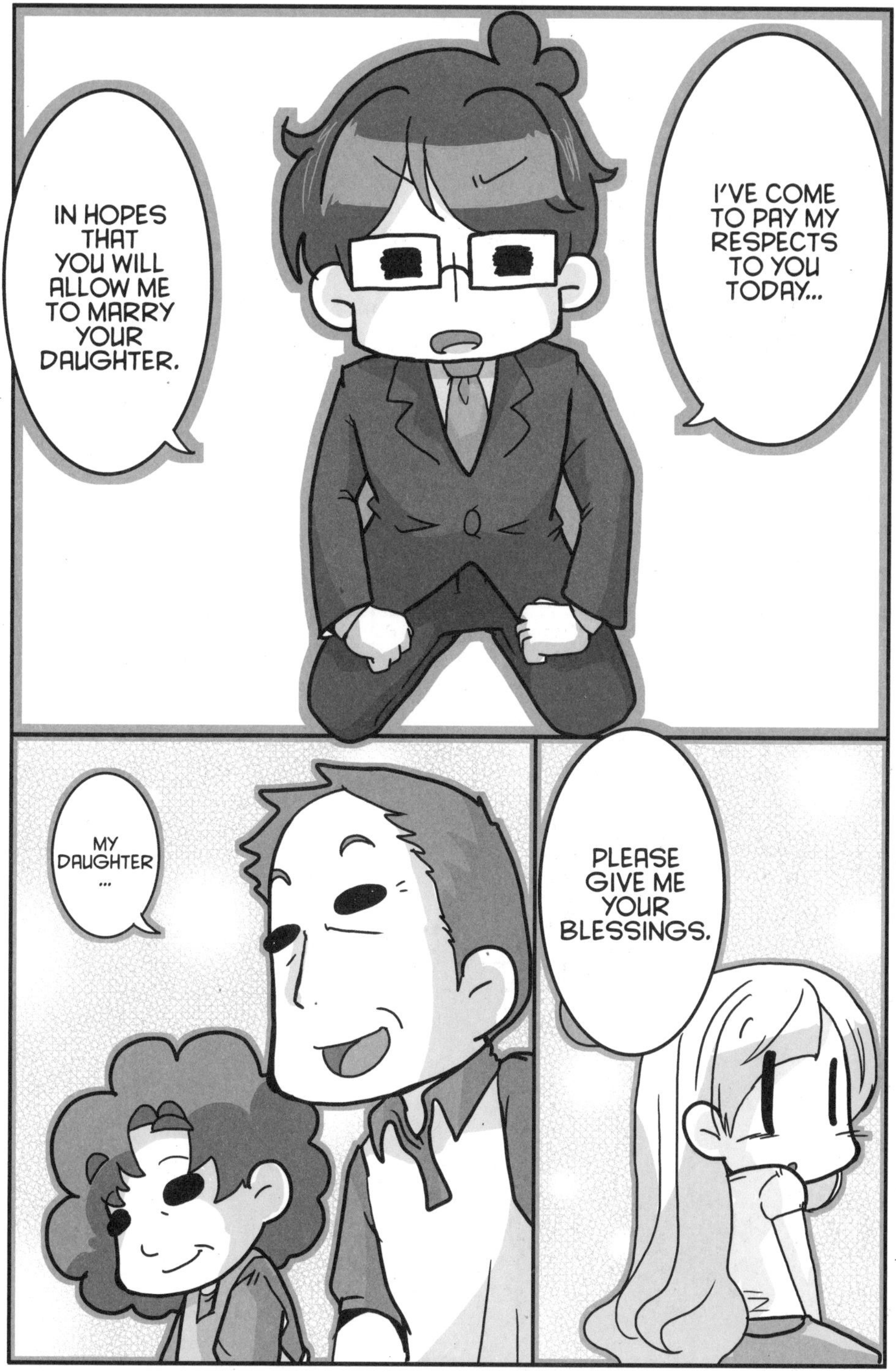
I'VE COME TO PAY MY RESPECTS TO YOU TODAY...
IN HOPES THAT YOU WILL ALLOW ME TO MARRY YOUR DAUGHTER.
PLEASE GIVE ME YOUR BLESSINGS.
MY DAUGHTER ...

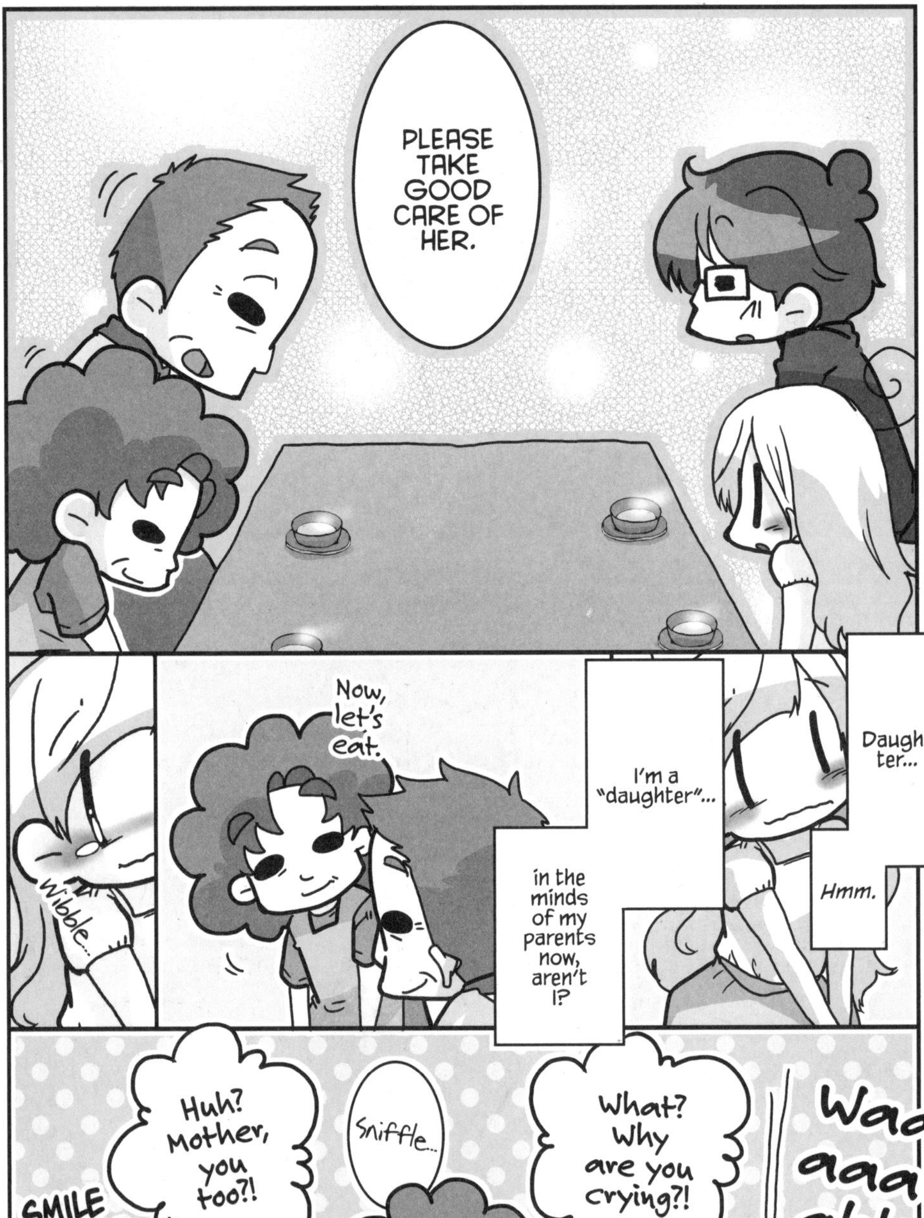
PLEASE TAKE GOOD CARE OF HER.
Daugh-ter...
Hmm.
I'm a "daughter"...
in the minds of my parents now, aren't I?
Now, let's eat.
Wibble...
Waa aaa ah!
What? Why are you crying?!
Sniffle...
Huh? Mother, you too?!
SMILE SMILE

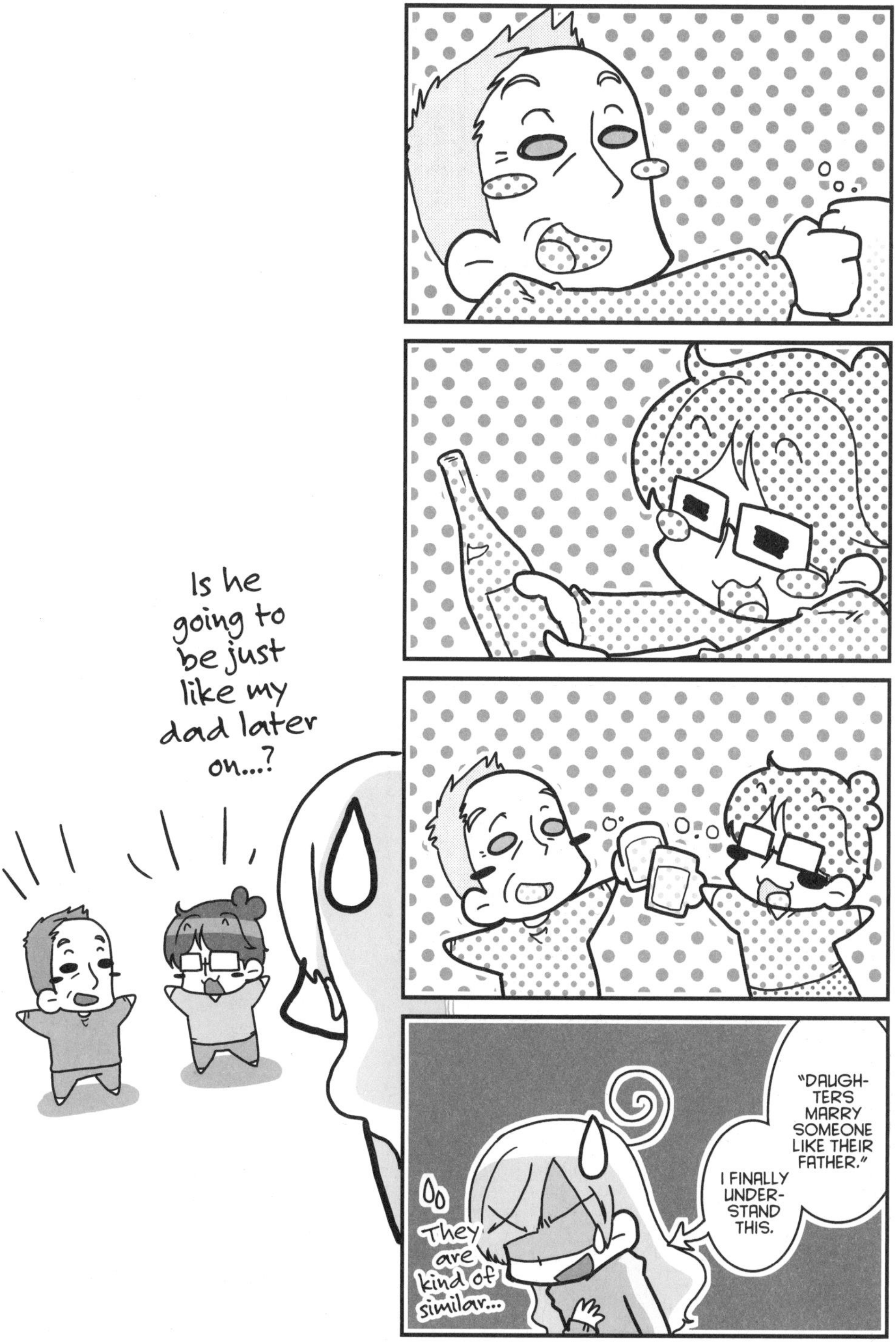
"DAUGHTERS MARRY SOMEONE LIKE THEIR FATHER."
I FINALLY UNDERSTAND THIS.
They are kind of similar...
Is he going to be just like my dad later on...?

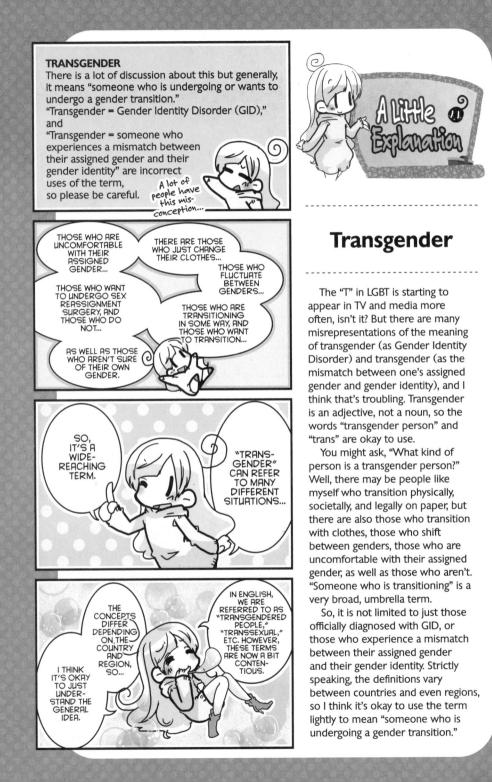

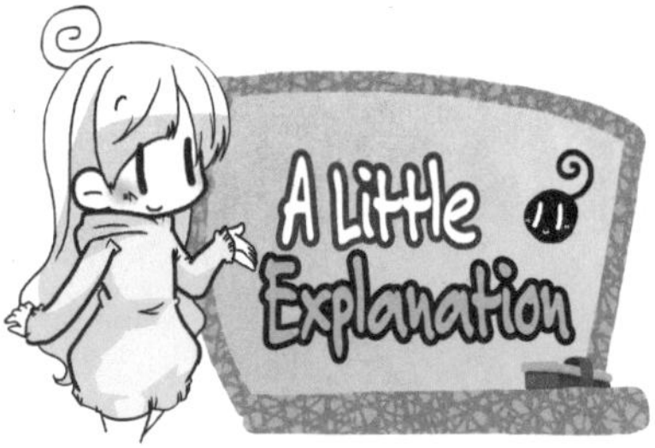
A Little Explanation

Transgender

The "T" in LGBT is starting to appear in TV and media more often, isn't it? But there are many misrepresentations of the meaning of transgender (as Gender Identity Disorder) and transgender (as the mismatch between one's assigned gender and gender identity), and I think that's troubling. Transgender is an adjective, not a noun, so the words "transgender person" and "trans" are okay to use.

You might ask, "What kind of person is a transgender person?" Well, there may be people like myself who transition physically, societally, and legally on paper, but there are also those who transition with clothes, those who shift between genders, those who are uncomfortable with their assigned gender, as well as those who aren't. "Someone who is transitioning" is a very broad, umbrella term.

So, it is not limited to just those officially diagnosed with GID, or those who experience a mismatch between their assigned gender and their gender identity. Strictly speaking, the definitions vary between countries and even regions, so I think it's okay to use the term lightly to mean "someone who is undergoing a gender transition."

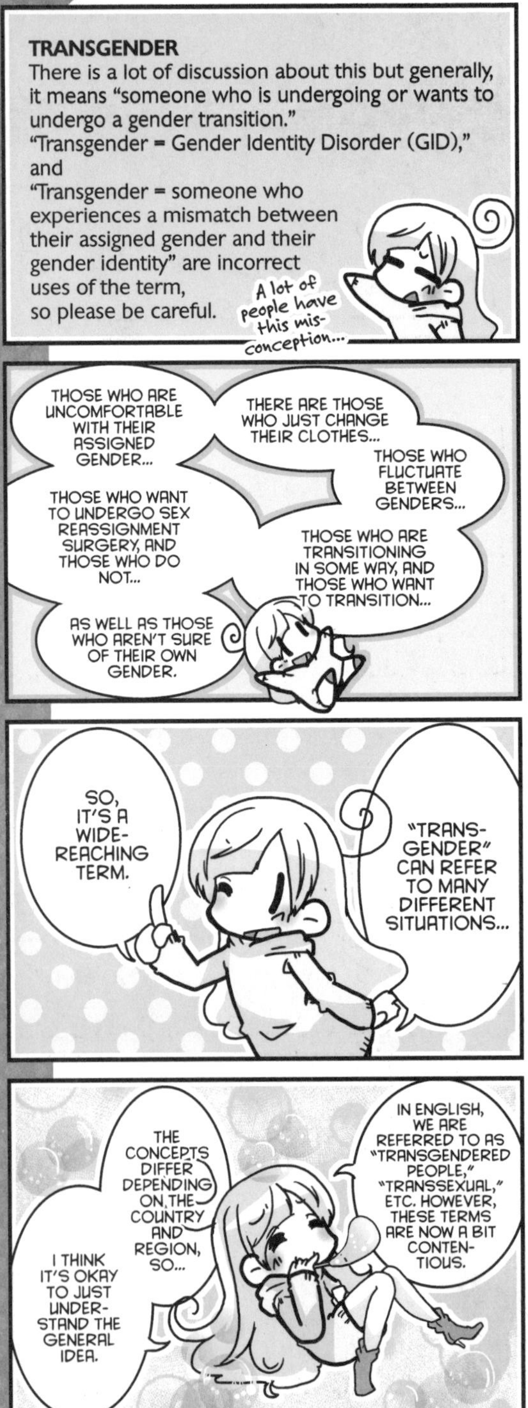
TRANSGENDER
There is a lot of discussion about this but generally, it means "someone who is undergoing or wants to undergo a gender transition."
"Transgender = Gender Identity Disorder (GID)," and
"Transgender = someone who experiences a mismatch between their assigned gender and their gender identity" are incorrect uses of the term, so please be careful.
A lot of people have this mis-conception...
THERE ARE THOSE WHO JUST CHANGE THEIR CLOTHES...
THOSE WHO ARE UNCOMFORTABLE WITH THEIR ASSIGNED GENDER...
THOSE WHO FLUCTUATE BETWEEN GENDERS...
THOSE WHO WANT TO UNDERGO SEX REASSIGNMENT SURGERY, AND THOSE WHO DO NOT...
THOSE WHO ARE TRANSITIONING IN SOME WAY, AND THOSE WHO WANT TO TRANSITION...
AS WELL AS THOSE WHO AREN'T SURE OF THEIR OWN GENDER.
"TRANS-GENDER" CAN REFER TO MANY DIFFERENT SITUATIONS...
SO, IT'S A WIDE-REACHING TERM.
IN ENGLISH, WE ARE REFERRED TO AS "TRANSGENDERED PEOPLE," "TRANSSEXUAL," ETC. HOWEVER, THESE TERMS ARE NOW A BIT CONTEN-TIOUS.
THE CONCEPTS DIFFER DEPENDING ON THE COUNTRY AND REGION, SO...
I THINK IT'S OKAY TO JUST UNDER-STAND THE GENERAL IDEA.

A Little Story about Getting Ready for the Wedding

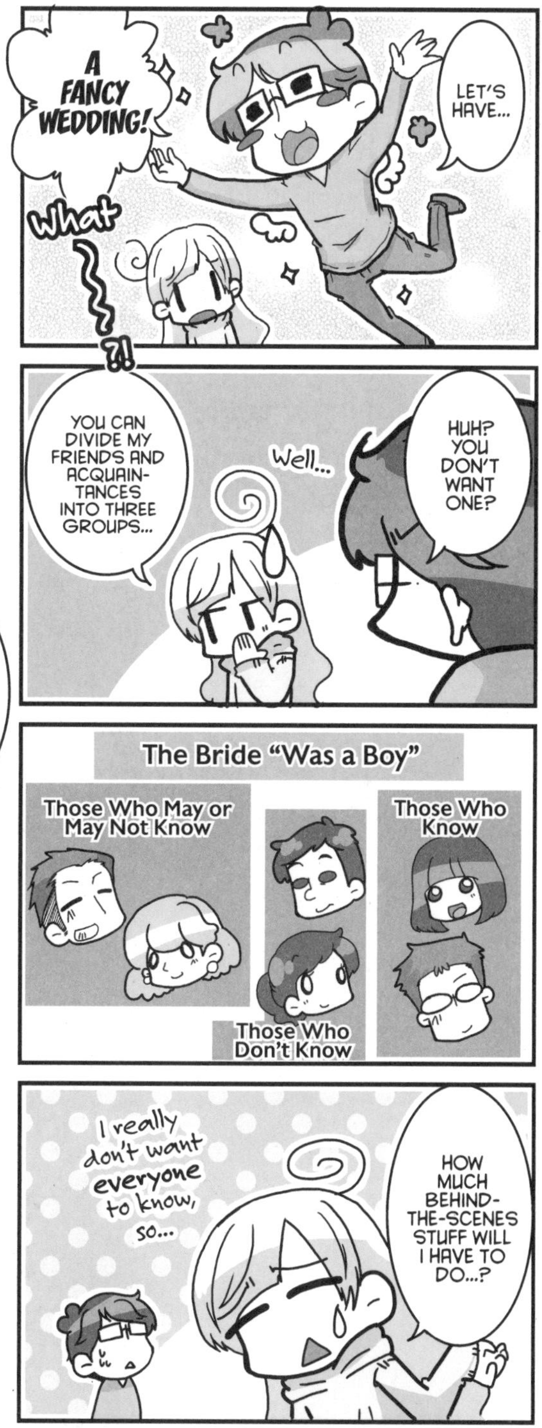
LET'S HAVE...
A FANCY WEDDING!
What ?!
HUH? YOU DON'T WANT ONE?
Well...
YOU CAN DIVIDE MY FRIENDS AND ACQUAIN-TANCES INTO THREE GROUPS...
The Bride "Was a Boy"
Those Who Know
Those Who Don't Know
Those Who May or May Not Know
HOW MUCH BEHIND-THE-SCENES STUFF WILL I HAVE TO DO...?
I really don't want everyone to know, so...

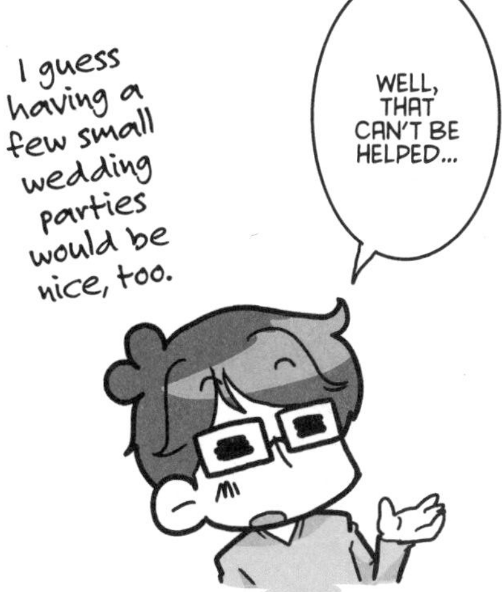
WELL, THAT CAN'T BE HELPED...
I guess having a few small wedding parties would be nice, too.

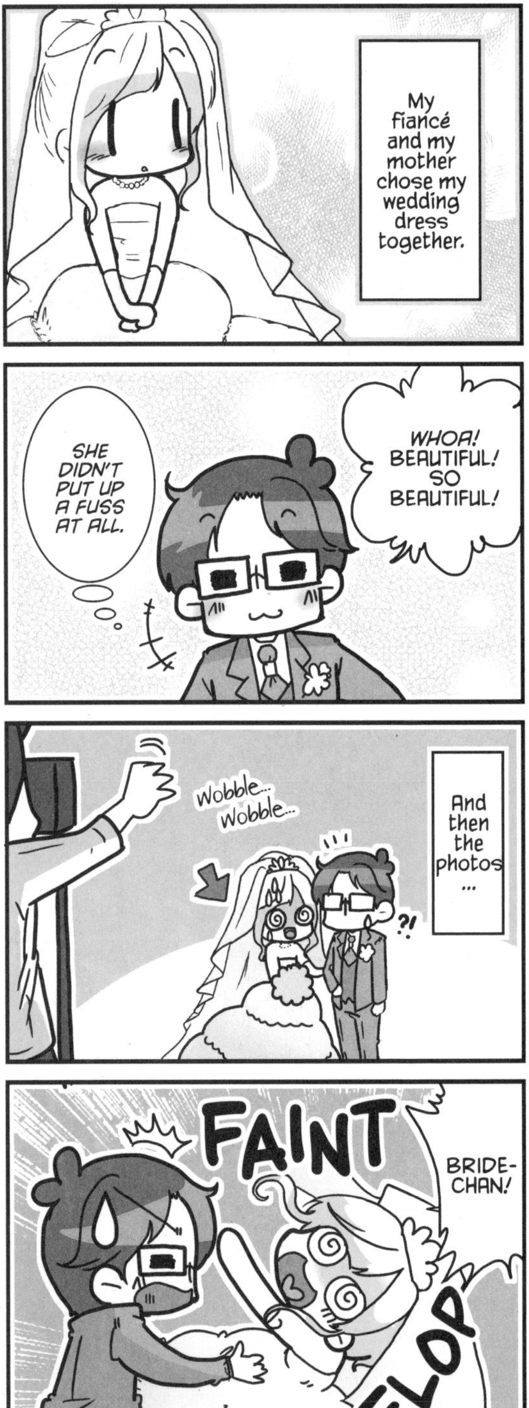
My fiancé and my mother chose my wedding dress together.
SHE DIDN'T PUT UP A FUSS AT ALL.
WHOA! BEAUTIFUL! SO BEAUTIFUL!
And then the photos...
Wobble... Wobble...
?!
FAINT
BRIDE-CHAN!
FLOP

A Little Story about Getting Ready for the Wedding

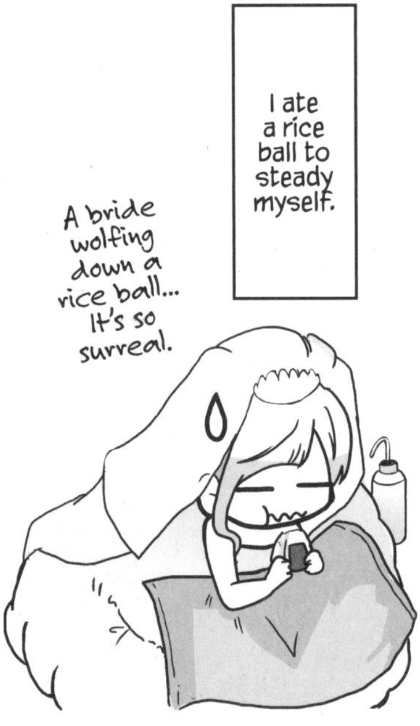
I ate a rice ball to steady myself.
A bride wolfing down a rice ball... It's so surreal.

A Little Story about Getting Ready for the Wedding

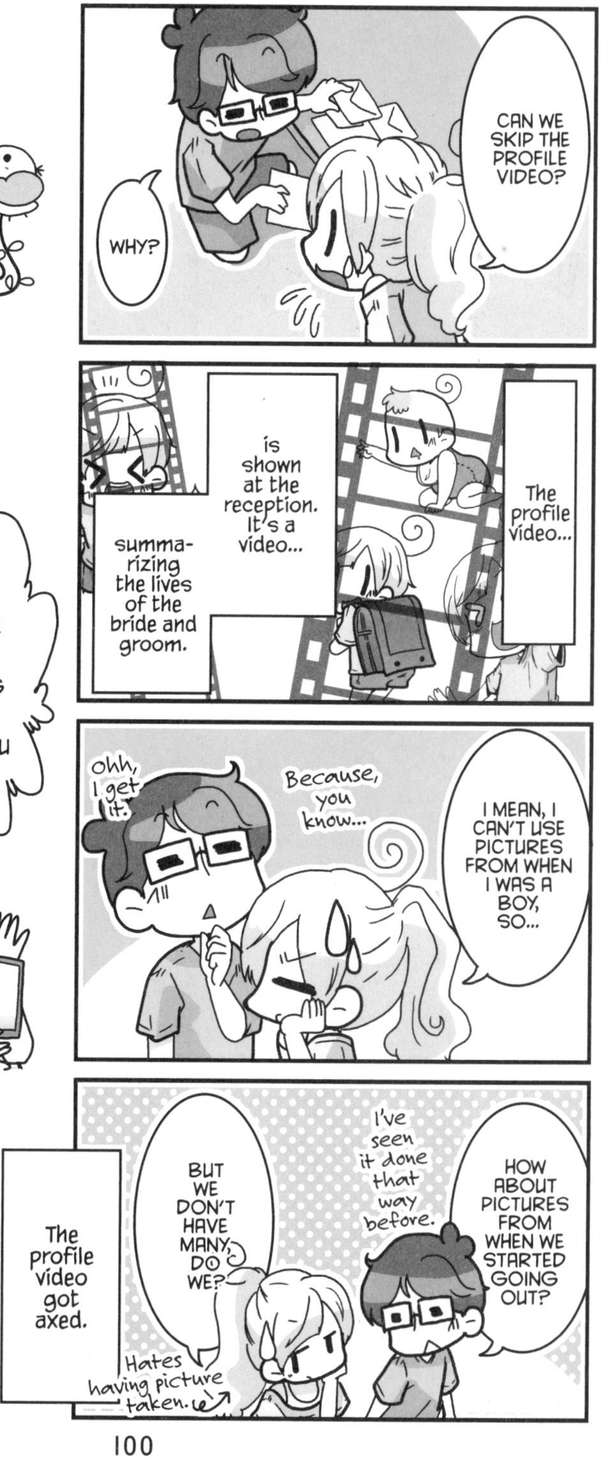
CAN WE SKIP THE PROFILE VIDEO?
WHY?
The profile video...
is shown at the reception. It's a video...
summarizing the lives of the bride and groom.
I MEAN, I CAN'T USE PICTURES FROM WHEN I WAS A BOY, SO...
Because, you know...
Ohh, I get it.
HOW ABOUT PICTURES FROM WHEN WE STARTED GOING OUT?
I've seen it done that way before.
BUT WE DON'T HAVE MANY, DO WE?
Hates having picture taken.
The profile video got axed.

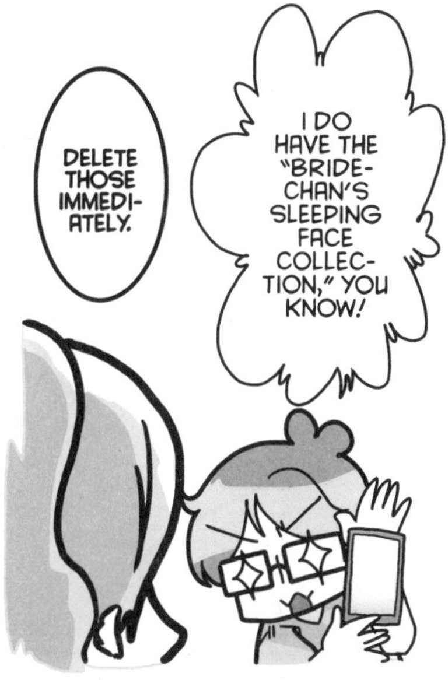
I DO HAVE THE "BRIDE-CHAN'S SLEEPING FACE COLLECTION," YOU KNOW!
DELETE THOSE IMMEDIATELY.

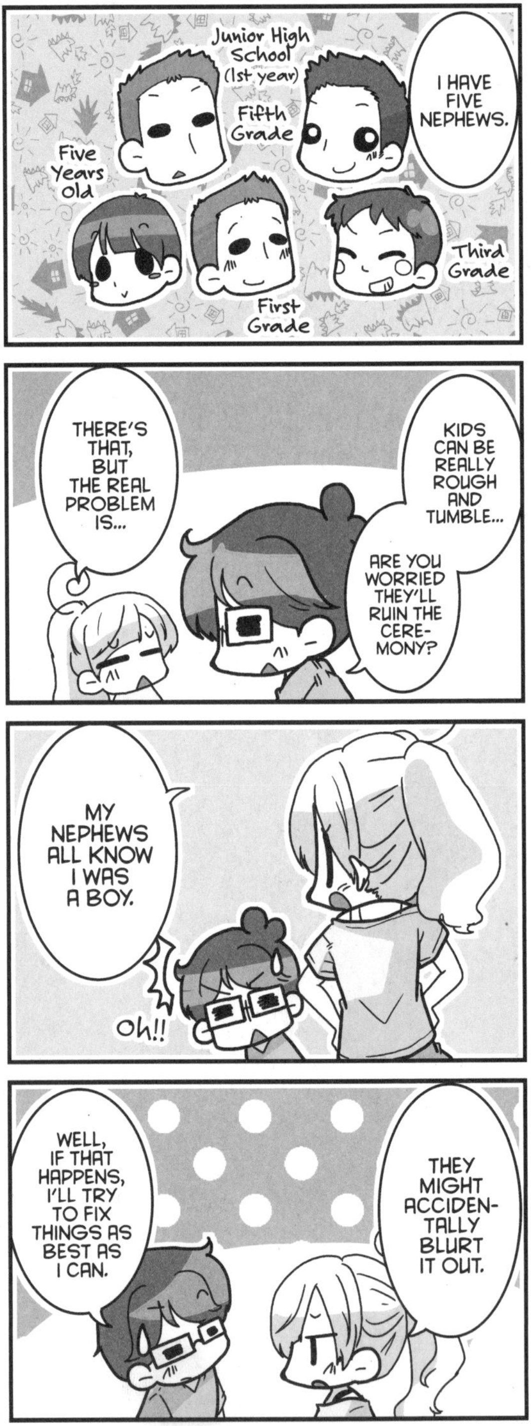
I HAVE FIVE NEPHEWS.
Junior High School (1st year)
Fifth Grade
Five Years old
Third Grade
First Grade
KIDS CAN BE REALLY ROUGH AND TUMBLE...
ARE YOU WORRIED THEY'LL RUIN THE CEREMONY?
THERE'S THAT, BUT THE REAL PROBLEM IS...
MY NEPHEWS ALL KNOW I WAS A BOY.
Oh!!
THEY MIGHT ACCIDENTALLY BLURT IT OUT.
WELL, IF THAT HAPPENS, I'LL TRY TO FIX THINGS AS BEST AS I CAN.

A Little Story about Getting Ready for the Wedding

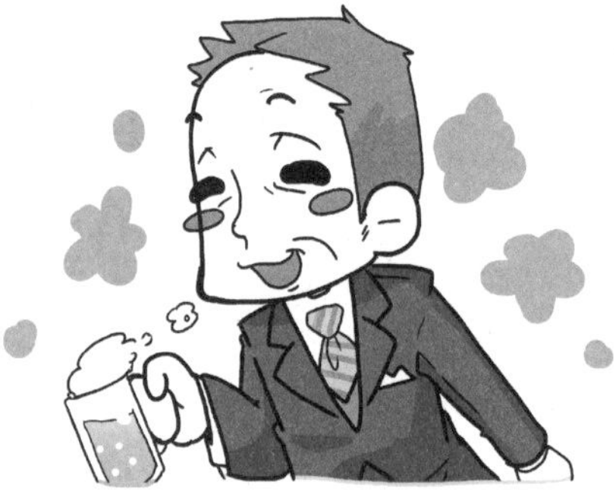

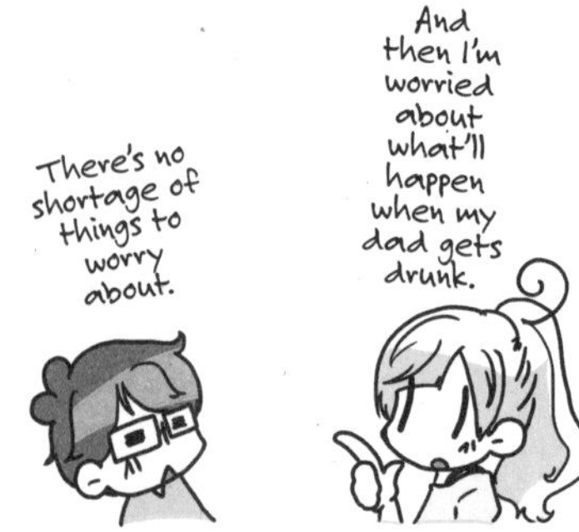
And then I'm worried about what'll happen when my dad gets drunk.
There's no shortage of things to worry about.

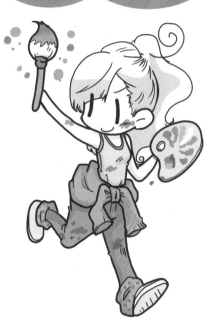

"Gay people and transgender people have a great sense of style, right?"

I myself draw, but have no sense of style whatsoever.
I don't think having a sense of style is limited to gay people and transgender people--or any group, for that matter. I think that there are just some people with amazing ideas--which leads people to say that they "have a great sense of style"-- and that those kinds of people are quite visible.
I wish they'd share some of their sense of style with me...

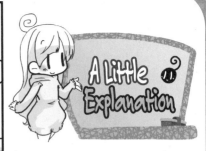

A Little Explanation

Sexual Minorities

In Japanese, we are referred to as "Seiteki Shousuusha (group)" and "Seiteiki Minorities." This is often abbreviated to "Seku Mai." This means that in our society, we are minorities in terms of sexuality. The media often uses terms like LGBT synonymously with that, and the expression "LGBT (sexual minorities)" is often seen. Strictly speaking, this is not a correct use of the term.

With regard to LGBT referring to sexualities and genders, the term "sexual minorities" also includes sexual preferences and is an even broader umbrella term. This term is not widely used because of negative connotations associated with the word "minorities" (meaning a small group within a larger societal group) and its overly broad meaning. I don't use it synonymously with LGBTs, either.

SEXUAL MINORITIES
This term refers to a small group of people who are at a disadvantage in society because of their sexuality and/or gender, or because their human rights are being denied.
Again, in Japan, this group is often referred to as "Seiteki Shousuusha," "Seiteki Shosuuha," and "Seiteki Minorities" and can also be abbreviated as "Seku Mai."
IT'S OFTEN USED AS A SYNONYM FOR LGBT, BUT...
Strictly speaking, the expression "Sexual Minorities (LGBT)" isn't correct.
THE TRUTH IS THAT IT DOESN'T MEAN JUST LGBT IN TERMS OF SEXUAL ORIENTATION OR GENDER IDENTITY...
It includes a whole bunch of stuff!
IT ALSO INCLUDES "SEXUAL PREFER-ENCES," SUCH AS BDSM.
minority??
SOME PEOPLE LIKE TO USE IT SINCE IT COVERS SUCH A BROAD SPECTRUM OF PEOPLE...
IN CONTRAST TO LGBT, WHICH HAS A SPECIFIC AND LIMITED MEANING.
ON THE OTHER HAND, SOME PEOPLE ARE UNCOMFORT-ABLE WITH BEING CATEGORIZED AS A "MINORITY."
THE WORD DOES HAVE NEGATIVE AND EXCLUSIONARY CONNO-TATIONS...
I don't use it very much, myself.
AND SO, IT DOESN'T REALLY SEE A LOT OF WORLDWIDE USE.

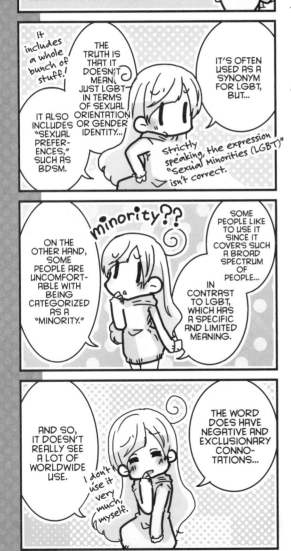

"It's the same thing as being gay, right?"

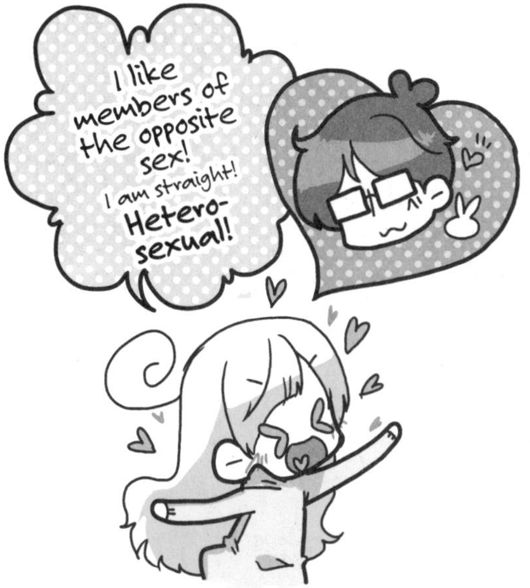
I like members of the opposite sex!
I am straight!
Hetero-sexual!

They are totally different. Gay is gay, those with GID have GID, transgender people are transgender people, and I am me.

Sometimes I try to simplify it by saying, "Gay is about the other person's gender and GID is about a person's own gender," but if you get into the details of sexual orientation, or of someone who identifies with a gender that is not the one they were assigned at birth, then the explanation would get really, really long. So at this point, I'd be happy if you could just think of them as being completely different.

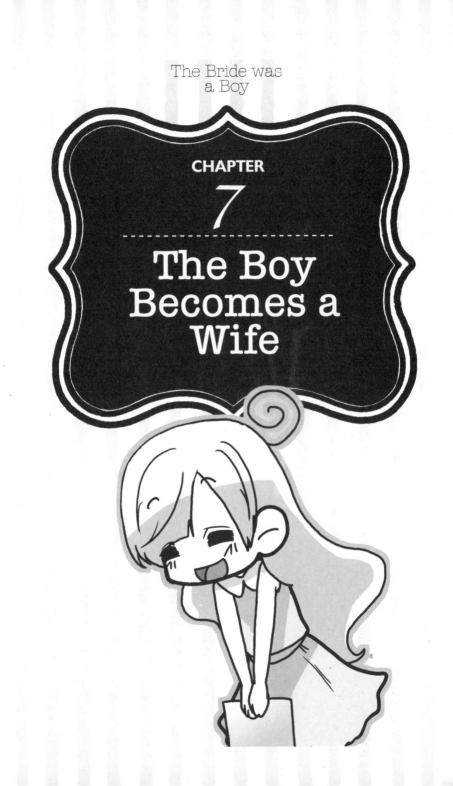

The Bride was
a Boy

CHAPTER

7

The Boy
Becomes a
Wife

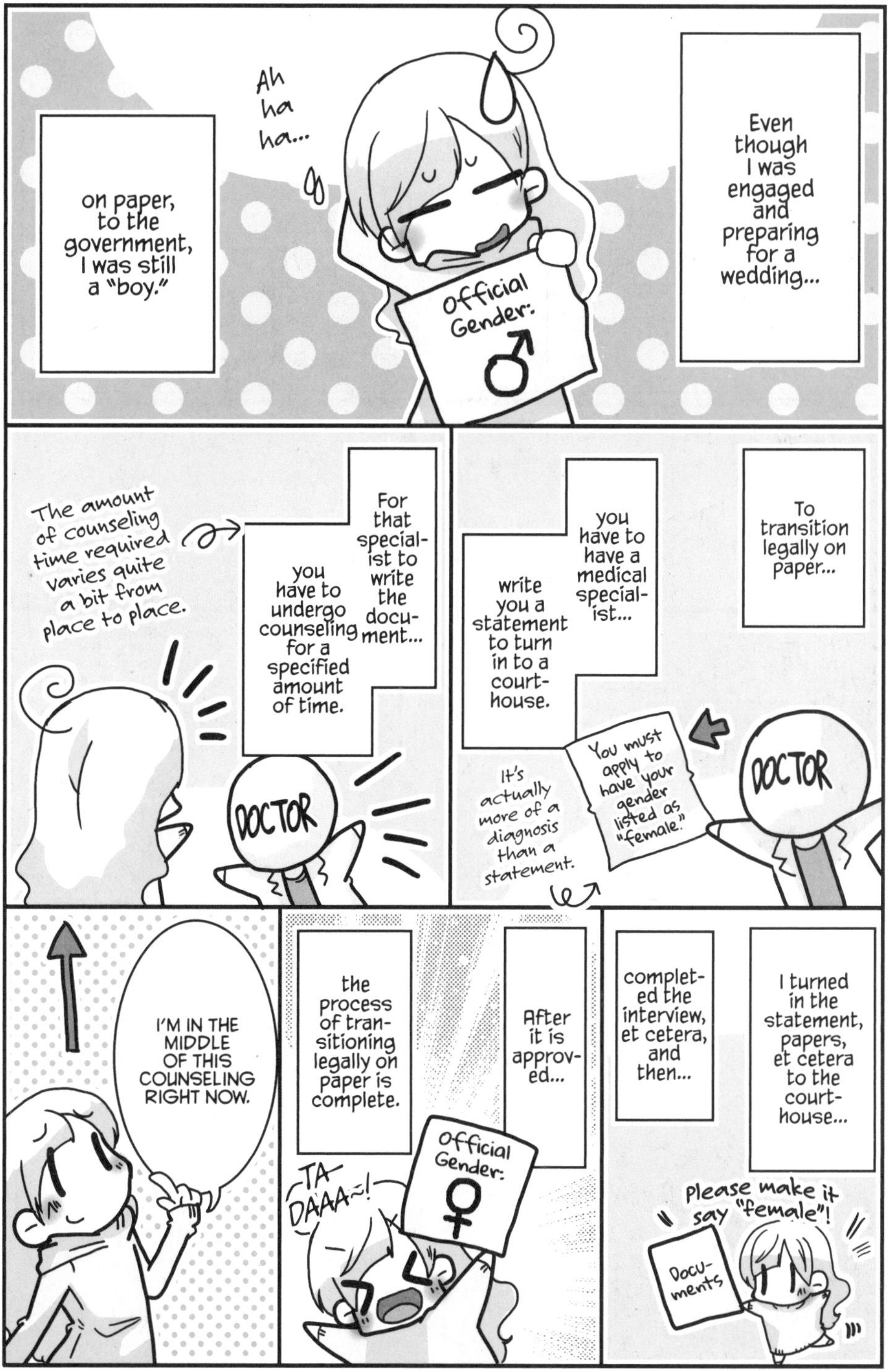
Even though I was engaged and preparing for a wedding...
Ah ha ha...
on paper, to the government, I was still a "boy."
Official Gender: ♂
To transition legally on paper...
you have to have a medical specialist...
write you a statement to turn in to a courthouse.
You must apply to have your gender listed as "female."
DOCTOR
It's actually more of a diagnosis than a statement.
For that specialist to write the document...
you have to undergo counseling for a specified amount of time.
The amount of counseling time required varies quite a bit from place to place.
DOCTOR
I turned in the statement, papers, et cetera to the courthouse...
completed the interview, et cetera, and then...
Please make it say "female"!
Documents
After it is approved...
the process of transitioning legally on paper is complete.
Official Gender: ♀
TA DAAA~!
I'M IN THE MIDDLE OF THIS COUNSELING RIGHT NOW.

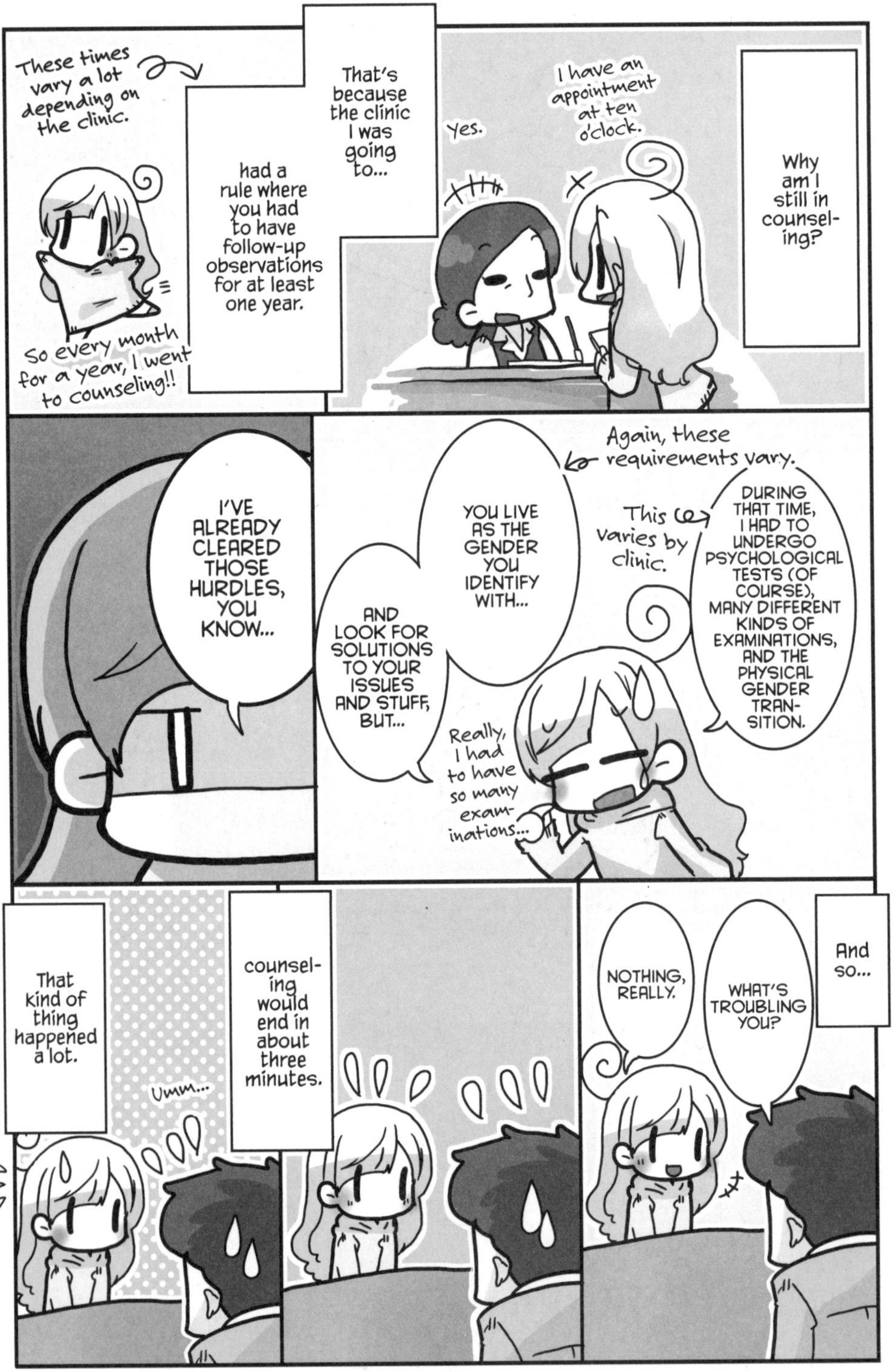

Why am I still in counsel-ing?
I have an appointment at ten o'clock.
Yes.
That's because the clinic I was going to...
had a rule where you had to have follow-up observations for at least one year.
These times vary a lot depending on the clinic.
So every month for a year, I went to counseling!!
Again, these requirements vary.
DURING THAT TIME, I HAD TO UNDERGO PSYCHOLOGICAL TESTS (OF COURSE), MANY DIFFERENT KINDS OF EXAMINATIONS, AND THE PHYSICAL GENDER TRAN-SITION.
This varies by clinic.
YOU LIVE AS THE GENDER YOU IDENTIFY WITH...
AND LOOK FOR SOLUTIONS TO YOUR ISSUES AND STUFF, BUT...
Really, I had to have so many exam-inations...
I'VE ALREADY CLEARED THOSE HURDLES, YOU KNOW...
And so...
WHAT'S TROUBLING YOU?
NOTHING, REALLY.
counsel-ing would end in about three minutes.
That kind of thing happened a lot.
Umm...

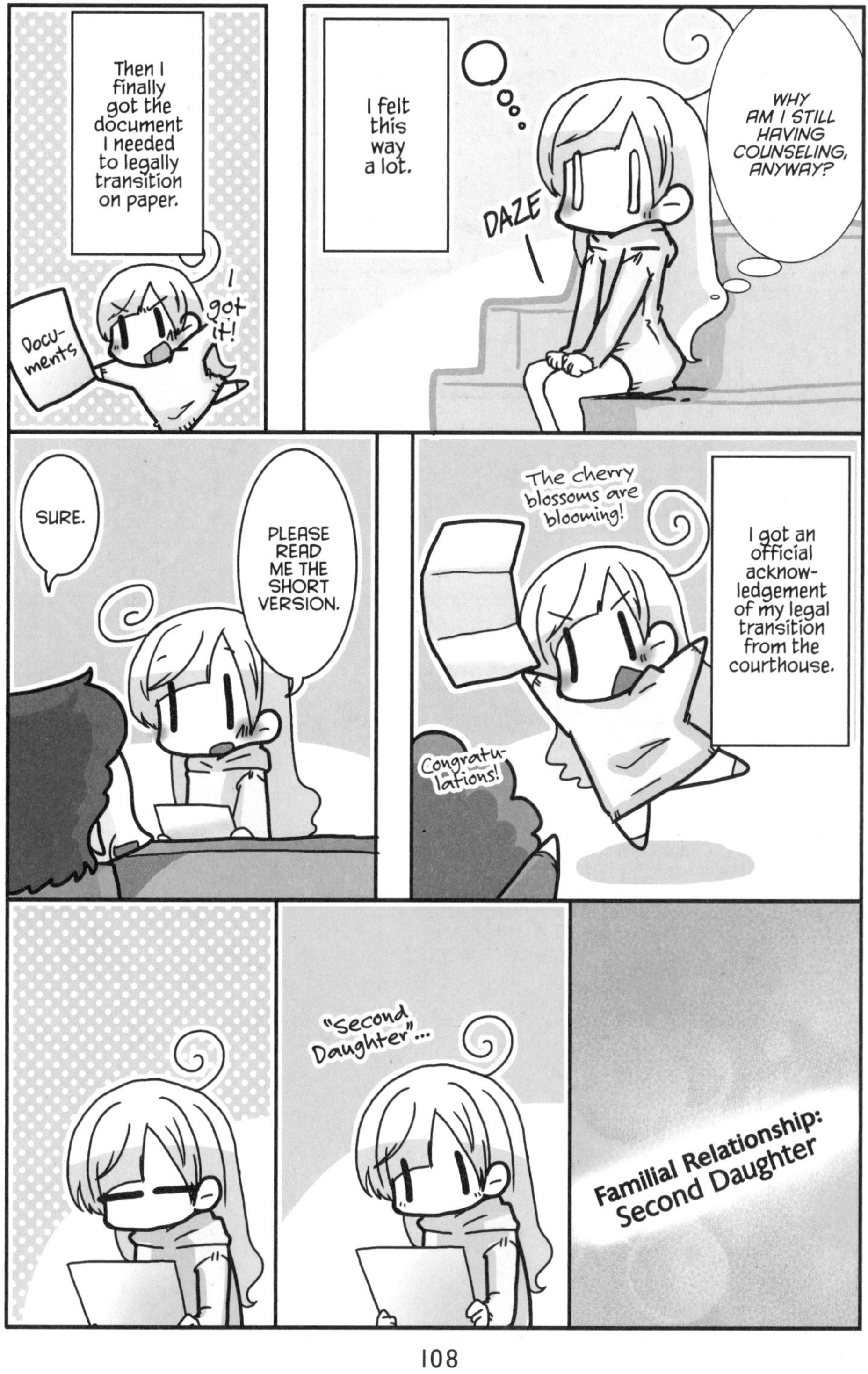
I felt this way a lot.
WHY AM I STILL HAVING COUNSELING, ANYWAY?
DAZE
Then I finally got the document I needed to legally transition on paper.
I got it!
Documents
I got an official acknowledgement of my legal transition from the courthouse.
The cherry blossoms are blooming!
Congratulations!
PLEASE READ ME THE SHORT VERSION.
SURE.
Familial Relationship: Second Daughter
"Second Daughter"...

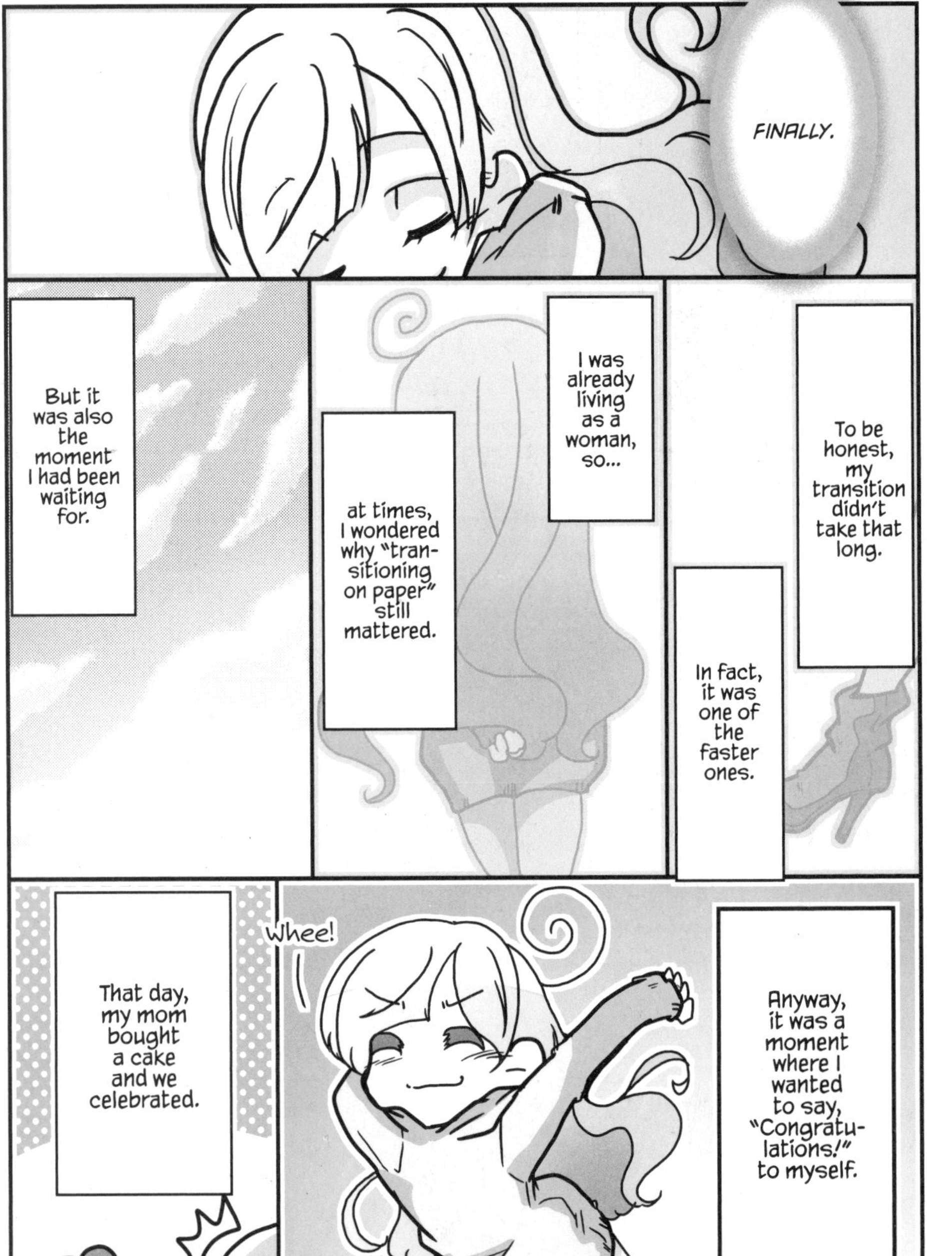
FINALLY.
To be honest, my transition didn't take that long.
In fact, it was one of the faster ones.
I was already living as a woman, so...
at times, I wondered why "transitioning on paper" still mattered.
But it was also the moment I had been waiting for.
Anyway, it was a moment where I wanted to say, "Congratulations!" to myself.
Whee!
That day, my mom bought a cake and we celebrated.

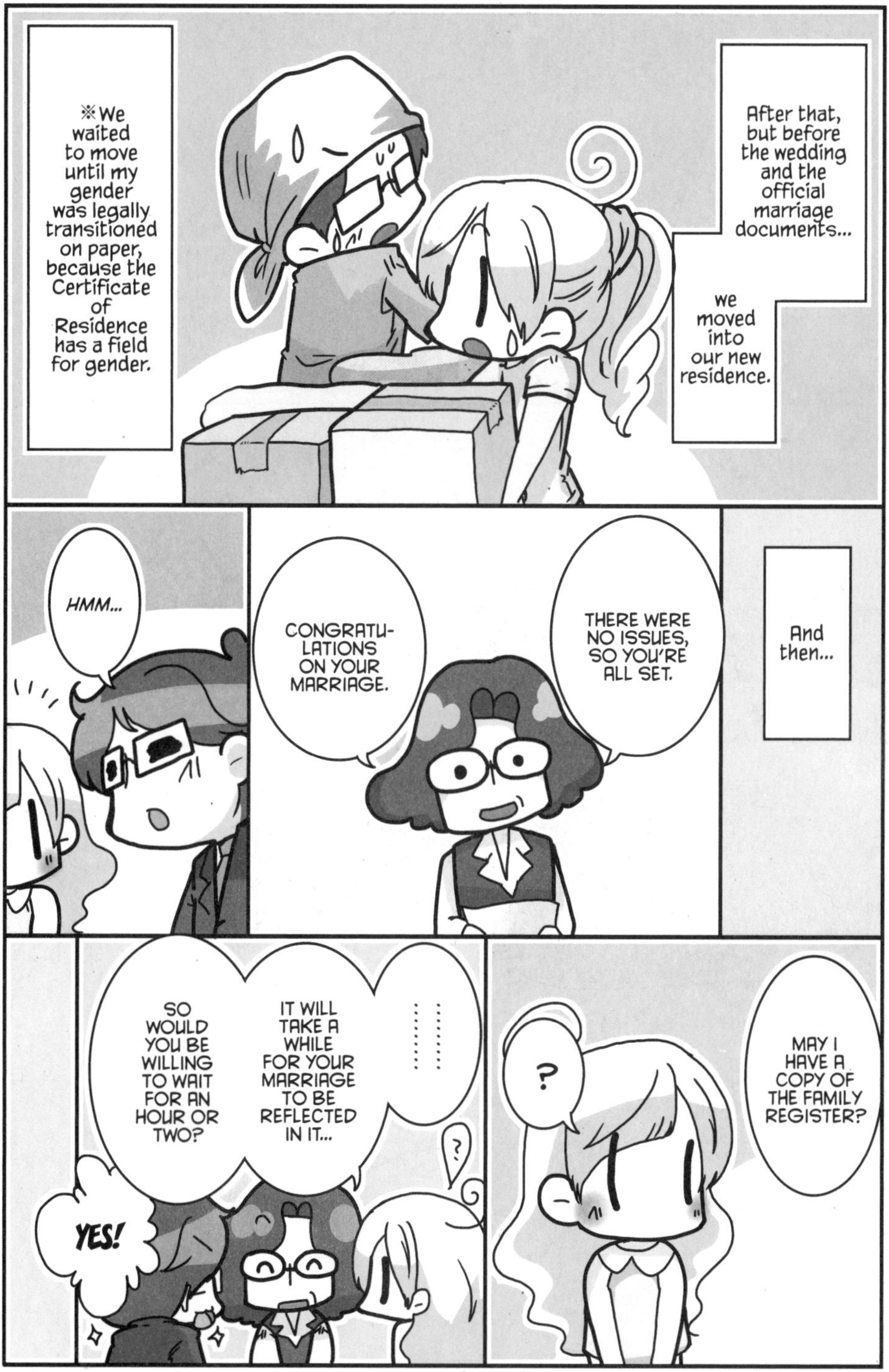
After that, but before the wedding and the official marriage documents...
we moved into our new residence.
※We waited to move until my gender was legally transitioned on paper, because the Certificate of Residence has a field for gender.
And then...
THERE WERE NO ISSUES, SO YOU'RE ALL SET.
CONGRATULATIONS ON YOUR MARRIAGE.
HMM...
MAY I HAVE A COPY OF THE FAMILY REGISTER?
?
......
IT WILL TAKE A WHILE FOR YOUR MARRIAGE TO BE REFLECTED IN IT...
SO WOULD YOU BE WILLING TO WAIT FOR AN HOUR OR TWO?
?
YES!

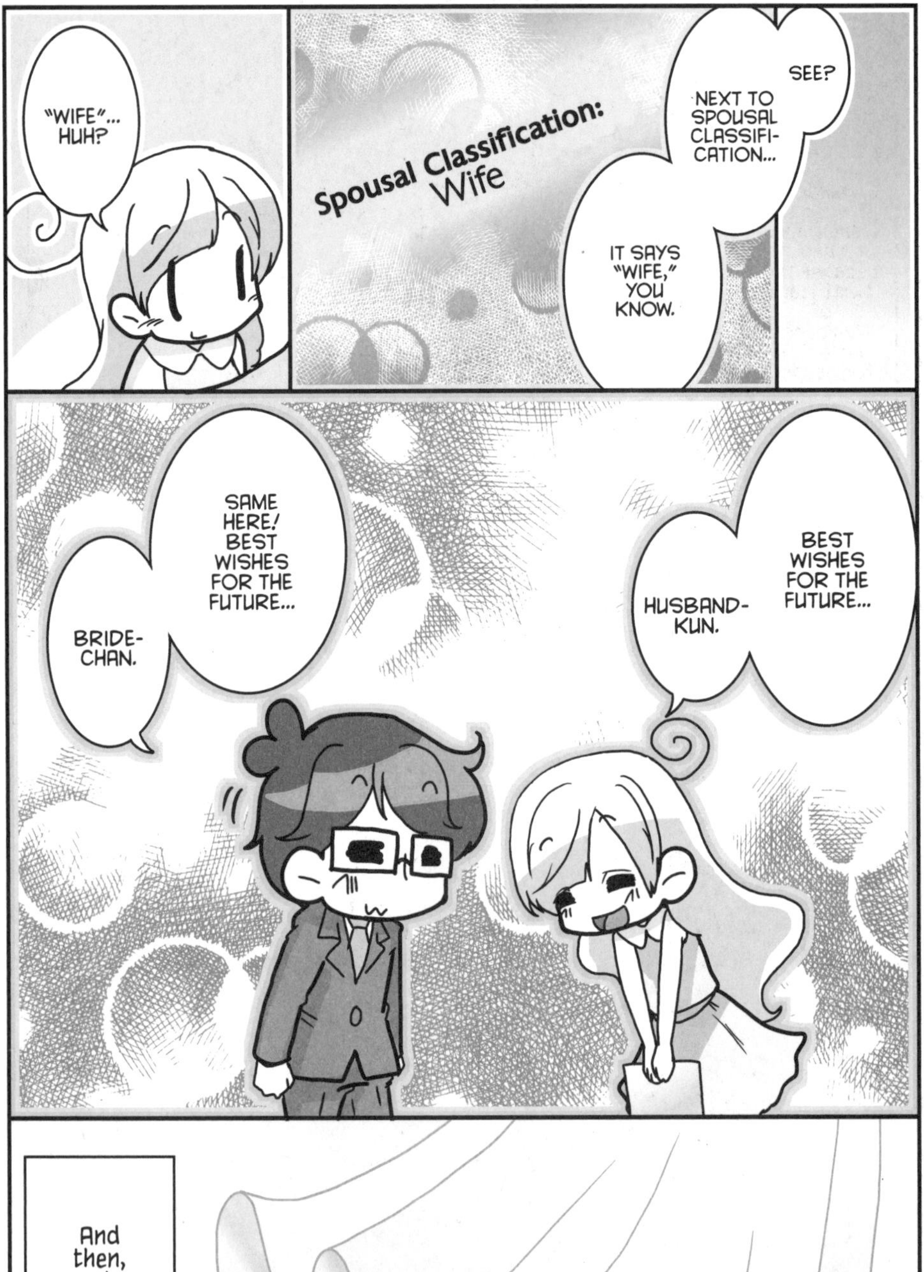
SEE?
NEXT TO SPOUSAL CLASSIFICATION...
Spousal Classification: Wife
IT SAYS "WIFE," YOU KNOW.
"WIFE"... HUH?
BEST WISHES FOR THE FUTURE...
HUSBAND-KUN.
SAME HERE! BEST WISHES FOR THE FUTURE...
BRIDE-CHAN.
And then, on to the wedding.

A Little Explanation: Longer Version
A Story About How to Legally Transition on Paper!!

I'm going to explain the Japanese law concerning how to legally transition on paper, which I briefly touched upon in the main story, in a shockingly simple way.

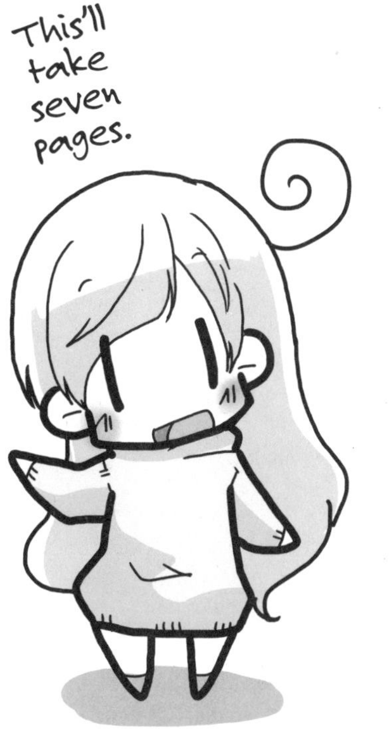
This'll take seven pages.

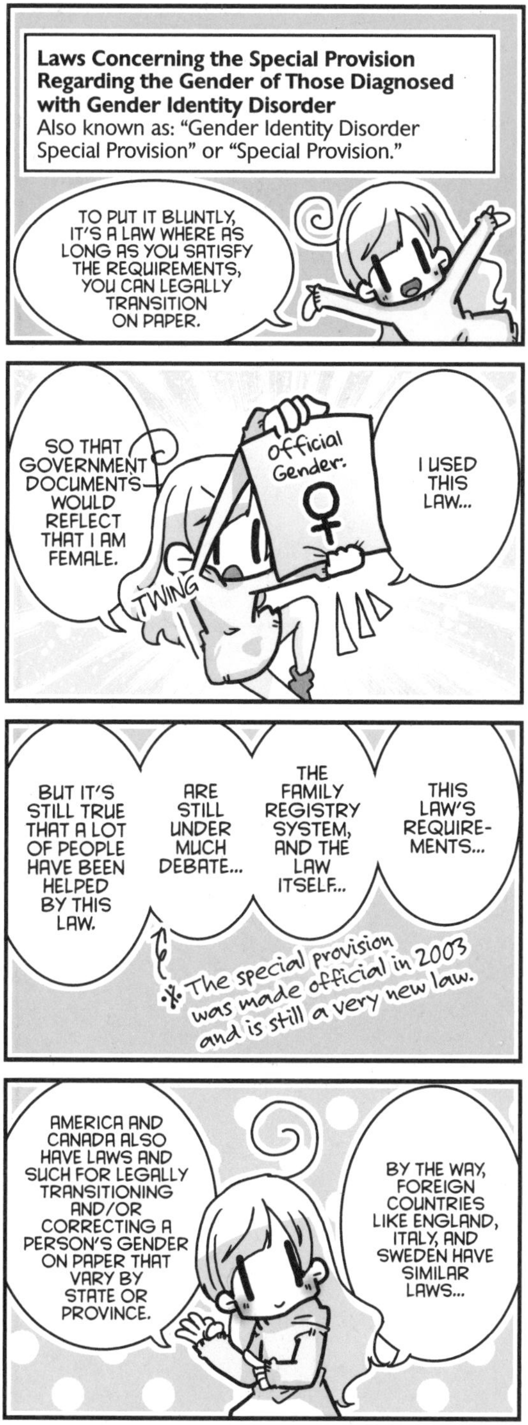
Laws Concerning the Special Provision Regarding the Gender of Those Diagnosed with Gender Identity Disorder
Also known as: "Gender Identity Disorder Special Provision" or "Special Provision."
TO PUT IT BLUNTLY, IT'S A LAW WHERE AS LONG AS YOU SATISFY THE REQUIREMENTS, YOU CAN LEGALLY TRANSITION ON PAPER.
I USED THIS LAW...
Official Gender: ♀
SO THAT GOVERNMENT DOCUMENTS WOULD REFLECT THAT I AM FEMALE.
TWING
THIS LAW'S REQUIRE-MENTS...
THE FAMILY REGISTRY SYSTEM, AND THE LAW ITSELF...
ARE STILL UNDER MUCH DEBATE...
BUT IT'S STILL TRUE THAT A LOT OF PEOPLE HAVE BEEN HELPED BY THIS LAW.
※ The special provision was made official in 2003 and is still a very new law.
BY THE WAY, FOREIGN COUNTRIES LIKE ENGLAND, ITALY, AND SWEDEN HAVE SIMILAR LAWS...
AMERICA AND CANADA ALSO HAVE LAWS AND SUCH FOR LEGALLY TRANSITIONING AND/OR CORRECTING A PERSON'S GENDER ON PAPER THAT VARY BY STATE OR PROVINCE.

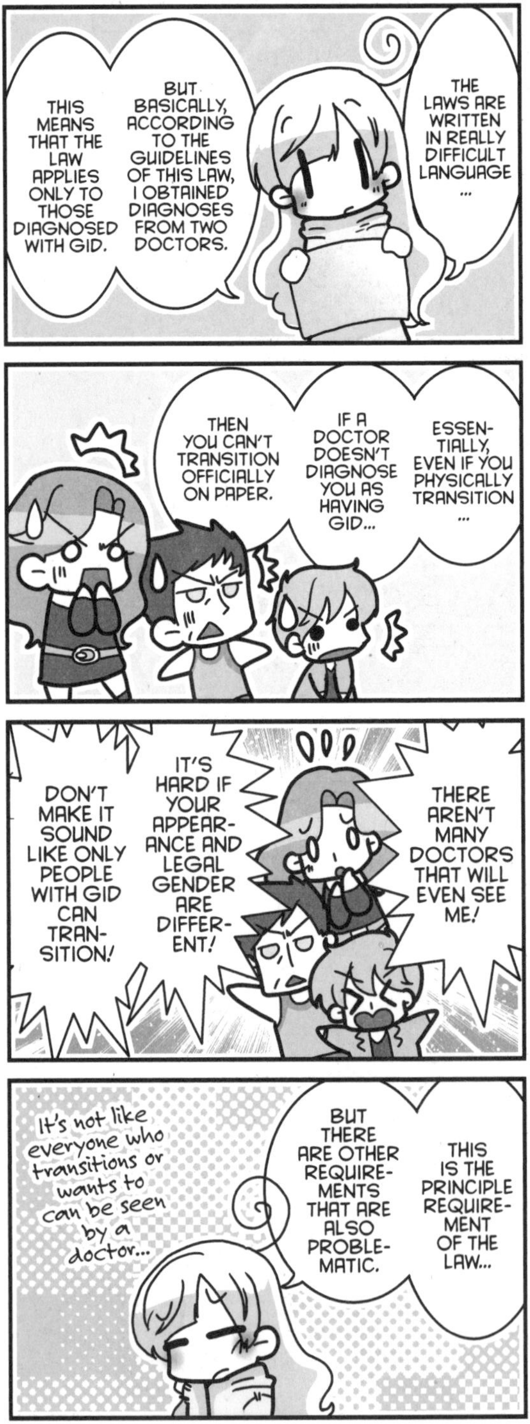
THE LAWS ARE WRITTEN IN REALLY DIFFICULT LANGUAGE...
BUT BASICALLY, ACCORDING TO THE GUIDELINES OF THIS LAW, I OBTAINED DIAGNOSES FROM TWO DOCTORS.
THIS MEANS THAT THE LAW APPLIES ONLY TO THOSE DIAGNOSED WITH GID.
ESSEN-TIALLY, EVEN IF YOU PHYSICALLY TRANSITION...
IF A DOCTOR DOESN'T DIAGNOSE YOU AS HAVING GID...
THEN YOU CAN'T TRANSITION OFFICIALLY ON PAPER.
THERE AREN'T MANY DOCTORS THAT WILL EVEN SEE ME!
IT'S HARD IF YOUR APPEAR-ANCE AND LEGAL GENDER ARE DIFFER-ENT!
DON'T MAKE IT SOUND LIKE ONLY PEOPLE WITH GID CAN TRAN-SITION!
THIS IS THE PRINCIPLE REQUIRE-MENT OF THE LAW...
BUT THERE ARE OTHER REQUIRE-MENTS THAT ARE ALSO PROBLE-MATIC.
It's not like everyone who transitions or wants to can be seen by a doctor...

REQUIREMENT:
"You must have GID."

And so, transgender people and those who are transitioning...

are not always considered to have GID.

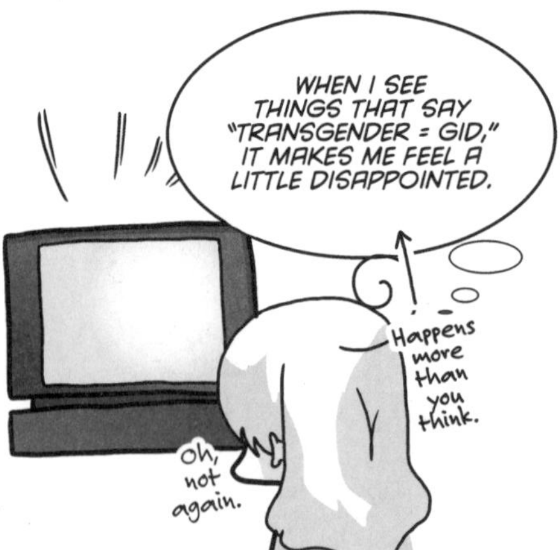
WHEN I SEE THINGS THAT SAY "TRANSGENDER = GID," IT MAKES ME FEEL A LITTLE DISAPPOINTED.
Happens more than you think.
Oh, not again.

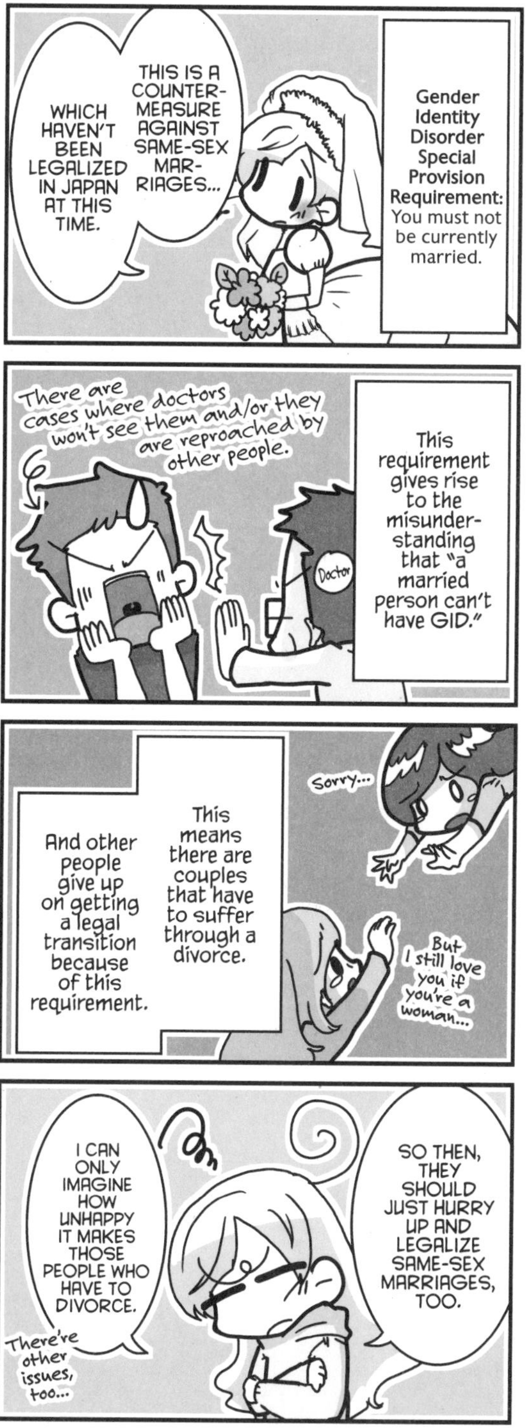
Gender Identity Disorder Special Provision Requirement: You must not be currently married.
THIS IS A COUNTERMEASURE AGAINST SAME-SEX MARRIAGES...
WHICH HAVEN'T BEEN LEGALIZED IN JAPAN AT THIS TIME.
This requirement gives rise to the misunderstanding that "a married person can't have GID."
There are cases where doctors won't see them and/or they are reproached by other people.
Doctor
Sorry...
This means there are couples that have to suffer through a divorce.
But I still love you if you're a woman...
And other people give up on getting a legal transition because of this requirement.
SO THEN, THEY SHOULD JUST HURRY UP AND LEGALIZE SAME-SEX MARRIAGES, TOO.
I CAN ONLY IMAGINE HOW UNHAPPY IT MAKES THOSE PEOPLE WHO HAVE TO DIVORCE.
There're other issues, too...

REQUIREMENT:
"You must not be currently married."

And then there's the fact that some people with GID are against legalizing same-sex marriage. This makes me feel bad.

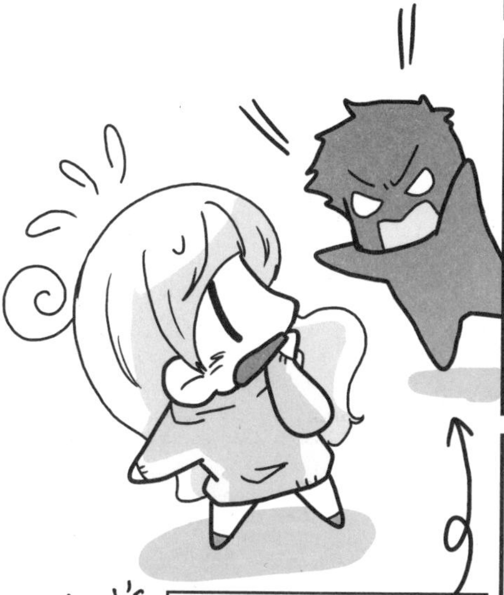

That's not true!!

I was pretty shocked the first time someone told me, "People with gender identity disorder oppose same-sex marriages with that special provision."

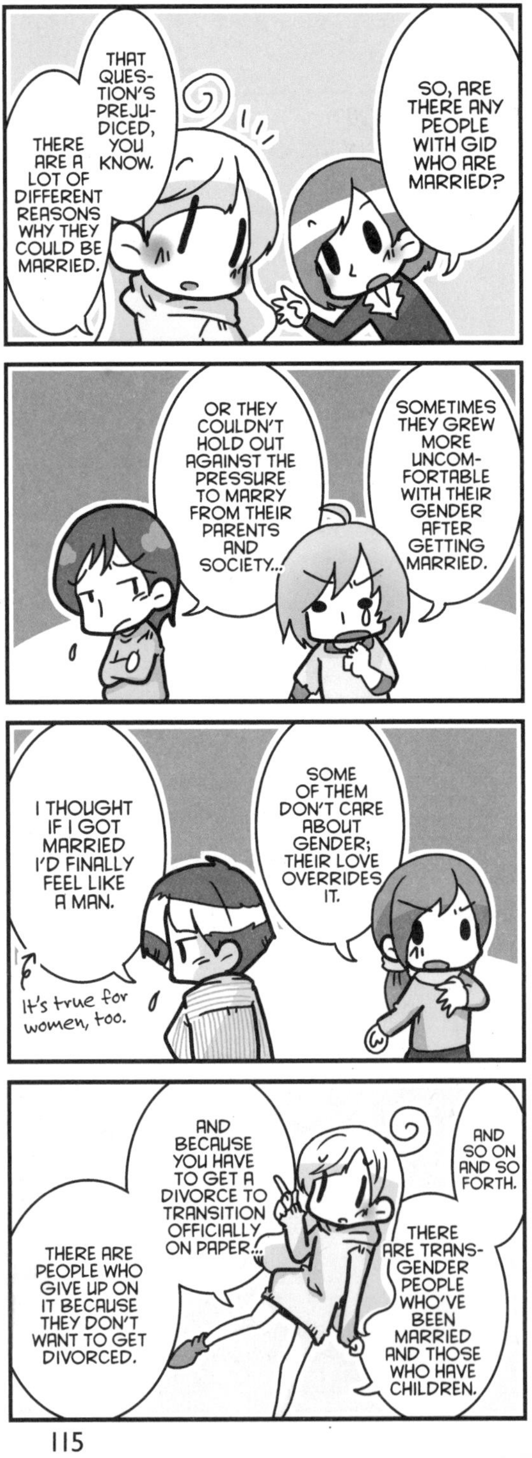
SO, ARE THERE ANY PEOPLE WITH GID WHO ARE MARRIED?
THAT QUES-TION'S PREJU-DICED, YOU KNOW.
THERE ARE A LOT OF DIFFERENT REASONS WHY THEY COULD BE MARRIED.
SOMETIMES THEY GREW MORE UNCOM-FORTABLE WITH THEIR GENDER AFTER GETTING MARRIED.
OR THEY COULDN'T HOLD OUT AGAINST THE PRESSURE TO MARRY FROM THEIR PARENTS AND SOCIETY...
SOME OF THEM DON'T CARE ABOUT GENDER; THEIR LOVE OVERRIDES IT.
I THOUGHT IF I GOT MARRIED I'D FINALLY FEEL LIKE A MAN.
It's true for women, too.
THERE ARE TRANS-GENDER PEOPLE WHO'VE BEEN MARRIED AND THOSE WHO HAVE CHILDREN.
AND BECAUSE YOU HAVE TO GET A DIVORCE TO TRANSITION OFFICIALLY ON PAPER...
THERE ARE PEOPLE WHO GIVE UP ON IT BECAUSE THEY DON'T WANT TO GET DIVORCED.
AND SO ON AND SO FORTH.

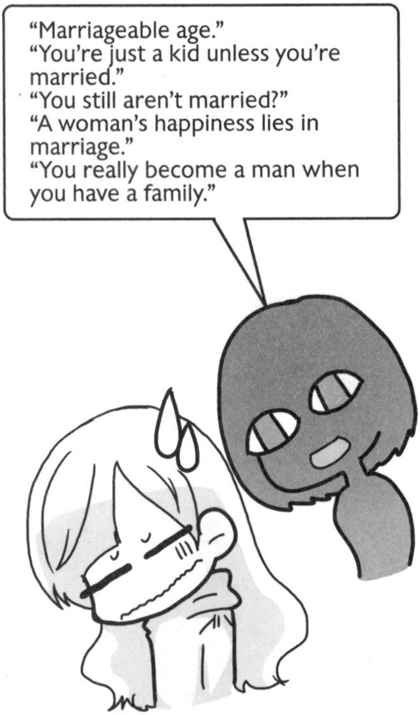
"Marriageable age."
"You're just a kid unless you're married."
"You still aren't married?"
"A woman's happiness lies in marriage."
"You really become a man when you have a family."

Et cetera, et cetera.
Pushing these views of marriage puts pressure on **everyone.**

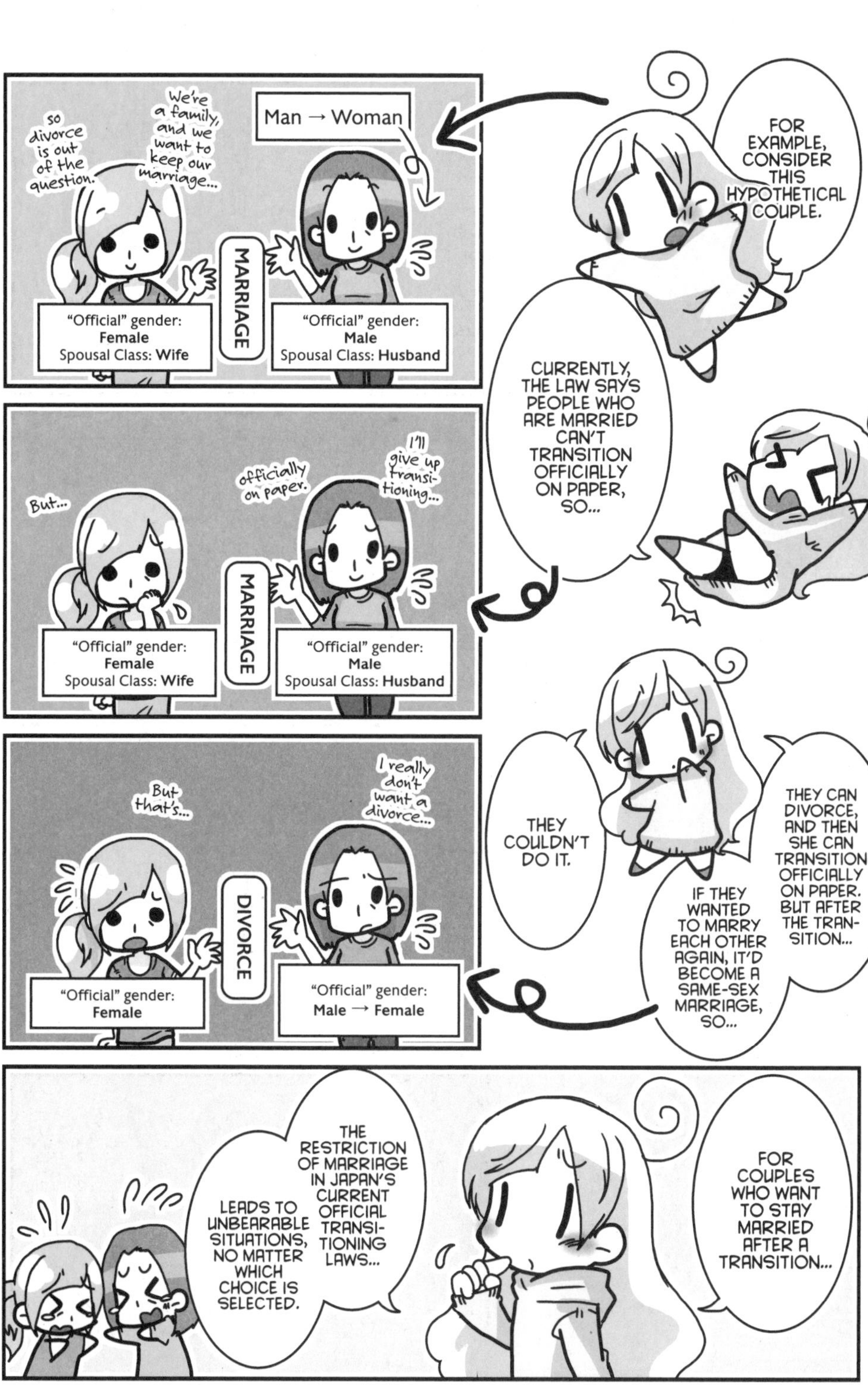
FOR EXAMPLE, CONSIDER THIS HYPOTHETICAL COUPLE.
Man → Woman
We're a family, and we want to keep our marriage...
so divorce is out of the question.
MARRIAGE
"Official" gender: Male Spousal Class: Husband
"Official" gender: Female Spousal Class: Wife
CURRENTLY, THE LAW SAYS PEOPLE WHO ARE MARRIED CAN'T TRANSITION OFFICIALLY ON PAPER, SO...
I'll give up transitioning...
officially on paper.
But...
MARRIAGE
"Official" gender: Male Spousal Class: Husband
"Official" gender: Female Spousal Class: Wife
THEY CAN DIVORCE, AND THEN SHE CAN TRANSITION OFFICIALLY ON PAPER. BUT AFTER THE TRANSITION...
IF THEY WANTED TO MARRY EACH OTHER AGAIN, IT'D BECOME A SAME-SEX MARRIAGE, SO...
THEY COULDN'T DO IT.
I really don't want a divorce...
But that's...
DIVORCE
"Official" gender: Male → Female
"Official" gender: Female
FOR COUPLES WHO WANT TO STAY MARRIED AFTER A TRANSITION...
THE RESTRICTION OF MARRIAGE IN JAPAN'S CURRENT OFFICIAL TRANSITIONING LAWS...
LEADS TO UNBEARABLE SITUATIONS, NO MATTER WHICH CHOICE IS SELECTED.

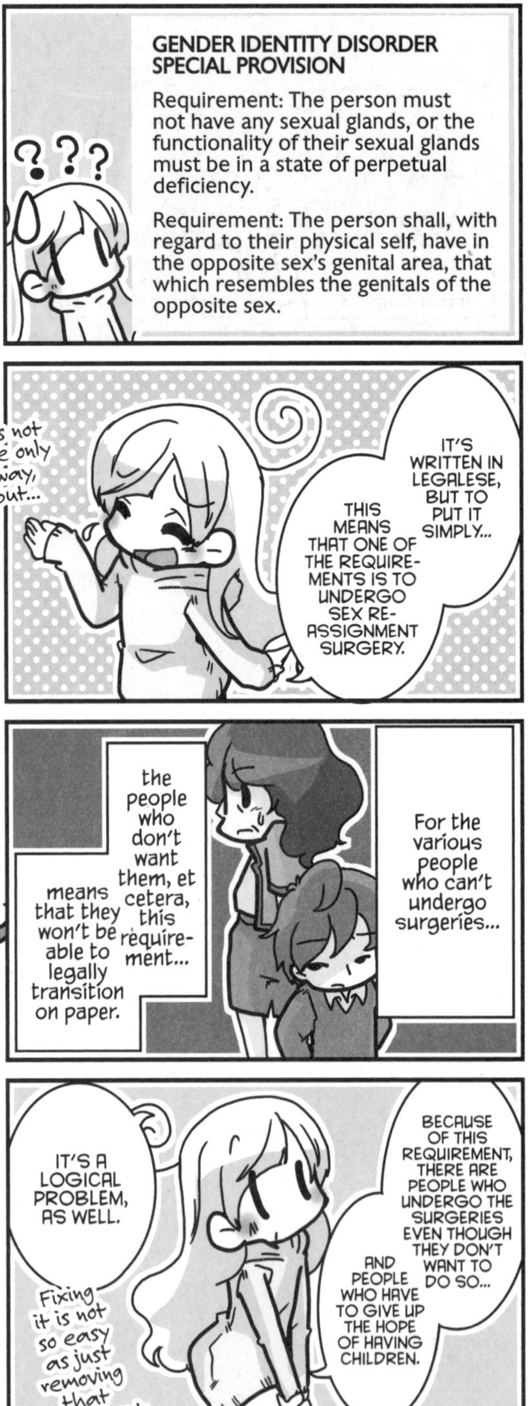
GENDER IDENTITY DISORDER SPECIAL PROVISION
Requirement: The person must not have any sexual glands, or the functionality of their sexual glands must be in a state of perpetual deficiency.
Requirement: The person shall, with regard to their physical self, have in the opposite sex's genital area, that which resembles the genitals of the opposite sex.
???
IT'S WRITTEN IN LEGALESE, BUT TO PUT IT SIMPLY...
THIS MEANS THAT ONE OF THE REQUIRE-MENTS IS TO UNDERGO SEX RE-ASSIGNMENT SURGERY.
It's not the only way, but...
For the various people who can't undergo surgeries...
the people who don't want them, et cetera, this require-ment...
means that they won't be able to legally transition on paper.
BECAUSE OF THIS REQUIREMENT, THERE ARE PEOPLE WHO UNDERGO THE SURGERIES EVEN THOUGH THEY DON'T WANT TO DO SO...
AND PEOPLE WHO HAVE TO GIVE UP THE HOPE OF HAVING CHILDREN.
IT'S A LOGICAL PROBLEM, AS WELL.
Fixing it is not so easy as just removing that requirement.

REQUIREMENT:
"Sex Reassignment Surgery"

I also get upset at the assumption people have where "transitioning" equals "sex reassignment surgery."

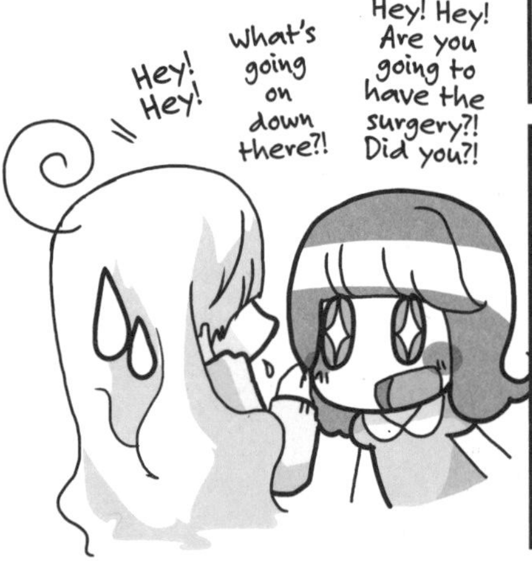
Hey! Hey! Are you going to have the surgery?! Did you?!
What's going on down there?!
Hey! Hey!

※OTHER REQUIREMENTS:
"You must be over 12 years old."
"You must not have any underage children at present."
These requirements are under debate, too.

This explanation is current for 2016.

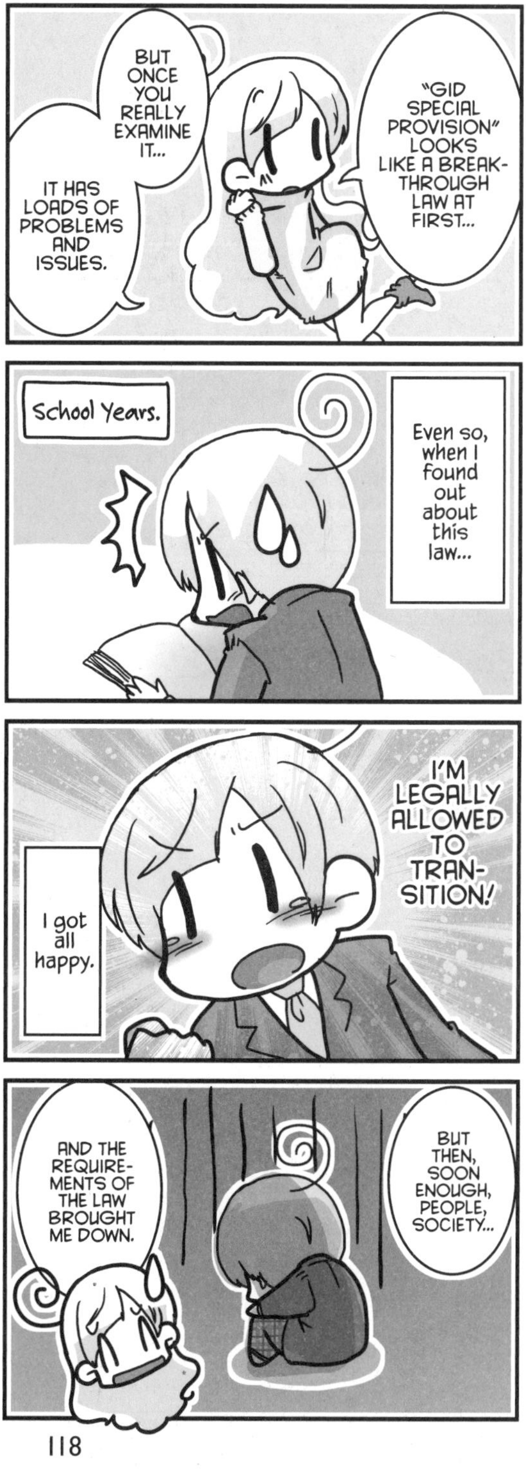
"GID SPECIAL PROVISION" LOOKS LIKE A BREAKTHROUGH LAW AT FIRST...
BUT ONCE YOU REALLY EXAMINE IT...
IT HAS LOADS OF PROBLEMS AND ISSUES.
Even so, when I found out about this law...
School Years.
I'M LEGALLY ALLOWED TO TRANSITION!
I got all happy.
BUT THEN, SOON ENOUGH, PEOPLE, SOCIETY...
AND THE REQUIREMENTS OF THE LAW BROUGHT ME DOWN.

Laws are important, but it's also important...

to create a society that accepts diversity and different genders.

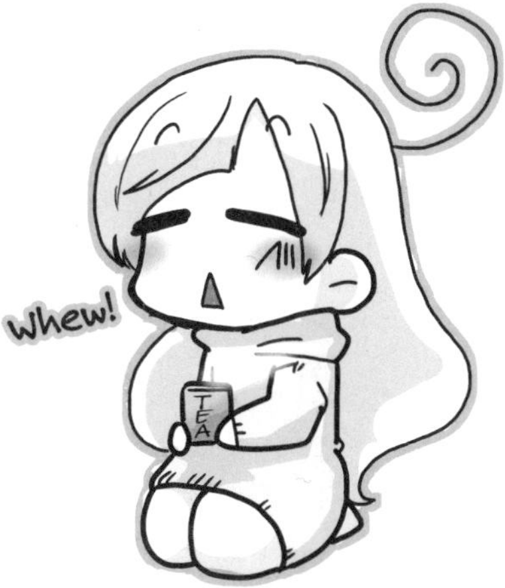
TEA
Whew!

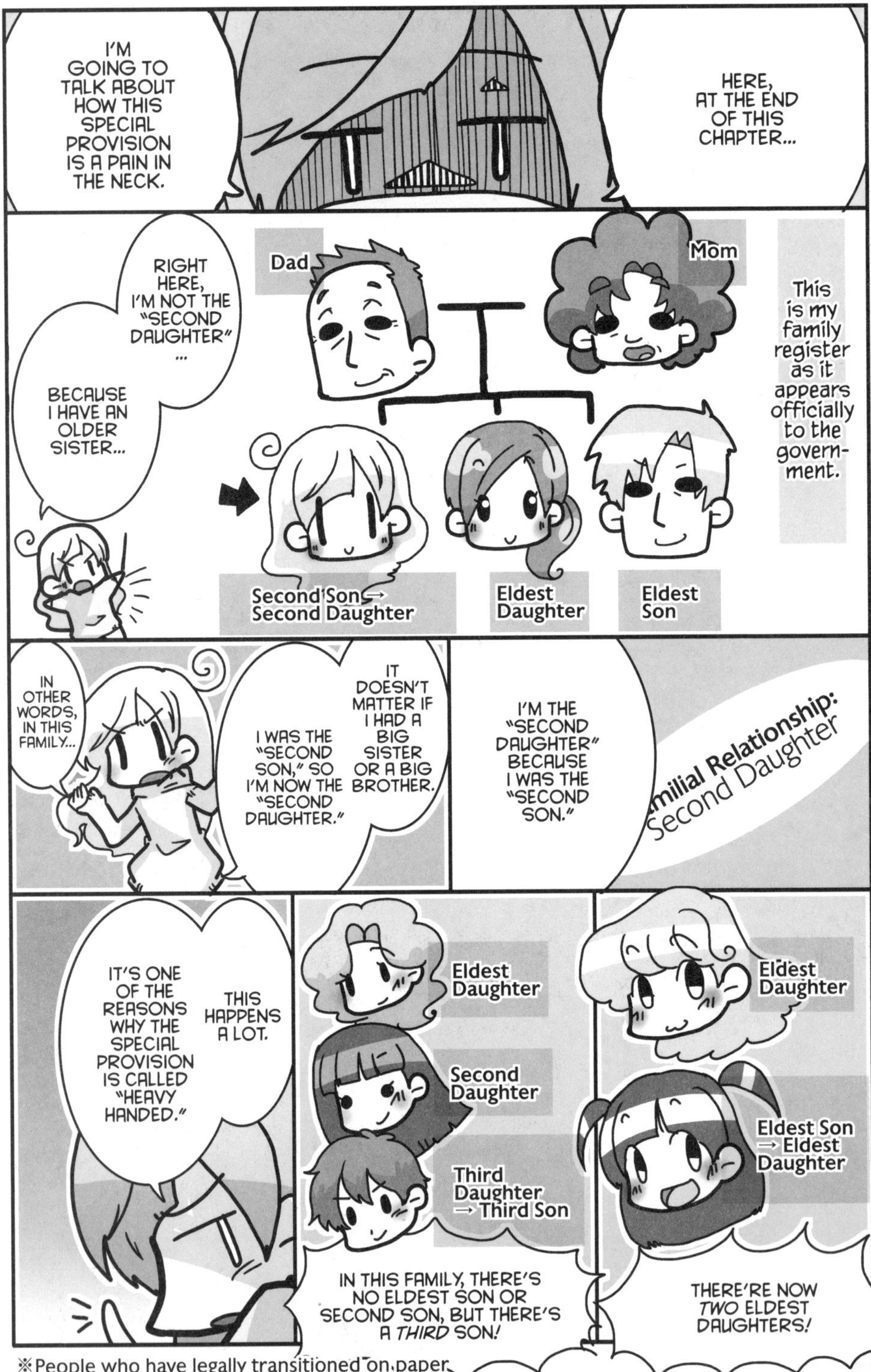
HERE, AT THE END OF THIS CHAPTER...
I'M GOING TO TALK ABOUT HOW THIS SPECIAL PROVISION IS A PAIN IN THE NECK.
This is my family register as it appears officially to the government.
Mom
Dad
RIGHT HERE, I'M NOT THE "SECOND DAUGHTER"...
BECAUSE I HAVE AN OLDER SISTER...
Eldest Son
Eldest Daughter
Second Son → Second Daughter
milial Relationship: Second Daughter
I'M THE "SECOND DAUGHTER" BECAUSE I WAS THE "SECOND SON."
IT DOESN'T MATTER IF I HAD A BIG SISTER OR A BIG BROTHER.
I WAS THE "SECOND SON," SO I'M NOW THE "SECOND DAUGHTER."
IN OTHER WORDS, IN THIS FAMILY...
Eldest Daughter
Eldest Son → Eldest Daughter
THERE'RE NOW *TWO* ELDEST DAUGHTERS!
Eldest Daughter
Second Daughter
Third Daughter → Third Son
IN THIS FAMILY, THERE'S NO ELDEST SON OR SECOND SON, BUT THERE'S A *THIRD* SON!
THIS HAPPENS A LOT.
IT'S ONE OF THE REASONS WHY THE SPECIAL PROVISION IS CALLED "HEAVY HANDED."

※People who have legally transitioned on paper become the principal of a single family register.

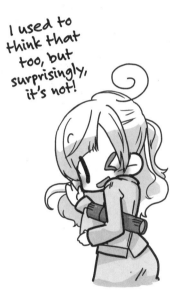

"Isn't it impossible for a man to live as a woman?"

I used to think that too, but surprisingly, it's not!

When I was a boy, I thought it was totally impossible for me to live as a woman. But I did it. Most people can. Of course, you need skills and know-how, too--but I think these are things that come when you actually start living that way. It just depends on how much work you put into it.

If I could say something to myself when I was a boy, I'd like to tell him, "It's not impossible, so just believe in yourself!"

CHAPTER 8

The Bride was a Boy

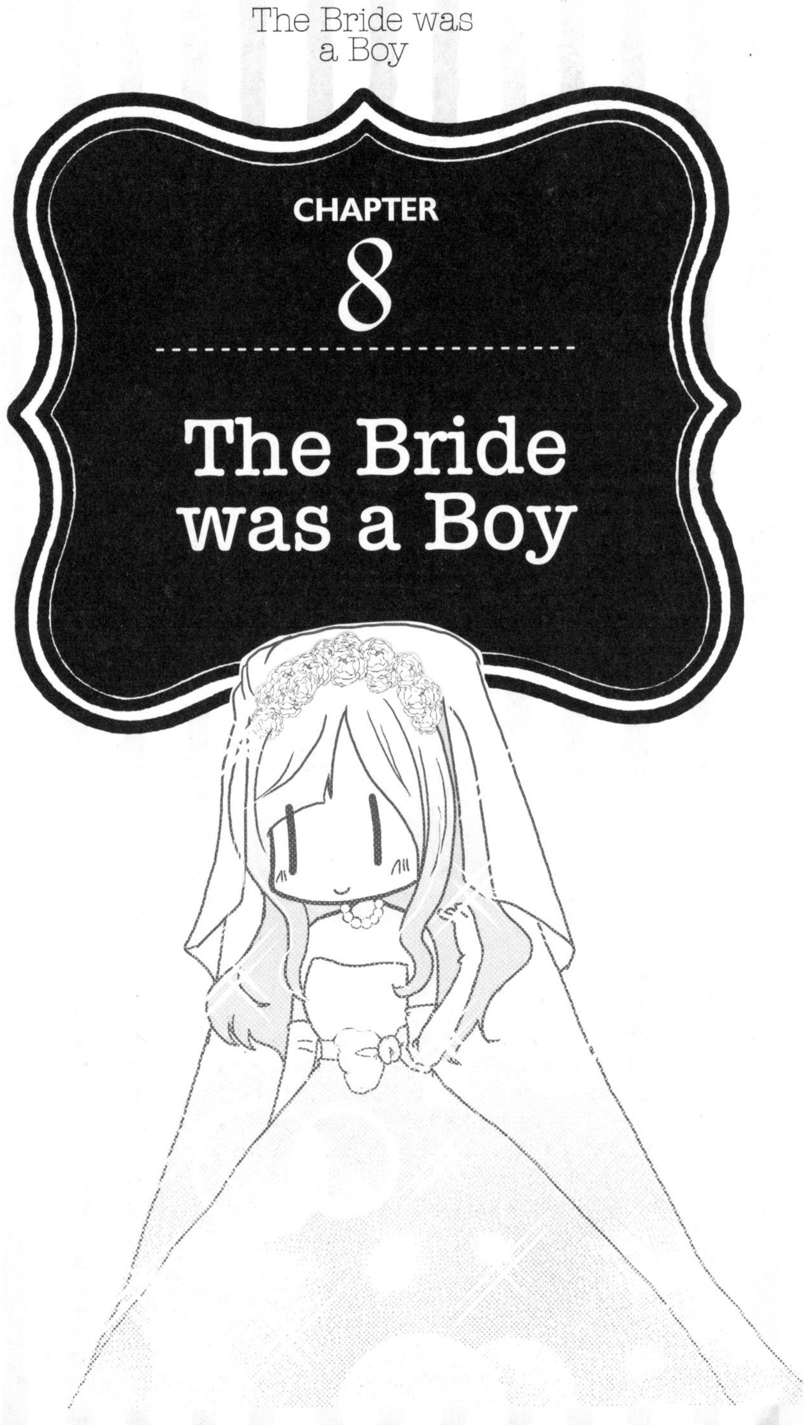

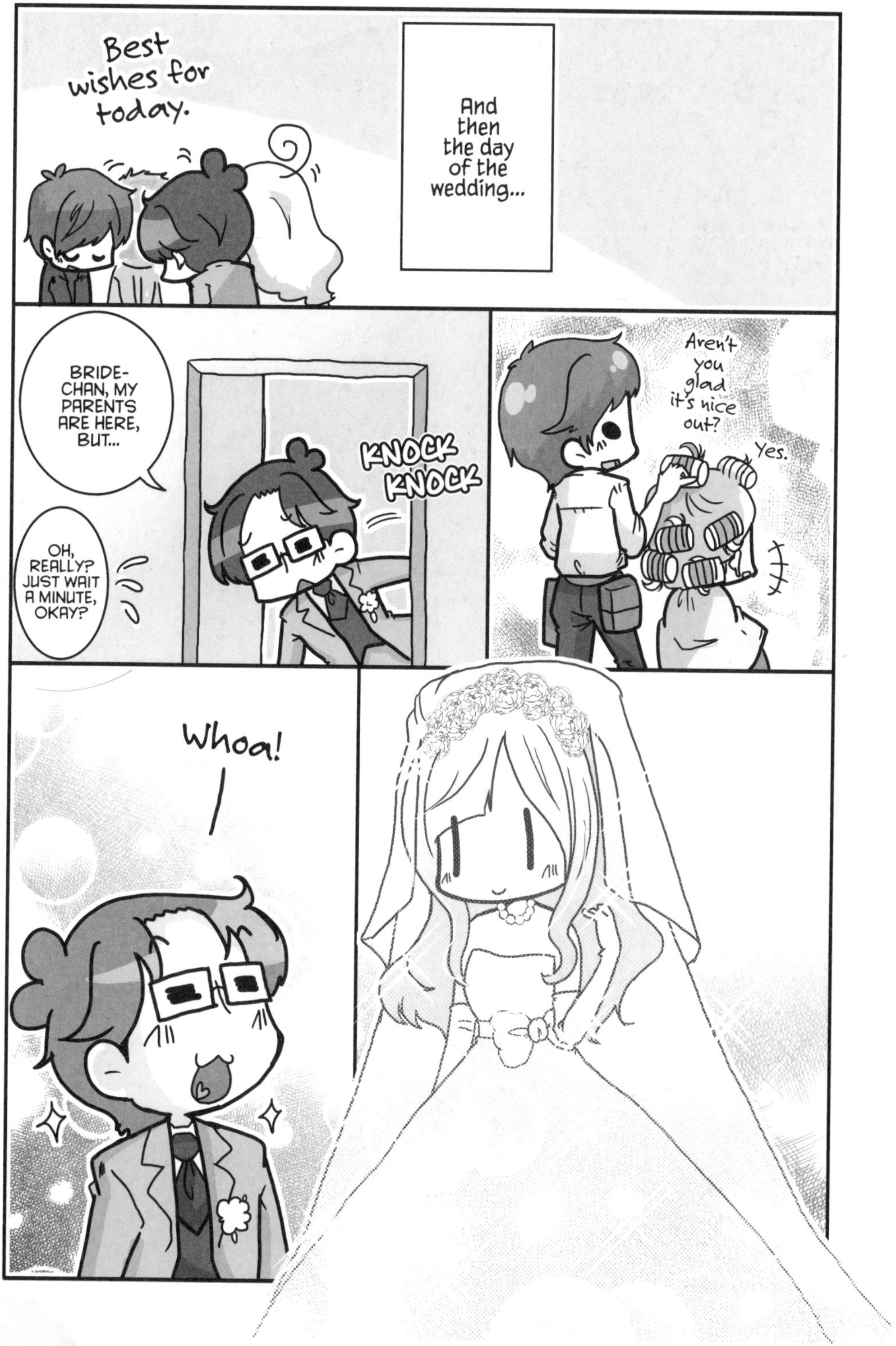
And then the day of the wedding...
Best wishes for today.
Aren't you glad it's nice out?
Yes.
KNOCK KNOCK
BRIDE-CHAN, MY PARENTS ARE HERE, BUT...
OH, REALLY? JUST WAIT A MINUTE, OKAY?
Whoa!

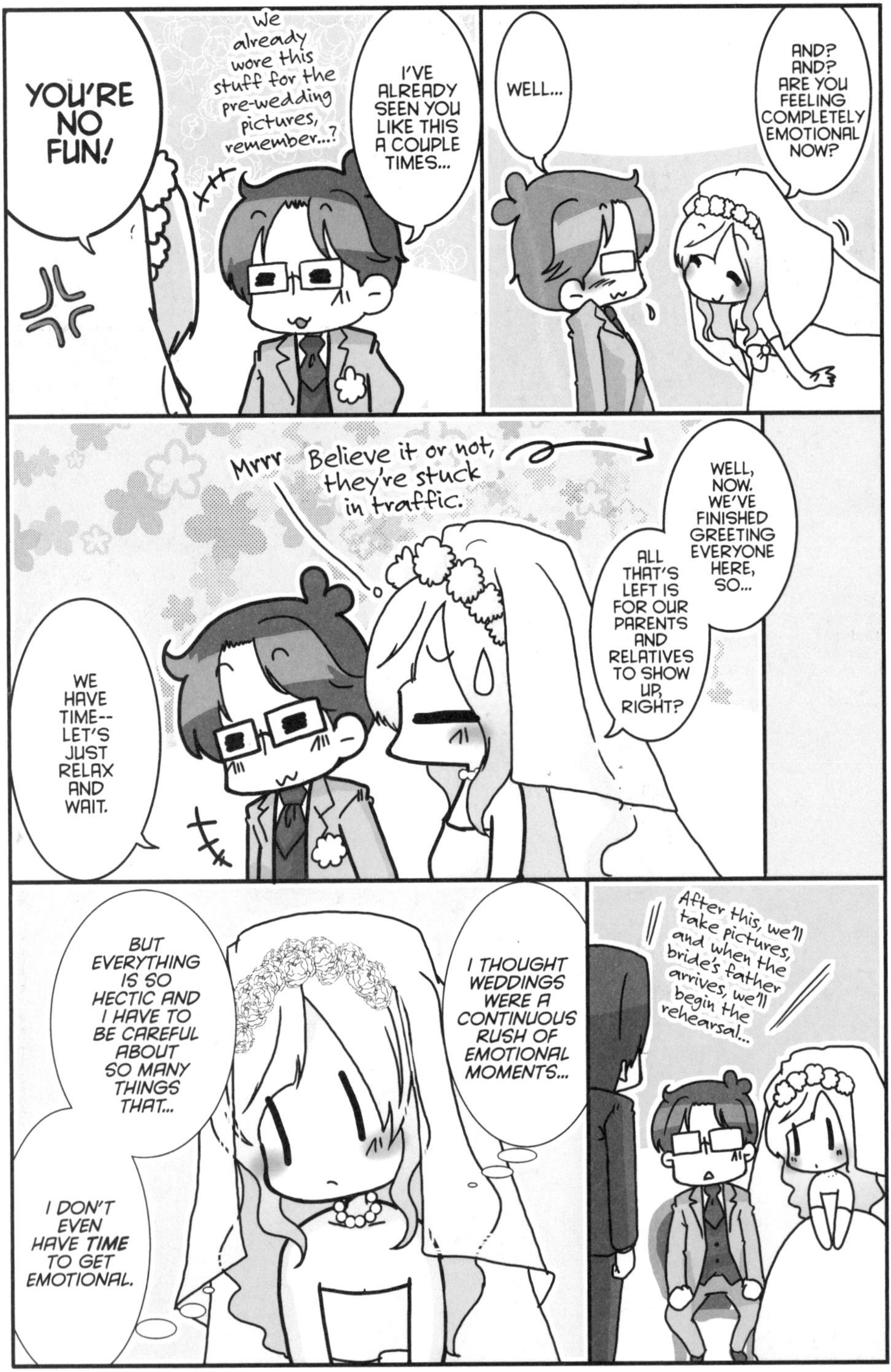
AND? AND? ARE YOU FEELING COMPLETELY EMOTIONAL NOW?
WELL...
I'VE ALREADY SEEN YOU LIKE THIS A COUPLE TIMES...
We already wore this stuff for the pre-wedding pictures, remember...?
YOU'RE NO FUN!
WELL, NOW. WE'VE FINISHED GREETING EVERYONE HERE, SO...
ALL THAT'S LEFT IS FOR OUR PARENTS AND RELATIVES TO SHOW UP, RIGHT?
Believe it or not, they're stuck in traffic.
Mrrr
WE HAVE TIME--LET'S JUST RELAX AND WAIT.
After this, we'll take pictures, and when the bride's father arrives, we'll begin the rehearsal...
I THOUGHT WEDDINGS WERE A CONTINUOUS RUSH OF EMOTIONAL MOMENTS...
BUT EVERYTHING IS SO HECTIC AND I HAVE TO BE CAREFUL ABOUT SO MANY THINGS THAT...
I DON'T EVEN HAVE *TIME* TO GET EMOTIONAL.

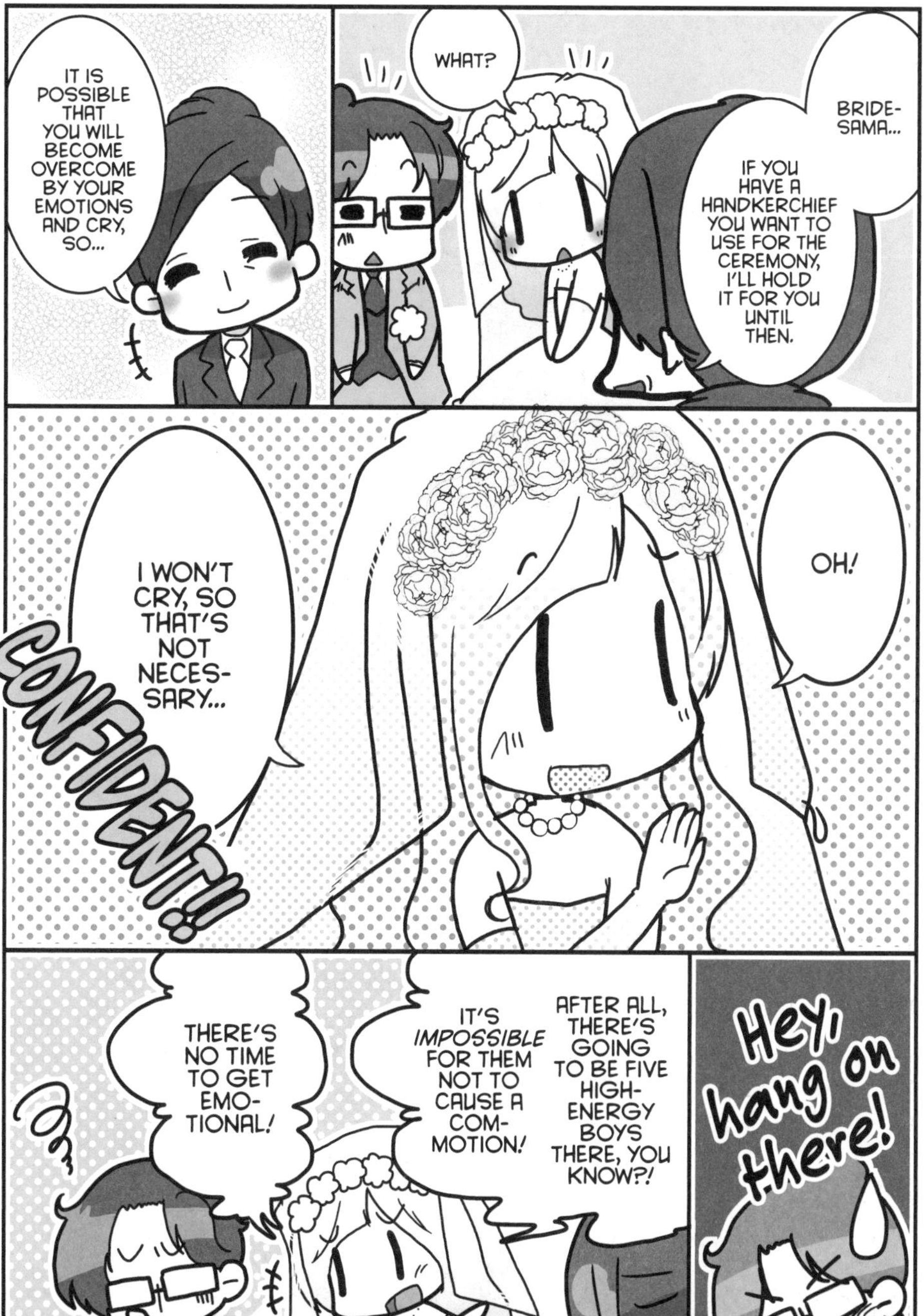
BRIDE-SAMA... IF YOU HAVE A HANDKERCHIEF YOU WANT TO USE FOR THE CEREMONY, I'LL HOLD IT FOR YOU UNTIL THEN.
WHAT?
IT IS POSSIBLE THAT YOU WILL BECOME OVERCOME BY YOUR EMOTIONS AND CRY, SO...
OH!
I WON'T CRY, SO THAT'S NOT NECES-SARY...
CONFIDENT!!!
Hey, hang on there!
AFTER ALL, THERE'S GOING TO BE FIVE HIGH-ENERGY BOYS THERE, YOU KNOW?!
IT'S *IMPOSSIBLE* FOR THEM NOT TO CAUSE A COM-MOTION!
THERE'S NO TIME TO GET EMO-TIONAL!

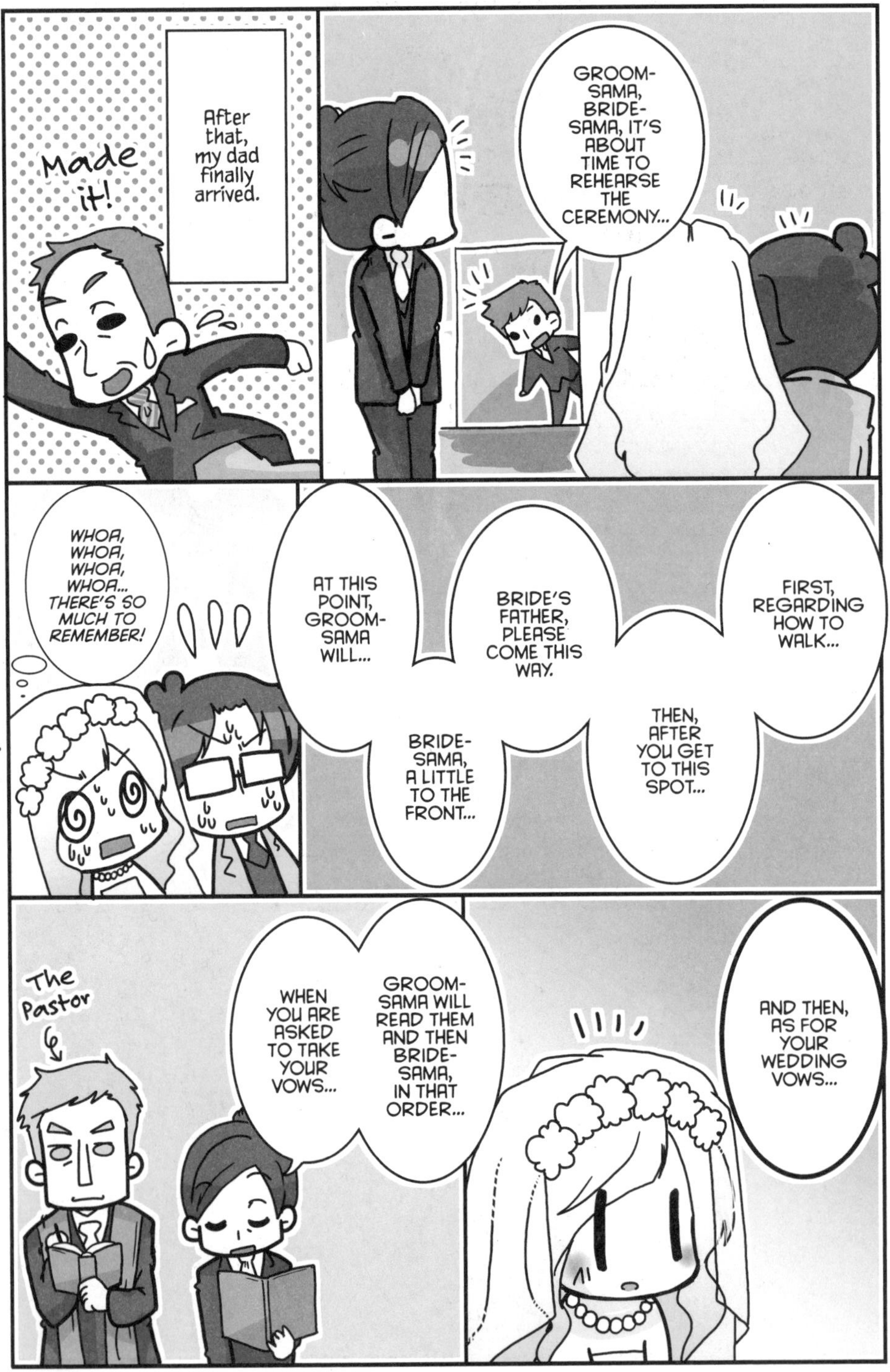
GROOM-SAMA, BRIDE-SAMA, IT'S ABOUT TIME TO REHEARSE THE CEREMONY...
After that, my dad finally arrived.
Made it!
FIRST, REGARDING HOW TO WALK...
BRIDE'S FATHER, PLEASE COME THIS WAY.
AT THIS POINT, GROOM-SAMA WILL...
THEN, AFTER YOU GET TO THIS SPOT...
BRIDE-SAMA, A LITTLE TO THE FRONT...
WHOA, WHOA, WHOA, WHOA... THERE'S SO MUCH TO REMEMBER!
AND THEN, AS FOR YOUR WEDDING VOWS...
GROOM-SAMA WILL READ THEM AND THEN BRIDE-SAMA, IN THAT ORDER...
WHEN YOU ARE ASKED TO TAKE YOUR VOWS...
The Pastor

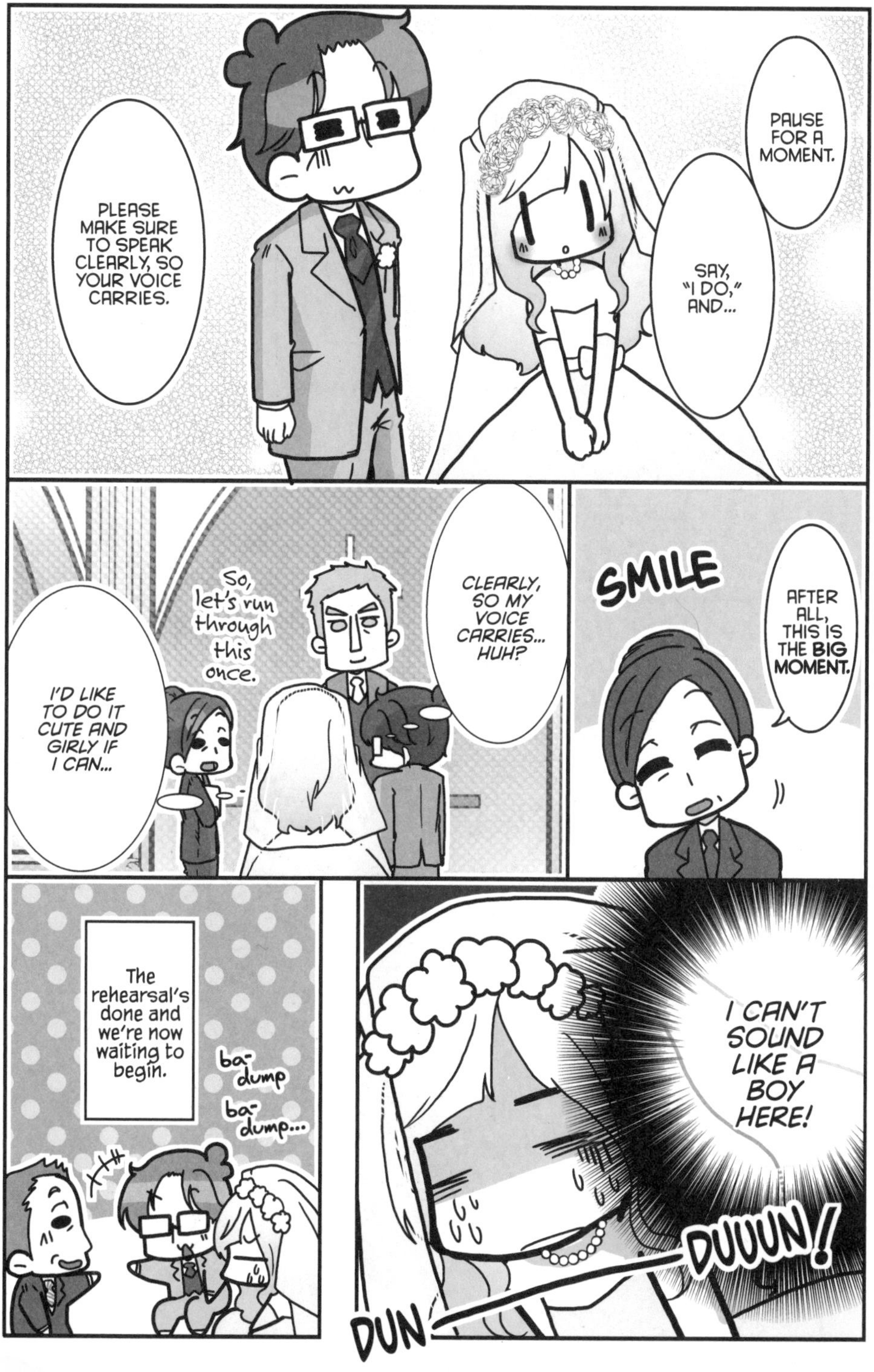
SAY, "I DO," AND...
PAUSE FOR A MOMENT.
PLEASE MAKE SURE TO SPEAK CLEARLY, SO YOUR VOICE CARRIES.
SMILE
AFTER ALL, THIS IS THE **BIG MOMENT.**
CLEARLY, SO MY VOICE CARRIES... HUH?
So, let's run through this once.
I'D LIKE TO DO IT CUTE AND GIRLY IF I CAN...
I CAN'T SOUND LIKE A BOY HERE!
DUUUN!
DUN
The rehearsal's done and we're now waiting to begin.
ba-dump
ba-dump...

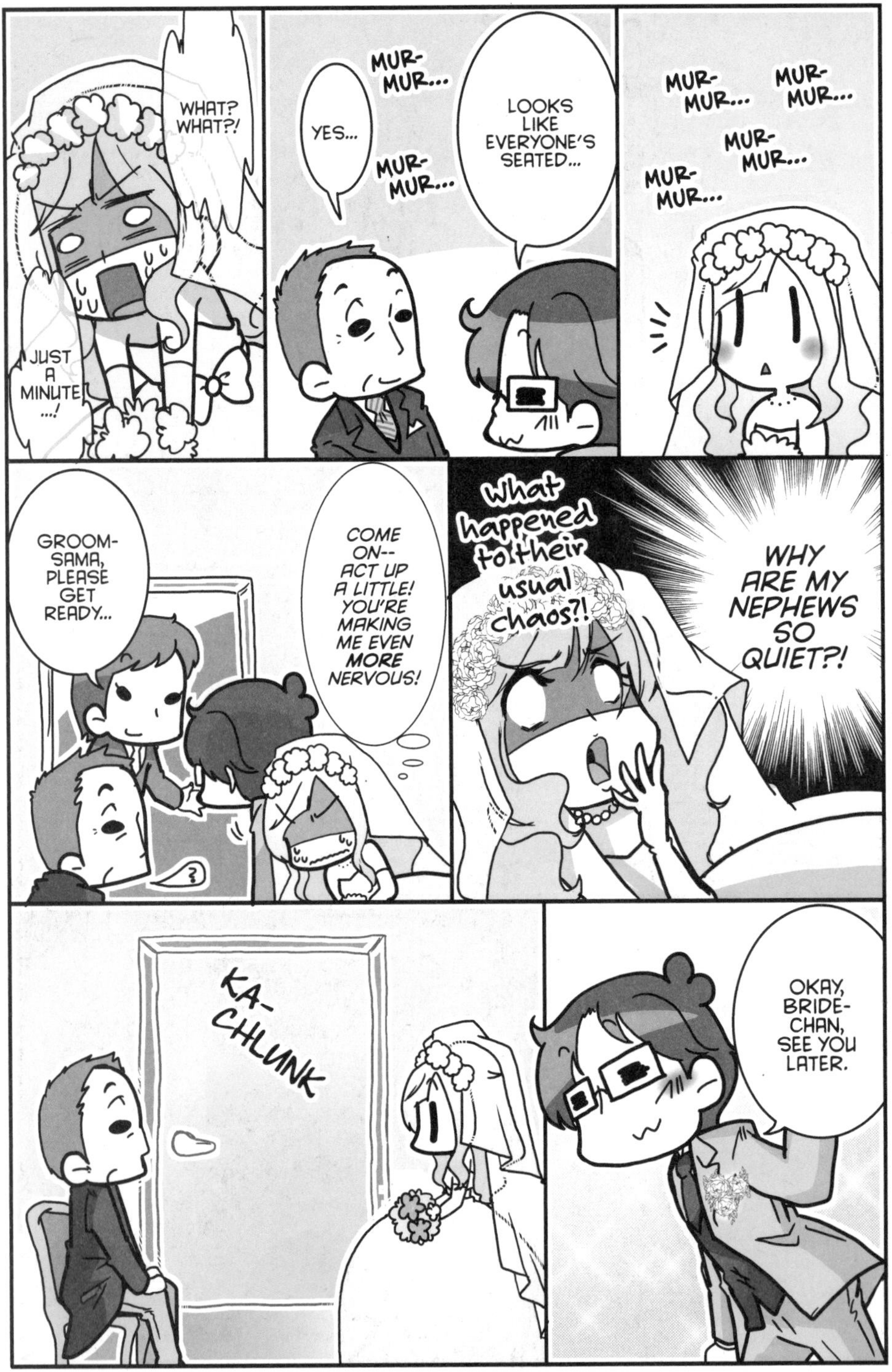
MUR-MUR...
MUR-MUR...
MUR-MUR...
MUR-MUR...
LOOKS LIKE EVERYONE'S SEATED...
MUR-MUR...
YES...
MUR-MUR...
WHAT? WHAT?!
JUST A MINUTE ...!
what happened to their usual chaos?!
WHY ARE MY NEPHEWS SO QUIET?!
COME ON-- ACT UP A LITTLE! YOU'RE MAKING ME EVEN **MORE** NERVOUS!
GROOM-SAMA, PLEASE GET READY...
OKAY, BRIDE-CHAN, SEE YOU LATER.
KA-CHLUNK

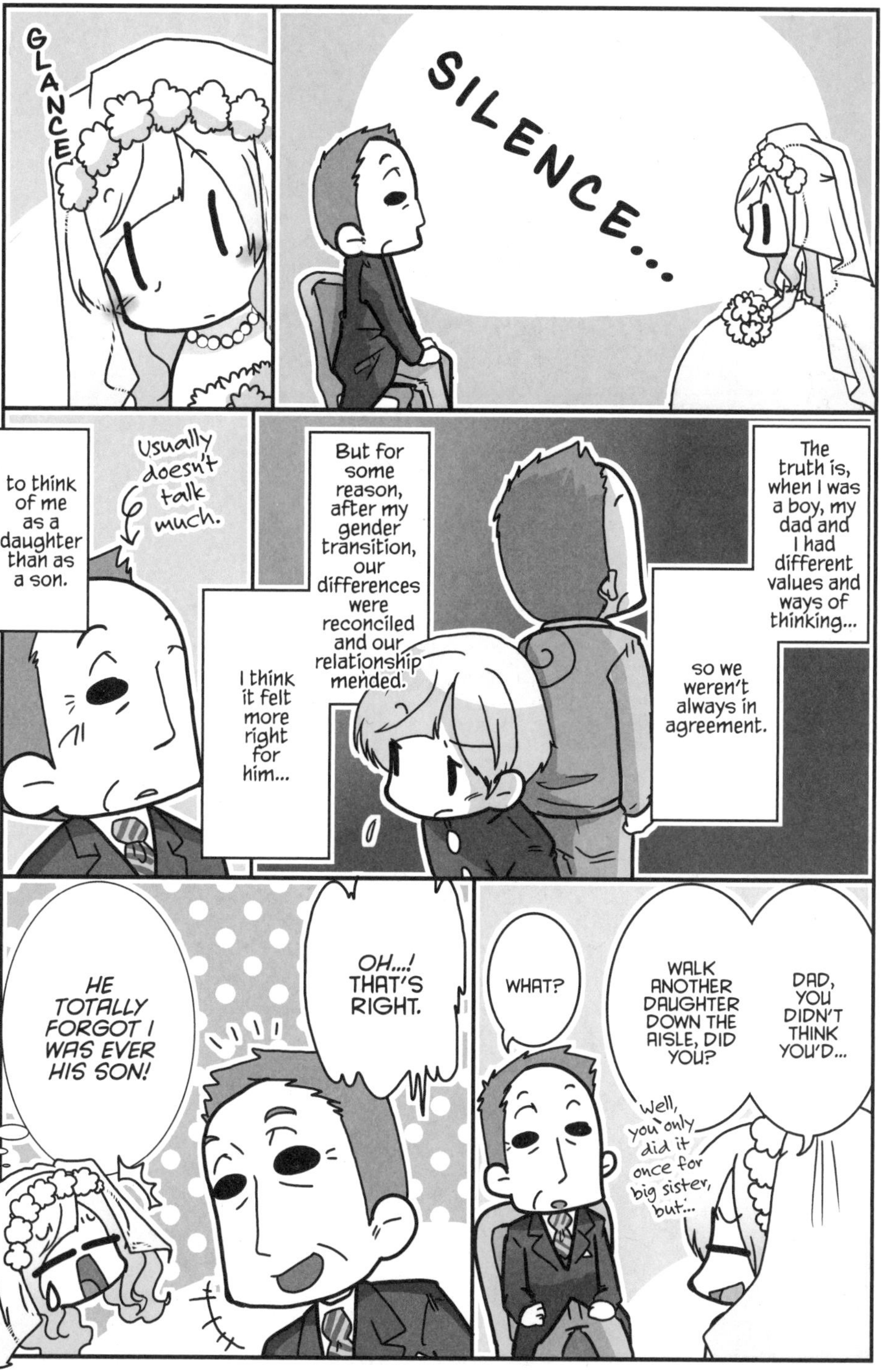
SILENCE...
GLANCE
The truth is, when I was a boy, my dad and I had different values and ways of thinking...
so we weren't always in agreement.
But for some reason, after my gender transition, our differences were reconciled and our relationship mended.
I think it felt more right for him...
to think of me as a daughter than as a son.
Usually doesn't talk much.
DAD, YOU DIDN'T THINK YOU'D...
WALK ANOTHER DAUGHTER DOWN THE AISLE, DID YOU?
Well, you only did it once for big sister, but...
WHAT?
OH...! THAT'S RIGHT.
HE TOTALLY FORGOT I WAS EVER HIS SON!

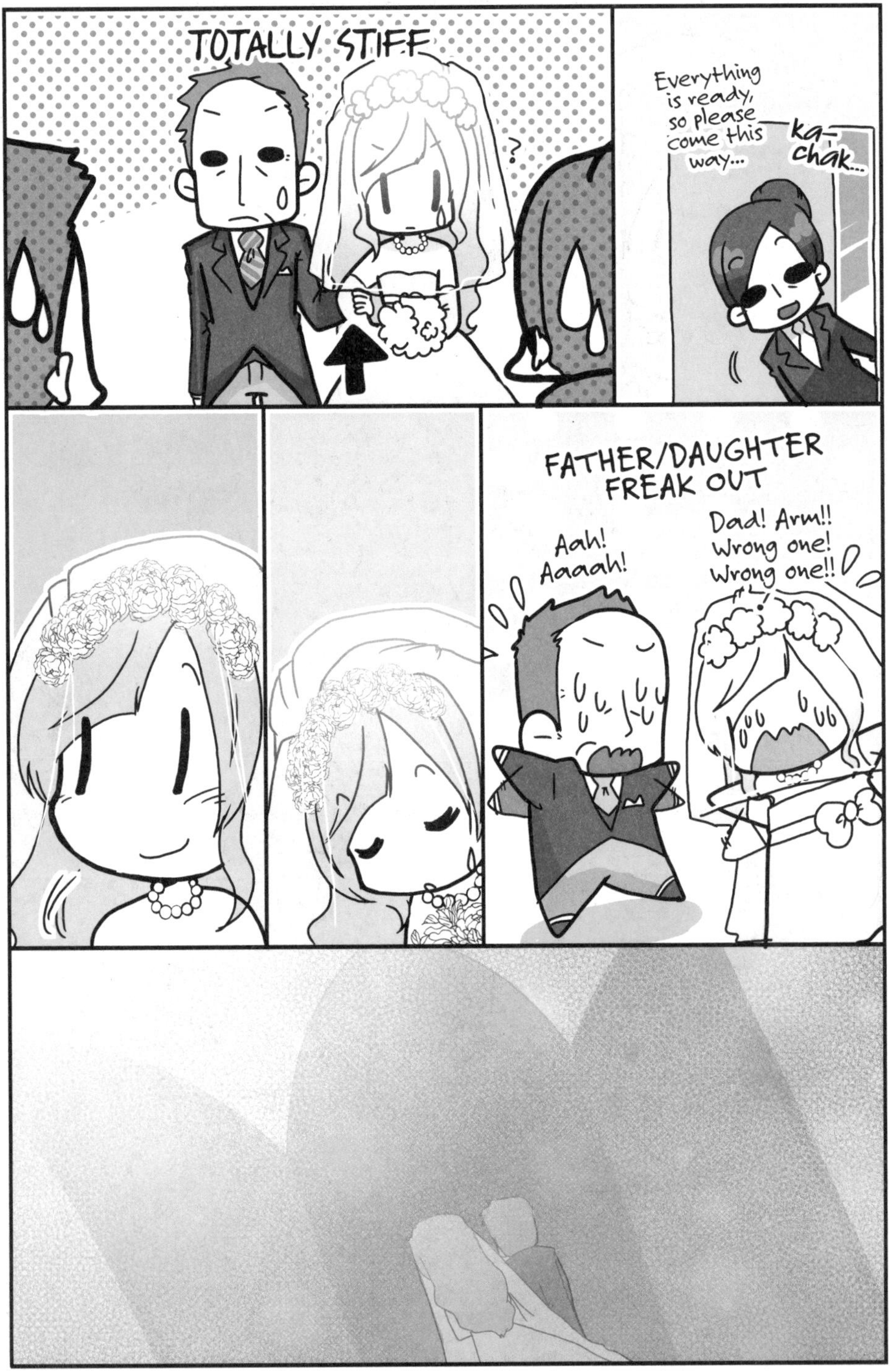
Everything is ready, so please come this way...
ka-chak...
TOTALLY STIFF
?
FATHER/DAUGHTER FREAK OUT
Dad! Arm!! Wrong one! Wrong one!!
Aah! Aaaah!

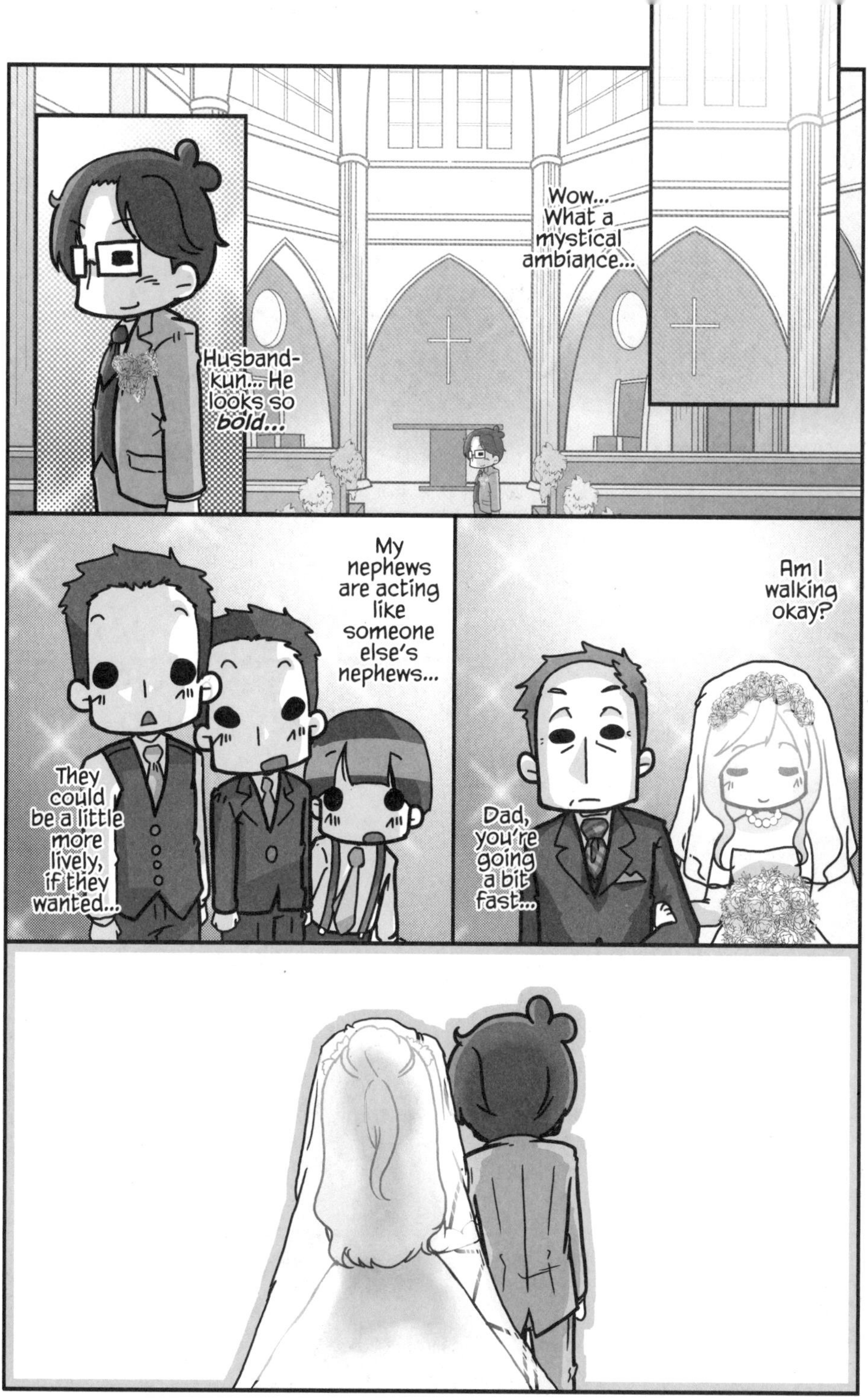
Wow... What a mystical ambiance...
Husband-kun... He looks so *bold*...
Am I walking okay?
Dad, you're going a bit fast...
My nephews are acting like someone else's nephews...
They could be a little more lively, if they wanted...

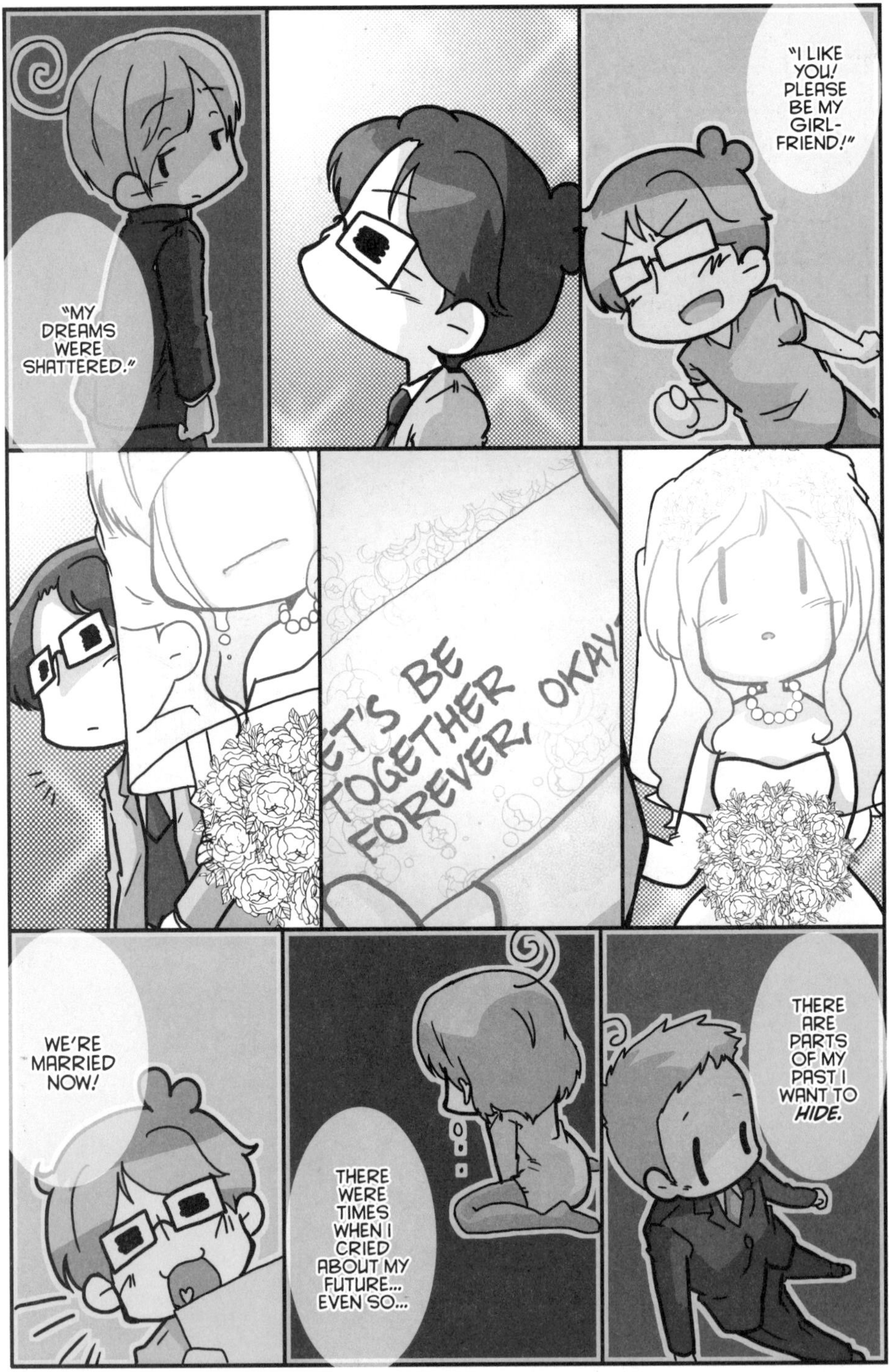
"I LIKE YOU! PLEASE BE MY GIRL-FRIEND!"
"MY DREAMS WERE SHATTERED."
ET'S BE TOGETHER FOREVER, OKAY
THERE ARE PARTS OF MY PAST I WANT TO *HIDE.*
THERE WERE TIMES WHEN I CRIED ABOUT MY FUTURE... EVEN SO...
WE'RE MARRIED NOW!

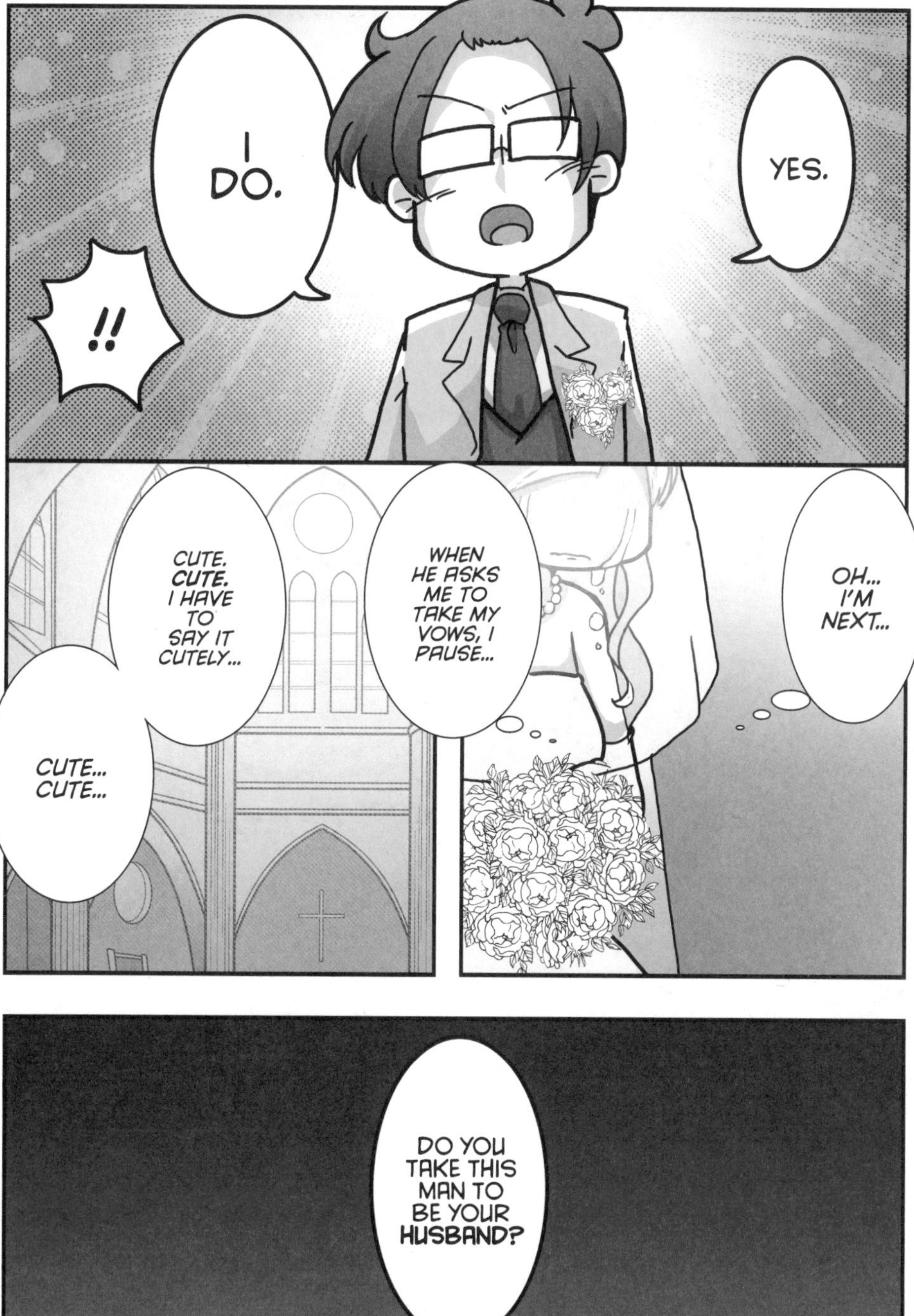
YES.
I DO.
!!
OH... I'M NEXT...
WHEN HE ASKS ME TO TAKE MY VOWS, I PAUSE...
CUTE. CUTE. I HAVE TO SAY IT CUTELY...
CUTE... CUTE...
DO YOU TAKE THIS MAN TO BE YOUR HUSBAND?

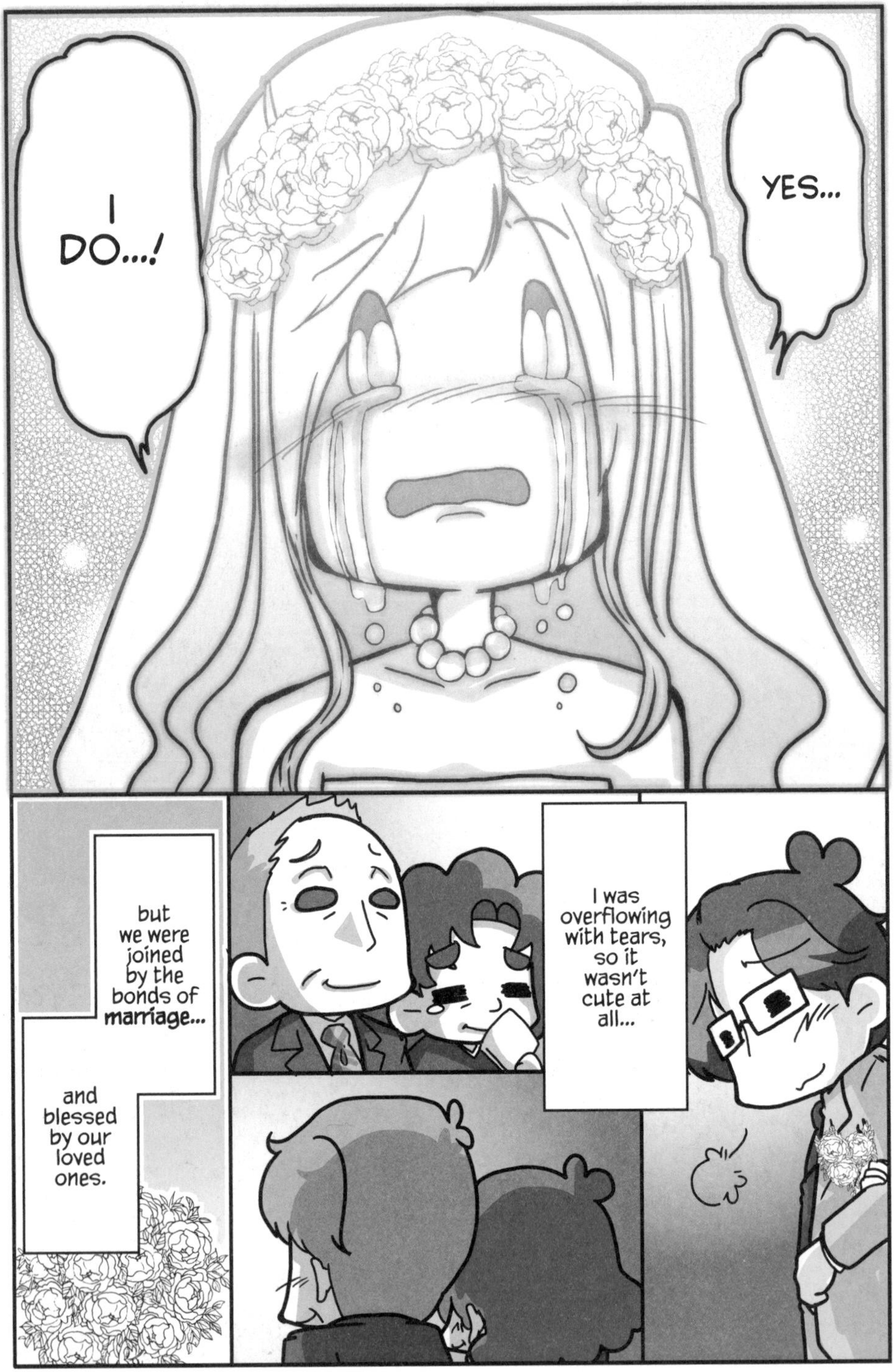
YES...
I DO...!
I was overflowing with tears, so it wasn't cute at all...
but we were joined by the bonds of **marriage...**
and blessed by our loved ones.

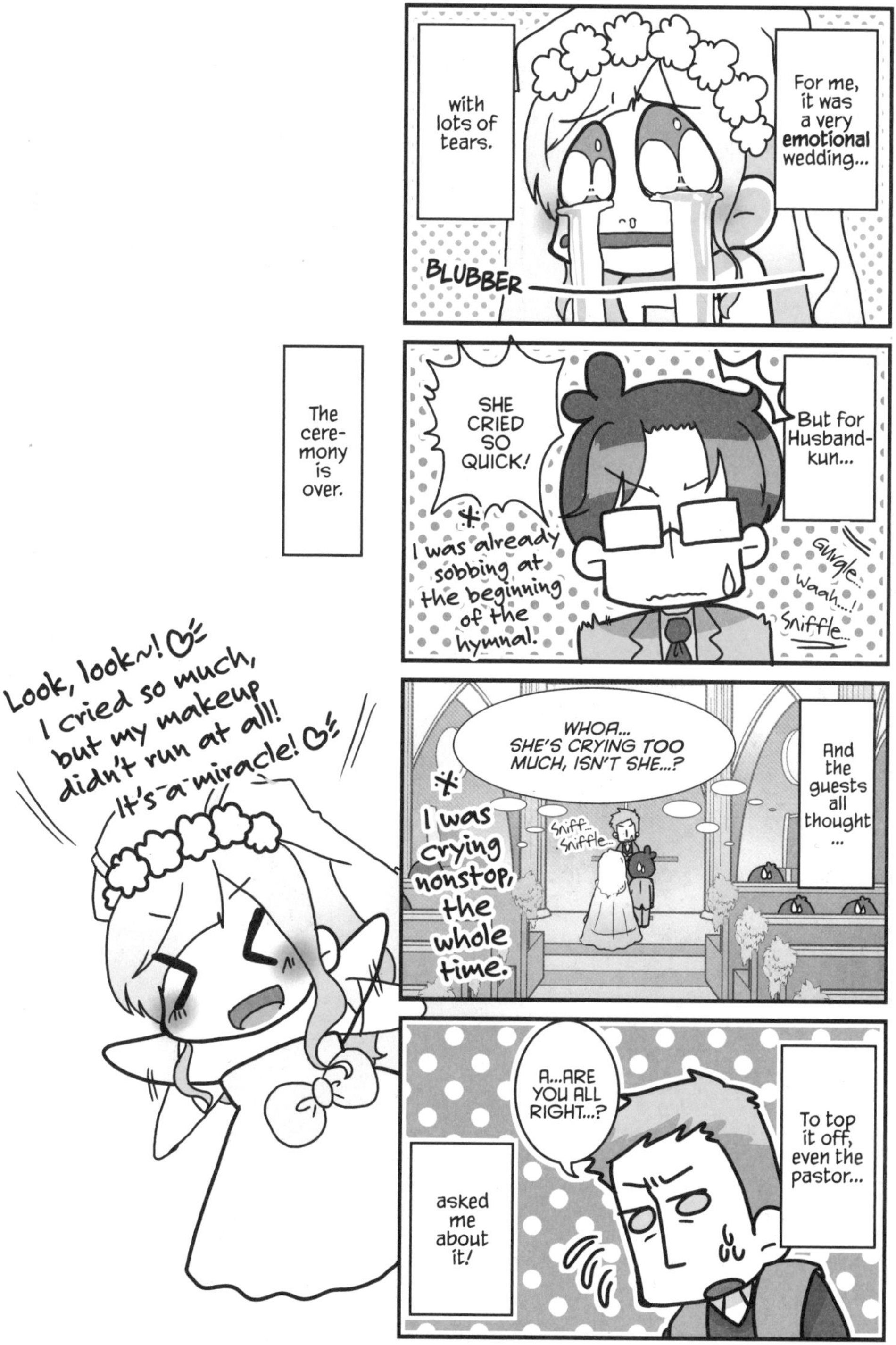
For me, it was a very **emotional** wedding...
with lots of tears.
BLUBBER
But for Husband-kun...
SHE CRIED SO QUICK!
*I was already sobbing at the beginning of the hymnal.
Gurgle... Waah...! Sniffle...
And the guests all thought...
WHOA... SHE'S CRYING TOO MUCH, ISN'T SHE...?
Sniff... Sniffle...
*I was crying nonstop, the whole time.
To top it off, even the pastor...
A...ARE YOU ALL RIGHT...?
asked me about it!
The ceremony is over.
Look, look~! ♡ I cried so much, but my makeup didn't run at all! It's a miracle! ♡

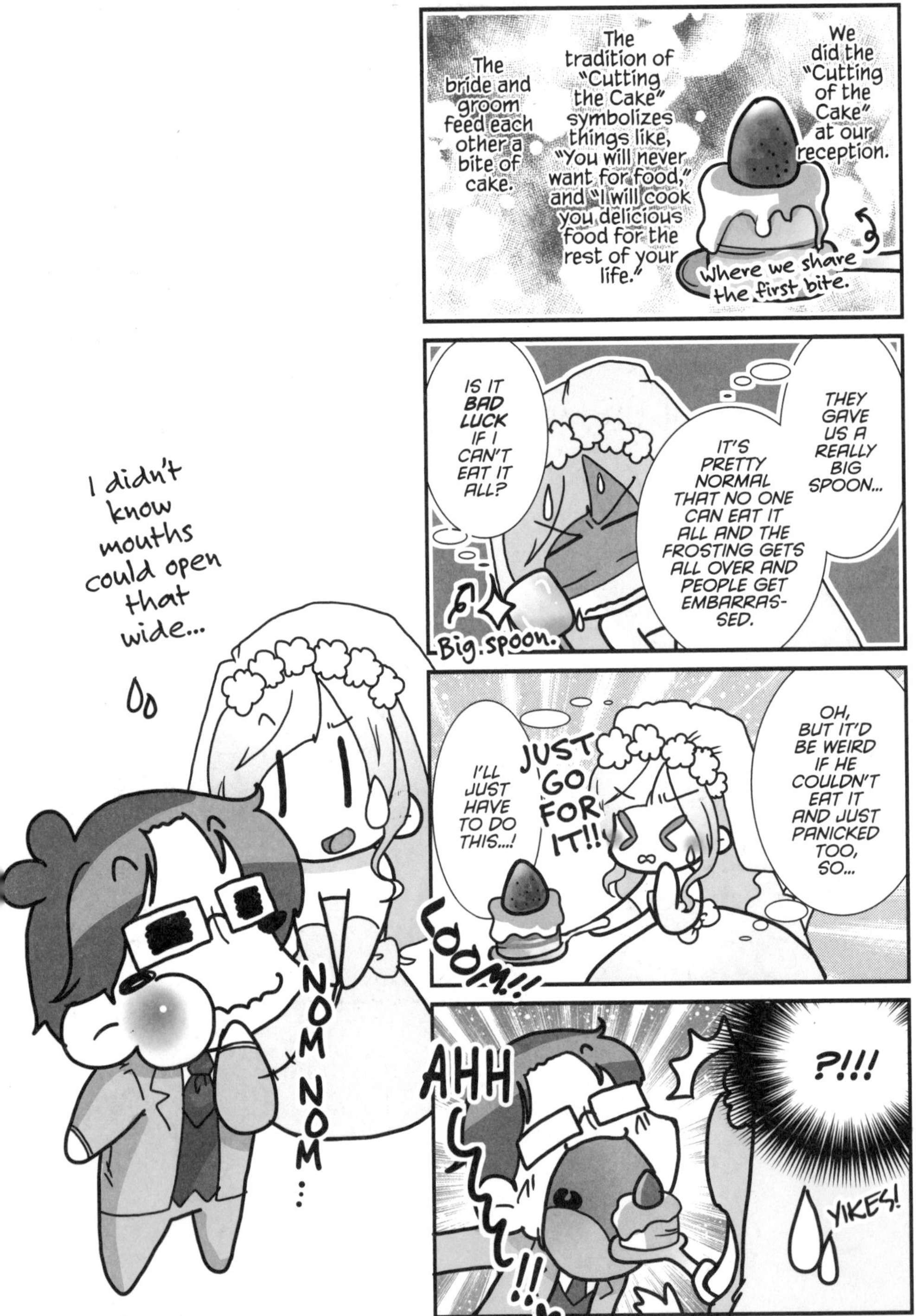
We did the "Cutting of the Cake" at our reception.
Where we share the first bite.
The tradition of "Cutting the Cake" symbolizes things like, "You will never want for food," and "I will cook you delicious food for the rest of your life."
The bride and groom feed each other a bite of cake.
THEY GAVE US A REALLY BIG SPOON...
IT'S PRETTY NORMAL THAT NO ONE CAN EAT IT ALL AND THE FROSTING GETS ALL OVER AND PEOPLE GET EMBARRAS-SED.
IS IT BAD LUCK IF I CAN'T EAT IT ALL?
Big spoon.
OH, BUT IT'D BE WEIRD IF HE COULDN'T EAT IT AND JUST PANICKED TOO, SO...
JUST GO FOR IT!!
I'LL JUST HAVE TO DO THIS...!
LOOM!!
?!!!
YIKES!
AHH
!!
I didn't know mouths could open that wide...
NOM NOM NOM...

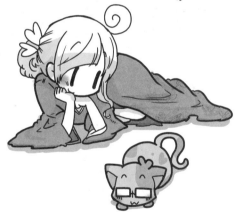

"You turned into a woman because you like men?"

I think it's not about "liking men," but rather that I wanted to be the woman I am.

There may be people who feel that way, but that wasn't the case for me. In my case, it was more that I was uncomfortable and disgusted with the fact that society said I was male. That's why I transitioned--it wasn't just because I am sexually attracted to men.

Feelings concerning this topic are highly individual, so I can only speak for myself--sorry!

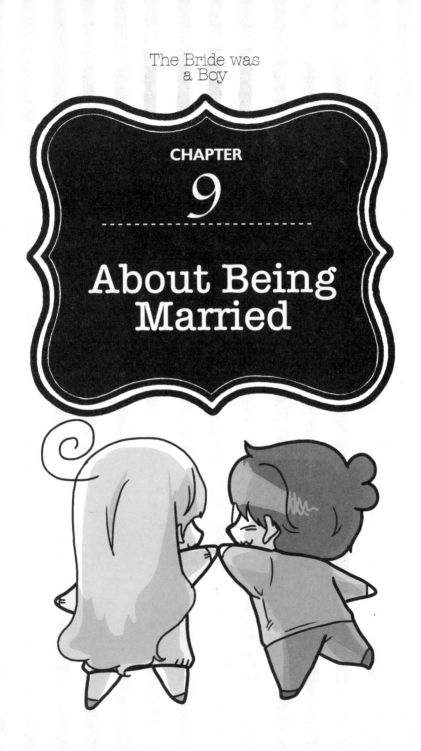

The Bride was
a Boy

CHAPTER

9

About Being
Married

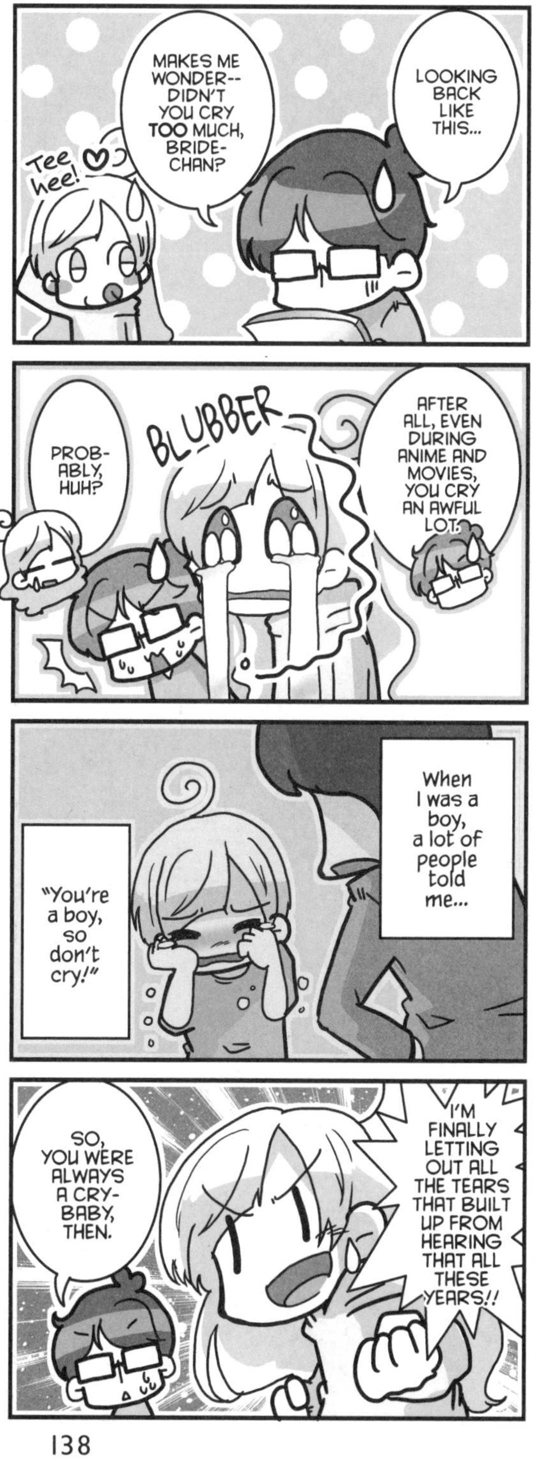
LOOKING BACK LIKE THIS...
MAKES ME WONDER-- DIDN'T YOU CRY **TOO** MUCH, BRIDE-CHAN?
Tee hee!
AFTER ALL, EVEN DURING ANIME AND MOVIES, YOU CRY AN AWFUL LOT.
BLUBBER
PROBABLY, HUH?
When I was a boy, a lot of people told me...
"You're a boy, so don't cry!"
I'M FINALLY LETTING OUT ALL THE TEARS THAT BUILT UP FROM HEARING THAT ALL THESE YEARS!!
SO, YOU WERE ALWAYS A CRY-BABY, THEN.

Really! I think the words...

"You're a boy, so don't cry!" are just horrible.

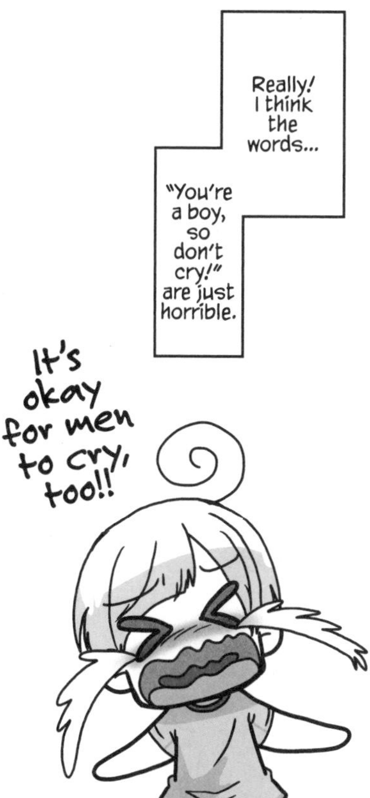
It's okay for men to cry, too!!

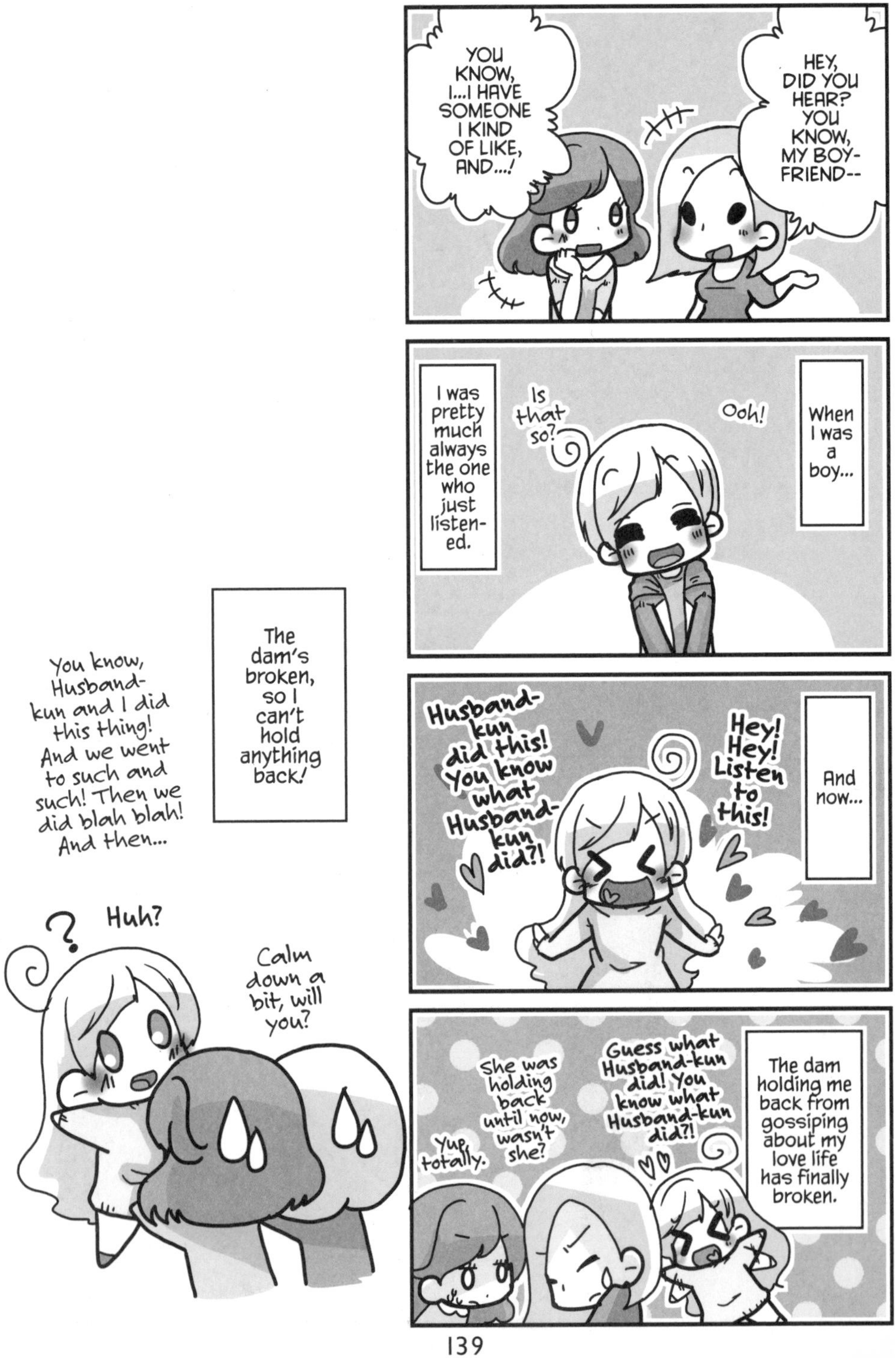
HEY, DID YOU HEAR? YOU KNOW, MY BOY-FRIEND--
YOU KNOW, I...I HAVE SOMEONE I KIND OF LIKE, AND...!
When I was a boy...
Ooh!
Is that so?
I was pretty much always the one who just listen-ed.
And now...
Hey! Hey! Listen to this!
Husband-kun did this! You know what Husband-kun did?!
The dam holding me back from gossiping about my love life has finally broken.
Guess what Husband-kun did! You know what Husband-kun did?!
She was holding back until now, wasn't she?
Yup, totally.
The dam's broken, so I can't hold anything back!
You know, Husband-kun and I did this thing! And we went to such and such! Then we did blah blah! And then...
Calm down a bit, will you?
Huh?

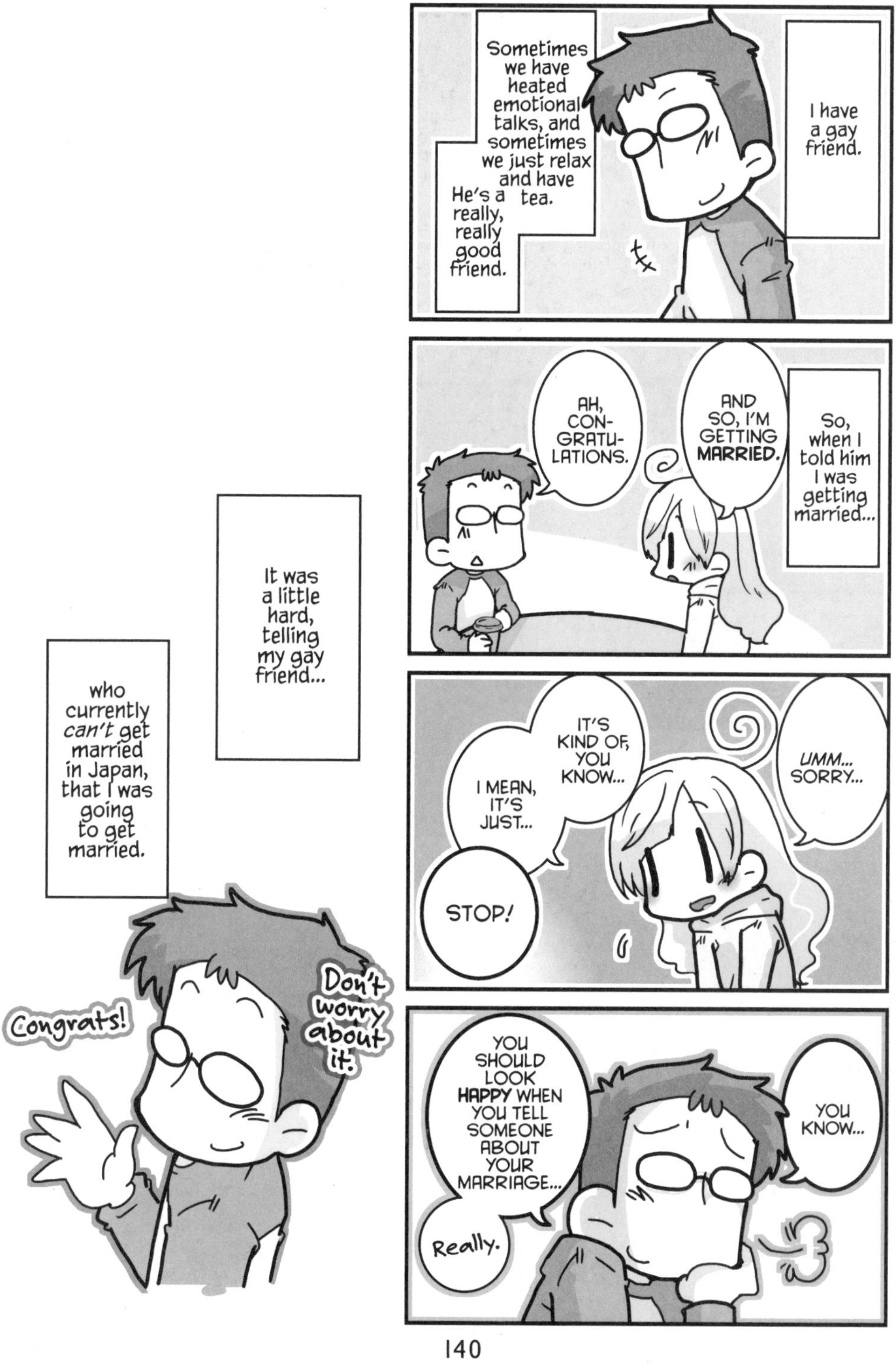

I have a gay friend.
Sometimes we have heated emotional talks, and sometimes we just relax and have tea.
He's a really, really good friend.
So, when I told him I was getting married...
AND SO, I'M GETTING **MARRIED.**
AH, CON-GRATU-LATIONS.
UMM... SORRY...
IT'S KIND OF, YOU KNOW...
I MEAN, IT'S JUST...
STOP!
YOU KNOW...
YOU SHOULD LOOK **HAPPY** WHEN YOU TELL SOMEONE ABOUT YOUR MARRIAGE...
Really.
It was a little hard, telling my gay friend...
who currently *can't* get married in Japan, that I was going to get married.
Don't worry about it.
Congrats!

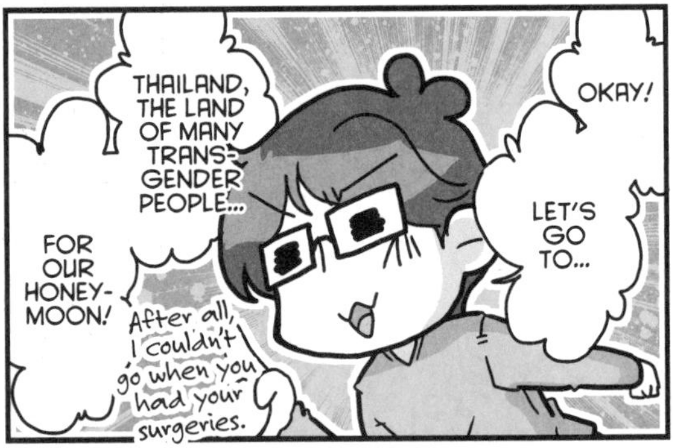
OKAY!
LET'S GO TO...
THAILAND, THE LAND OF MANY TRANS-GENDER PEOPLE...
FOR OUR HONEY-MOON!
After all, I couldn't go when you had your surgeries.

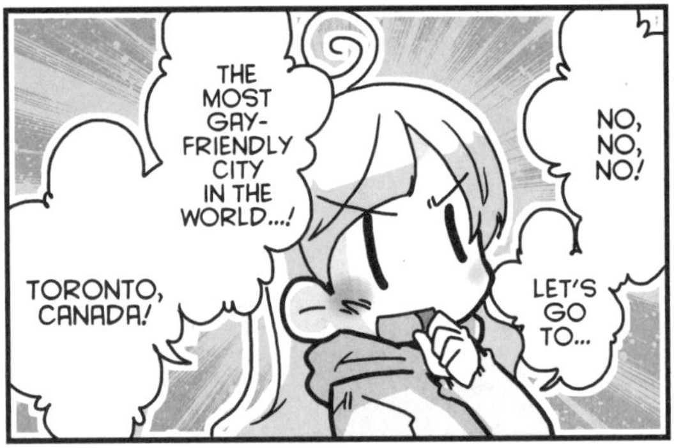
NO, NO, NO!
LET'S GO TO...
THE MOST GAY-FRIENDLY CITY IN THE WORLD...!
TORONTO, CANADA!

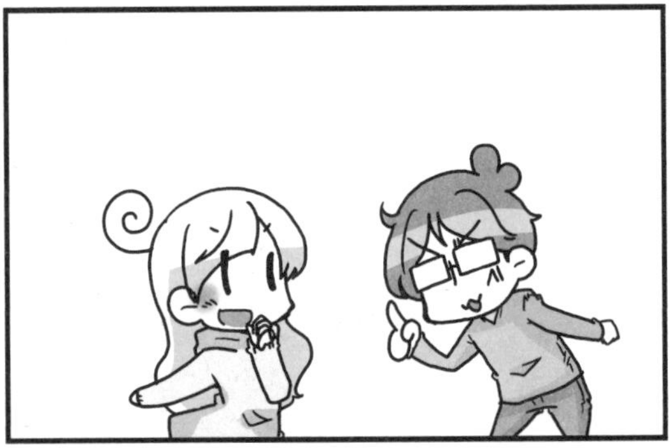

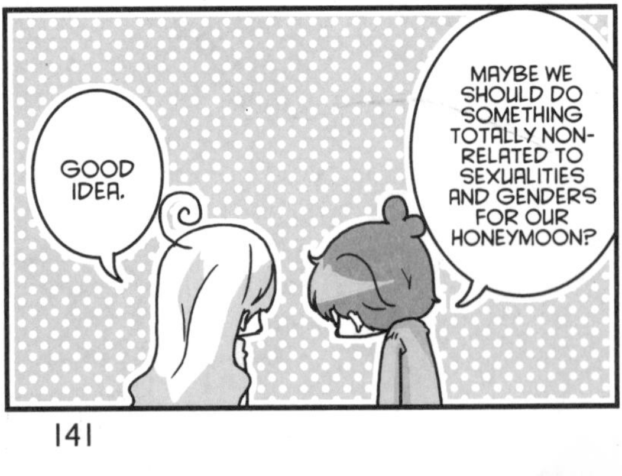
MAYBE WE SHOULD DO SOMETHING TOTALLY NON-RELATED TO SEXUALITIES AND GENDERS FOR OUR HONEYMOON?
GOOD IDEA.

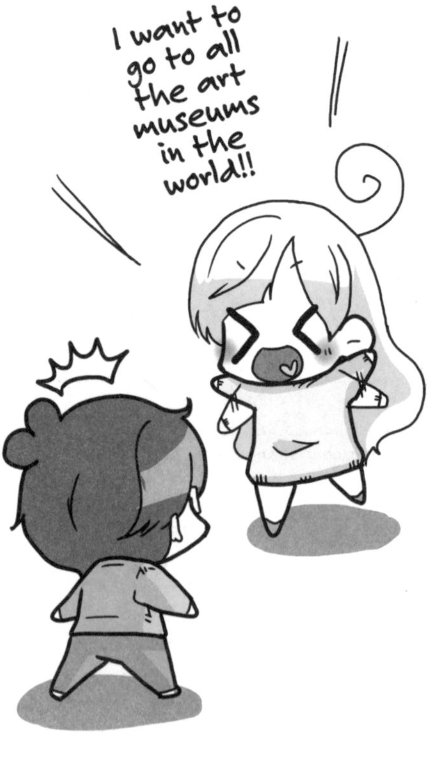
I want to go to all the art museums in the world!!

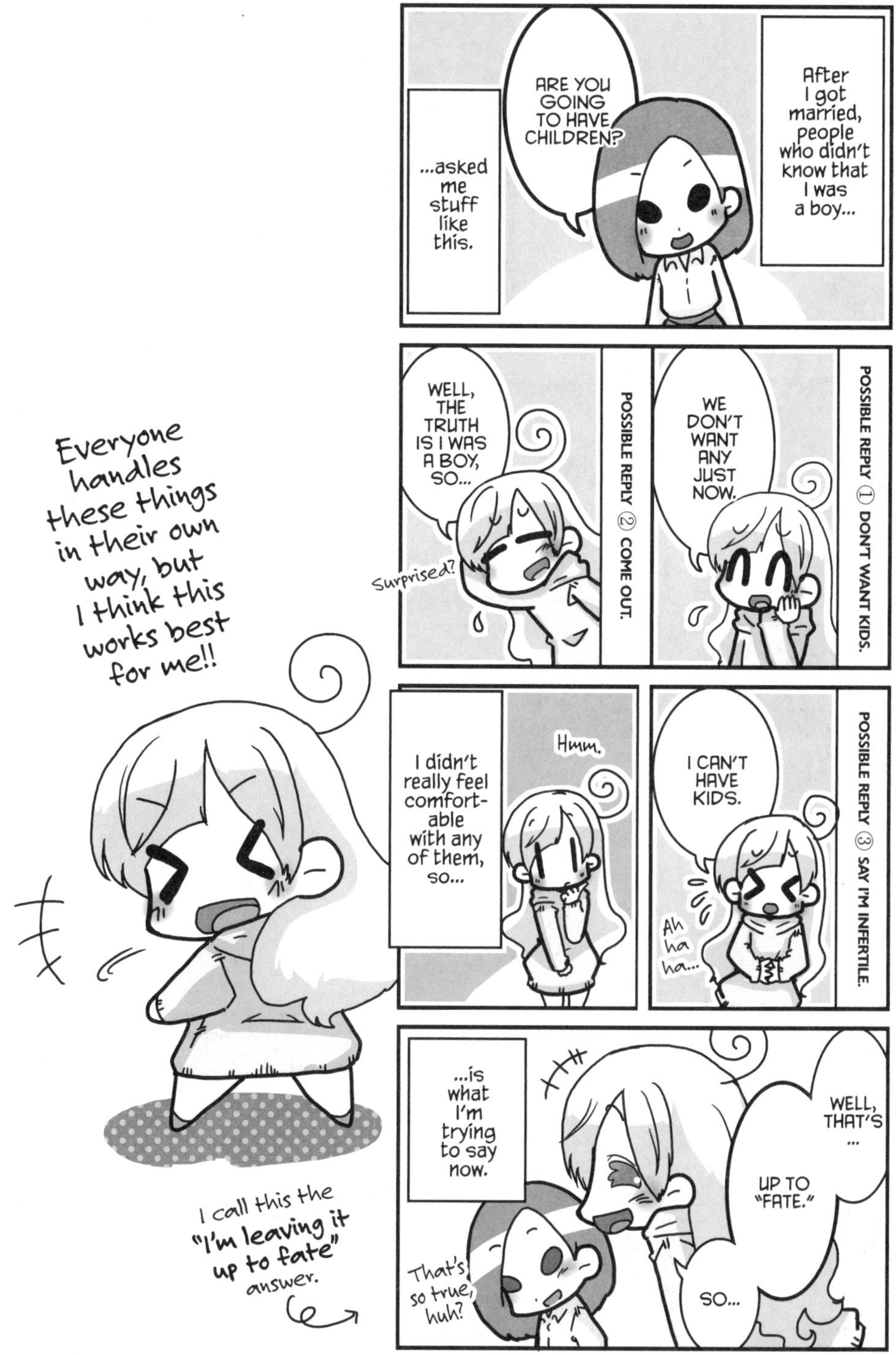

After I got married, people who didn't know that I was a boy...
ARE YOU GOING TO HAVE CHILDREN?
...asked me stuff like this.
POSSIBLE REPLY ① DON'T WANT KIDS.
WE DON'T WANT ANY JUST NOW.
POSSIBLE REPLY ② COME OUT.
WELL, THE TRUTH IS I WAS A BOY, SO...
Surprised?
POSSIBLE REPLY ③ SAY I'M INFERTILE.
I CAN'T HAVE KIDS.
Ah ha ha...
Hmm.
I didn't really feel comfortable with any of them, so...
WELL, THAT'S ...
UP TO "FATE."
SO...
That's so true, huh?
...is what I'm trying to say now.
Everyone handles these things in their own way, but I think this works best for me!!
I call this the "I'm leaving it up to fate" answer.

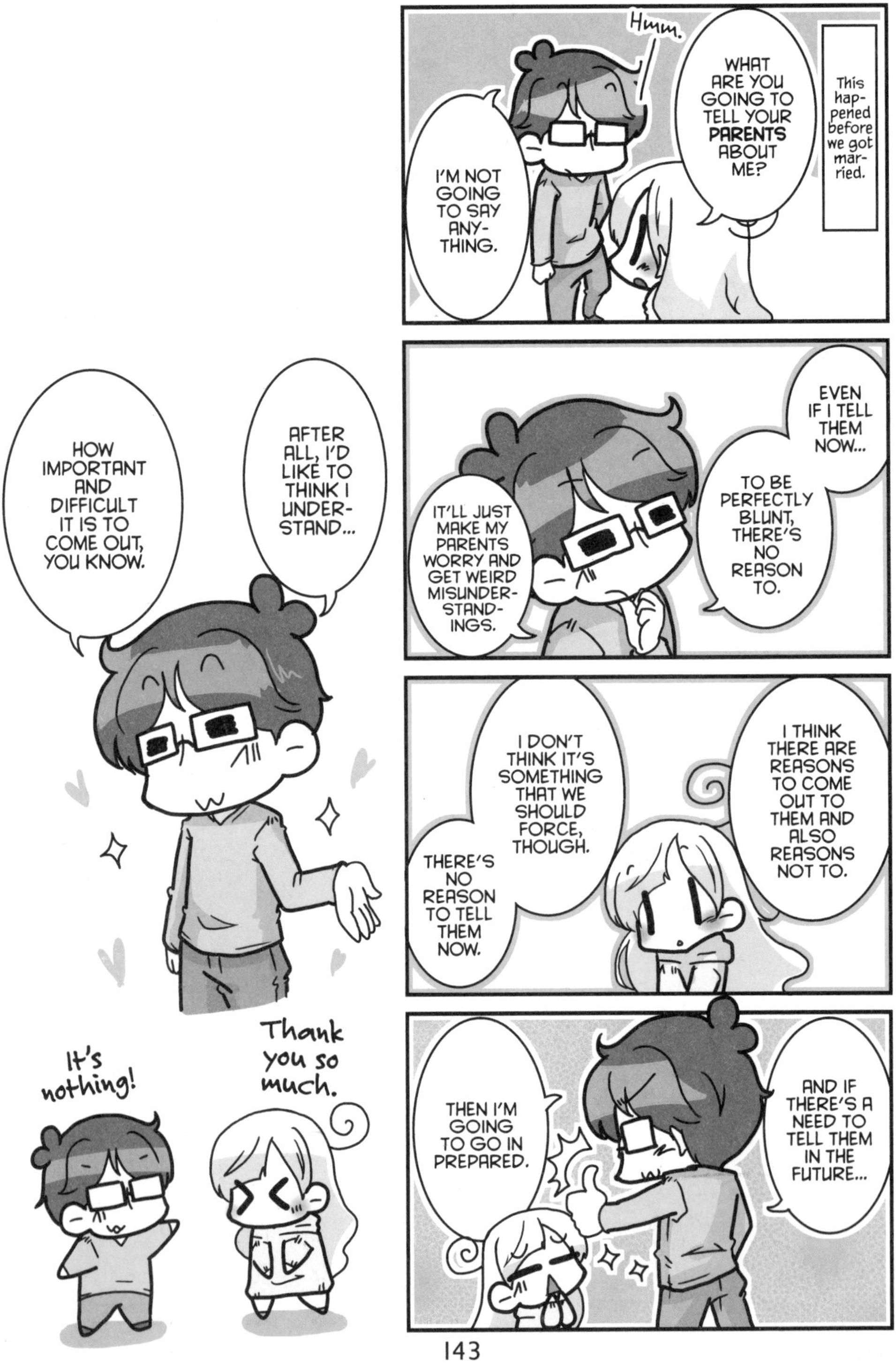

This happened before we got married.
WHAT ARE YOU GOING TO TELL YOUR **PARENTS** ABOUT ME?
Hmm.
I'M NOT GOING TO SAY ANYTHING.
EVEN IF I TELL THEM NOW...
TO BE PERFECTLY BLUNT, THERE'S NO REASON TO.
IT'LL JUST MAKE MY PARENTS WORRY AND GET WEIRD MISUNDERSTANDINGS.
I THINK THERE ARE REASONS TO COME OUT TO THEM AND ALSO REASONS NOT TO.
I DON'T THINK IT'S SOMETHING THAT WE SHOULD FORCE, THOUGH.
THERE'S NO REASON TO TELL THEM NOW.
AND IF THERE'S A NEED TO TELL THEM IN THE FUTURE...
THEN I'M GOING TO GO IN PREPARED.
AFTER ALL, I'D LIKE TO THINK I UNDERSTAND...
HOW IMPORTANT AND DIFFICULT IT IS TO COME OUT, YOU KNOW.
Thank you so much.
It's nothing!

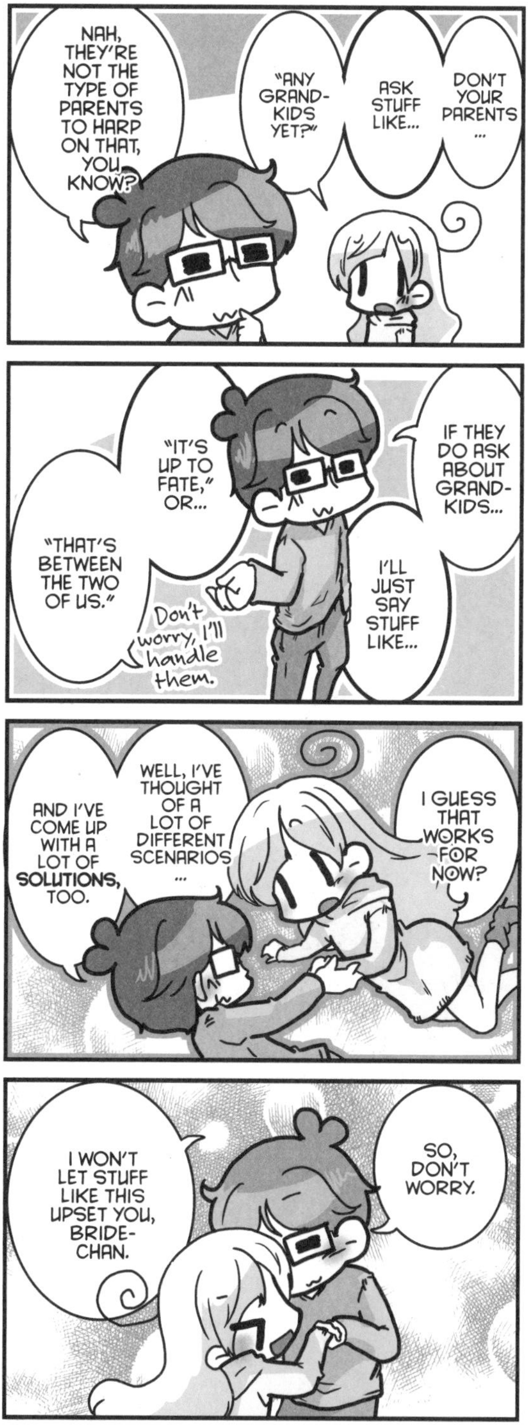
DON'T YOUR PARENTS...
ASK STUFF LIKE...
"ANY GRAND-KIDS YET?"
NAH, THEY'RE NOT THE TYPE OF PARENTS TO HARP ON THAT, YOU KNOW?
IF THEY DO ASK ABOUT GRAND-KIDS...
I'LL JUST SAY STUFF LIKE...
"IT'S UP TO FATE," OR...
"THAT'S BETWEEN THE TWO OF US."
Don't worry, I'll handle them.
I GUESS THAT WORKS FOR NOW?
WELL, I'VE THOUGHT OF A LOT OF DIFFERENT SCENARIOS...
AND I'VE COME UP WITH A LOT OF **SOLUTIONS**, TOO.
SO, DON'T WORRY.
I WON'T LET STUFF LIKE THIS UPSET YOU, BRIDE-CHAN.

I think it depends on a lot of things, like what kind of relationship you have with your parents and other relatives...

so I don't think there's any one right answer.

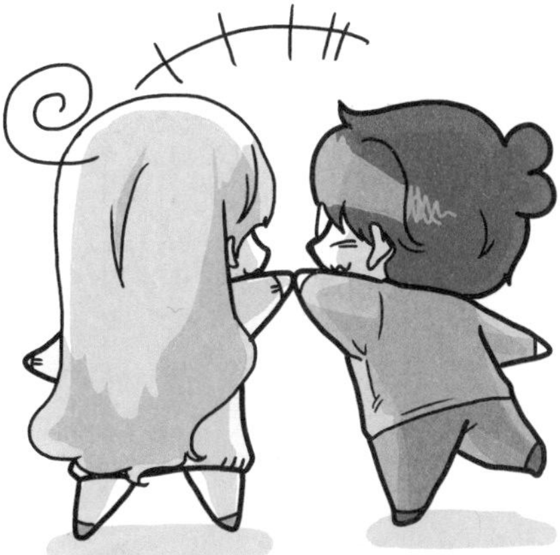

Even so, if people could just understand...

that this is one kind of family, that'd make me happy.

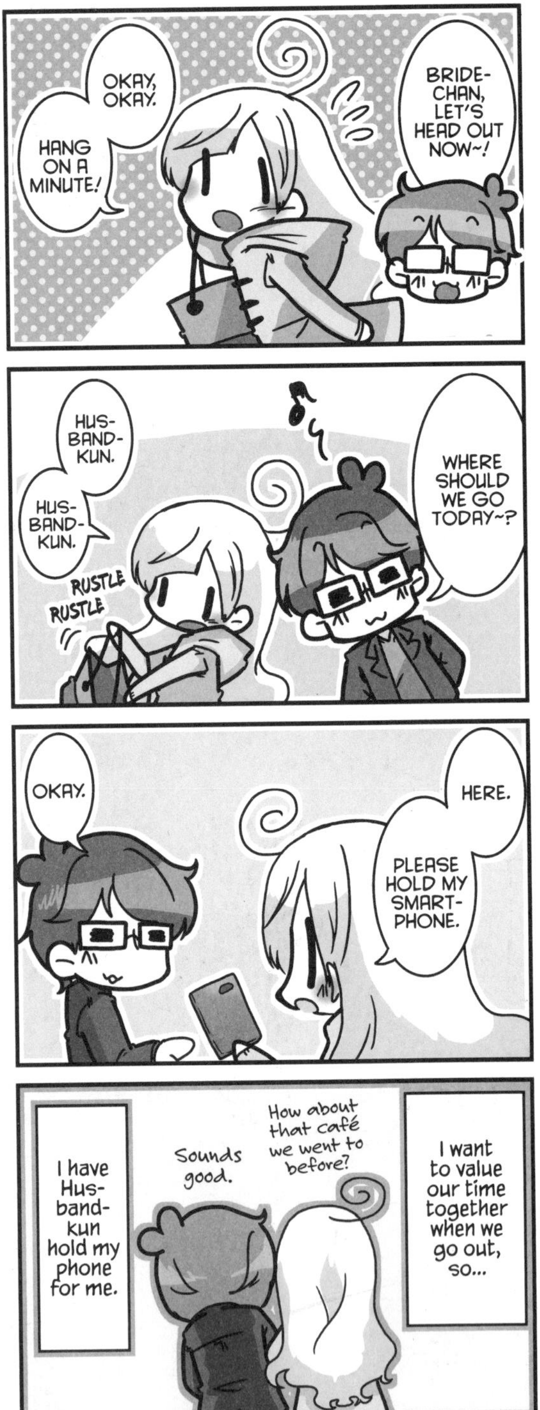
BRIDE-CHAN, LET'S HEAD OUT NOW~!
OKAY, OKAY.
HANG ON A MINUTE!
WHERE SHOULD WE GO TODAY~?
HUS-BAND-KUN.
HUS-BAND-KUN.
RUSTLE RUSTLE
HERE.
PLEASE HOLD MY SMART-PHONE.
OKAY.
I want to value our time together when we go out, so...
How about that café we went to before?
Sounds good.
I have Hus-band-kun hold my phone for me.

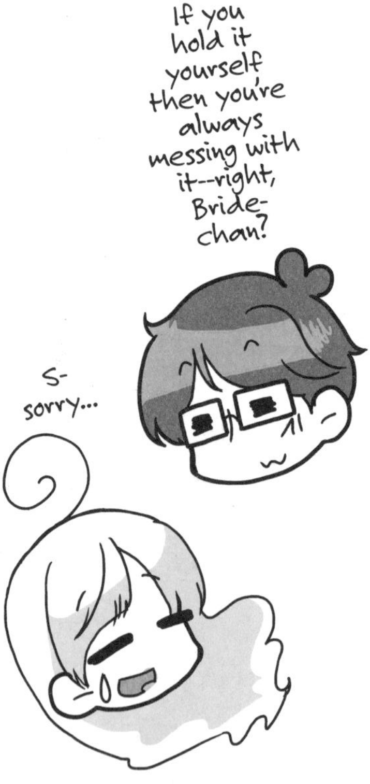
If you hold it yourself then you're always messing with it--right, Bride-chan?
S-sorry...

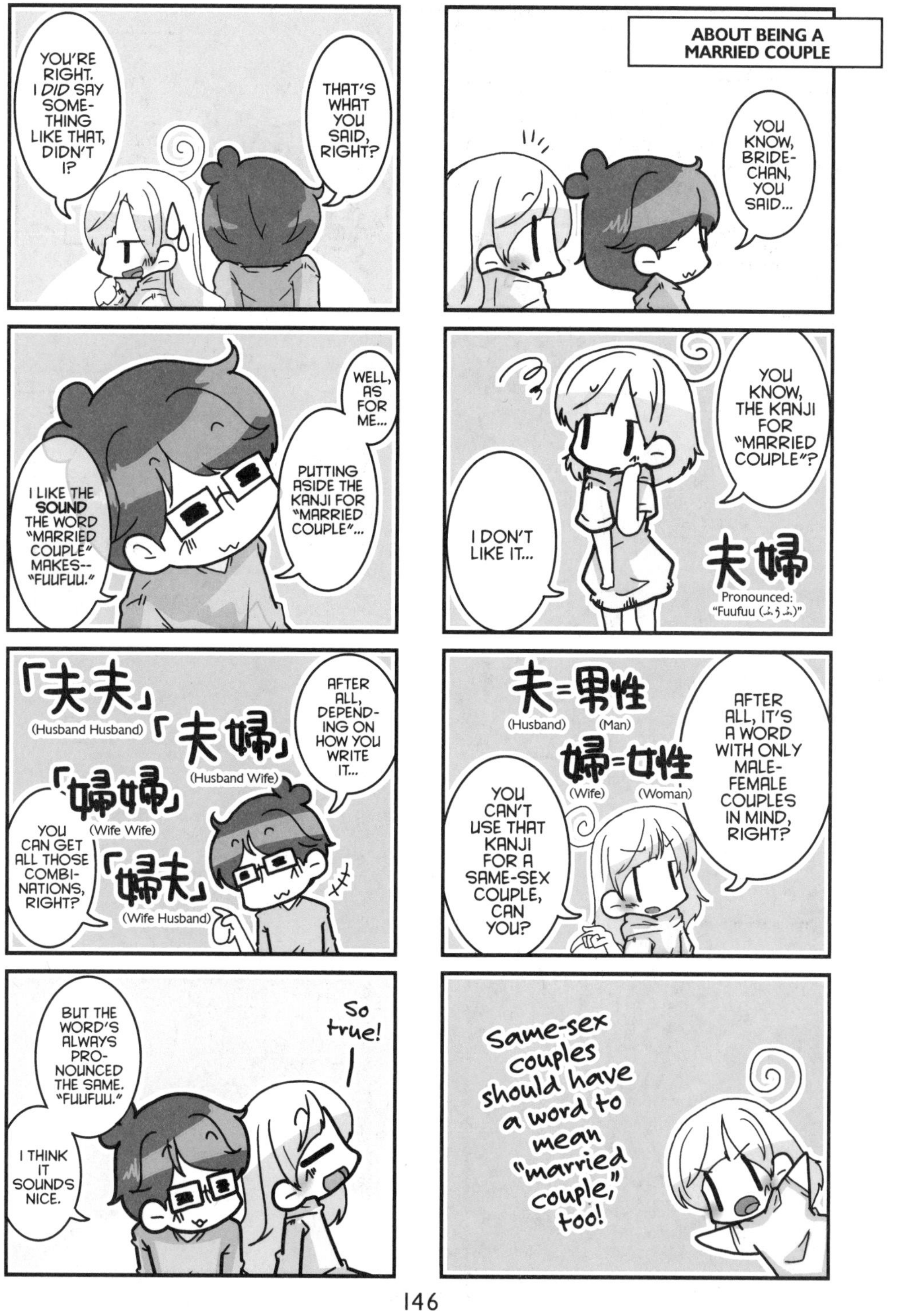

ABOUT BEING A MARRIED COUPLE
YOU KNOW, BRIDE-CHAN, YOU SAID...
YOU KNOW, THE KANJI FOR "MARRIED COUPLE"?
夫婦
Pronounced: "Fuufuu (ふうふ)"
I DON'T LIKE IT...
AFTER ALL, IT'S A WORD WITH ONLY MALE-FEMALE COUPLES IN MIND, RIGHT?
夫=男性
(Husband) (Man)
婦=女性
(Wife) (Woman)
YOU CAN'T USE THAT KANJI FOR A SAME-SEX COUPLE, CAN YOU?
Same-sex couples should have a word to mean "married couple," too!
THAT'S WHAT YOU SAID, RIGHT?
YOU'RE RIGHT. I *DID* SAY SOMETHING LIKE THAT, DIDN'T I?
WELL, AS FOR ME...
PUTTING ASIDE THE KANJI FOR "MARRIED COUPLE"...
I LIKE THE **SOUND** THE WORD "MARRIED COUPLE" MAKES-- "FUUFUU."
AFTER ALL, DEPENDING ON HOW YOU WRITE IT...
「夫夫」
(Husband Husband)
「夫婦」
(Husband Wife)
「婦婦」
(Wife Wife)
「婦夫」
(Wife Husband)
YOU CAN GET ALL THOSE COMBINATIONS, RIGHT?
So true!
BUT THE WORD'S ALWAYS PRONOUNCED THE SAME. "FUUFUU."
I THINK IT SOUNDS NICE.

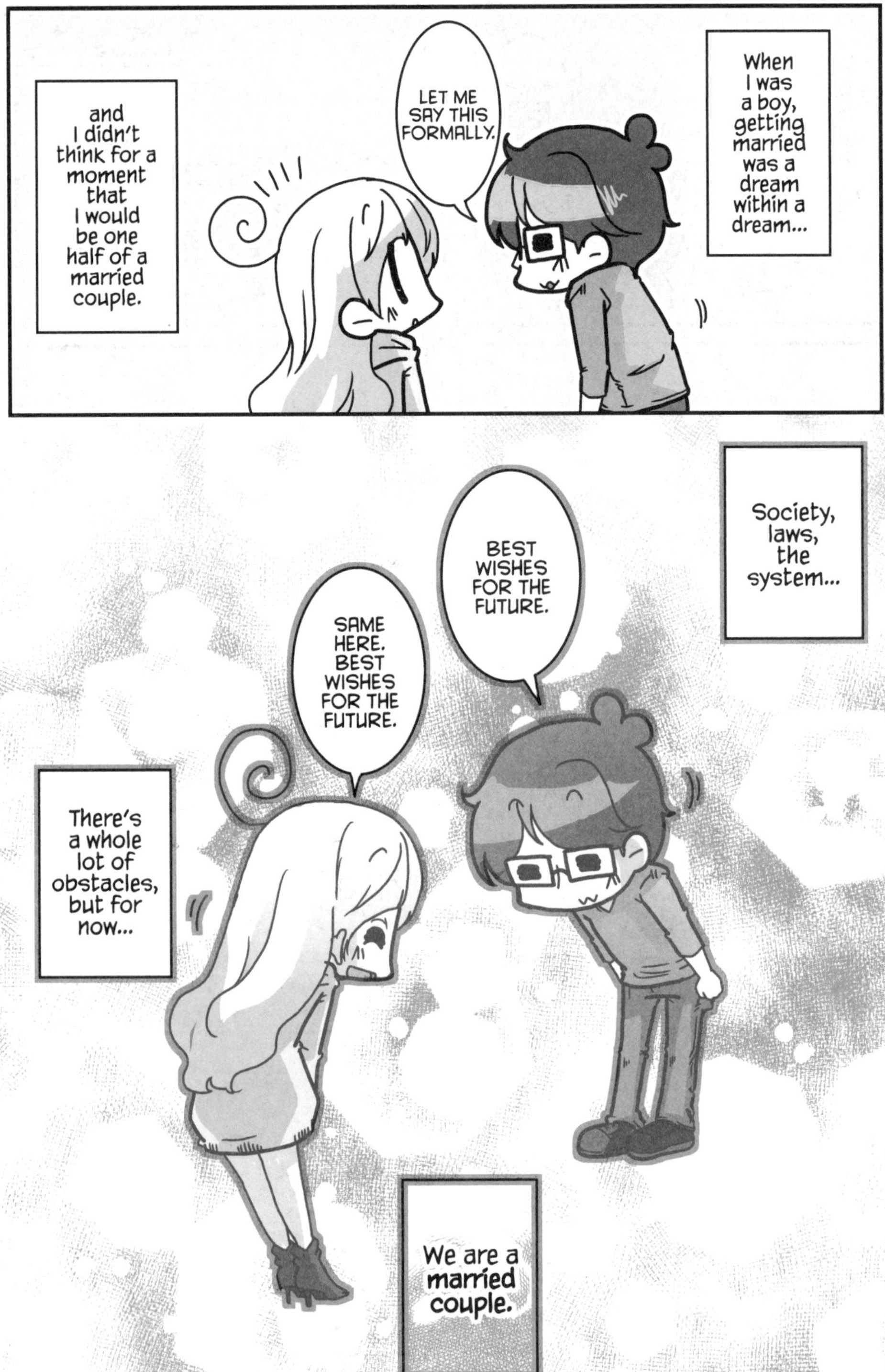
When I was a boy, getting married was a dream within a dream...
LET ME SAY THIS FORMALLY.
and I didn't think for a moment that I would be one half of a married couple.
Society, laws, the system...
BEST WISHES FOR THE FUTURE.
SAME HERE. BEST WISHES FOR THE FUTURE.
There's a whole lot of obstacles, but for now...
We are a married couple.

Did you enjoy *The Bride was a Boy*?

The blog I started as a "record for myself" became a four-panel manga strip because someone said, "Wouldn't it be fun if the everyday life of someone who was a boy became a manga?" That was the impetus that led to this book here.

When most people hear the words "sexualities and genders," they think that it sounds like such a difficult and delicate issue, and they are completely right. It *is* very difficult and delicate, but that's because there are so many different views relating to it. This makes the subject very interesting, colorful, and new--as well as educational.

I would like to take this opportunity to thank:
those who helped me publish this book...
those who read this book...
those who read my blog and cheered me on...
my father...
my mother...
my family, and...
my husband, who supported me in many ways while I converted the blog into a book.

Thank you so very much.

Bride-chan, a.k.a. "Chii"

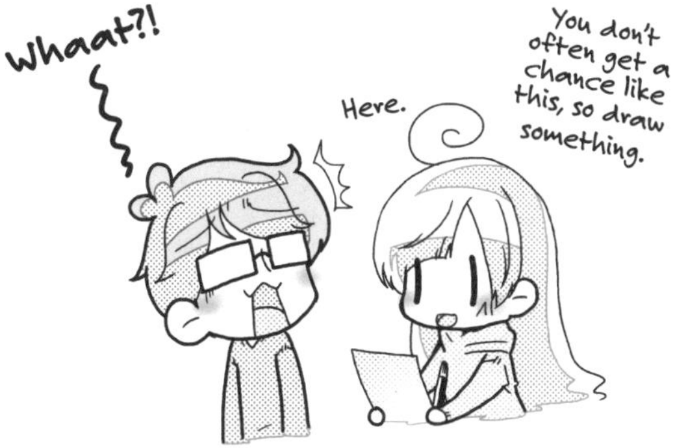
You don't often get a chance like this, so draw something.
Here.
Whaat?!

Thank you for taking *The Bride was a Boy* into your hands. This is Husband-kun.

When Bride-chan discussed making her blog into a book, even though I was even happier about it than *she* was, I was secretly worried because creating a book is a lot of work.

In truth, comic essays differ from those created for a blog, and when I saw how Bride-chan was troubled and had suffered through much trial and error, I thought that maybe I shouldn't have encouraged her to make the book.

However, as the decision had already been made, I threw myself into acquiring things that were said to soothe tired eyes and shoulders, and did my best to support her in all the ways I could, aside from actually authoring and illustrating the book, as Husband-kun's illustrative efforts are surprisingly...unique (LOL).

This book may have given you the image of Husband-kun as a perfect human, but the truth is, I was often fraught with worries and anxieties. I had envisioned a more dramatic proposal to Bride-chan, but the results were what you have read in the book (LOL).

I hope that we may live together peacefully to old age.

Thus says Husband-kun.

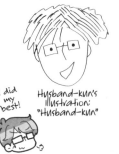

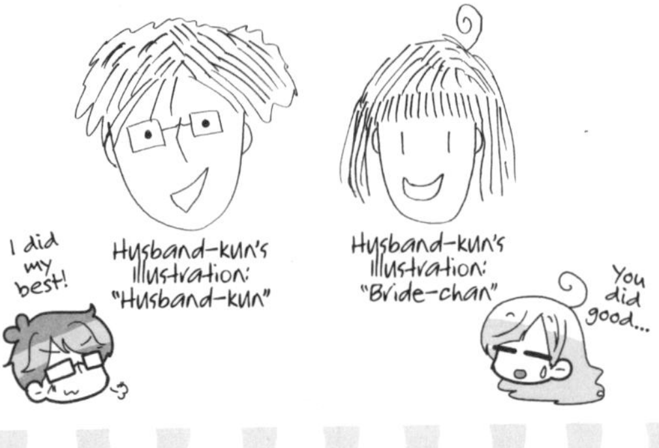

I did my best!

Husband-kun's Illustration: "Husband-kun"

Husband-kun's Illustration: "Bride-chan"

You did good...

Works Cited

Baird, Vanessa. *Seiteki Minority no Kisochishiki* [The No-Nonsense Guide to Sexual Diversity]. Translated by Tetsuo Machiguchi. Sakuhinsha, 2005.

Harima, Katsuki, Toshiyuki Ooshima, Aki Nomiya, Masae Torae, and Aya Kamikawa. *Seidouitsusei Shougai to Koseki – Seibetsuhenshi to Tokureihou o Kangaeru* [Problem Q&A, Gender Identity Disorder and the Family Register – Thinking about Gender Change and Special Provisions]. Rokufu Shuppan, 2007.

Huegel, Kelly. *LGBTQ tte Nani? –Sexual Minority No Handbook* [LGBTQ: The Survival Guide for Gay, Lesbian, Bisexual, Transgender, and Questioning Teens]. Translated by Seko Udea. Akashi Shoten, 2011.

Kawasaki, Masaji, and Katsuki Harima, eds. *Seidouitsu Shougai No Iryou to Hou – Iryou·Kango·Houritsu·Kyouiku·Gyousei Kikansha Ga Shitte Okitai Kadai to Taiou* [Medicine and Law Regarding Gender Identity Disorder – Medicine·Treatment ·Education·The Issues that Government Officials Want to Know and How to Handle Them]. Ono Chieko Representative Edition. Medica Shuppan, 2013.

Nomiya, Aki, Toshiyuki Ooshima, Takao Harashina, Masae Toare, and Yutaka Uchijima. *Seidouitsu Shougaitte Nani? – Hitori Hitori No Se No Ariyou o Taisetsuni Surutame* [Problem Q&A: What Is Gender Identity Disorder? – Treasuring Each and Everyone's Gender Problems Q&A]. Rokufu Shuppan, 2003.

Yanagisawa, Masakazu, Maki Muraki, and Junichi Gotou. *Shokuba No LGBT Dokuhon – "Arinomama No Jibun" de Hatarakeru Kankyou o Mezashite* [The Book of LGBT at Work – Working toward the Goal of a Work Environment where "I Can Be Myself"]. Jitsumu Kyouiku Shuppan, 2015.

Sei no Mondai Kenjyuukai. *Zukai Seitenkan Manual – Counseling, Hormone Therapy Kara Kakushun Shujutsu, Koseki No Hensji Made* [Illustrated Sex Change Manual – From Counseling and Hormone Therapy to Surgeries and Legal Documentation Changes]. Doubun Shouin, 1999.

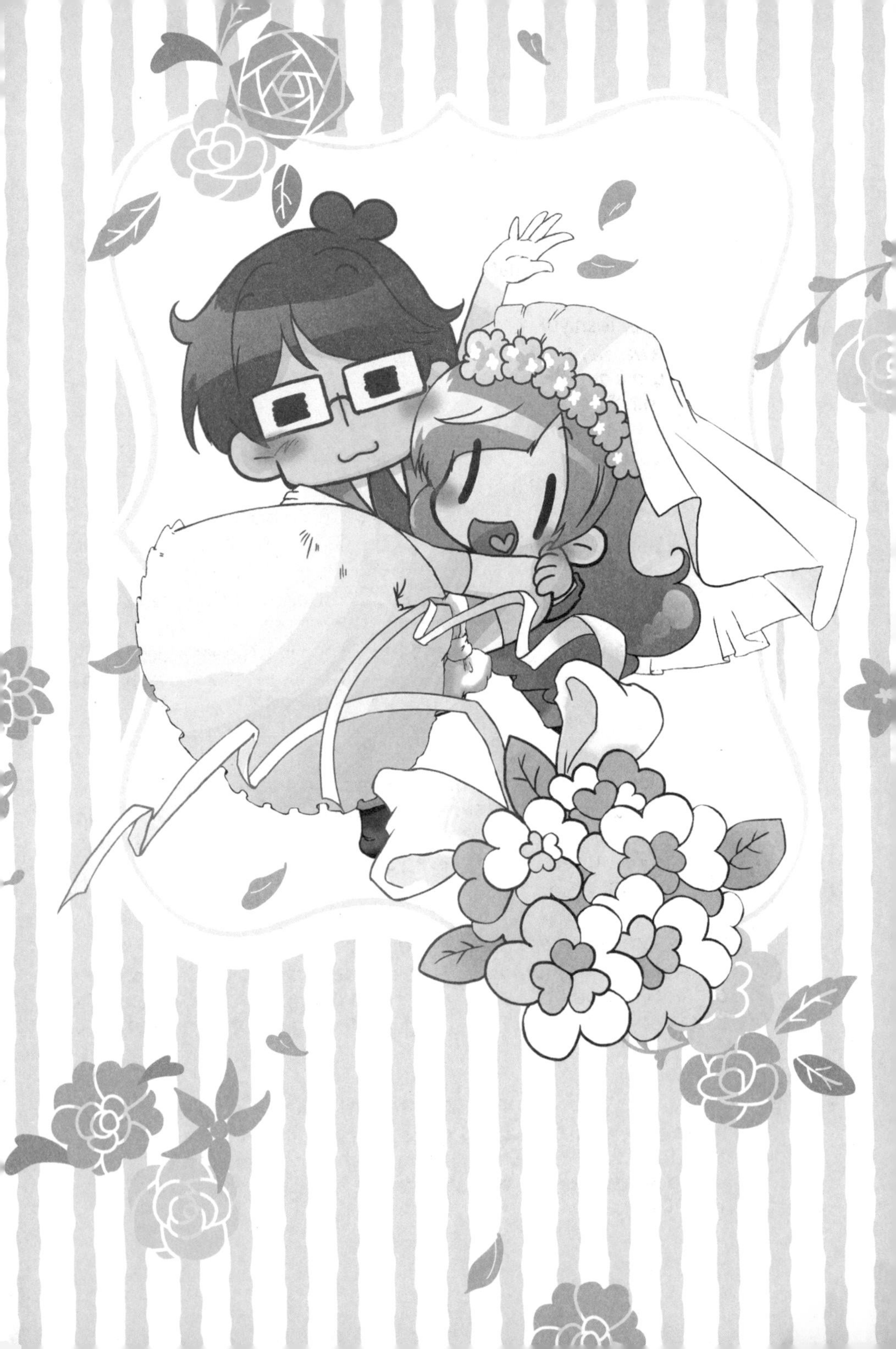

Bonus! 1st Anniversary

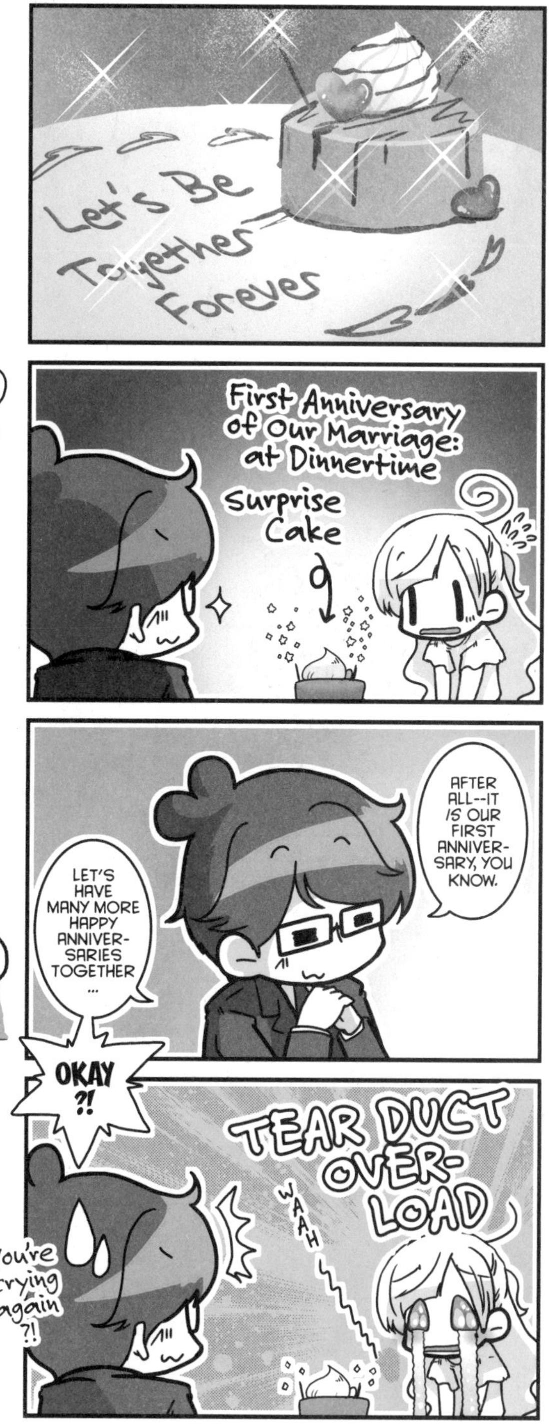
Let's Be Together Forever
First Anniversary of Our Marriage: at Dinnertime
Surprise Cake
AFTER ALL--IT IS OUR FIRST ANNIVERSARY, YOU KNOW.
LET'S HAVE MANY MORE HAPPY ANNIVERSARIES TOGETHER ...
OKAY ?!
TEAR DUCT OVER-LOAD
WAAAH
You're crying again ?!

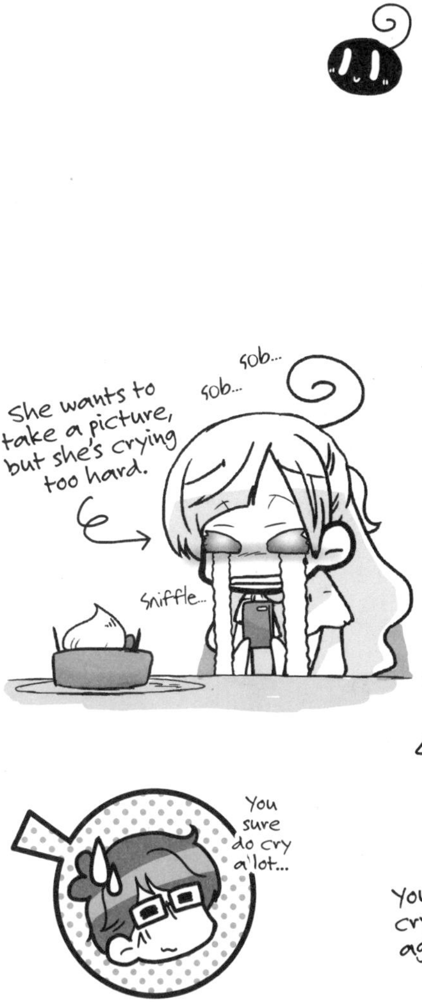
sob...
sob...
She wants to take a picture, but she's crying too hard.
Sniffle...
You sure do cry a'lot...

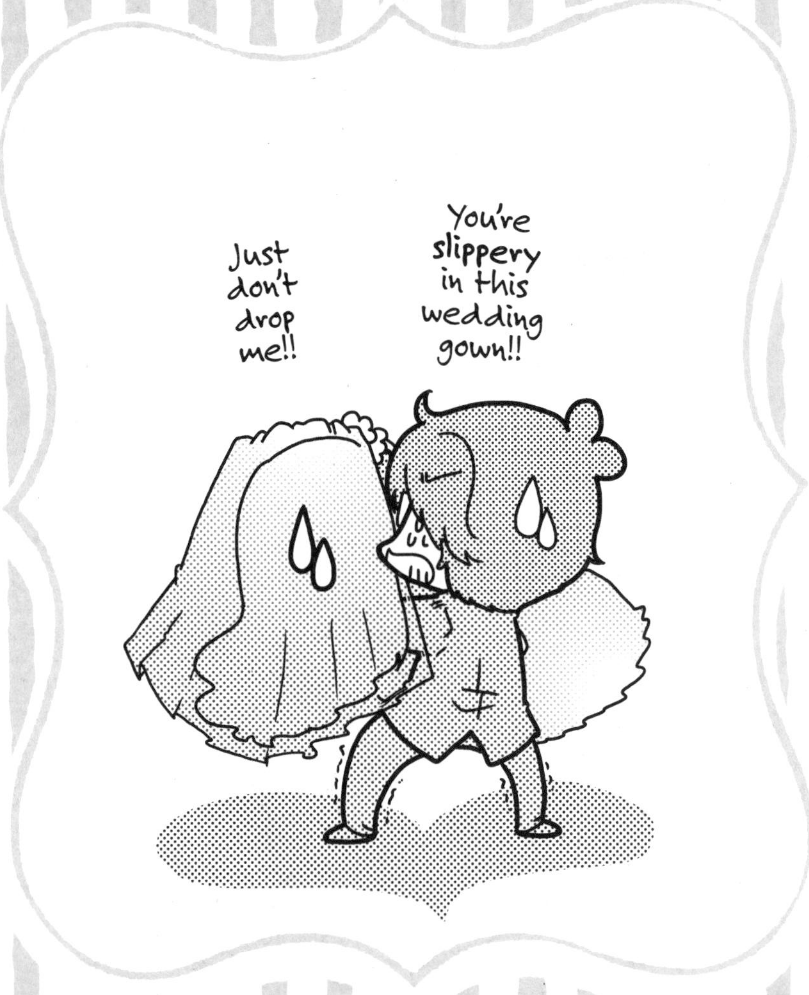
You're slippery in this wedding gown!!
Just don't drop me!!

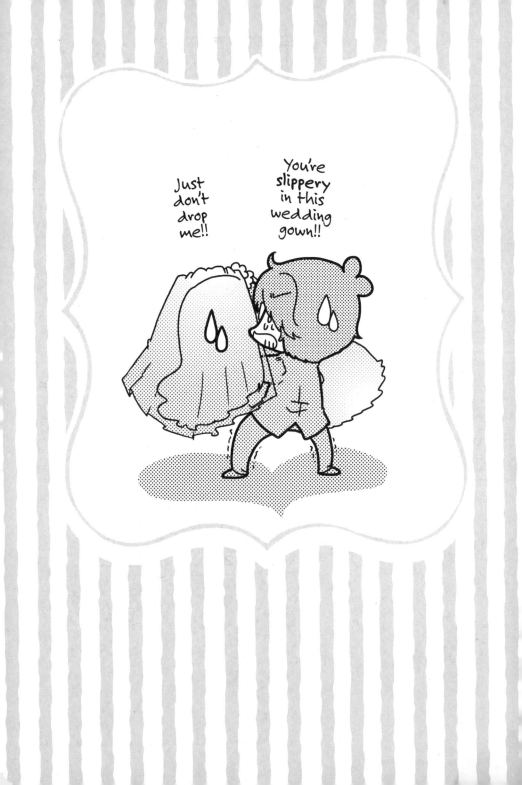

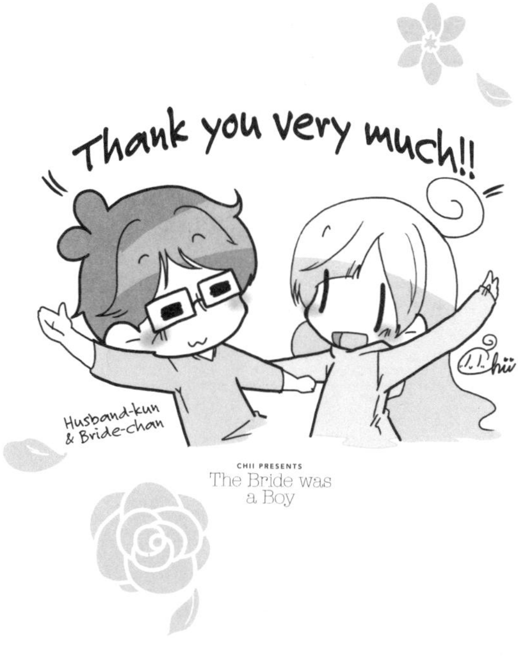
Thank you very much!!
Husband-kun
& Bride-chan
Chii
CHII PRESENTS
The Bride was
a Boy

Chii

...published her four-panel manga about when she was a boy, her experience with gender transition, and LGBTs-related topics on her blog "My Bride-chan was a Boy" and on Twitter.

Blog: "My Bride-chan was a boy."
http://ameblo.jp/infection1985
Twitter: @chii_gid_mtf

CHII PRESENTS
The Bride was
a Boy

SEVEN SEAS ENTERTAINMENT PRESENTS

The Bride was a Boy

(true) story & art by CHII

TRANSLATION
Beni Axia Conrad

ADAPTATION
Shanti Whitesides

LETTERING AND RETOUCH
Karis Page

COVER DESIGN
KC Fabellon

PROOFREADER
Kurestin Armada
Lianne Sentar

SENSITIVITY READER
Casey Lucas

EDITOR
Jenn Grunigen

PRODUCTION ASSISTANT
CK Russell

PRODUCTION MANAGER
Lissa Pattillo

EDITOR-IN-CHIEF
Adam Arnold

PUBLISHER
Jason DeAngelis

HANAYOME WA MOTODANSHI.
© Chii 2016
Originally published in Japan in 2016 by ASUKASHINSHA, Tokyo.
English translation rights arranged with COMIC HOUSE, Tokyo,
through TOHAN CORPORATION, Tokyo.

Seven Seas books may be purchased in bulk for educational, business, or
promotional use. For information on bulk purchases, please contact Macmillan
Corporate & Premium Sales Department at 1-800-221-7945 (ext 5442)
or write specialmarkets@macmillan.com.

Seven Seas and the Seven Seas logo are trademarks of
Seven Seas Entertainment, LLC. All rights reserved.

ISBN: 978-1-626928-88-6

Printed in Canada

First Printing: May 2018

10 9 8 7 6 5 4 3 2 1

FOLLOW US ONLINE: *www.sevenseasentertainment.com*

READING DIRECTIONS

This book reads from *right to left*, Japanese style. If
this is your first time reading manga, you start
reading from the top right panel on each page and
take it from there. If you get lost, just follow the
numbered diagram here. It may seem backwards at
first, but you'll get the hang of it! Have fun!!

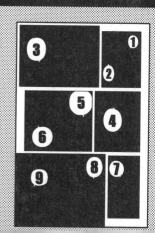